Cryptobyte

Cat Connor

"Cryptobyte, with its original and intricate plot and gutsy intelligent protagonist, is the kind of blockbuster book where you have to stop and catch your breath once you've finished reading."
- Nikki Crutchley, writer

The Delta team is back! In Cryptobyte, Cat Connor delivers a fast-paced story complete with an eerie mystery, a cryptic puzzle, action and wit. Time's short and the danger's close as the team uncovers a frightening truth hidden beneath an innocent surface. Cryptobyte will keep you guessing while you're reading and thinking after you're done.
- Margot Kinberg, author of the Joel Williams mysteries

For information regarding permission email the publisher at 9mmpressnz@gmail.com, subject line: Permission.

Paperback ISBN : 978-0-473-48904-5
ISBN ePub: 978-0-4734890-5-2
ISBN: 978-0-4734890-6-9
Draft2Digital ISBN: 978-1-0670072-7-0

Life Saver/emergency editor: Jayne Southern

For Joshua (aka The Boy Wonder)

"What greater thing is there for human souls than to feel they are joined for life - to be with each other in silent unspeakable memories."
- George Eliot

Chapter One
John, I'm Only Dancing

"Move!" Lee's deep voice boomed across the vast warehouse to Dane.

Kurt and I opened fire into the room behind us. Someone yelped. I suppressed the desire to escape, controlled my thundering heart, aimed at the sound, and squeezed the trigger. Someone moved. A glimpse of blue fabric near a truck tire. Kurt fired. I fired. A squawk of pain, the fabric vanished behind the rear wheel. From our semi-covered position behind a solid wooden workbench I saw Dane disappear through a doorway. Gunfire erupted. Guess they weren't done with us yet.

Delta A: riling bad guys since Twenty-Oh-nine.

"There's a shit ton of stupid happening here," I whispered. Kurt nodded. "On two."

Lee crept in beside me. "With me, boss."

Great. I groaned inaudibly. I'm in the middle again. *Bam*, music filled my soul. Not now, brain. Not now. A small thud into the workbench jerked me out of the song.

I squeezed Kurt's shoulder as Lee squeezed mine. He gave a quick nod and moved toward the door. We stayed low and moved as quickly as possible. Flashes in my peripheral sent tiny spikes of pain into my gray matter. Rounds hit machinery with a metallic *ptink* sending sparks into the air.

Breathe.

More flashes.

Ptink.

Clunk. Ping.

Thud. Dust hung in the air sparkling in slivers of sunshine.

Dane provided cover fire from the doorway.

That was our cue. We darted past him, Kurt to the left, I ducked right, Lee spun into position next to Dane. A round whizzed through the doorway where we were and sank into the wall opposite. Followed closely by another. I glanced at the wall as another bullet dug in – nice grouping – and tugged my phone from my pocket to call Andrews.

Another bullet hit a clock on the wall with a *whack*; glass tinkled to the floor.

"I live for your calls, Iverson," Andrews said with a chuckle. Several bullets hit the wall at once, raining more dust upon me.

I scrunched lower and fired through the gap in the doorway. "We needed you an hour ago."

"Fuckadoodledo, Iverson. You do find trouble."

"Wouldn't do to be boring."

"Cavalry incoming, I got your location."

That was fast. Technology is on our side today.

"We're in a garage/warehouse. The truck we were looking for is in here too. We don't know exactly what the load is, chemical of some sort."

"Hazardous?"

"Yeah, maybe acetone."

I heard him moving around and all of a sudden the sound over the phone changed, hollow. He was in his truck. The engine fired with a rumble.

"With you in twenty. Don't die," Andrews said. "Sparks are not your friend if that truck carries acetone."

"Do my best."

I hung up and shuffled close to Kurt.

"SWAT's on the way."

"Did you get a look at the hazard symbols on the truck?" Kurt asked as more rounds smacked into the drywall and pinged off heavy machinery. "Ricochet. We need to get out of here. Jacked truck or not."

"I saw a hazardous load symbol. Think I saw the word acetone."

"Lee," Kurt whispered harshly. "Try not to hit the truck."

"Trying."

"Try harder, that truck's carrying a volatile liquid," I said. "We don't wanna attempt outrunning an explosion."

Delta A settled in, trading fire with whoever wanted to play, until Andrews's SWAT team arrived, full noise. Green clad men with semi-automatic rifles made short work of the hijackers. Weapons fell, clattering onto the concrete floor. I watched as SWAT herded six men, two wounded but walking, into the middle.

Andrews barked at the group. "Sit. Hands on heads."

One of his team moved and plasti-cuffed each man.

Andrews sauntered over to me. "Nothing like a bit of fun to start the day right," he said with a smile, our left hands slapped together in a high-five.

"Thanks for coming." I holstered my Glock and surveyed the sorry looking gunmen sitting on the floor. We weren't done yet.

"Always fun being part of your chicanery," Andrews said; his eyebrows waggled.

"If you and your team take charge of the prisoners, we'll take a good look at the truck and contents."

"We got them, no worries. You carry on." He flicked me a half-assed salute then swirled his arm in the air. "Pack this lot up. We're taking them in."

"Hey, Andrews," I said, grabbing his attention. "Hand over to Delta B, Claude will be waiting in interrogation."

"Sure thing, Iverson." He continued on his trajectory.

I called Claude. "Truck hijacking incoming for you. Andrews is bringing six males in for questioning. Two require medical assistance, have medics standing by. I'll input everything we find into Sentinel on my way back."

"Everything okay, SAC?"

"Just peachy."

I hung up. Kurt was on his phone to request a forensic team. Dane and Lee had already snapped on nitrile gloves and headed for the truck. Lee found the keys still in the ignition. He unlocked the back doors and swung them open. Racks of large plastic containers filled the truck. Each container bore a hazardous chemical sign and labeled 'Acetone.'

"Why would someone want a truckload of Acetone?" I said, staring at the flasks. "That'd remove a shit ton of nail varnish."

Kurt stepped up beside me. "That'd dissolve a shit ton of fat."

Two hours later, we trundled into the office in search of sustenance and coffee. I glanced at my wristwatch as I strode down the corridor. I had five minutes to clean up before a meeting.

Five minutes later, Sandra handed me a sandwich as I hustled to my meeting with the Chief and the Special Agent in Charge of cyber. Twenty minutes later I paced the carpeted outer office of our resident psychologist waiting for my team.

Twice a year we had a team session with Psychologist Ashley Williams. None of us looked forward to it, but it was a Delta requirement.

Chapter Two

As Tears Go By

The door opened behind me. I turned to see Lee step in, followed by Dane, and Kurt.

"We ready?" I asked, my eyes skimmed each face and received affirmation.

The main office door opened, and Ashley greeted us with a smile. "Nice to see you all again," she said, her faded Texan accent added a sincerity to her words. "Come on through."

We dutifully filed into the room and sat in the squishy armchairs already arranged in a circle. Ashley took her seat last; her eyes flicked across each of our faces.

"Doctor Henderson," she said, pausing at Kurt. "Anything you'd like to address today?"

Kurt's lip twitched into a half-smile. "Not that I can think of."

Good answer.

She moved to Dane, the youngest and newest Delta A member.

"Agent Smith, how are you doing?"

He met her gaze head-on. "Okay, actually."

"Coping since the death of your brother?"

She sure jumped in with both feet.

"There are days and there are *days*," he replied.

"What's the spread like?" She jotted something on

her pad.

"More good than bad." Dane held her eyes with his. "I'm aware grief is not straightforward, and the ratio of good and bad is fluid."

She nodded. "Is there anything you'd like to share, perhaps a memory of Stewart?"

A weight pressed me until I thought it'd push me right through into the back of the chair. The invitation to share a memory was a can of decaying worms, and I wasn't prepared for it today. Dane spoke about something that happened before he and Stewart joined Delta A. I tried to hear his words but all I heard was rapid fire and wood splintering. Muzzle flashes lit the screen. Hauling my mind back, I heard Dane's voice, pulling further back I heard him laugh.

I blinked. Dane grinned, Lee and Kurt chuckled, even Ashley had a smile on her face. And I was back. Until Dane looked at me and pressed words into my mind, I thought I'd escaped without anyone noticing my absence. Dane's words danced out and around me, tantalizing, as they waltzed in the air. I swished left with a finger. White words spun in front of me, leaving an imprint. *It's not your fault.*

Ashley spoke. Dane's word's exploded into tiny balls of light.

"Agent Iverson, how are you doing? Still blaming yourself for Stewart's death?"

Sure, why not jab spikes into an open wound? How about a sprinkling of salt as well? I took a breath and tried not to hold it. Even though I knew there weren't supposed to be any right or wrong answers, honesty felt like it'd be the wrong way to go.

"Sometimes." Fuck! Apparently I cannot control my mouth.

"Can you elaborate on that?"

Yes, but I do not want to.

She knew immediately she'd asked the question the wrong way to get a response from me. A fleeting smile crossed her lips.

"Yes, but I don't want to," I said. Wouldn't do to disappoint.

"Please elaborate on how you *sometimes* blame yourself for Stewart's death?"

"Stewart was wounded because of my decision to stand and fight," I said, with precision. Truth is truth. It was my decision. Sometimes doing my job is not fun.

"But not his death, Ellie," Ashley said.

Truth threatened to spill forth. "Yes, his death. A blood clot killed him. That would not have happened had he not had surgery," I replied. "If we're going with the truth here, then that's the truth."

"It's not sometimes is it?" Ashley said but didn't wait for a response. Instead, she changed the subject. "How are you and Dane getting on?" She looked from me to Dane and back. "Has this caused any relationship problems? Are you two still able to work as a unit?"

"We're good," Dane confirmed.

"We *are* good," I added, with a smile.

"You've both reported an extraordinary ability to tap into each other's consciousness," she said. "Still?"

I nodded. Dane nodded.

"Can either of you tap into anyone else's mind like that?"

Was she worried that we could read what she was thinking? Knowledge of a smile emerged before it reached my lips.

"My husband and I share a mental connection similar to the one Dane, Stewart, and I share." I rethought my wording. "Shared. The three of us shared."

Ashley nodded. "But not with Lee and Kurt?"

I shook my head. "Not like that, no. A connection, yes, but, different."

"How about with Sam Jackson?"

Shit! A heavy door banged shut. We're done here.

A tiny sliver of light peeked from under the door. A voice echoed in a hallway. "Breaching!" I turned away from the door as a shotgun boomed. Looking back, I saw him. Special Agent Sam Jackson. He pushed the door all the way open and filled the doorframe with his muscular six-feet-six body. Sam's bald head shone in the light. Giving the appearance of a halo. He grinned, looking every bit like a cross between Denzel Washington and Mr. T. "Chicky babe, I've missed you."

Not as much as we miss you.

Sam faded into a pool of twinkling stars.

"Agent Iverson?"

"Uh-huh?"

"How about Sam, did you share a connection as you do with Dane?"

I shook my head. "No, we were close. We're all close. And before you ask, I do miss him, but I don't blame myself for his death." Much. Some days.

Lee cleared his throat. "Ashley, we all miss Sam. He left a gaping hole in Delta A. Dane here, well, he came along with Stew at the right time. He fits right in." He looked at Dane. "They both did."

Kurt had something to add. "Rather than focusing on what we've lost as a team, how about we focus on what we have built over the years. A strong unit of people who genuinely care for each other both at work and out of work."

Ashley nodded, and wrote some more. Sometimes having a doctor on the team is a really good thing. She turned to Kurt. "Agent Henderson. How are things with you?"

He smiled. "Good, thanks."

Suppressing a smile was tricky. She'd have to work harder to get anything from us. Any Delta issues were Delta issues and we handled them together. Outsiders not invited. The only reason we had a standing appointment with Ashley was to satisfy a requirement for review. We dealt with the worst of humanity on an ongoing basis. Made sense that the FBI wanted to make sure we didn't go off the reservation, guns blazing. My belief is that the only thing stopping that scenario from happening is us.

"Nothing you need to talk through?"

"Like Ellie, Lee, and Dane, there are times that I miss Sam and I miss Stewart. But other than that, I'm good."

And just like that, we were back on me. I thought she'd moved on with Lee in the firing line. Wrong.

"Ellie, hallucinations, are you still having them?"

The question stalled me. Not what I expected to be asked at all.

"What?"

She turned a few pages in her pad and read for a moment. Ashley looked at me and carefully said, "You were having hallucinations featuring your dead husband a while ago. Does that still happen?"

A ball of ice formed in my gut. That was years ago. Can't we put that fine chapter of my life to bed?

"No." It was the truth. I hadn't *seen* Mac in a long time. I had no need to elaborate. Mac morphed into Christopher Chance a few years back. I didn't see a problem with having an imaginary friend. Even Kurt didn't seem to mind Chance's visits and observations, though we liked to keep Chance under wraps.

"They stopped?"

"Yes."

"How do you feel about that?"

"Relieved." Now that was honest. Once I shot Mac in the head and he quit popping up and annoying me, a weight lifted. Best I never mention that I thought I'd shot his ghost in the head.

"What do you think caused the episodes?"

Crackerjack, now they're episodes. Of what? The worst soap opera ever?

Kurt jumped in. "We determined they *were* a tool for Ellie to make sense of information she was otherwise unable to assimilate." He paused. "Things she knew and gleaned from body language and environment, but couldn't justify knowing."

"That's interesting."

"The mind is a fascinating place, as you know, Ashley," Kurt said. "And Iverson's mind gathers information most of us don't notice. Makes her extremely valuable to Delta A and an astute leader."

Whoa. A compliment? I left it alone.

"I imagine having a mind like that is an asset." She wrote again then looked up. "Agent Davenport, how are you getting on without your partner of many years?"

And just like that we were back on stirring up Sam feelings. What is her problem?

Lee nodded. "I'm not going to lie. It's tough going. But we move forward."

We do.

She spun back to Dane. "How is it for you, coming in and having Sam's ghost hanging over you?"

Fucking what?

Dane looked at me then back to Ashley. "Sam's ghost doesn't hang over me. I knew Sam, not long, but I knew him. We are a team."

Lee fist-bumped Dane.

Good try, lady. We're solid. We're ready for whichever road she takes next.

"Did I ask last time we met how the release of the Qu pathogen impacted on you all?"

The air pressure changed as my team stiffened. Batter up, Ellie.

"Qu affected us less than the loss of Director O'Hare. However, Qu affected Virginia in deep and still evolving ways." I let that settle for a split second. "Our losses during its release and while the pathogen ran its course are irreplaceable people who were close to us and whose existence made our jobs easier, but none of them died from Qu."

Qu killed many people. But most of the people we came across in our investigation who died, did not die from Qu but from the actions of those involved with the release of the pathogen. Hit and run. Horse riding accident. Gun shot. Drug overdose. Drowning.

Pages flipped.

Ashley shot me a questioning look. "There is no mention of human loss at earlier sessions."

Yeah, well, maybe we weren't ready to talk about our friends.

Lee moved his foot. "We'd rather not discuss Qu-related losses," he said, quietly.

"It's an important part of the life of Delta A. Dealing with the loss of friends and colleagues can be challenging."

Dane leaned forward, his elbows rested on his knees. "We got this, Ashley."

"I'm letting you all know I'm available."

"And we appreciate that," Dane said.

So ended her enquiries into the team psyche surrounding the Qu pathogen. Ashley dropped her pen. It rolled, stopping at my feet, I picked it up and handed it to her.

"Thank you," she said.

I smiled. "No problem."

"Is there anything you'd like to discuss, Ellie?"

"No. We're good."

She turned her attention to Lee again. I watched a little white ball of spittle form near the corner of her mouth. As she spoke, it elongated, relaxed then changed into a fat creamy maggot. It swung from her top lip, wriggling blindly, until it plummeted toward her lap. At the very last second, a fluffy yellow duckling popped out of her cardigan pocket and snapped up the juicy maggot.

With a furtive glance in Dane's direction, I saw him struggle to suppress a smile. He slid words into my mind: *Not fair*. Once upon a time, Kurt told me I wasn't insane. The term he chose to use was *mentally hilarious*. No doubt about it, I fully embraced the hilarity for better or worse.

Chapter Three

100 Years Ago

Half an hour later, relieved to be back in my office, I settled in to decompress, but looked up when I felt a presence.

A surprise Wednesday afternoon visitor. Mike Davenport's hand paused in mid-air as he returned my smile, his blue eyes warmed. Somewhere deep in my skull, I heard David Bowie's, 'John, I'm only dancing.' A memory of time spent with Mike surfaced then bleached as the rest of the recollection sucked the color away. A turbulent time for Delta A during which I was on the run from the FBI because Owen, the Wicked Queen, decided I had something to do with my ex-brother-in-law's death. I became a private detective named Laura Graham to help protect Mike Davenport, who the world knows as Mike Fisher, the actor, from a crazy person. It ended in our fake marriage and Laura's death. Do I know how to have fun or what?

"Hey, what are you doing in town?" I said and waved him in.

"Promo gig for the next season of my TV series. Thought I'd say hello. I come bearing an office-warming gift." He jiggled a gift bag in his hand and grinned. Mike stood in the middle of my office and surveyed it. "This is nice. Corner office. I noticed a new nameplate on the door."

Same name, different designation. Shit happens. Things change.

"I take it Lee signed you in." I glanced at the visitor tag attached to his breast pocket.

Mike placed the bag on my desk. "Hope you like turmeric."

Don't know that I have feelings regarding turmeric. I peered into the bag and pulled out a tall thin bottle of golden brown liquid. *Lee-thal Latte*. Interesting. I read the directions on the bottle before setting it aside.

"Thanks."

"It's tasty. Reminds me of pumpkin pie." His smile crinkled around his eyes. "Something other than coffee."

Good, another person who thinks I need something other than coffee. He and Kurt should get together and compare notes.

"Have a seat, Mike." I closed the laptop and gave him my undivided attention.

He lowered himself into a chair opposite my desk. "How is it every time I see you, you look more incredible than the last time?"

"How is it you're more full of shit by the year?" I said. "You should come by the house while you're in town."

His grin broadened. "Sure. Dinner would be good, I hear Mitch can cook."

I arched an eyebrow at him. "Smartass."

He ignored my comment and moved on. "What's it

like being the Special Agent in Charge, and where's Grafton, that's his name right?"

"It's all right. Bigger office, more responsibility, and a ton more paperwork, but apart from that, not much has changed." I tried to work out what the visit was all about, maybe he just dropped in to say hello? "Caine is our new EAD."

"EAD." He paused. "Exasperated Assistant Director?"

"Can't argue with that." A grin that lit my voice. "It's supposedly Executive Assistant Director, but I like yours better."

"So what do they call you now you're the boss?"

"SAC."

An eyebrow rose as a smirk played across his lips. "This place is full of acronyms."

"Actually, it is full of initialisms."

"Pedantic this afternoon, Ellie."

"You didn't bring coffee," I quipped, and glanced at my phone screen a split second before it lit with a message. An unknown origin phone number and a single word: Cryptozoology.

Weird. I read the word again. Be a good one for *Words with Friends*.

"Problem?" Mike said.

"Nope," I replied, and wrote the phone number on the pad on my desk and closed the message. It could be a wrong number. A smile flickered around my lips. Wrong number. Let's go with that.

"What happened to Owen?" Mike stretched his legs out. "Lee said she's gone and it sounded final."

Final. That's the right description.

"Deceased." I didn't even blink. I tried to feel bad for the woman when she was dying months ago, it didn't take. In all honesty I was relieved she wasn't screwing things up here anymore.

"Qu?"

I shrugged. "Maybe." A sigh leaked out. "Can we not talk about her or Qu?"

Faces of the dead drifted across the screen in my mind, the first one caught on a broken branch from an oak tree, the others banked up behind it. I willed the dam to hold.

"Too soon?"

"I think it'll always be too soon. Too soon and way too close to an apocalyptic event."

He nodded and lightened his inquiries. "Tell me about your new job."

"It's extra paperwork, more meetings. I know a helluva lot more about our budgets now, and the real bonus is I have more people to worry about," I replied with a smile. "This is the quietest afternoon I've had since I took over."

"You love it, don't you?"

"I do."

"You're still in the field with Delta A though, right?"

"Do you think I'd give up the fun part?"

He laughed and shook his head. "I once tried to

imagine you sitting behind that desk while the team was out doing their thing. I'm an imaginative guy, but that was a struggle."

"I don't know how Caine did it for all those years. Now I understand why he was so keen to help out in the field after Sam—"

He sure was helpful when we were down an experienced agent, and I think he enjoyed the return to the field.

A message alert sounded from my phone. The message was from the same number as before. This time it said: Cryptomnesia.

And just like that weird got weirder. Could be someone was helping someone with *Words with Friends* or *Scrabble* and it was a wrong number. A little niggling wiggle of a notion in my gut told me it wasn't a wrong number.

If it's not a wrong number then perhaps someone wants me to know something. Curiosity peaked.

"Catch up with you later?" I said to Mike. "I'll put the word out that dinner is at our place on Friday night. Time we had everyone together for a meal."

Mike rose. "Sure. Sounds good."

"Seven, and you're bringing the wine and beer."

"Coronas and red or white?"

"Yes."

Mike smiled. "Okay, I can handle that. See you Friday night. I'm staying at Lee's by the way." He paused at the door. "Open or shut?"

"Open."

Chapter Four
Lookin' Out for #1

Opening a handy piece of software on my laptop, I added the phone number from the earlier text messages. The query came back fast. No name attached to the phone number. No surprise the number belonged to an unregistered mobile phone. Great.

An email notification popped up on the corner of my screen. The subject both intrigued and worried me: *Second family vanished.* I clicked on the notification.

A police officer I knew out in Missouri sent the email. He'd included an email from a colleague of his about another missing family. I read it twice. Then hopped into Law Enforcement Online and looked up the cases. We hadn't received an official invitation to meddle, but Gary wanted to know what I saw and thought. A straight-up second opinion. That I could do.

The first missing family disappeared eighteen months ago from a suburb of Wichita, Kansas. The second family on November fifteenth twenty-nineteen from a suburb of Jefferson City, Missouri. I read through the notes from the investigating officer's files. Entire families don't usually disappear.

Unless ... I stopped and checked the names of the parents against federal criminal cases from around the time of the disappearances. Nothing. Probably not WITSEC then.

Unless ... I dug around some more and ran a search for all crimes in the particular cities around the time the families vanished. On the surface, I saw plenty of crime but none that would require families to go into protective custody or make families want to up and leave.

Back to the first missing family: the Johnson family. An elementary school teacher noted the absence of seven-year-old Janine Johnson. No one could make contact with the family. Police weren't notified until a week after the child was first noted as absent from school.

A similar pattern occurred with the Abbots, the second family. Once police received notification, a short investigation showed that neither parent had turned up for work, and two of their three children were absent from elementary school. The third child, although too young for school had not been to daycare in a week.

Whole families. Mom, Dad, and two kids. Mom, Dad, and three kids. Whatever happened to the families more than likely took place over a weekend. The kids last seen at school on a Friday, the adults last seen at work on a Friday. As far as police could determine the families appeared normal. None of the adults had ever come to police attention before. Nor the kids either. They were regular families. Both parents worked. Kids attended school and did normal after-school activities. Both church-on-Sunday type families.

Zero history of mental illness.

I sat back and thought about it for a moment. A family that disappeared would've made the news. A group of people doesn't disappear like that. One person might. Two might run away together. But a whole family? Unless people assumed the families had moved away, it was suspicious. And why would anyone think a family would up and move like that? They weren't isolated families. They were part of a community. School. Work. Church. Sports clubs. Neighborhoods. People with ties and lives.

I was still trying to find information when Kurt walked into my office.

"Got a minute?" He moved the chair Mike had vacated a bit closer to the desk before he sat.

"Be right with you." I wrote an email reply to Gary and told him I wanted to look into the missing families cases and asked if he minded and who I needed to contact in Wichita. As soon as I hit send I looked at Kurt. "What's up?"

"A couple of text messages from an unregistered mobile phone."

"Oh, snap," I said. An eyebrow rose. "What'd yours say?"

"Cryptozoology then cryptomnesia."

"Same as mine."

Dane appeared in the doorway with Lee right behind him.

"Boss," Dane said. "Something weird is going on."

"Lemme guess, text messages? One says cryptozoology and the other cryptomnesia?"

Dane's forehead wrinkled into a slight frown as they joined us.

"Delta A is getting weird messages. Any ideas?" I said, swinging my chair from side to side. I looked at Lee. "Word of the day stuff is right up your alley. What do you make of it?"

Lee cleared his throat. "It's pretty obvious that someone conducted an investigation into Big Foot and came across research they thought was new but in fact, it's a forgotten memory." His straight-faced delivery was impressive. "They've plagiarized themselves and are now ready to report it."

A laugh rolled from Dane and ended in a snort. Kurt spluttered coffee. Dribbling like a two-year-old, he wiped his hand across his mouth and chin.

"Hang on, there's a flaw in your logic," I said. "In twenty-eighteen researchers proved that Big Foot did not exist, once and for all. So, I reckon the sender of the text is talking about Leviathan."

"Biblical Leviathan or *Supernatural*?" Dane said, his mirth spilled forth.

"Sea monsters versus something so awful that they were locked in purgatory because God couldn't control them?" I said, dropping my feet to the ground and bringing my chair upright. "Looks like we've got quite the battle in front of us. Anyone got any ideas on how to subdue or kill Leviathan?"

Kurt coughed, reached for tissues from my desk, and wiped up the coffee in his lap.

"Meanwhile back on dry land and in the real world," Dane said. "We all got the same text messages, so there must be a reason."

I'd like to think someone made a mistake. I'd really like to think that. I really would.

An email notification hung in the corner of my screen. It was from Officer Gary Singe. The official invitation to help investigate the missing family in Missouri and a contact in Wichita. The weird text messages would have to wait.

"We have a potential new case," I said and opened the email. "For now it's research-based."

Everyone's head lifted. Kurt balled up soggy tissues and tossed them at the waste paper basket.

"Who, what, where, why?" Lee moved his chair closer. Dane followed suit.

"Two missing families," I said, and scanned the email for information to share. "They went missing fifteen months apart from different cities and states." The energy in the room homed in on me. "The first disappearance was in Wichita, Kansas. The second in Jefferson City, Missouri."

"Why aren't FBI in those cities involved?" Kurt said.

"Mostly because there is no evidence of foul play, as strange as that seems."

"Hard to imagine that families would vanish without

foul play."

My right eyebrow arched in his direction. Exactly what I thought. "A couple more reasons for our invitation, we're the experts in serial crime and also because a cop I know asked me to have a look at the files."

"Two isn't serial," Kurt replied quietly.

"No, it isn't. But something about this case tells me there's more going on. Hence, research."

"Do we know if they're witnesses or criminals within the Witness Protection Program?" Dane said.

"I did a quick look at cases around the time of their disappearances. Zilch jumped out to make me think WITSEC is involved."

"But they just disappeared," Dane said. "That's a WITSEC trademark."

Sure is. I filed the thought away with the intention of talking to Debbie Barnes, our resident expert on new identities.

"Let's leave that to simmer and in the meantime, I want to know if any other families have disappeared. If so when and where. Nationwide."

Dane made notes on his iPad.

"Why do you think there are more?" Kurt said, he glanced around the room then back at me. "Chance? A song?"

"Not this time. Just a big ol' twinge in my gut."

Lee looked up from his phone. "Media has reports of a missing family in Carson City, Nevada. Twenty-one months ago."

"Any details?"

"The Gatewood Family. Scott and Kirsty Gatewood and their twelve-year-old twin daughters, Josephine and Julie, were last seen at school and work on Friday April thirteen." He looked at me for a beat. "It's possible they went missing over the weekend even though they weren't reported missing until two weeks later."

"Why did it take so long to report the missing family?" Dane asked.

"The parents signed the girls out of school for a week from that Friday. They planned a family camping trip before Scott Gatewood continued his cancer treatment."

Not good. "Did they go?" I said. Maybe they were they eaten by bears.

"No one knows," Lee said.

I scrolled through the information I had about the other two families. All three families were last seen on a Friday. Maybe it wasn't the Friday ... they could've disappeared at any point over the weekend.

"Weekends," I said.

"Let's look into that," Kurt said. His pen scratched across a page in his notebook. "What events do families attend on weekends?"

He looked at me but didn't see me. I waited for a revelation from my team.

To my surprise, all heads came up and eyes focused

on me. When did I become the expert on family weekend adventures?

Nope. Not even close to a starter for that role. "I'm new to this family business and my girls are a bit young to take to weekend events." My thoughts scrambled about in the dust and cobbled an answer together. "But, I imagine, when they're older we'll go to movies, parks, fairs, circuses, art galleries, museums, parties, theaters, concerts, and they'll probably play some sport."

Heads went down. Pens and fingers added information to either notebooks or tablets. To locate all the events and places families could go in each city and within a reasonable day-trip distance from each city or town would take time. I envisaged spreadsheets and other aggravations.

In truth, I imagined me with a coffee and comprehensive brief once the tedious stuff was done. Once again I proved the existence of my vivid and active imagination.

The Gatewood family from Carson City, Nevada, felt like an anomaly. We had no evidence to suggest the other two families disappeared from anywhere but their home cities. The Gatewood's may have vanished from the campsite, or never reached their destination, or taken part in some activity before the trip. More variables than the other families.

Maybe the families took part in the same event but in different states, and different months and years.

What would people do that is the same month after month and year after year?

I heard the word in my head before it tumbled off my lips. "Circus."

Lee's eyes met mine. "Carnie folk."

Nope. Not going there. I jammed the circus thought into a mental safe and clanged the door shut.

Chapter Five

Jump

Thursday morning's sun streamed through the windows in my office. Emails chimed their arrival as they popped up on my screen one by one. I hit mute on my keyboard and silenced the alerts. Somewhere in the middle of the many emails on my screen I saw a subject line that gave me pause. One click confirmed its importance. My eyes darted across the screen.

I picked up the phone and pressed three numbers into the keypad. Two rings.

"Boss?" Dane said.

"Provo, Utah. There's another missing family this one is dated October twenty-seventeen."

"We have two from twenty-nineteen, one twenty-eighteen, and one twenty-seventeen?"

So far. "Yep. We have a span of over two years."

"Same deal? Nothing different?"

"Nothing different that I can see in the reports I've been given. The Provo family were last seen on a Friday, parents didn't show up for work on Monday, kids never showed at school."

"How'd you find this one?"

"Word's out that we're interested in missing families," I said, and typed an email with one hand to thank the police officer who alerted us to the Provo family. "I'm putting a timeline up in my office." I hung up, and left Dane to ponder the news.

From my drawer, I took a couple of whiteboard markers. I had an entire whiteboard wall at my disposal in my brand new office. It wasn't just a whiteboard; it was a smartboard. With my phone in my left hand and a marker in my right, I faced the board.

Instead of the family names, I used location as the identifier. Every case becomes personal: I needed distance to arrive at an overview of the whole picture before they became moms and dads and their kids. Before I named each person and committed their faces to memory. And carried them forever.

I started with Wichita and wrote all the information we had about that family.

By the time I finished, I was sick of the smell of whiteboard markers and in need of a coffee. I scooped my wallet and phone from my desk drawer and left my office.

A run down the dimly lit stairs is always fun. I swung open the last smoke-stop door and entered the brightly lit reception area of the building. A few blinks let my eyes adjust.

Our friendly agent manning the reception desk grinned at me from behind the desk.

"Knew it was you, SAC." Frank tipped his head to the stairwell door. "Good echo in there, huh?"

"Yep," I replied with a laugh as I pushed the glass entrance door open. Fresh warm air hit me. Fall hadn't really started yet. It thought about it a few times, then summer kicked back in. Couldn't say I was unhappy about the extended summer days and warmth.

I turned right and walked along the sidewalk. Autopilot guided me like a coffee-fueled missile. The return trip included delightful sips of rich, black nectar of the God's. They'd made my coffee for me for so long, all I had to do was walk through the door, wait, and pay. The staff even added four pieces of ice to my coffee so I could drink it on the way back to work without third-degree burns.

Each sip was delicious. Each footfall eased and lulled my mind allowing clean space to sift through the case details.

Two is a coincidence, three is a pattern, four is a problem.

What connected the families?

What made these particular families vulnerable?

How did entire families disappear? The C-word perched on the edges of my conscious mind. How many circuses are still operational? How many travel state to state? A nugget of information I'd read about a German circus came to the fore. They were using holograms instead of live animals. Not sure even that would make me want to take my girls to a circus. A clown holding a red balloon waved to me. I reined in the thoughts, we could come back to the circus once we've exhausted other options. All other options.

I stopped at a light-controlled crosswalk and waited. Traffic moved past me. Someone waved from a black sedan. I knew who it was before I *knew* who it was and waved back. US Marshal Cara Wells. The lights changed. On the other side of the street I stopped and looked at the intersection. Red light cameras. Turning on the spot I saw four more cameras. If I disappeared at that moment, at least one person I knew saw me at the crosswalk, and probably all five cameras would've picked me up. And that did not include the ATM near the corner.

How did entire families disappear without a trace? I swung through the door of our building and ran up the stairs without spilling a drop of coffee.

Frank's voice followed me up the first flight of stairs, "Didn't your mother ever tell you that running on stairs is dangerous?"

My mother didn't parent, she checked out.

The smell of whiteboard marker lingered in the air of my office. I stood and finished my coffee while I took in all the information in front of me.

Maybe ten years ago families could disappear in a puff of smoke, and even then I'd imagine someone somewhere saw something or knew something. Now surveillance was everywhere. People had dashboard cams. Many houses had external motion sensitive video capability. Everyone carried cellphones and took pictures and videos constantly. Images and videos were uploaded at a phenomenal rate to Facebook and Instagram and other social media sites. CCTV operated in most schools grounds and in the hallways of the buildings. You couldn't go far without being captured on film.

Where did they go?

The C-word appeared again, followed by a creepy clown. There is nothing good in a circus.

My phone buzzed on my desk. Without real thought, I propelled myself toward the buzz and away from the whiteboard of misery.

A quick glance at the screen told me I didn't want to open the message.

Unknown caller.

Again.

The message faded to black and left a shadowy residue imprinted on my mind. Cryptosporidium. I was pretty sure that was some kind of gastrointestinal illness. It sounded nasty.

Lee's voice rang out. I spun around to see him walking toward me.

"Cryptosporidium," he said, his phone in his hand.

"Did everyone get it?"

"Yeah, but let's hope no one does." He grinned and threw me a pocket-sized bottle of hand sanitizer.

Ha! Mr. Hilarious was the chosen emissary. "Great. Any ideas?"

Lee shook his head. "It's something, but I don't know what."

Snap! I Googled cryptosporidium just to get the facts. The Center for Disease Control said it was 'a microscopic parasite that caused diarrheal disease and can live in the intestine of humans and animals and is passed in the stool of an infected person or animal.'

Delightful.

'The parasite is protected by an outer shell that allows it to survive outside the body for long periods of time, making it resistant to chlorine-based disinfectants.'

Yuck. I wondered if there was a link between our cryptic text messages and the missing families. A stretch, but stranger things have happened. I squirted a dollop of hand sanitizer into my palm. Even talking about illnesses woke my inner germaphobe. Before Qu, I didn't even know I had an inner germaphobe. The things you learn if you survive long enough.

"Any of the missing people doctors?" Because that would give me a tie and maybe make sense of something.

"Not a hundred percent on that. Hang tight," Lee replied. He shoved the bottle I handed him into his jeans pocket. He scrolled through information on his phone.

"We have a doctor in the house." He turned his phone to show me the screen. "Sherrie Anderson, Provo, Utah. She's a psychiatrist."

We stared at each other for a beat. Stuff wriggled in my cerebrum like a parasite. A psychiatrist, now that was something, but not a parasitic disease specialist kinda of something.

Okay, maybe a parasitic disease wasn't a link then.

"Stick a pin in that, Lee." No. Wait. Shit. "Cryptomnesia."

"Whoa," Lee said. "I'll find out if that has anything to do with Sherrie Anderson."

Kurt walked through the doorway and waved an envelope. "You've got mail."

"Doesn't a cart usually come round with mail? Or do you work in the mailroom now?"

He glanced over his shoulder then back at me. "The mail person went past. I said I'd give this to you." He skimmed the envelope toward me.

The fingers of one hand snatched it from mid-air as I reached behind myself with the other and picked up a letter opener from my desk.

"Does no one just pass anything to me anymore?" I muttered. The envelope felt silky and weighty compared to bill envelopes. Cursive writing in what looked like fountain pen adorned the front, my full title and name, and a complete address. Not just 'Agent Iverson, Hoover Building.' Even though the mailroom screened all mail, I gave the envelope a gentle shake. The contents moved as a cohesive unit. I turned it over and read the return address and name of the sender. Mrs. M. Falacco. Intrigue from oozed from my bones. With a quick flick, the blade sliced the top edge of the envelope.

Habit made me peer into the envelope before I extracted a tri-folded piece of top quality stationery. I didn't get mail like that every day. I didn't get mail like that ever. There's a first time for everything.

Before I unfolded the heavyweight silky paper, I paused.

"Problem?" Kurt said.

"Did you look at the sender?"

"No. I'm just the delivery boy. Someone you know?"

"Someone we know. Mikki Falacco or as the thriller world knows her, Mikki Kennedy."

"The youngest O'Hare, Mikki Kennedy, the author?" Kurt said.

"The very same," I replied.

"Unconscionable," Lee said.

My eyes widened. Kurt's eyebrows rose.

"Really, that's the word you've been desperate to use?" A small strangled laugh escaped. "At a pinch it might work, maybe." My head shook. "Nope, I can't make that work."

Thoughts buzzed across Lee's face, several settled then flew away before he said, "A letter from our deceased Director's sister is outrageous ... unconscionable."

Kurt high-fived him.

"Wow." I was reasonably impressed that he squeezed that out. "Can I read it now?"

"Sure, go ahead."

The beautiful penmanship dragged me into the world of the sender. Mikki Kennedy: world-famous thriller author. By the time I'd finished the second sentence I knew why Mikki reached out to us. Police weren't interested in her particular issue because it hadn't yet reached danger level and Delta A had a long relationship with her family.

The wound left by the death of her sister, and our former Director Cait O'Hare, still wept and stung. I looked up, Kurt and Lee's curiosity simmered under the surface and subtly tweaked their expressions.

"Mikki needs advice. She remained in Virginia after Cait's death, so she's not far away."

"Serious?" Kurt looked from me to the whiteboard on the wall.

"The potential is there." My eyes flicked to the whiteboard and back to the men in front of me. With luck, we could nip the situation in the bud and all would be well. "We're multitaskers from way back. This is not a problem for us." That was awful positive of me. Pollyanna lives.

"And the problem?" Lee shoved his phone in his pocket.

"An over-zealous fan." I skimmed over the letter again. "We need a face-to-face with Mikki to get all the information. Where's Dane?"

"He's deep in missing person land on the hunt for families that might fit our whiteboard," Lee said, with a nod of his head toward the timeline.

"Lee, I want you to stay with Dane." I added a label to the case file on our system. "From now on this case is Operation Disney." He rose from his seat. "Update the whiteboard as you uncover information."

"Of course. Alert and safe, Ellie." Lee and I ran our palms across each other's catching our fingers briefly before he left the room.

"I'll call Mikki now, and we'll go over to her place," I said to Kurt.

"I'll let Sandra know. Meet you at the car in ten."

Mikki picked up on the fourth ring. Counting rings is a habit. "It's Ellie Iverson here, Mikki. Kurt and I are on our way to you. Hope that's okay." I didn't offer a choice.

"You got my letter." Her voice lilted and tipped to a smile. "I'm home all week and between books, so this is the perfect time."

"Excellent. We'll be there within the hour."

"Thank you Ellie, I appreciate you taking this seriously."

Yeah, well, I know what over-zealous fans can be like from personal experience. Not fun. Never fun.

"No problem, we'll see you soon."

Chapter Six

Bounce

Kurt pulled our black Suburban into the lower driveway of Mikki Falacco's expansive home. The wrought iron gates stood open, inviting us further into the grounds. Kurt eased the car up the driveway toward the house and parked. The expansive manicured front lawns spoke of a gardener's hand. Sure enough, a young man appeared with a wheelbarrow. He stopped as we approached the front door.

"Can I help?"

"We are here to see Mrs. Falacco," I said with a smile.

A hint of distrust lurked under his pleasant demeanor. Or was it a smidge of unease?

"Mrs. Falacco is in back garden. She is expecting you?"

"Yes. We're old friends," I replied with a smile. The man remained cautious and aloof. Rather than push him, I opted for a gentle approach. "We can wait here if you'd like to check with Mrs. Falacco. I am Ellie Iverson and this is Kurt Henderson." Special Agent Iverson and Special Agent Henderson didn't sound friendly enough.

He nodded. "Please. I'll be right back." He left the wheelbarrow and hurried away down the side of the house.

Kurt gave me a look. I shrugged. Moments later, the young man appeared from the side of the house.

"Please follow me," he said.

"What's your name?" Kurt asked as he caught up to the man.

"Carlos."

"Have you worked for Mrs. Falacco long, Carlos?"

"I take care of the grounds for the last four years." Carlos held open a high wooden gate. "Mrs. Falacco is on the back patio. Follow the path through the trees."

"Thank you, Carlos," I said.

The gate shut. Birds twittered on branches above the path. Our footsteps sank into the ground below. No concrete or gravel. The path was dirt. The entrance to the back garden reminded me of a nature trail or a horror movie. No matter how hard I tried to push that away it stuck.

"Is the patio in New Jersey?" Kurt muttered.

A small laugh slipped from me. "Probably."

Bright light filled the path ahead. As we reached the light, an expanse of green fitted all available space in front of us. To the right I saw the house and patio. A loveseat swung gently. From where I stood, legs came into view.

"Mikki!" I called as we walked across the manicured lawn.

A hand waved from somewhere above the legs swinging the loveseat. I walked up the porch steps.

Mikki rose from the seat. Her blonde hair

shimmered in the sun. She smiled, warmly. "Thank you for the visit," and shook my hand then Kurt's.

"Not exactly a hardship." I waved an arm around her secluded back yard. "This is beautiful."

"A small sanctuary secreted in suburbia," Mikki said with a wink. "Tea?"

Kurt's smile widened. "I'd love tea." He looked at me with a challenge in his eye. "Iverson?"

Not biting.

"Coffee?"

"Of course," Mikki said and rang a small bell on a table near the swing. She motioned to an outdoor table and chairs at the other end of the porch. "Shall we?"

The chair I tried to pull out from the table felt surprisingly heavy. I looked down at the seat and a large black cat opened an eye and looked at me.

"Sorry, puss," and gave it a gentle pat on the head before moving to another chair.

"That's Kincade," Mikki said. "He's a dreadful mouser, fussy as can be, and generally cranky, but I like him."

"Sounds like Kurt," I mumbled.

He shot me a look.

The door opened and a woman emerged and approached Mikki. "Ma'am?"

"Tea for two and a coffee, please," Mikki said.

"Yes, ma'am." The woman left and closed the door behind her.

"Okay, Mikki, what's the story here?" I said. Kincade

opened an eye and watched me for a moment and then instantly fell asleep. Nice to be a cat.

Mikki shook her head slowly. "It's a strange situation."

"We're pretty good with strange." Kinda our thing.

"The worst part is that I think I created it myself without realizing." She looked across the table at me. "He's a friend … but he seems to have created a fantasy world around me."

Crazy fan shit.

"Walk us through this from the beginning," Kurt said. "We need a sense of the build-up to the current situation."

Mikki nodded.

"About six years ago he got in touch and said he was an avid fan of my latest series. It's lovely to hear from people who read and doubly so when it's an old friend." She smiled and adjusted her cream cardigan. "Was nice to reconnect, I've known him and his sister since we were all in our twenties." She buttoned two buttons and then unbuttoned them. "He told me he was writing a book. And before long he wanted me to read it."

Mikki paused as the tea and coffee arrived. Her housekeeper left us to pour. Once we all had our beverages I prompted Mikki to tell us more.

"It's good to encourage new writers," she said, and took a sip of tea from the delicate bone china cup then set it on the matching saucer.

"I suppose it is," I said. "What was it like?"

"Hard to read. Long-winded. Never quite got to the point."

"That good?" Kurt said with a smile. "I don't envy you. Must be hard to read for people like that."

"It's no fun when it is mansplained waffle and you have to tell them so."

"How did that go?"

"Oh, he defended each comment. But after a few days, he seemed to grasp what I had said." She sipped her tea again. "Then he announced he wanted to write a tie-in book to my current series and use my characters, and that I could write some of it as well."

Cheeky and a bit too sure of himself, considering she'd just told him his book was crap.

"And?"

"I let him write, I was never going to be part of it. Each new story idea stumbled around the page like a one-legged duck that couldn't find a pond. His main character was a thirteen-year-old girl I wanted to throttle because all she did was whine."

"I'm sorry, what? He's how old and he's writing about a thirteen-year-old girl?"

She nodded. "Thirty-nine."

"That doesn't sit well with me."

"Me either. It's worse when you know it's first person."

"Oh, wow." I placed, my coffee cup on the table. "Why was he writing a young female character?" No matter how much I didn't want to dwell on that, I knew my mind would file it all away to drag out later. A male in his late thirties writing from the point of view of a thirteen-year-old girl ramped my alarm system up several notches.

"I don't know. I advised against it, but he played with that character for quite a few years."

"A few years? Mikki, why has this gone on so long?"

"I thought I could help, that I'd be able to get through to him and he'd improve." She sighed. "Some people really want to write. He is one of them."

"I almost don't want to ask what happened next ..."

"The quality of the writing didn't improve." She shrugged. "At all. I think it got worse."

"How did we get from a creepy guy writing from the point of view of a young kid to today?" Kurt asked.

"Slowly, over years. The process was painful. I fought the urge to poke my eyes out at every revision. Eventually, I turned to my editor and publishers and asked what I should do. Bearing in mind that he was a friend."

Smart move.

"My editor reminded me to check my contract. So I did. I went to him and said he can't use my characters due to copyright and I can't write the story with him because it would have to be under fifty-thousand words. He'd written over eighty-thousand awful words by this stage." She smiled. "For a minute it looked like a great out."

"And?"

"He ignored me as is his pattern. He doesn't hear what he doesn't like. I repeated the same message for weeks until he finally heard me. But he really didn't. I travel, as you know, and every time I came back, he'd hound me about this godawful story again."

"Any other behaviors?"

"Constant need for contact. He used to call all the time until I made him understand that it's too intrusive when I'm working. He then moved to texts. Some days I'd get ten or twelve wanting me to call him or to meet with him."

"Your response?"

"I ignored ninety percent of all contact or was short with my response."

"What happens when he does see you?"

"He goes on and on about himself and his story, and how he's had yet another idea. I did manage to persuade him not to use a child, so he made the character eighteen." She sighed and shook her head. "But honestly, all he did was change the age, as in he *says* she's older in the story. She's still a thirteen-year-old in every other way. And an eighteen-year-old girl isn't even close to the thirty-five to forty-year-old male I wanted him to write."

"Clearly he isn't getting the message here," I said. "And you cannot have your name associated with what sounds like a horrendous story." Career suicide.

"Absolutely."

"What'd you do next?"

"When he told me he'd finished it. Stupidly I thought this was finally over. I said to send it to me." She traced the roses on her saucer with her index finger. "I was appalled when I read it, utter bullcrap, from the first to last sentence. I went to mark it up, but it would take too long and I don't have that kind of time." Mikki poured a fresh cup of tea. "I sent it to a friend who is an editor and asked her for her professional opinion. It was clear, brutal, cut to the quick. I sent it to him and he turned around the next day and said he had an idea how to change the story."

Exasperation wriggled like a worm on a hook. A fluffy yellow duck squeezed out of the teapot spout with a plop. It shook and waddled across the table, snapped at the threads of exasperation that hung from Mikki's lips. I blinked. The duck disappeared.

"He doesn't understand?" Kurt asked. "Is he capable of understanding?"

Mikki smiled. "Are you asking if he's thick?"

"More mentally impaired."

"I don't think so, but I doubt he can feel empathy or put himself in an imaginary situation."

I moved in my chair. Sociopath? That didn't feel right.

"Is there a chance he's deliberately writing badly to have a reason to seek you out?" I said.

"That crossed my mind a few times over the last year, but I discounted it because I've known him a long time."

She just second-guessed herself and thinks she was wrong. "What, Mikki? What do you know?"

"A few months ago I met someone, a fan and a friend of his. I knew who she was before I'd met her. From my Facebook page and also he had mentioned her a few dozen times over the years. I met her in person because she sought me out." Mikki looked at me. "We met at your sister-in-law's bookshop when Holly invited me to do a book signing. We had a chat about the books and then she mentioned our mutual friend, Ellis. I changed the subject. We talked about books some more and that was that."

"Did you say Alice? His name is Alice?" Wow. I'm out of touch if Alice is a boy's name. And it wasn't that long ago we were thumbing through name books to find the perfect names our babies. We nearly called Grace, Alice.

Mikki smirked. "Yes, I said Alice, except it is spelled E-L-L-I-S. Ellis."

"And it's a male name?"

Mikki regarded me for a moment. "You know, I'd never considered that. We've known each other a long time, but I've never given his name much actual thought."

Kurt coughed. "I don't think it matters what gender this person identifies with or what sex his parents thought he was. It's the behavior that we're interested in."

Back on track, my next question fired at Mikki.

"How did this woman you met change your perception regarding Ellis?"

"How'd you know it changed?"

"Because otherwise why tell us about a fan ..." Unless the fan is another lunatic.

Mikki laughed. For a split second, I saw Cait in her. "We got together for a coffee. I don't usually go out for coffee with fans, but she seemed nice. We talked. She told me all she hears from Ellis is Mikki this and Mikki that, and what good friends we are and how he's writing a book with me. I told her he ignores my husband if he's around when Ellis is, doesn't even say hello. And I'd noticed some behavior patterns around that."

"What sort of patterns?"

"Ellis ups his level of contact before I travel and when I come home, and before my husband arrives and after he leaves. Generally, when he's here or we're away I don't hear from him at all. There are no sudden book emergencies or concocted reasons for contact."

"What else?"

"He seems to have no other friends. Certainly, no male friends that I know of. He makes himself out to be quite the hero at work. He used to bug Shelly as much as he bugs me. They worked together, so I guess there was more opportunity. When Shelly got married he stopped." Her fingers traced the edge of the saucer. "Really, it shouldn't have taken marriage. Shelly isn't interested in men."

I guess some idiots would see that as a challenge. "This new friend is Shelly?"

"Yes."

"And she worked with Ellis?"

"She said so and he used to talk about her." Mikki smiled. "Now he's suddenly followed me on all my social media accounts when he's never bothered with social media before."

I raised an eyebrow.

She arched hers in reply. "I blocked him."

"There's more isn't there?"

She nodded. "He's started making excuses to come over. Like he had a book he said he'd borrowed, but I didn't lend him one. He had two copies of a DVD, did I want one? There is an urgency to his contact. And that annoys me. Then if I didn't reply to his messages, he'd come over in case my phone was broken or there was an emergency." Her nose wrinkled. "It's a slow suffocation."

"You've seen him?"

She shook her head. "No. My staff were briefed. It'd be quite hard to get past Carlos."

I nodded. "He's good."

She laughed. "He should be for what I pay him." She wiped her mouth with a napkin and scrunched it into a ball. "I spoke to a psychologist. He thinks Ellis may have built a fantasy life around me. I gave him all the information I have and Doctor Henshaw is convinced that Ellis has over time concocted a life that centers on contact with me ..." she grimaced, "... and a special relationship that only he is aware of. Doctor Henshaw warned me that this type of internal fantasy is common to stalkers and that the stalker/fantasy creator may think that everything I say publicly or write in my books is meant for him. A special code of sorts that means I'm reaching out." She shuddered before she could control the impulse. With a slight smile Mikki said, "Even if he was the last man on earth I would not be interested."

"And you've never shown any interest?" Kurt needed clarification.

"None whatsoever. I've been polite." Another sigh. "Sometimes not even polite, there have been times over the years that I have outright shouted at him to fuck off or shut up." Her voice trailed off and sounded almost apologetic.

"How did he respond?" Kurt said.

"He left me alone, or shut up, but never for long. Maybe a day or two at most. Guess he thought I would be over it or forgotten about it in a couple of days. Then he was right back to his old tricks, with the same concocted urgency that surrounds all his ridiculous attempts."

All the drama. All the time. But of course it would be, he'd be worried she'd cut him off completely, and I imagine that caused panic. He'd grab at anything that meant contact.

"Wonderful. And this other friend, Shelly?" I said

then drained my cup.

"She filled in some blanks or maybe made me more aware of his behavior. But I think she's right and that he purposefully manufactures reasons to make contact. Therefore I don't respond, but then it escalates. *Catch-22* for me. All he's ever done is whine about how he does his best. Doesn't matter what the tale is, he does his best."

"We can change that *Catch-22* situation." I looked at Kurt. "What is it that Sean Connery said about losers in *The Rock*?"

Kurt grinned. "Something along the lines of 'Losers whine about doing their best while winners go home and fuck the prom queen.'"

"Yes!" Mikki said with barely suppressed delight at Kurt's butchered movie quote. "He does a lot of whining, and I'm sure there's never been a prom queen."

"Give us his details and we'll track him down and have a word." Kurt passed Mikki his notebook and pen. "I promise to try to make sure he doesn't think it's some secret coded communication that will escalate this crazy shit any further."

"Carlos is here all day?" Mikki's security concerned me. If she was worried enough to reach out to us, then we needed to take all possible precautions.

She nodded. "He and Christelle are married and live in the guest cottage on the grounds."

Good. "Alarm system?"

She smiled. "What does my big brother do?"

Sean O'Hare, security expert. He owned the biggest security firm in Virginia: scene guard contracts, security analysis, monitored alarms, and bodyguards. Delta A used his scene guard company and had done for a long time. In a private capacity, I'd hired his bodyguards to protect my family, and my house had a state of the art O'Hare monitored security system.

"Does Sean know?"

She shook her head. "He's been in Mauryville with Ethan since Cait's death."

"I suggest you tell him. You need to get in first on this one. Tell Sean we're on it, but I want you to have a team of bodyguards. At the very least you need a driver and a companion."

"Seems like overkill—"

"I hope it is. But people who are out of touch with reality concern me."

Kurt nodded in agreement. "Mikki." His tone changed to instructive. "Call Sean. Or we will."

I shot her a grin. "Where's Ed?"

"South America."

"Will he be away long?"

"Another month to six weeks."

"Does he know about this Ellis situation?"

"Not all of it."

"Uh-huh, and would he cut his trip short if he did?"

Mikki nodded. "He's scouting locations. I don't want to pull him back for this."

"Fair enough. You should tell him, though. Let him know we have the situation handled but tell him," I said. "Secrets, Mikki, they always come out."

Mikki looked at me for a moment. "You sounded like Cait."

Time froze. With a sudden jolt, the world came back. A bubble swelled inside me, I couldn't place it right away, then I did. Pride. Sounding like the woman who mentored me throughout my career was one helluva compliment. I missed her.

"Do you have a copy of the story this Ellis person wrote?" I said, the smile on my face reached all the way to my eyes. I felt it there, like a beam of sunshine.

"For?"

"Analysis. There could be clues within the text that tells us more than it tells you."

She nodded and picked up her phone. My phone vibrated a few seconds later. I glanced at the screen and saw an invitation to a shared document.

"Thank you. I'll let you know if we find anything useful."

"I'm sorry in advance for what you have to read."

The name Ellis flapped about until it landed on a reference. Harry Ellis. *Die Hard.* Yapping on about how he could fix the John McClane situation and how he was his buddy. Act like a hero and fuck everything up. Perfect.

Kurt frowned, checked his phone, and then motioned that we needed to go.

Chapter Seven
Summertime

An alert sounded on my phone as I climbed into the car. The look on Kurt's face said he knew what it was.

A message from our random text buddy. Again a lone word: `Cryptocurrency`.

Kurt turned the key and said nothing.

I called Lee. "Hey, get a text?"

"Yeah, me and Dane. Guess you both did?"

"Cryptocurrency?"

"Uh-huh. Whoever this is they sure like crypto-shit."

A snigger welled up as I thought of the previous text, cryptosporidium. Shit indeed.

"We're on our way back in, think we need a team meeting."

"We'll be around."

I dropped my phone into my lap. Kurt drove in silence. The movement of the car lulled me into a stupor. No thoughts. Zero brain wanderings. A void instead of a thinking mind. Ain't that just peachy.

* * *

Sandra waved as we swung through the stairwell door onto the Delta floor. I signaled that I was going to my office. At my desk, Kurt pulled a chair closer.

"Do you still know how to make words come out of your mouth?"

"Smartass."

"Not like you to be this quiet, Iverson."

"Mikki gave me a lot to think about, Henderson."

"We need to talk to Sean, A-sap."

He was right. We did. It wasn't that I didn't trust Mikki to tell him, but I didn't want to withhold information from him either. There was another reason, the earlier silence was a smokescreen created by my subconscious. Now that I was in my office it was firing thoughts and ideas at a rapid rate on three fronts. Because, whether I liked it or not, we now had three situations to deal with. Missing families. The crypto-weirdo. Mikki's stalker-slash-friend gone wrong situation. This is what we do. We deal with other people's shit and make it less stinky.

I dialed Sean O'Hare's number. We go back too far to screw around. I waited for the inevitable voicemail message then the beep.

"Sean, it's Ellie Iverson, pick up!"

A click then a real voice flowed down the line. "You just caught me before I headed your way," Sean said. Before I could ask he continued, "Mikki called a few minutes ago."

"Good. Can you put a close protection detail on her while Kurt and I have a chat to the wannabe-in-Mikki's-life-guy?"

"Already notified one of my CPD teams, switched them from another case."

"Diego Juarez?"

"Yeah, and Casey O'Rouke."

"They had different partners when they worked a job for me ..." I struggled to recall who they were partnered with back when Mitch's brother was kidnapped.

"A lot has changed since Qu. We're down a few guys."

We're all down some good people. "How far away are they?"

"They were in New Jersey. It'll take them a couple of hours to get to Mikki. What's her security like?"

"She has a groundsman who seems capable and one of your monitored security systems ... wanna give me access to her camera feed until you get here?"

"Yes, I do. I'll text the details now. Uses the same app you already have on your phone for your system."

My cell phone screen lit up on my desk with the codes for Mikki's cameras.

"See you when you get in. Take it easy, Sean."

We hung up. I looked at the text message and added Mikki's login and passcode to my security app. Seconds later, her camera feed popped onto my screen. I set the app to text me whenever the motion detectors triggered and closed the program. I figured Carlos would trigger them often and it'd become a pain in the ass. Better that than risk missing Ellis and his special brand of madness. That would not be good. There was something very strange about the guy so fixated on writing with Mikki.

"What type of mental disorder could it be?" I met Kurt's eyes. "A personality disorder?"

"Potentially. I thought Erotomania to start with, because he seems to think there is a special relationship between him and Mikki. But that's also quite a simplistic view and I don't believe it's the whole picture."

"Borderline Personality Disorder?"

"I need to talk to this person. But now, with the information from Mikki I'm tempted to lean toward ASD but it's not my field."

Might not be his field but I trusted his opinion.

"You think he's on the spectrum. Like Autistic?"

"I do. Probably undiagnosed. OCD might be prominent in the mix as well. I want him in a room with me."

Yeah, that sounds like a good idea. Emails popped up on my computer screen and distracted me for a few minutes. When I looked up, Kurt was gone. A split second of confusion followed until he spoke from the other side of the room. He'd read the timeline.

"We could do with approximate populations for these cities." He pointed to the board with two fingers.

We had access to some very useful databases, one of which gave us population for every town and city in the United States. I typed Wichita into the database search field.

"Wichita is approximately three hundred and forty-thousand." I glanced up from my phone. "I'll find them, you write them."

"Deal." The green whiteboard marker in his hand

squeaked on every downward stroke.

"Jefferson City is forty-three thousand." I tapped on my phone screen. "Carson City is approximately fifty-four thousand, and Provo is one hundred and seventeen thousand."

I crossed the floor, and stood next to Kurt. He placed the cap back on the green pen and picked up the red one. He circled Jefferson City and then Carson City.

"Lowest populations." My eyes skimmed the board. "The lower the population, the bigger the impact. The more the local media will carry the story, the more friends and family will search."

"Exactly."

"We'll concentrate on the low population cities first. Let's see what we can turn up from their communities."

"Road trip?"

I shook my head. "Not yet anyway, not with the Mikki situation and the crypto-whatnot." My mind spun on with possibilities. We could Skype people if we got local police or local FBI to lend a hand.

"Enlist local police and FBI. Get a list of everyone who knew that family. I don't care how many times they've been spoken with thus far, we need to conduct some interviews and also have transcripts of any previous interviews."

"I'll ask local FBI to set us up a video interview room," Kurt said. He handed me the red pen. "Then I'll give Dane and Lee a nudge while I'm at it."

"Thanks. I'll compile an interview list." I drew a red

line under the words Jefferson City. "We start here and dig deep. Somebody knows something even if they don't know they do."

Kurt left my office and I stared at the board for a few more seconds. The cities twirled like a crazed ballerina in my gut. I touched a button on the wall and scrolled through maps until I found a map of the United States of America with the states and main cities noted. With a swish of my hand, the map appeared on a large screen to the left of the whiteboard. I chose pushpins from a drop-down menu, pinned them on the relevant cities, then stood back and surveyed the map.

My head shook before my brain engaged enough to utter a mumbled, "Shit."

The lost families cut a swathe through the middle of the country. A trail. A pattern. I focused on the pattern. Not quite a straight line but I could see a path. What connected those families and those cities? Two state capitals on the map. Jefferson City and Carson City. Was that an investigation line?

No.

If we had four state capitals, then I'd say yes. I filed the capital cities out of the way but close, just in case.

I tapped the board and traced a red line with my finger from Carson City, Nevada to Jefferson City, Missouri. I made sure to intersect Provo in Utah and Wichita, Kansas. The line ran through Colorado. Colorado Springs to be exact.

I leaned over, picked up my desk phone, and pressed

three numbers and waited. Sandra's voice echoed as I tapped the speaker button.

"How can I serve, O Leader of the Rebellious?"

"I need a police contact in Colorado Springs, please."

"I'll get on it. Stand by."

I replaced the receiver.

The day ran on; restlessness took over. I paced the corridors but no answer bounced from the doorways. So I ran up and down the stairs. Cowboy boots on concrete. The stairwell echoed with my footfalls.

Halfway down the stairs for the third time, my phone rang. It wasn't a number I recognized. "Special Agent in Charge Iverson."

"Agent Iverson this is Sergeant Jim Kowalski from Colorado Springs Police Department. I was asked to give you a call."

"Yes, thank you for your call, Jim. I'm Ellie Iverson. Doing some research out here in D.C. in regard to missing families. Do you have any cold cases or current cases of any family disappearances?" I walked back up the stairs and down to my office while Jim thought about my question. By the time I was settled behind my desk, Jim had something for me.

"You still there, SAC?"

"Yep."

"Back in twenty-sixteen, a young family went missing. The Davis family."

I started taking notes. "Were they found?"

"No. Miles and Caroline Davis were last seen on

June seventeen, twenty-sixteen, along with their infant son, Jeremy."

I checked the perpetual calendar app on my laptop. June seventeen was a Friday. The Davis disappearance fitted.

"Any idea what happened to them?"

"None. Speculation that Miles got a job out of state and they moved. Caroline was a stay at home mom. The baby was only eight weeks old. They were a delightful family according the neighbors and friends."

"Did they rent or own their own home?"

"Owned their home. Like most of us, had a mortgage."

"Did they sell the house or rent it out?"

"No. If they had, everyone would've thought they'd moved for sure."

"Is the mortgage still being paid? What about utilities?"

"Bank records showed the mortgage was paid automatically until the money ran out eight months after they disappeared."

"The house?"

"The bank wanted to foreclose, but we got a judge to tell them to back off. As far as we're concerned this is an open case albeit a cold one."

The house is sitting there waiting for them to come home. I didn't imagine the bank would be too happy about that situation.

"How long before you have to release the house to

the bank?"

"Another four months and they can take it and do whatever with the house. The contents will be turned over to family members."

"Family?"

Papers flicked. "Family is in California. Miles came here for work and they liked it enough to buy a home."

"You've been in touch with family?"

"Yes. Caroline's brother is Army. Deployed at the time of their disappearance and spoke to his sister about a week before the disappearance."

"Did he know what they were doing that weekend?"

"He said they mainly talked about the baby. There's a note here that says he mentioned his sister was planning a surprise for him."

Probably not the disappearance of the entire family. That'd be more of a shock than a surprise.

"Other family? Did they have living parents?"

"Miles's parents live in Benicia, California. They heard from their son and daughter-in-law on Friday seventeen June."

"That was the last time anyone saw them?"

"We're not a hundred percent on that, but it's certainly the last day anyone spoke to them, and Miles never turned up for work on the following Monday."

"The parents have any idea what they were doing that weekend? Did they notice anything different?"

"They said both Miles and Caroline were happy, the baby was doing well. They were excited about a surprise they had planned."

"Do you know what the surprise was?" The surprise was a sticking point. Could that have gone horribly wrong?

"No. We found nothing in the house to indicate they were planning anything."

"Okay. And there have been no sightings since June twenty-sixteen?"

"None. Not even their car."

"One or two cars?"

"One."

"Can you send me what information you have, please? I think this case fits ours."

"Sure. Originals or copies?"

"Copies are fine." I leaned back in my chair and imagined Colorado Springs on my map. We had a solid line. "Thanks for your help." WITSEC wriggled around until it flopped off my tongue. "Hang on, Jim. Did you consider this could be WITSEC?"

"I did. First thing I thought of because the whole family was gone. Can't get a confirm or deny from the US Marshal's Office and I am not aware of any crime either adult could have witnessed or been involved in. They've certainly never been in any trouble here."

"Thanks, Jim." An afterthought reared. "If you come up with more information reference Operation Disney in the email subject line."

"Sure. Good luck."

* * *

A quick glance at my wristwatch told me I needed to get home. We had a deal, Mitch and I. Unless there was a dire emergency, we were both home every night for dinner with our toddlers. As tragic as Operation Disney was, it would not keep me from my family. Thoughts of the swathe of disappearances kicked the need to go home up a gear.

Chapter Eight

Just One Look

In the driveway, I removed my belt, badge, and the holster containing my Glock. I shoved it all into the glove compartment with my phone. I opened the front door to Mitch's parents' home and closed it again while I called out, "Hello!"

Joan's voice floated down the hallway on a wave of toddler noise, "We're in the kitchen."

Of course. It's always been the most used room in the house, and with our babies there every weekday it continued to be the most used room of the house.

I passed open doors and baby gates. The only doors without child protection were the living room and the kitchen. Nothing is as fast or unpredictable as an eighteen-month-old on the run. Except two of them. Two small heads swiveled as I stepped into the kitchen.

"Mama!" Grace squealed and wriggled to get free of the confines of her granddad's arms. Alan laughed and set her down. She propelled herself at me on her sturdy little legs. In one swift movement, I bent and scooped. Her arms tightened around my neck as she giggled. I held her against me and kissed her head before she slid to the floor. And she was off at a run down the hallway toward the front door. Guess she was ready to go home.

Isabella clambered to her feet on a chair, her little

arms thrust into the air. I leaned over the back of the chair and lifted her into my arms.

"Mommy. Miss you," Isabella said, her face buried in my hair.

"Missed you too, Isabella." I looked at Joan and Alan over her head, with a raised eyebrow. "Has she been okay?"

Joan's gentle smile settled on her lips. "She missed you. We had a lot of mommy talk today." That was when I saw the photo album on the table. That's what everyone was doing at the table, looking at photos. I adjusted my hold on Isabella, her fingers wound tightly in the length of my hair.

Grace thumped on the front door and yelled, "Mama! Home!"

"Hold on, Grace." The open page in the album interested me. I took a closer look. Mitch and I when we were about the girls' age.

Isabella leaned from my arms and pointed at a photo. "Bell-la."

Joan laughed. "Mommy." She touched the photo.

"Is-bell-la!" The quiver in her lip spoke volumes.

Alan smiled. "Isabella. Who is that?" He pointed to the second baby in the photo.

A small frown formed, her fist tightened in my hair, "Race?"

"Daddy," Alan said.

Wrong answer. Isabella let loose an almighty wail. "It's okay baby, shhhh." I hugged her tight and rubbed her back. The noise changed to a small sob. "That's a picture of Mommy and Daddy when we were babies."

Her head swiveled so she could see the picture. "Mommy and Daddy."

"Yes."

"No Is-bell-la." Her head shook. "No Race."

"Clever girl." She tried to reposition herself on my hip but I held her so she couldn't. "Shall we go home and see Daddy?"

"Home," she said on a sob.

"Tired baby," I whispered. "Mommy needs you to walk."

Isabella twisted in my arms. I put her down and she took off to the front door and Grace. Joan passed me their backpacks.

"Thank you." I smiled and hoisted a backpack on each shoulder. "See you tomorrow."

Joan walked me to the door and opened it for us.

"Girls, hands," I said. Grace grabbed Isabella by the hand. Isabella grabbed my hand. "Good job. Let's get you in the car."

Joan stood on the porch and watched.

I dropped the kids' backpacks on the backseat between their car seats then put Grace in her seat. Always Grace first. Isabella and I walked around to the other door. Then it was her turn. I took my phone from the glove compartment and dropped it on the front passenger seat. Within reach, just in case.

The trip home was quick, with little traffic. As I

pulled up in front of the house, my phone rang. I saw Mike's name on the screen and let it go to voicemail with a mental note to call him tomorrow.

The front door opened. Both girls squealed, "Dad-dee!"

Mitch laughed, and opened my door for me. I climbed out and into his arms with the girls' chorus of chortles and joy behind me.

"You're home early," I said and tipped my head back to see his face before I kissed him.

"Might have to play catch-up and do a bit of work once the munchkins are in bed," he said.

With one last kiss, we separated and released the kids from the confines of their car seats.

Inside, with the door shut, I set Grace down and she took off to the kitchen. Mitch lowered Isabella, who followed. Both girls garbled words that I couldn't interpret.

"Where's Argo?"

The sounds of delight from the kitchen told me the girls found him.

"He decided to wait on his bed for them," Mitch said with a laugh. "He's learning."

Yeah, it's easier to just lay there and accept the love than to greet them at the door and have them hang off him. Smart dog.

From the kitchen door, I watched our girls smother the patient dog in love. He'd let them pet and hug him for as long as it took. Little hands gently petted him.

Little arms hugged him. He licked as much skin as he could reach.

"I'll take him to work tomorrow," I said. Argo looked at me. "Did you hear me, boy?" His tail thumped on his bed.

Mitch wrestled the girls away from Argo. The two little bundles of energy giggled. With a smile, I walked into the laundry and opened the backdoor and rejoined the fun in the kitchen.

"You three can play outside until dinner." I struggled to be heard over the noise. Argo looked up at me. "Outside."

He stood, stretched, shook, and meandered toward the laundry. Grace caught sight of him moving and hurled herself after him. Argo picked up the pace a bit. I saw him run across the back lawn pursued by Grace and Isabella.

That'd tire them out. Mitch handed me a tall glass with a twist of lime.

"Shall we join them?"

I sipped my tequila, lime, and lemonade and followed him. My foot kicked Grace's bag. I bent down to move it and saw a piece of paper in the side pocket. I pushed the bag aside, took the paper, and joined Mitch on the patio.

"What's that?" He put his glass on the table.

"We're about to find out." I unfolded and smoothed it against the table surface. A flyer for a photographer. In the middle of the page was an image of two people standing in a person-sized snow globe with a winter wonderland backdrop.

Mitch picked it up and had a closer look.

"Human-sized snow globes," I muttered, and watched the girls run around after the dog. He loved this game. He'd slow down until they almost caught him, then power off. He left giggles and grabby hands in his wake. Sometimes he'd let them catch him, and they'd all roll around in a furry leggy pile on the grass. I laughed as Argo changed direction and sidestepped the girls. One day they'll figure out they're a team and he'll be done for.

"Might be fun," Mitch said.

I tore my eyes off the backyard hi-jinx and paid closer attention to my husband.

"Fun?"

"Yeah, a family photo. It could be a tradition."

My head nodded before it was pulled up by my brain. Traitor. Family photos sounded like trauma and tears. Halt that thought. No. Don't let your childhood ruin theirs. I sipped my drink. Family photos would be kinda cool.

"A photo in a snow globe?"

"Not particularly the snow globe, but in general."

"Good to know, because I'm not sure I want to be in a giant snow globe."

"It's not an elevator."

A laugh escaped. "I'm pretty sure they could make that backdrop and my nightmare would be complete."

Isabella ran to me. "Bella drink?" Little hands grabbed for the glass in my hand.

I lifted it out of the way. "I'll get you a drink, Isabella. This is Mommy's special drink." I stood and headed inside with my glass in my hand. Isabella squawked. I didn't look. I knew that squawk. That was the 'Daddy's got me and I can't follow you' squawk. I took two sipper cups from the fridge, hooked my fingers on my free hand under the handles and returned to the patio table. Isabella was over the horror of my disappearance. Mitch took the cups from me and handed her one.

"Thank you," he said as she took the cup.

"Thank you," she repeated.

"Put your cup on the table before you go and play," I said as she turned to return to the game. With one last suck on the spout she pushed the cup onto the table and ran back to join her sister.

"I imagine Mom thought the snow globe photograph idea was a good one," Mitch said then downed the last of the whiskey in his glass.

"No doubt that's how it got into Grace's bag. Do you think we can ignore it?"

We watched Argo run around the lawn and the kids for a few minutes.

"I think we can ignore it," Mitch said. "Or at least let's not bring it up until it's mentioned."

"I like that plan. I need to go change then we'll make dinner?" Dinner. "Friday night, team dinner here and

Mike Davenport is in town so he'll be here too."

"Sounds good. You change." Mitch watched the hi-jinx in the yard. "I'll supervise the game while you're gone."

"Starting to get a bit cooler out here." I kissed him before going inside. If I was lucky no one would notice I'd left. No cries followed. That was a good sign. I retrieved my messenger bag, belt, badge, and weapon from the car then climbed over the baby gate and walked upstairs. From our bedroom window, I watched the girls chase the dog. It was as it should be. Children playing outside with a dog.

I locked my weapon, belt, and badge in the bedside drawer. Dropped my phone onto the bed. Then changed into leggings and a hoodie. My phone rang.

Mike.

I answered. "Hey, still on for dinner tomorrow night?"

"Yes, just wanted to check on the wine. Did you say red or white?"

"I said 'yes.'" I laughed. "Make it both, cover our bases."

"In that case, I'll add a bottle of bubbly too."

"Sounds good."

"Done."

"See you tomorrow, Mike."

I hung up, stuffed my phone in my hoodie pocket, and checked out of the window one last time before going to the girls' room to get their pajamas and towels ready. Grace lay across Mitch's arms as he flew her around the yard like an airplane. Isabella sat with Argo, and watched. Dinner, bath, story and bed. Our nightly ritual filled me with contentment.

Chapter Nine
Turn! Turn! Turn!

A knock outside my office startled me. Bright eyed and bushy-tailed Dane grinned from the doorway. A reminder of how suited he was to his nickname, Squirrel, even though that's not where it came from. Argo's tail thumped against my ankle but he didn't move. His favorite place in my office was to lie near my chair, half under my desk.

"Morning. How's it going?"

"It's getting interesting," I replied. "Come in here, Squ— Dane." Almost. "Take a look at this." I waved a hand at the map and the whiteboard where I'd added Colorado Springs.

"So there is one in Colorado too?"

"Yep. Confirmed by Colorado Springs Police Department before I left yesterday." I chewed my bottom lip. "The Davis family disappearance in Colorado is the earliest on our timeline. Twenty-sixteen. That also makes it the coldest trail."

He nodded.

"What do you need?"

How about if we have a serial killer whose victim preference is families? But for now we focus on one family. The Abbots. We had better prospects of turning up actionable information because the population was lower in Jefferson City.

"Everyone focused on this," I pointed to Jefferson City, "and every detail about the lives of the Abbot family."

A bell-like noise rang somewhere. Unsure if it was a warning or not, there was definitely bell activity – connected to the Abbots? I concentrated and listened. Not a bell as such, an old fashioned cash register noise. *Ka-ching*. Shania Twain's voice filled the room as she sang about a credit card mess and how people spend money they don't have.

I wanted to see the Abbot's financial records.

"Ellie?"

I blinked and focused on Dane. "Yep?"

"You want the financials?"

"Yes, I do." Dane had abilities akin to mine and not unusual for him to hear my thoughts.

"Shania Twain?"

I shrugged. "I get what I get." More weird and wonderful stuff from my ever-entertaining prophetic abilities. "But that song seems relevant."

"Okay if I work in here?"

"Sure. Let Kurt and Lee know. This office is big enough for all of us."

Dane smiled. "I'll be right back."

The files within Sentinel open, I searched for all financial information that pertained to the Abbot family. Dane came back just as I'd started going over bank statements belonging to Joseph Abbot.

"Kurt is in his office with their medical records."

Dane got comfortable on the sofa and used the coffee table as his desk. "Lee has clubs and organizations and is working with Sandra."

I glanced over. "Does that include sports?"

"Yes."

"And you?"

"I'm all over the co-workers and business associates."

All on the same wavelength, we believed the disappearance was more about the parents than the kids. That made sense, but it paid to keep all investigation channels open. I'd come across cases before where it looked like it was about the parents but underneath was child trafficking.

The life-numbing crawl through bank statements that dated back five years was my task If there was a financial motive, it more than likely built up over time. I compared outgoings and incomings on Joseph Abbot's accounts. He ran a checking account and two savings accounts as well as three credit cards. Two hours later, coffee and a walk were imperative. I'd successfully matched all his bills to regular outgoing payments and highlighted two payments without a bill attached to them that I could find. One amount of a thousand dollars left his account on the fourteenth of the month and went to another account with the same bank. He hadn't attached a name to that account and it wasn't one of his. Another thousand dollar amount left his account on the fifteenth of every second month to a different bank.

Maybe he had a couple of secret accounts, or it was a college fund for his kids.

I stood and stretched. "Coffee?" I said to Dane.

He frowned at the screen in front of him. "Please, our coffee or real coffee?"

"Real. I need to stretch my legs. We won't be long." I tapped my leg. Argo rose, stretched, and yawned. I clipped his leash to his harness.

"Didn't even know you were there, boy," Dane said, when Argo nudged his hand away from his iPad. He gave Argo a head rub.

"He's patient. Bet he needs to get outside for some air though," I said as we left the room.

On my way to the stairwell, I messaged the team and asked for coffee orders. No one else wanted a coffee.

The happy hormones kicked in after I'd run down the stairs and hit the smoke-stop doors at the lobby. Argo looked up at me, tongue lolling, tail wagging. Yep, it's fun to run.

Frank grinned at me from the desk.

"Like a herd of elephants," he said with a head shake. "Cowboy boots and a dog."

"You get what you get." I stepped into the sunlight, and pushed on my sunglasses with one hand. Warm exhaust fumes from passing traffic stuck in the back of my throat. People stood in small groups chatting. I recognized a couple of agents, who waved.

I walked with Argo for a couple of blocks. He

enjoyed the different scents and occasional pat from dog-friendly people. A couple of fire hydrants appealed to him. We circled back toward the office. Traffic noise became white noise. By the time I'd picked up the coffee, the white noise coalesced into words.

Follow the money.

Back in the office, I unclipped Argo's leash and handed Dane his coffee. Argo flopped onto the floor and I sat at my desk. Intent on following the money, I searched out the accounts that received the regular amounts from Joseph, starting with the monthly amount that went to another account with the same bank.

A phone call to his bank manager was in order.

"Hello, this is Special Agent in Charge Ellie Iverson of the FBI. We are investigating the disappearance of one your customers. I need information on money transfers he's made to another account at your bank."

"Ma'am, you'll need a warrant from a judge to access financial information."

"I have a warrant attached to the case. Case number zero-seven-nine dash HQ dash six-six-six-nine. That number should match your records for Joseph Abbot. Please refer to the investigative nature of the warrant." I crossed my fingers. A bit of extra help wouldn't hurt.

"One moment, Agent. I'll put you on hold."

Silence, then music. Tapping on my desk in time with the music, I stopped myself from singing along. It was amusing and also fitting that a bank used songs about money as its hold music; I heard the tail end of 'Money Honey' by Lady Gaga before Donna Summer kicked in with 'She works hard for the Money.'

The music cut out. "Agent, do you have the account number the money is transferred to?"

"Yes." I read off the number and waited.

She confirmed the string of numbers. Fingers on a keyboard and program beeps followed.

"The account is owned by a Mrs. Jennifer Abbot."

His wife's name is not Jennifer. "Do you have a date of birth attached to the file?"

"Nineteen ninety-nine."

Not his mom then. "Where does Jennifer live?"

"Oklahoma."

This just got really interesting. "Can you send me the information regarding transfers and the account of Jennifer Abbot?"

"Yes, I'll do that now."

"Thank you for your help."

"I hope you can locate the Abbot family, Agent. Best of luck."

The email from the bank with the information I required arrived a few minutes later. I saw the payments from Joseph Abbot into the account but nothing else in relation to the account. The payments started in January twenty-thirteen.

Jennifer Abbot intrigued me. Who was she? Not just Jennifer Abbot but Mrs. Jennifer Abbot. A sister would hardly be a Mrs. Abbot unless she married an Abbot.

How lucky would that be? Sister-in-law perhaps? Time for a births, deaths, and marriages search. I started searching for Joseph Abbot in Missouri. The sister-in-law idea seemed feasible right up until I found Joseph Abbot's birth certificate and his parents' names. His parents were married to each other and there were no other children recorded from their union. Mr. Abbot senior had no previous marriages or children. He was the only son from a family of four daughters. The mysterious Mrs. Abbot wasn't an immediate blood relative or an in-law.

Why would Joseph send her a grand a month? Alimony? Child Support? There was no record of a previous marriage. And the dates didn't work. The payments to Jennifer started while he was married to Lily not beforehand.

I turned my attention to Oklahoma and Jennifer Abbot: Jennifer McDermott married Joseph Abbot on November fourth twenty-twelve. My bigamy alarm sounded just like a cash register. *Ka-ching*.

So was the disappearance of the Abbot family related to the other disappearances, or an anomaly? Why had no one found Mrs. Abbot part *deux*? Because they looked at recent bank activity such as cash withdrawals, credit card, and debit card use, not banking history.

I turned my attention to the second regular amount that left his account. Every two months for this one – to another Mrs. Abbot. This time in Ohio. He'd married twenty-year-old Andrea Green in twenty-sixteen, November again.

Three wives. Three states. That's one helluva back-up plan.

Each wife had ample motive for murder, if they knew about the others. As far as I could tell, there were no other off-spring. The only fruitful marriage was the one with Lily; it was also the longest.

He traveled a lot. I bet. Checking on the interviews with neighbors, no one was concerned when he wasn't seen for days or weeks. No one recalled arguments or any noteworthy behavior.

Time to talk to the remaining Mrs. Abbots. I needed to know what they knew.

I made a call to the second Mrs. Abbot. Jennifer Abbot. The call went to voicemail. I left a message to let her know I'd call back tomorrow and who I was, but not what it regarded.

The next call went to voicemail. I left the same message for Andrea Abbot.

"What did you find?"

I jumped. Dane laughed and apologized.

"Forgot you were there," I said with a smile. "I found that Joseph Abbot likes getting married."

Dane frowned. "He what?"

"Must like getting married. He's got three wives."

"Apart from illegal and crazy. That's motive."

"Possible motive," and carried on digging around in the murk that Abbot created.

"Does this mean the Abbot case is not connected to the other cases or ...?"

"Are bigamists targets?"

"Yeah."

"I've no idea, but we will find out."

Someone had information; we just needed to find that someone. I leaned back in my chair and surveyed the whiteboard willing it to reveal more information. Argo grumbled in his sleep, his back leg twitched.

A tweak in my gut became a gnaw as I stared at the board. A rat was trying to eat its way out of my stomach.

"Hey, Dane. How's your investigation channel?"

"Hard to find data that stands out," he said without looking up. "The Abbots appear to be the perfect family."

"That in itself is significant. No one's good, nice, conscientious, or kind, all the time. Unless we are looking into the disappearance of the first saintly family."

He dragged his eyes off his screen and looked at me. "It'd be exhausting being saintly. Doubly so trying to hide the existence of two extra wives."

"Yeah. It would. Someone must've known about Joseph's penchant for marriage."

"Where are they now?" He smiled at my frown. "The extra wives, I mean."

"Not answering phones so I have no idea. Maybe at work," I said as I looked up at the clocks above my office door. Yeah. They could easily be at work. Ohio was Eastern like us, and Oklahoma was only an hour behind. I wrote a big question mark in my notebook. Then added their names to a program we used to pull information from a multitude of social media and also our databases.

"Background check?"

"Running their names now." The social media thought wiggled. "Did you come across Facebook or MeWe or some form of social media Joseph and Lily use?"

"Found nothing for Joseph, but now we know he's a bigamist, that's not surprising. Lily Abbot uses Facebook."

"Get Sandra to get us a cyber warrant for all forms of social media relating to Lily Abbot. I'd like to see who Lily has been messaging."

Dane hauled himself to his feet but stopped at the door. "Do you want to add the other wives to this warrant?"

"Absofuckinglutely."

Chapter Ten

The Happening

Lee's voice rang out from the outer office as we waited for the warrant, "Kurt!" Argo was on his feet and at the door before I was.

We don't raise our voices on this floor.

Lee leaned on the outer office doorframe, his right hand wrapped around his left forearm, a pained expression on his face. Red dripped from his tightly closed fingers. Argo sat in front of him. He turned to me and whined, then watched Lee.

"Problem?" I turned to Dane. "First aid kit."

A cabinet opened and closed.

"Where's Kurt?" Lee said still leaning on the doorframe.

"How about you sit down and we sort this. Then we'll worry about where Kurt is."

Red dripped all over my new pale gray office carpeting; we'd need a crime scene clean-up team to restore it to a usable state. Lee stepped into the room properly, as I guided him to a chair I saw blood spreading across the back of his shirt. Dane indicated he'd seen the spreading blood. Argo positioned himself close to Lee. His go-to move for anyone hurt was to get close and provide warmth and comfort.

"I'll find Kurt," Dane said. On his way out he closed the outer door. No need for anyone to see what was happening in my office. It'd just start more rumors.

"Wanna tell me how you ended up bleeding on our floor?" I said, opening the first aid kit and removing two dressing packs. "Show me your arm."

He pulled his sticky fingers away. A five-inch gash gaped, pumping blood. I used the biggest butterfly closures we had in the kit to secure the edges together, then wrapped a pressure dressing around his arm. I put a roll of bandaging in his inner elbow and told him to fold his arm to his shoulder to slow down the bleeding.

"Thanks, Chicky," Lee muttered. "I'm not a fan of angry lunatic fucks."

"No one likes lunatic fucks. Which lunatic fuck in particular are we talking about?" I said, putting pressure on his shoulder so he'd turn and I could see his back. I cut away his bloody shirt with the scissors in the first aid kit. "Looks like a stab wound."

"It is. The asshole came up behind me. No clue who he was or maybe still is."

"Where is the person now?" Suppressing a smile and pressing a dressing onto his back, I stemmed the blood flow. With my free hand I found wide crepe bandaging and wrapped it tightly over the dressing and around his torso.

Kurt walked through the door. "An ambulance was outside the building. Unconscious male." He stopped at the sight of Lee. "This is related I take it?"

"Sure is. I was jumped."

Kurt peered at my bandaging and smiled. "You or the dog do that?"

I grinned. "Argo did it. He's getting real good."

"Good job. Let's get a bus for Lee." He walked away talking into his phone.

Dane hurried through the door. "I couldn't—" An eyebrow rose. "What the?"

"He found us," I said, turning my attention back to Lee. "While we wait for that ambulance, I'd like to know why one of my most seasoned agents ended up bleeding in my office."

Like a rookie.

Kurt finished his call and joined us. "I have a feeling this is going to be pass the popcorn good," he said, settling into the large brown leather sofa. "Grab a seat, Dane."

"Whenever you're ready, Lee," I said.

He winced as he turned in the chair to face into the room, Argo leaned against his leg. "I ducked out for half an hour to have a coffee with my bro." Lee smiled at me. "He said he's coming for dinner tonight."

Which reminded me that I'd better check in with Mitch to see what we needed. "Yep. Everyone. My place. Tonight. Now how'd the red slippery stuff get free of your circulatory system?"

"There was a guy sitting on one of the bollards. I said 'hi' as I passed him. He jabbed a knife into my back. I spun around and blocked his next attempt." That explains the arm wound. "And elbowed him in the side of the head. He dropped like a bag of potatoes. I swear his head bounced."

"You recognize him?"

"Nope and I think he fell on the knife."

Good job.

"I'm sending Claude from Delta B over to the hospital to find out who the assailant is and why he thought it was a good idea to attack Lee." I made the call to Claude then while it was still a fresh notion I rang Mitch and reminded him we had dinner guests. My last call was to Mike. I stood and walked into my office with my phone.

"Hey, Lee's been stabbed. He's all right. He's with us waiting for transport."

"I was just—"

"I know. You didn't see anyone, no one followed you?"

A small pause.

"No."

"Okay, dinner, seven tonight."

"He's really okay?"

"It's Lee-nine-lives-Davenport ... yeah, he's okay." I walked back to the outer office and passed Lee my phone. "Tell Mike you're okay, please."

Kurt, Dane, and I waited while Lee reassured his brother. The call ended with a laugh.

Kurt pulled me aside. We stepped into the corridor. "I don't think this is random. A random knife-wielding lunatic would not pick on a guy the size of Lee

Davenport."

"That's why I sent Delta B over to get an ID on the stabby fool. Something is most definitely up."

Kurt's phone rang. He answered it fast then pocketed it again. "Ambulance is here. Paramedics are in the lobby."

"He can walk out, right?"

Kurt nodded. "I'll take him down."

"I need to see everyone. Let's turn dinner into a work meeting." Mike wouldn't care, I was sure Mitch could entertain him.

"Good idea. I'll stay at the hospital with Lee, and bring him straight over to your place."

"Get him a change of clothes first," I said with a grin. "I'll make sure Sandra has a dinner invitation."

***

My boots hit the stairs, drawing a smile to my lips. Frank was waiting, eyes glued to the stairwell door, he gave me a slow head shake when I emerged.

"Hey, Frank, you get any usable footage from today's antics?" I said, striding across the floor space to his desk.

"Come around and have a look," he said.

I joined him on the other side of the desk, grabbed a chair and sat down. Frank handed me his open notebook. I read the page.

"Four times in the last two days and twice today?"

"He was watching for someone."

"Show me the footage, Frank. I find it hard to believe

anyone would be waiting to stab a guy like Lee."

Frank cued the video to the relevant times and days. The first time he found the Unsub was in a car across the street. Second time, he went into the Hard Rock Café. Logical if he was surveilling the Hoover Building. There were a couple of good places to look down on the street corner and the entrance to the underground garage. The third sighting was near the public entrance to our building. The fourth time, he walked down 10th on the other side of the street and then back up again half an hour later.

"SAC, the only time I've found any of Delta A outside the building alone over the last two days was when Agent Davenport was attacked."

His words rumbled around gathering momentum until a question forced its way out. "What about the other Delta team members?"

"They're in and out as much as the Delta As, found instances of most people walking out or in alone." Frank pointed at his screen. "Watch this." He touched the space bar.

The Unsub walked past the building on our side of the street, then back on the opposite side of the street. I watched the time stamps. Half an hour between sightings. Then just less than forty-five minutes later he showed up sitting on the edge of one of the bollard planter boxes outside the entrance we use the most. And there he waited until Lee walked past him. I saw Lee's mouth move as he spoke to the man.

"Thanks for this, Frank. It's definitely not a random event." Why stab Lee? Plenty to think about. "And facial recognition didn't ping him until you ran a search and the first instance was two days ago?"

"Correct."

My phone chimed. One of my many afternoon meetings bought forward. Dammit.

"Gotta run," I said.

Back upstairs, I sent the whiteboard and map images to my phone for later and hustled to the meeting. Within the hour, I was back at my desk and wading into a trench of paperwork. Dane took Argo out for a comfort break during one of my mid-afternoon meetings. This was my life now: extra paperwork and more meetings than I thought possible crammed into an already full day.

The warrant hadn't arrived by the time I was ready to leave, but that didn't matter too much. I didn't think we were in a time-sensitive situation; that at least meant we could take a break and eat together. Time to call Mitch.

"Babe, I'm heading home. What do we need?"

He gave me a grocery list and said he too was heading home. I'd do the grocery shop and he'd pick up the twins from his parents. Teamwork. I glanced at Argo.

"You coming with me. Like it or not, pal. You're my grocery buddy."

Chapter Eleven

It Takes Two

The bright supermarket lighting hurt my eyes. I slid my sunglasses off my head and over my eyes. Better. There were a few things in life I disliked, one was supermarket shopping. The potential for shopping cart rage was high. Argo sighed. He knew. I glanced at the list on my phone as I pushed the cart, avoiding elderly people who'd stalled in the middle of the aisles and younger people wandering aimlessly in search of inspiration. I was on a mission. I had Argo's leash clipped to my belt. He wore his FBI vest and badge. I left my badge visible. Maybe that would deter some of the supermarket annoyances. A voice in my head said, "They're people, Ellie. Just as much right to shop as you." I swiped the disembodied voice away, it skittered sideways into a dark cupboard. The door banged shut.

Focused. Ticking things off my list like a crazy person. The sooner I could get to the checkout, the sooner I'd be on my way home. As usual I picked the slowest checkout operator in the store. She was friendly. Great. A Chatty Cathy. I watched the conveyor belt move in tiny increments unbefitting a conveyor belt. I had no idea they could move that slow. The groceries barely noticed they were being purchased. The lady in front of me quacked on to the checkout operator about her day. Just when all hope faded a small fluffy duckling squeezed from a box of old person cereal and pooped all over the woman's groceries.

I choked on a laugh. The checkout operator and old lady turned their heads to me. No groceries moved for a good three seconds as they stared.

Like a grown-up, I pretended to check my phone. Obviously the laugh was not related to an invisible duckling shitting all over the groceries …

With much relief I loaded the groceries and Argo into the back of my car and left hell for home. My phone rang before I pulled into our driveway. I let it go to voicemail and parked behind Mitch's car. With a mental note to garage the cars I climbed out and opened the back door for the grocery unload.

Mitch stepped through the front door grinning. "Babe, you made good time."

He pulled me into his arms for a long slow kiss. Leaning back in his arms so I could see his face, I smiled. "This is why I come home."

Argo whined in the car. I glanced at him. Ears erect, his tail swished across the seat.

I opened the back door and unclipped his seatbelt. He leaped out and shook.

"Hey, buddy," Mitch said, reaching down to give his head a scratch. Mitch and I gathered the grocery bags and deposited them on the kitchen bench. "It's quiet. Where are the girls?"

"Napping."

"You're kidding me." I checked my watch. "They'll be

up half the night."

Mitch grinned. "Napping at Mom's."

"Are we picking them up later?"

"Tomorrow."

A night off. "Okay." Maybe. A voice in my head mumbled. 'Maybe's ass.' I went back to the car for my bag and phone, followed by Argo. Even though he'd been with me all day, he was super attentive. No babies to play with. No giggles. No snuggles. No little blonde bundles of energy. I walked into the kitchen. "It's not okay."

Mitch stopped putting the groceries away.

"Babe. One night."

My head shook. "I'm calling your mom and going to get the girls." I was already dialing. Mitch watched, accepting that he wouldn't persuade me. I grabbed my keys with the phone still ringing in my hand and headed for the door. I put my gun and holster in the glove compartment.

Joan answered as I fired up the engine. "Sorry, Joan, Mitch must've forgotten our plans tonight. Could you get the girls ready, please?"

"Oh, of course." She sounded taken aback but said nothing else.

"I'm on my way."

Alan met me at the door with a smile and a hug. "You okay, El?"

"Yes. Everyone is coming over tonight and a friend has arrived from Los Angeles so it would be nice if the girls were there." That wasn't it at all. It was an excuse. Something deep within me wanted my babies home, safe.

The safe bit seemed like something I should explore.

Grace barreled toward me, curls bobbing. "Mama!"

"Grace," I said, scooping her up for a cuddle.

Alan laughed and said, "Incoming ..."

Isabella tackled my knees. I shifted Grace to my left hip and scooped up Isabella onto my right. Her little arms wrapped tight around my neck as I adjusted my hold on them both. "Mom-my."

Yep, this was right.

Joan had their bags ready. I thanked her over the top of the girls.

"You know we love having them, Ellie. We'll make another night that we can have them sleep over. Perhaps next Friday?"

"Next Friday sounds good." Yeah, next Friday. I had a whole week to get used to the idea. Weird. It's not like we hadn't been apart before. "Thank you both."

I carried the girls to the car, setting them both on the driveway before putting them in their car seats. Alan passed me their bags. Joan waved to the girls from the porch.

Alan touched my arm. "She had something planned this evening, a surprise for you and Mitch," he whispered.

"I'm sorry. I ruined it, didn't I?" I said, putting the girls' bags on the floor in the back. Grace grabbed my hair. I extracted my ponytail from her hand before straightening up.

"I don't think so. She'll reschedule for next Friday evening."

"Ah, thanks. I'll make sure you do have the girls then."

Alan winked and walked back to the porch with Joan.

Chapter Twelve
Friends In Low Places

The smell of dinner cooking permeated the house and met us at the front door, along with a very happy Argo. Both girls squealed with glee at the excited greeting from their four-legged protector. Grace tugged her hand from mine to wrap her arms around Argo. He gave me a look. I laughed. One day she'd be big enough. Isabella clung tight to my other hand but stretched herself to capacity to try to reach the dog. He moved closer taking Grace with him. Isabella smiled and babbled at him.

"You three go find Daddy, while I get your bags."

Grace tugged Argo's collar. "Find."

Instructions given by Grace got the dog moving. Isabella's hand grasped mine tighter.

"Go on, Isabella. I'll come in a minute. We have a surprise tonight."

Her big blue eyes looked up at me, sparkling with thought. "'Prise!"

"Uncle Lee is coming for dinner."

Her delighted smile radiated. "Un-cool Lee."

"Yes, now go find Daddy."

Isabella squealed and called, "Un-cool Lee." As she ran down the hall leaving me to think how much of a kick Sam would've got out of the Un-cool thing. Dammit, Sam, you're missing so much.

With a sigh, I shut the front door, and moved my car to the garage. My phone alert sounded. Mikki's CCTV. I watched the screen for a moment to determine who triggered the alert. Carlos. No problem. Pocketing my phone, I took the spare keys for Mitch's car from the garage wall safe and moved his car. I pulled the bags out of the back of my car, replaced the keys in the safe and entered the house from the interior door. The happy noises of the girls playing with the dog filled me with joy.

It was as it should be.

"Hey," I said, walking into the kitchen, trying to determine what dinner was going to be. Garlic, basil, and a deep richness spoke of something Italian. "Something smells amazing."

Mitch turned, brandishing a wooden spoon.

"Lasagna. Just making the béchamel sauce. We'll be ready to layer soon."

A big pot of delicious ground beef in Mitch's famous tomato-based sauce bubbled on the stove. On the counter was a large dish, already prepped ready to receive the layers of delicious meat sauce, fresh lasagna sheets, béchamel sauce, and extra cheese. The man knew me. Judging by the mountain of grated cheese on the chopping block, he knew me well.

"Want me to make the salad?" I said swiping a pinch of cheese and shoving it in my mouth before the girls spotted me. They liked to share. Everything. All the time.

A loud crash on the tiles gave cause for pause. Giggling followed. Argo climbed into his bed. If I were him, I'd be tempted to hop up onto the window seat and get right out of the way. The contents of the upended toy box scattered across the family area of the kitchen. A toy car zoomed under the table. The girls rifled through the pile of toys looking for whatever it was they were after.

Our attention returned to dinner.

Mitch finished the lasagna and put it in the oven to bake. I made coleslaw and a green salad and stored them in the fridge. By the time half our guests arrived, the girls were fed, bathed, in pajamas and ready to be as cute as they could possibly be.

Isabella hung back, staying close to me. Mike, Sandra, and Dane deposited wine, beer, and dessert in the kitchen, said their hellos to Argo and then joined us all in the living room, where Grace was in full social butterfly mode. It didn't matter that she'd only met Mike once before and she was too small to remember. He was getting a tour of her favorite toys. Isabella managed a shy hello to Sandra and a smile for Dane; she barely acknowledged Mike before she climbed into my lap, placed a hand either side of my face to get my attention and turn my face to her.

"Mom-my. Un-cool Lee." Isabella was not happy.

"He's coming, Isabella."

Mike heard. "Did you know Uncle Lee is my brother?"

Isabella frowned. Grace interrupted Mike with another toy that needed inspection.

"Who wants a drink?" Dane said.

Hell, yes. "Everyone," I replied.

Mitch stood. "I've gotta check on our dinner. Let's go get those drinks, Dane."

At a noise near the front door, Isabella looked at me wide-eyed. Before I could speak, she was off my knee and running to the door, followed by Argo.

Mitch smiled at me as he and Dane headed in the opposite direction.

Voices.

Moment's later, Lee came into view with Isabella in his arms. I noted he wore long sleeves and clean clothes. Kurt appeared behind him with Argo.

Argo surveyed the room then disappeared, off duty.

"You all right with her?" I said to Lee.

"Yep. Little Bella is like a feather."

If feathers had grabby hands, a hard head, and wriggled.

Isabella beamed down at me from high in Lee's arms. "Un-cool Lee."

"Your fan club is enthusiastic," Sandra said, taking a drink handed to her by Dane. "Thanks, Dane."

"I'll get you two a drink now you're here," Dane said, with a grin, and a quick fist bump with Lee then Kurt. "Is your wife coming?"

"Rachel has taken our daughter away for the weekend," Kurt said. "Where's that drink?"

"Coming right up." Dane left the room.

"Sit down, Bro," Mike said. "You sure you're all right?"

"Flesh wounds. I'm fine," Lee said, easing himself into an armchair and shifting Isabella to his lap. "You want to go play, little lady?"

Isabella shook her head and leaned back on his chest. I had a feeling she'd fall asleep on Lee before long. Lee wrapped his injured arm around her as she snuggled down. I picked up her cuddle-rug from the floor and draped it over her. Her fingers wrapped around the satin edge. Yep, she'd be asleep soon.

"This is the best part of the week," Lee said, kissing her curly blonde head. "Hands down the best part."

"We are blessed," Sandra said, before taking a sip of her drink.

Kurt knelt next to me and handed Grace a toy that had escaped.

"Blessed is definitely what we are," he replied. "Lee's fine, but I don't want him chasing down perps for a week."

"This case doesn't seem like it will involve a lot of chasing."

Kurt looked at me, eyebrows raised. "Can't believe you just said that."

Yep. I jinxed it. We were screwed. "Get your running shoes on," I said with a laugh. "Shit's about to get real."

Dane appeared with drinks and a piece of paper. He handed out the drinks, then showed us all the piece of paper. I'd seen it before. Snow globes. Not on my watch.

"We could do this for a team Christmas card this year," he said. "Team Christmas card, yeah, it'd be fun."

A chorus of groans and "Oh hell, no." filled the room. No need for a team Christmas card. No one needs to have that particular brand of hell inflicted on them.

"What even is that?" Sandra asked, extending her hand for the paper. Dane gave it to her. She gave the spiel a quick read. "Photoshoots in snow globes. Now I've heard everything."

Oh, man. Joan was planning a surprise. Joan left that flyer in Grace's bag. I held my hand out for the paper. Sandra passed it via Kurt.

The photoshoots were Friday evening or Saturday mornings at their studio in Fairfax, Virginia. Times were booked online.

"I can think of plenty of better ways to have a photo taken," I said, passing the paper to Kurt.

"Says they hire the globes out for proms and work functions," Kurt said. "Bet they cost a bit. Giant snow globes. There would have to be a piped air supply if they're sealed, which they look to be."

Even more reason to never get inside the snow globe. Suffocation.

"Mitch, I think your mom is planning to stick our girls in a snow globe and get photos taken." As they suffocate.

He picked up on my thought. "They won't suffocate El, Mom and Dad will be there with them."

Hang on a minute. He knew. My eyes narrowed. "She told you."

Snapped.

Guilt settled in his eyes but left as he smiled. "It's a surprise. You're not supposed to know."

I held my glass out for Mitch to take and chose not to continue the conversation. "I think Isabella is asleep, I'll take her up."

I lifted her from Lee, wrapped her in her cuddle-rug and carried her from the room. When my foot hit the first stair, all our phones sounded at once. Isabella's eyes flickered then settled. I carried on up the stairs.

Chapter Thirteen

More Than A Feeling

Isabella stayed asleep as I put her down. The power of cuddles with Lee. Grace had faded by the time I was back in the living room.

Mitch swooped in and removed the sleepy and about to lose it little Grace, letting me finish my drink and check my phone. I noticed my team had their phones in their hands.

I checked mine.

Another cryptic text: `Cryptomania`.

"Oh good, a made-up word," I said, closing messages.

"We all got it," Lee said. "Don't you wonder where this is going?"

"I have a feeling it'll get interesting and not in a way that makes us want to share the story," I replied. Putting my drink on the coffee table, I started picking up toys and putting them in the basket that lived under the coffee table. Mike and Kurt helped. How one small person can spread toys so far is a mystery. Just like the crypto-Unsub.

The delicious smells of dinner wafted down the hall. My stomach growled. We needed to eat and put the crazy crypto person aside. Texting the team with the crypto words was weird but not threatening, although each text intrigued me more. Wouldn't hurt to get

Sandra to do some digging into the phone number.

"I'm going to go see how far away dinner is," I said to the group, who were all talking about the text message. Lee was telling Mike all about it as I left, I heard Mike's laugh. Gotta admit, I struggled to find the crypto texts funny.

Mitch had removed the lasagna from the oven. It rested on a wooden chopping board on the countertop, filling the room with delicious smells and making my stomach growl louder than before.

"You all right?" Mitch asked. His eyes flicked across my face for a second before he turned to the fridge and extracted the salads.

"Yep," I said, taking a platter from a cabinet and piling fresh bread rolls on it.

"Again, this time with feeling," Mitch said. His smile reached his voice and his eyes at the same time.

"I'm okay. Just thinking. There's a lot to think about at the moment."

"Work?"

"Yes."

Because I'm not thinking about your mother putting our babies in a snow globe. That is not happening.

"All work?" He passed me tongs.

I placed them on the platter with the rolls and took butter from the cabinet. Margarine has no place in our kitchen.

"I'll take these through to the dining room," I said, ignoring his question. I had no real reason to dislike the nice thing Joan and Alan wanted to do by having the girls photographed professionally for us, so arguing about it wouldn't work. Best to ignore the question.

I disappeared with the bread rolls and butter. Then returned for the salads and salad servers.

"When did you set the table?"

"While you were picking up the girls," Mitch replied, carrying the hot, heavy lasagna into the dining room still on the large wooden chopping board. "Shall we?" We stood at the end of the table and surveyed the dining room and table. Mitch slung his arm around my shoulders and stole a kiss. "When you want to talk about the snow globe thing, we will."

A smile lay on his face.

"Such a smart ass."

"I know you, remember?" he said, and kissed me again. "Let's feed this noisy crowd."

Lee, Dane, and Kurt were the first three to the table. Sandra and Mike came into the room together, deep in conversation. Their conversation halted enough for them to take their seats and for Mike to pour the wine.

Interesting. I hadn't seen Sandra so relaxed since Sam. I swallowed the instant lump in my throat. It was still hard. I missed him a lot. Sandra laughed at something Mike said and I smiled without realizing. Tonight was good. We needed this.

Mitch sliced the lasagna into squares. While I enjoyed the conversations around the table, he slipped a slice onto my plate. I sipped my wine and winked at him. We usually sat next to each other at the table. Tonight we were opposite each other. The head of the table was empty: a reserved space for our missing colleagues and loved ones. Lee sat beside Mitch and then Dane. Beside me, I had Kurt then Sandra. Mike sat at the end of the table.

"Mitch, this is great," Kurt said, with a forkful of lasagna hovering near his mouth.

A chorus of affirmation sprang from around the table. It really was great. I felt lucky to have such a capable husband. Pretty sure the team was relieved I hadn't cooked. My cooking still needs work, but my coffee is magnificent.

Above the chatter, I heard something I didn't expect. A knock on the door. That meant the gates were still open.

I shifted in my chair, ready to stand, while I tried to determine if it was a knock. My eyes searched for Argo. As if he heard me, he nudged my leg, letting me know he was close.

The dog hadn't reacted to the door.

I relaxed when Argo jumped to his feet and growled, a split second before a knock resounded from the direction of the front door. Everyone's chairs moved as they readied to stand.

Mitch looked at me, then Argo. I raised an eyebrow and shrugged. My hand dropped to my hip, but my gun was safely in the glove compartment in my car. A voice inside my head told me normal people don't need to be armed to answer the door. I let my internal voice tell my mother to back off. Next thing I knew I was standing at the closed front door with Argo and Mitch and no recollection of the walk through the hallway.

Silence from the dining room felt reassuring: my team were prepared to act.

Mitch swung the heavy door open. "Can I help?" he said, pulling the door wider.

"I have a delivery for Ellie Iverson."

I moved closer to Mitch. Face-to-face with a courier, I smiled. Argo emitted a low growl from between us and took a step forward. The courier stepped back and thrust a courier envelope at me. "Ellie Iverson?"

"Yes."

I took the bubble-wrap pre-paid courier envelope. Flipping it over, there was no return address or sender information.

"Have a good night," he said and turned to walk to his van, parked halfway down the driveway, illuminated by the security lighting.

"Where did this come from?"

He shrugged. "Our depot. I don't know. I just pick up from the depot and deliver."

"Didn't know you delivered at night?"

"Just doing my job, lady. If a client insists on a delivery, we deliver."

"Good to know. Thanks."

Argo grumbled. The courier quickened his pace. I closed the door and flipped the lock.

"That's weird, right?" Mitch said, indicating the envelope in my hand.

"Definitely."

"You going to open it?" He watched me feel the contents through the bubble-wrap.

A small object, about two inches long, maybe a quarter-inch deep, and a half-inch wide. Felt like a flash drive and that compounded my feeling that something hinky was going on.

"Yeah, carefully in my office." On my way to my office I stuck my head around the dining room door and caught Kurt's attention. "Got a minute?"

He rose and followed me. Mitch joined everyone back at the table.

Flipping the light on, I closed the office door behind us. I took a pair of blue nitrile gloves from a box marked medium in the cabinet on the back wall and handed them to Kurt. He tugged them on before taking the envelope. Lucky me got the small pink ones. The pink nitrile snapped against my wrist.

"Feels like a flash drive," he confirmed. Kurt switched my desk lamp on for closer inspection. "You want to check for latent prints?"

"Don't think there is much point covering the envelope in black dust but the contents, yes."

He held the envelope under the lamp and checked every inch of the outside for anything untoward. "Shame we can't use a light source to determine exactly what's inside."

"Yeah." Might be time I had a scanning device in the house or a portable X-ray unit. I jammed a red pin in that thought and hung it on the hessian note board in my head. "Would be handy to know if it will explode or spray us with Sarin, or if it's covered in poison." Maybe an X-ray could detect an explosive or a device that could emit a gas, but it wouldn't pick up a poison coating.

"Jesus, Iverson. Could just be a flash drive." His tone suggested otherwise. "I felt nothing that suggested wires or a trap." He tipped the envelope back and forth in his hands with care. "Pretty certain there is only one object in here."

We stared at each other. It didn't have to have more than one object to be lethal. It didn't have to be any bigger than a flash drive to blow someone to pieces. The best devices are the innocuous-looking ones.

Fishing around in my desk drawer I found scissors. Kurt lay the envelope on the desk in front of my keyboard. I lifted the very edge of the envelope and sliced between the layers.

Taking my time, I placed the scissors back in the drawer and pushed it closed.

"Are we opening it?"

Impatient.

"In a hurry to die?" I muttered, lifting the open edge of the bag and peering inside. "It's a flash drive."

Kurt pulled a piece of printer paper from a ream on the shelf above our heads and put it on the desk so I could tip the flash drive onto a clean surface.

"Fingerprint kit?" He asked, looking around.

"Bottom right-hand drawer."

I slid the dark blue flash drive to the white sheet of paper. Kurt opened the fingerprint kit. Swirling dust he uncovered two partials on the top of the small device. He photographed the images with the app on his phone and set the database search in motion. Flipping the flash drive over, he dusted the other side. Another two partials. He dealt with those the same way.

"Well, that was easy." I took tissues from a box on the shelf to wipe the dust away so we could handle the drive. A little too easy. "That tells me the person who sent this isn't in a system or doesn't care if we find them."

Yay, a newly minted bad guy.

I paused that thought. Did the flash drive have to be bad? A laugh erupted from deep within.

I picked the drive up with the tissue. It didn't have a removable cap but a retractable end. Catching myself holding my breath I slid the end out.

Nothing bad happened.

I breathed.

"This could contain anything," I said. What I needed was a laptop that was not connected to the internet. Something that was reserved especially for dodgy flash drives and could contain potential trojans or malware. Sean had a laptop like that. We'd used his equipment in the past. And he was on his way to Northern Virginia or was possibly even already here. "Let's give Sean O'Hare a call."

I reached for the landline on my desk and jumped as the Rolling Stones blared from my office speakers. What the? Jeez.

I blew air through pursed lips. 'Jigsaw Puzzle.'

"Sorry," Kurt said and touched the screen on the entertainment system, turning the volume down. "What is this?"

"*Beggars Banquet*, 'Jigsaw Puzzle.'" I picked up the handset and dialed Sean's cell. Most people stopped committing phone numbers to memory when phones became smart. I like numbers. I also like knowing that if I don't have my phone or access to my phone, I can use anyone's phone and get the help I need.

Chapter Fourteen

Puzzle Pieces

Kurt and I left the office and rejoined the foray in the dining room. The flash drive wasn't going anywhere.

"Everything all right?" Lee said as I passed his chair.

"Uh-huh."

"Bullshit," he whispered.

"I'm about to make an announcement. Gimme a sec." I stooped and kissed Mitch on my way to my seat. Warmth from his hand seeped through my shirt into my lower back.

"Okay?"

"Yep," I said, with smile, and walked past the empty chair at the head of the table to mine, across from my husband.

Conversations fell from the air. They writhed on the table cloth like magical threads of spaghetti, capable of being the most delicious meal or a cold slimy noose.

I blinked. Glittery words replaced the spaghetti. Remnants of conversation now lay, draped across plates and glasses. Another blink cleared the images. Questioning eyes waited. Kurt's held more questions than the others. He'd switched from SSA Henderson to doctor mode. I smiled at him. More to throw him off than anything.

"Okay. This is what's happening." Focus carried me through the rest of the explanation regarding the courier, flash drive, and that we were waiting for Sean.

Lee spoke first. "The last flash drive was from Iain Campbell, wasn't it?"

"Yes," I said. "Those were some fun CIA times."

Sandra piped up, "That was a song with a hidden file within it, if I recall correctly."

"Yes. A Kevin Costner and Modern West song."

Lee and Sandra nodded. Mike leaned forward, resting his elbows on the table, attentive.

"'Maria Nay,'" Sandra said after a moment of silence.

Good times. The only thing I knew for sure about the flash drive in my office was that it was not from Iain Campbell. He was killed by a hit and run driver connected to the release of the Qu pathogen. I pushed the sadness away. Not now. That won't bring him back.

"So what's this about?" Mike asked.

"Dunno yet," I said. My hand closed around my glass. I downed the last mouthful and refilled it. Not a bar pour either. I wanted a proper amount. "First, we all get text messages saying the same things and now a flash drive."

It smacked of more cryptic shit. A little flame stirred within and reminded me how much I like puzzles. Might not be all bad.

"Does it have anything to do with the cold cases you're investigating?" Mitch asked, refilling his glass but opting for half.

Good call. He'll be on baby duty later if this flash drive contains serious material. Not if. When. I knew it was significant.

"I don't think so. The first text came before the query from a cop in Missouri over a missing family. No one could've predicted him contacting me when he did."

Even though I said the words and they felt right, a cymbal crashed – a warning – and I jumped. Maybe someone did know the cop would contact me. I pulled up the email until it was front and center on my internal screen. It seemed fine. I didn't think I'd missed anything. Thunder rumbled and a flash of lightning speared the email from the cop.

Okay, I have missed something.

Kurt's voice jolted me back to the table conversation. "Iverson, what's going on in your head?"

Another rumble of thunder let loose.

"A storm," I replied with more honesty than I intended. "Thunder, lightning, the whole nine."

"Because?" Kurt said with his usual calmness.

"What if someone did know about the missing family case and this crypto-bullshit is related?"

You could've heard a pin drop or a buzz from the gate. My head swiveled to the hallway. A buzz from the gate. Did I close the gates after the courier? I didn't remember closing the gates, the envelope distracted me.

Mitch was on his feet.

"Did you close the gates?" I said, pushing my chair back and joining him at the dining room door.

He grinned. "Yep. I used the control panel in the hall."

"I'll get the gate," I said, "You finish eating."

His arm circled my waist and pulled me close for a second. "I'll come with, then rejoin our guests."

Hand in hand, we walked to the front door and the control panel. I touched the intercom button.

"How can I help?"

A crystal clear voice came back. "It's Sean O'Hare."

Sean had his own gate code. Odd that he didn't use it.

I looked at the control panel as I pressed the gate button. The gate lock flashed orange. It was on hard lock auto, it would lock again once Sean entered the grounds. Mitch smiled and inclined his head to the panel.

"Smart," I said, returning the smile. That's why Sean couldn't let himself in. Hard lock was like a deadlock on a door. It stopped all codes but mine and Mitch's from opening the gate. Guess Mitch didn't like the courier getting to the door any more than I did. Maybe my paranoia has rubbed off on him.

A car engine hummed then stopped. Mitch opened our front door wide as Sean walked up the steps to the porch with a black case in his hand.

"Thanks for coming," I said, moving in to shake his hand, but getting a hug instead.

"Always happy to help."

He shook Mitch's hand.

"If you're hungry we have plenty of lasagna," Mitch said, inviting him in and ushering him down the hall before closing the door on the night.

"I wouldn't turn down your lasagna," Sean said with a laugh. Then stopped and looked at Mitch square on. "It is yours, yes?"

"Sure is."

"Then plate me up a slice!" He gave Mitch a good-natured pat on the shoulder.

I could've opted to be offended at the inference but to be fair, I wouldn't eat my lasagna either.

A chorus of greetings rose from the dining room as Sean stopped in the doorway.

"Howdy, folks, nice to see you all." He looked at everyone in turn, then stopped at Mike. "Mike Davenport, it's been a while."

"It has."

Sean clapped a hand on his shoulder. "Pleasure or business?"

"Both."

"Good answer. We'll catch up soon. I'll go take a look at the problem flash drive."

"You can eat first, doubt it'll go anywhere," I said.

"Let's get this done."

"Okay, it's your dime."

Mitch waited until Sean and I moved away before he headed to the kitchen for a plate.

The murmur of the dining room conversations filtered down to the office.

Sean opened his black case on the desk and removed a laptop. "It's fully charged and ready to rock." Sean sat in my chair. Didn't look comfortable at all. My chair was perfect for someone five feet nine inches tall, me. Sean stood at an impressive six feet seven. A smile flickered. It took him a few seconds to adjust my chair. I was amazed he could still get his legs under the desk.

I passed him the drive.

"Ready?" he said, holding the drive near one of the USB ports on the laptop.

"Yep. Let's do this."

Sean pushed the drive into the port. I exhaled. Nothing exploded when the power hit the drive. That was positive.

An icon popped up on the home screen. The drive had a name. Cryptomania.

Well, that felt like proof it was related to the text messages.

"Cryptomania?" Sean said as he moved the cursor until it hovered over the icon.

"Yeah. Matches some texts we've been getting."

Sean looked at me for a beat then clicked the icon and opened the drive. A blue light flashed.

Inside the drive were a document and an executable file.

"Let's have a look at the document first." Sean right-clicked on the file and opened it within a text editor. I dragged a spare chair to the desk and sat down. On the screen were instructions.

Someone likes to play games. We get all the fun bad guys. My eyes rolled.

"It says the executable file is a puzzle. It can be played three times before it will self-destruct." The *Mission Impossible* theme filled my head and refused to be dislodged so I could carry on reading the document and paraphrasing. "There's a lot of words and not much information," I muttered. "So, we can play whatever game this is three times. Unsub says we've already had clues."

I leaned on one elbow and rubbed my temple.

"Is this making any sense?" Sean asked.

"Not really. I think the clues referred to are words all starting with crypto."

I read on. Then re-read the whole document. So many words, mostly padding. But hidden among the waffle, the Unsub mentioned a timer. Sean pointed to the paragraph I'd just read.

"A timed game."

"Yeah, that'll probably make it tricky." The next paragraph said we had ten minutes initially to solve the puzzle. The second time the game started over, we had eight minutes. The third time, the game started over, we had six minutes. "Ah, shit."

Sean nodded.

"I can get this onto a big screen, if you want, before we look at this game?"

"Yeah, that would be a good idea. It might take all of us to figure this out."

"First, let me have a look and see what we're dealing with."

"Could the game have a tamper code in it?"

"Sure could. I'm hoping that it doesn't."

"Worst case scenario?"

"It turns the laptop into a bomb."

"What the fuck, Sean!"

He grinned. "You asked."

"Seriously?"

"It didn't burn out my laptop when I inserted the USB drive. How serious is the Unsub about wanting you to unscramble his or her puzzle and act on the information?"

"That I don't know. But I do know that usually, people don't send us clues if they don't want us to solve them. Unless. And this is big. Unless they think they're much smarter than us and this is how they get off." In which case I expect there's a way for the Unsub to know that the destruction code has been triggered. It'd annoy the Unsub if he could not find out. Hard to revel in your cleverness if you don't know you out-smarted your target.

"What do you know about this Unsub?"

"That the person has Delta A cell phone numbers and has been sending us text messages from a burner phone for the last few days."

"Tracked the phone?"

"And got nowhere. It's Washington, D.C, do you have any idea how many burners are operating at any one time?"

He nodded and shrugged. "It's D.C." Par for the course. "What do you want me to do, El?"

What did I want?

The Unsub. Answers. To know what we were dealing with. Motive. What did I think was happening here? I poked around inside everything I knew looking for clues. Nothing in my gut said the Unsub wanted to destroy us. How did my gut know? Because where's the fun in destroying something before you say whatever it is you want to say?

"How serious are you about the laptop frying?"

"Very. Usually though, it happens when the drive is inserted to the USB port."

I'm sorry what? Usually?

"So this is an actual thing?"

"Yeah. Back in twenty-fifteen, the Russian's developed a killer pen drive and used it to destroy laptops and computers. It basically fried the equipment."

"This is something that happens and you have experienced?"

"Yes." He nodded. "I wish I could say I hadn't and it was all a smokescreen put up by the Russians to make everyone think they had this technology. But it's real. And now there are even smarter ways to achieve the same result. Kinda like Stuxnet. Remember that?"

"I do." We'd dealt with a similar program once upon a time. Hence I knew about Sean's fancy purpose-built containment laptop. "How does a flash drive fry a computer?"

"If you create a piece of software that overrides internal controls ... the theory is that it's not possible for the hardware to prevent all the damage to physical systems."

"But you said it was real so it's not a theory is it, Sean?"

He shook his head. "It was a theory, and they tested it."

I don't know why I had such a hard job accepting Sean's explanation. Maybe my brain was still a bit mushy?

"Clarify. Computers do have hardware safeguards to protect themselves from overheating and turning into a fireball?"

"Yes."

"But there is a way around them—"

"Yes, and we learned here this evening to never, ever, insert a flash drive or pen drive into a device if you don't know its origin."

"It's always so educational when you're around, Sean."

He laughed. "Your geek knowledge has grown."

"Okay, we're going to play the game. Are you all right with that?"

Thought I should check. His equipment is expensive. And who knows what the game will do once it's running.

"Sure am. I'll project the screen if you like?"

"Good thinking." I had a drop-down projector screen on the back wall of my office. Sometimes we needed to see things really big and clear, and I like techy-type gear.

Moments later, we stared at a big gray puzzle mat and puzzle pieces lining the edges.

"Let me try something," Sean said. He snapped a few screenshots of some of the pieces and dropped them into an image-editing program. He roughly cut out the pieces. When Sean sat back, he'd managed cut out seven pieces from one side of the puzzle screen and one of them was a corner.

"I think those two work together?" I said, pointing to the lone corner on his white background and another straight-edged piece. Both were a solid sea-blue. Nothing distinguishable picture wise. They almost fitted together. Close enough that we knew they would fit in the real puzzle.

"This is not going to be easy, El."

Understatement of the year.

"I'll get the troops."

Chapter Fifteen

It's A Game

Conversation halted and heads swiveled when I walked into the dining room.

"We have a file, an executable game file, according to a document supplied with it. The problem is we have limited time to solve the puzzle."

"You're the puzzle solver," Lee said to me with a grin. "You can do it."

"We're about to find out if that's true. I need all your eyes for this one." I turned to leave. Chairs scraped as everyone moved.

Mike's voice met my ears. "I'll take off if you're working."

"No, stay. I have a feeling you're good at puzzles," I said, shooting him a grin over my shoulder. "Am I right, Lee?"

Lee laughed. "He was always good at dishing them out ... let's see how good he is at solving them."

As the team plus Mitch and Mike filed into the office, I was again thankful that I'd opted for a large workspace at home and plenty of room for the well-built men that filled my life. Sandra caught my eye and pulled a face at the room full of testosterone. Sean spotted her and asked to come sit with him; I heard their low voices but not their conversation. Everyone else turned to face the wall by the door and stared in silence at the gray puzzle mat and surrounding haphazard puzzle pieces on the projector screen in front of them.

"One hundred and twelve pieces maybe?" Kurt said, pointing out the number at the bottom left of the screen.

"Could be."

Three buttons ranged along the bottom of the screen beside the number. Play. Reset. End. Finally there was a timer.

"How long can we look at this screen? Is there a limit?" Lee asked snapping some pictures of the visible puzzle pieces.

"The timer is still on zero," I said. "I'm hoping it doesn't kick off until we hit play."

My index finger crossed my middle finger as I resisted the urge to rap my knuckles on the nearest wooden surface.

Mike let out a low whistle. "That's a lot of pieces. We got any clues as to what we're looking at?"

"Nope. But if you look at the monitor on the desk, you'll see Sean and I have assembled a few pieces." Honestly, they didn't look very assembled. "It's not great, but it's as good as we could get it using photos and cutting them up."

Lee used the PC. He added the photos he'd taken and pulled them up on the monitor. He enlarged the images, making it easier to see each piece. We all tried to work out exactly what we were looking at and get a game plan happening.

"Two corners," I said touching the screen. "And that piece there fits into the first corner."

"What is it?" Kurt said, finding pieces that appeared to work together.

"There are pieces under pieces. This is not going to be easy," Dane mumbled on a sigh. "Lee, can you cut out some of these and move them around? Maybe if we get a few more pieces close enough we'll be able to see something."

We all stood staring at the PC screen then swiveled on the spot to look at the projector screen. I had zero idea what I was looking at. The only thing I did know was we were not looking at a ten-minute puzzle. Figuring it would take an hour or more to assemble the puzzle did nothing to settle the rising anxiety in my gut.

"I have an idea," Sandra said. "If I can use the computer, I'll see if I can match some images to the corner you've made. I have a nifty little program that searches far and wide for image matches."

"Of course. Use it. If we get a background that might help us build the foreground."

Lee relinquished the PC to Sandra.

Mike pointed out creamy colored pieces that showed a slight curve. "That one and the one on the other side of the image seem related."

Everyone agreed.

Sandra's typing punctuated the air around us.

Phones snapped images of the pieces we could see.

"Maybe we should just play it," Dane said. "We might get close."

"About that, there are rules. We only get ten minutes. We can only play three times and the time reduces each round" Sean said.

Yeah. But. What if we did it once and photographed every step until time ran out? Surely that would make round two faster? Nothing internal refuted my idea. "Let's do it. But we photograph every step. See what happens. At least then Sandra should have more pieces to run through her program."

"That would help, currently that one corner piece you two tried to assemble has millions of possibilities." Sandra looked up at me. "I have sampled the color of five pieces in the image Sean has. I used the right-hand corner, a left-hand pale curve, the brightest piece of visible red, the brightest blue I could find, and a neutral tan color. That's given me five html codes. I'm searching for images containing all five codes."

"Will that narrow the millions to something manageable?"

"If we're very lucky. It also depends on the image used. If it is a photograph taken by the Unsub we have little chance of finding it in our databases or by searching the internet."

Excellent point. Hope slipped away and my mood dampened. "We better do the puzzle then."

"That would be ideal," Sandra said. "I'm also

running the five sets of HSV numbers."

"The what now?"

"Hue, Saturation, and Value."

"Yeah, I'm going to need more than that."

Sandra smiled. "The HSV model is a color wheel or a cone, depending. Color is expressed as angles from zero to three hundred and sixty. Saturation, which is the amount of gray in the color, is expressed as a percentage. Value is the brightness. That's also a percentage with zero being black and one hundred being the brightest which reveals the most color."

Learning all the time. "Will that help?"

"Can't hurt. I'm running two different programs looking for the combinations of those five colors, one in HSV and the other in html."

"Okay." Anything was worth a shot. "Sean you ready?"

He was in charge of the play button and the moving of pieces. He swiveled in the desk chair, laptop on his knee. "Ready."

"I'll take the pictures," Mike said.

"Me too," Sandra added.

Two photographers. Phones at the ready. "You two stand front on to the screen on either side of us," I said. "Take a couple of test photos now so we can check how good the quality is off this screen."

Might have to move them in front of the screen on Sean's laptop, or go with screenshots, which would pull Sean away from his task, moving pieces.

Test shots taken. I looked at Sandra's first. Surprisingly the project screen enabled clear photographs. Mike's were the same.

Then I got them to take photos from Sean's laptop screen. Mike's laptop photos were clearer than his projector screen ones.

"Mike, you stick with Sean and photograph his screen. Sandra, you're on the projector screen."

"I'll get as many screenshots as I can as well," Sean said. "Are we ready?"

Mike sat in the chair next to Sean. We were ready. I pushed aside all the doubts niggling about our ability to solve this puzzle.

A jigsaw is just a different kinda code. That was all I needed to know. "Press play," I said.

Sean did, the screen changed. The timer started. He immediately moved the pieces we'd already seen and thought they matched. The minute a piece neared its partner, it stuck fast and could not be moved. Sandra and Mike took photos.

Dane, Lee, and I pointed to pieces for Sean. I started to feel sorry for him. Instructions flew and he moved pieces as fast as he could.

All of sudden the main part of the puzzle screen went black. At the bottom, the timer registered zero.

Fuck a duck. "Okay, what did we get?"

Mike passed me his phone. I scrolled through images. We got more than I thought.

"Sandra, can you do something with the partial

puzzle?"

"I can," she said, motioning to Mike to shift from the chair. "Let me see how far my color coding got us then I'll load up Mike's images and mine."

I handed Mike his phone. Sandra glanced at it for a moment. "Hey, Mike, Airdrop those images to me, will you?"

"Sure."

Without warning the black projector screen sprang to life. The puzzle sat on the screen as it had in the very beginning and taunted us with the incompleteness.

"Shit," Sean said. "The timer started again."

Dane, Lee, and I scrambled to reassemble the pieces and then add more before we were out of time. Mitch stepped up and took the photos for us.

"That should have a face," I said, pointing to a group of pieces we'd assembled. We scoured the screen looking for a face. "There!"

Sean slipped the puzzle piece into its match.

"Who the fuck is that?" Lee muttered.

"A man, maybe," I said.

We joined the entire top edge before the timer ran out and the screen went black. This time I knew we didn't have time to let Mitch Airdrop the photos he'd taken before the timer restarted.

"When it starts up," Sean said. "It's six minutes and this is the final round."

"And that means?" Dane said, never taking his eyes off the screen.

"The program has a built-in self-destruct. We think."

The screen sprang to life. The timer pinged into action. My heart thumped against my ribs. All or nothing.

Sean moved at speed reassembling all we knew from memory while Dane and Kurt joined me in trying to find the next pieces to the puzzle.

It's just a different type of code. Focus.

Phones buzzed. No one checked. All our attention was on the screen and the puzzle.

"That," I said pointing to another piece. "Grab it, Sean, it's part of that man."

He slid the piece home. "It's a man with a kid."

With that the screen changed. A big yellow 'Boom' flashed up then disappeared taking the puzzle screen with it.

Gone.

I looked at Sean. He was typing fast. His screen was black. Green words and symbols spewed from his fingers.

"It's corrupted itself. We can't get it back."

Shit.

Chapter Sixteen

Out of Time

Mick Jagger pranced from the wings to take center stage with both hands wrapped around the microphone, his unmistakable vocals rocked my world. He was right, I had no idea what was going on and I sure as hell was 'Out of Time.'

Maybe I should've paid more attention to 'Jigsaw Puzzle' when I heard it earlier. My office transformed, first into shades of gray, then the more familiar traditional comic-book colors complete with rich black outlines. A page turned as a door opened. Chance grinned at me.

"Long time no see," he said as he crossed the floor.

"It has been a while. How are you, Chance?"

"I'm great." His eyes roamed over my face. "Something going on, El?"

"Why would you ask?"

"Because I'm here." His dimples deepened with his smile. "I exist in your wacky head to serve."

Well, that's true, I guess. "Can you help?" I stuffed my hands into the front of my jean and rocked on my heels.

"It is possible. Now, what were you thinking about the Rolling Stones?"

"That when I heard 'Jigsaw Puzzle,' I should've picked up a clue in that song, but I can't see it."

"All right, what's the first thing that comes to you when you hear that song?"

"That someone is lying on the floor doing a jigsaw while life happens around them."

He nodded. "Did you consider that the jigsaw might be a scene with all the people he sings about in it?"

The song filled the room. Chance and I listened from the beginning.

"The jigsaw could be him lying on the floor on a rainy day doing a jigsaw with all the other scenes in it." I thought about that for a moment then shook my head. "That's fucked up and doesn't really help me."

"Why do you think the song is important?"

Incredulity poured from my eyes, bathing Chance in the skeptical glow.

"Because it's me. It's a song. And I heard it right before discovering the puzzle."

"And it's a jigsaw right?"

"Right."

"What else have you got?"

"A series of text messages that make no sense but are all words prefaced by crypto."

"And you are sure they make no sense as a group?"

"I don't see a link between cryptomnesia, cryptozoology, cryptocurrency, cryptosporidium, cryptosphere, and cryptomania. Apart from the obvious."

"The last two aren't even real words."

"I know, right?"

"A series of texted words that appear to make no sense and a song that makes no fucking sense."

"That about covers it."

"Who got the texts?"

"Delta A."

"Let's forget the texts and look at the song. It's a series of scenes containing people."

I leaned on the desk. "Chance, the jigsaw we failed to complete, I think a man and a kid were in one part of it. That'd be a scene." But not one that matches the song. Why do I think they're connected because I'm sure as hell not seeing the connection?

"Bet there is more to the scene than a man and a kid. Could you see any background?"

I shook my head. "There was a background, but we couldn't decipher it. Sandra is trying to find the images using her fancy software."

"What could connect a series of unconnected people and places?"

"If I knew that, Chance, I wouldn't be lurking in your comic-book office hoping for answers."

"You do know. Think, El, think."

I tore my gaze from the rug on the floor and met Chance's cool blue stare. "The same thing that connects my missing families."

We weren't looking at the puzzle properly.

"How clear was the father and child image?"

"I don't know." But I needed to find out. Was that one of our missing dads? "Why would the crypto-weirdo have a photo of one of our missing dads?"

"Someone always knows something, El. Someone always knows."

Because life is now lived in a goldfish bowl. A snap-happy goldfish bowl. "Whoever the crypto-crazy is, they could be our person who knows." Here I go again, creating a theory that needs proving instead of looking at the facts and drawing a conclusion.

"You know more than you think, El. Trust that gut of yours a little bit longer."

"Thanks, Chance."

"Happy to help." He winked from the doorway. As he stepped through, the black lines shimmered and faded. Life replaced the comic-book drawings piece by piece.

I blinked and realized I was staring at the PC screen and the jigsaw pieces we'd assembled and photographed. Voices around me buzzed. Sandra typed. Sean was still working to recover the file.

Dane nudged my arm. "A word?"

I nodded and followed him from the noisy office.

"Problem?"

"Not with me," he said. "That was Chance?"

Oh, he saw that then. Ain't it great how I can project my own special brand of crazy into other people's heads?

"How much did you see?" Because his brother used to be able to see Chance when he was around, but I didn't know Dane could. Maybe he'd evolved to take

Stewart's place as the second weirdo of Delta A.

"A comic strip. You were drawn just like Chance. The whole room was drawn and different."

"Cool, huh?" Yeah, let's go with cool. It's not freaky. At. All.

"Pretty much."

"Did you hear?"

"Yes."

Right, we're on the same page. "Back in we go then, Dane. Let's see if Sandra's magic extends to matching faces from a tiny piece of a jigsaw."

Kurt shot me a questioning look as we entered the room. I smiled and shrugged. Nothing for him to worry about.

"Sandra, can you do something with that image of the man and kid?"

"Like?"

Work magic. "Like get an ID?" Match him to one of the many missing persons in our case.

She looked up at me, hands poised over the keyboard, and frowned. "This is not the best quality image, a photo of a photo that's been jigsawed and our version, taken from a screen. I can try."

"Do or do not, there is no try."

"Yes, O Yoda of the Delta Teams." With a flourish of her hands, she began to work magic.

If we were lucky. If we could get an identity and if it matched one of the missing families, we'd have a link. A freaking weird one, but a link. One that could lead us to the puzzling Unsub and, maybe, all the way to missing families. A shot at closing some long-standing cold cases seemed within reach, and the potential to stop any more families disappearing.

Did I really think there would be more? Yes. Yes, I did.

Mitch tapped me on the shoulder. "I've made coffee," he said quietly in my ear. I turned to face him.

"Thank you."

"It's all quiet on the baby front. Fatherly dutiful check on the sleeping princesses is complete."

I smiled, gave him a quick kiss, and watched as he left the room. When it's right, it's right.

Chapter Seventeen

Dream Weaver

While Sandra tried her talented hands at magic, Kurt crossed the room to me. Sean stood, placed his laptop on the desk, and stretched. "I smell coffee," he said. "Anyone else want one?"

I shook my head. Dane nodded and followed Sean out the door.

"Did you see the text?" Kurt asked, his phone in his hand.

Nope. I'd forgotten about it until that very second. I checked my phone. Sure enough, there was a text from the same number that sent the crypto texts and possibly the same person who sent the flash drive. This time the text said: Do I have your attention now?

"Okay, that's it. No more ignoring this fool. I'm engaging," I said. "Lee, can you see if you can find this person on the map?"

I hoped my reply would generate a conversation and we'd see the phone pinging from a cell tower somewhere; maybe we could get a location.

"Yep, go," Lee said, he was using my laptop and some fun software designed for us.

"Okay."

I replied: You sure have. How about you

come into the office tomorrow and have a chat?

Kurt and I grinned at each other. Suppose we could've replied earlier, but no one wanted to encourage our cryptic Unsub. We had enough to do without looking for trouble.

My phone buzzed in my hand. "We have a reply." I opened the message and read the text aloud. "That won't work for me."

I replied: What will work for you?

Seconds later another reply: You work this out. I've helped enough.

I replied: Work what out?

Seconds ticked by, then a minute, then another minute.

"Dammit. Might have lost him," I grumbled.

My phone buzzed: I've helped enough.

"Lee, did you get anything?"

He shook his head. "That phone is pinging off a tower."

Sounded like we could get something then.

"Okay, is our Unsub close?"

"The problem here is he's pinging off a tower over three and a half thousand miles away."

"What the fuck?"

"He's in London. According to our software, he's texting from the United Kingdom."

"That's going to make knocking on the door tricky. But how is he doing that?"

Sandra turned to face me. "He could be texting from a computer using proxy servers and using one of the many internet sites that allow you to text phones for free." I smiled at the air quotes framing the word texting.

"Texting from a computer is an old trick but obviously still effective," Lee said. "Or he could be running a VPN app on a smartphone."

"Virtual Private Network, yes?" Mike said then bent down near Sandra and asked if she wanted a coffee.

"Yes, it is a VPN and no thanks to coffee, but I wouldn't say no to another glass of red."

"How does that work?"

"You grasp the bottle and pour the contents into my wine glass," Sandra replied without a pause.

Mike chuckled. "You've been around Ellie too long ... you're starting to sound like her."

His comment elicited a snort from me. I waved a hand down my body. "Maybe the world needs two of all this wonderful."

He laughed. "That is *not* what the world needs." His attention diverted back to Sandra. "How does the VPN thing work?"

"It's pretty cool actually. The connection between the smartphone, tablet, or computer, and the VPN is secure, but the connection between the VPN and the rest of the world or internet is not. We could trace ping him back to the VPN IP address but not back to his own IP address."

"What if you use the VPN with a browser like Tor?"

"Then that provides extra security and anonymity." Sandra smiled up at him. "That's how I work when I'm poking around in places."

"Places?"

"Uh-huh, sometimes we don't want anyone being able to ping us back."

We never want anyone to be able to ping us back.

"If you pay for a VPN service, wouldn't there be a record?"

"Yep. But we'd need to know who we were looking for. Also, you can use free VPN. Then you'd create an account and more than likely not in your own name, or with a known email address."

"Okay. That's enough geek-speak for me." Mike smiled. "Red wine?"

"Please."

"Anything else to add, Sandra?" I said, staring at my phone screen as if it held all the answers.

"Not really, it's my opinion that he's using proxies. He doesn't want us to get close."

"He doesn't want us to know who or where he is, but he wants to tell us something, in such a way that we have to work it out for ourselves." I was thinking aloud. "Odd behavior."

Or this person is a dick and gets his or her kicks from taunting the FBI.

"Stop," I said. "Before we go any further." Meatloaf hit me square on the jaw. I shoved him, putting my body weight behind me and yet felt myself slipping backward as he stood his ground. From nowhere another pair of hands joined the foray. Together we pushed and pushed until he toppled from the makeshift stage. I heard a motorbike roar. Meatloaf disappeared in a cloud of noise and exhaust. The extra hands that high-fived me belonged to Dane.

"What the hell?" Kurt said, shaking his head slowly.

"What?"

"Nothing, I thought I heard 'Paradise by the Dashboard Light.' You know, that Meatloaf song."

Dane and I looked at each other, then at Kurt and shrugged. "Hearing things?"

"I'd like to believe that, but I get the impression that you two know why I think I heard Meatloaf."

We said nothing.

Kurt dropped it. "Okay, so, why have we stopped everything?"

"Because this Unsub might have tried to make contact before and there has to be a reason why he's doing it now."

Why now? It's not like we talked to the media about this case or appealed for information through any public forums. We've only just started investigating the strange phenomena of missing families. All we have done so far is gather police files and look at re-interviewing anyone connected to the Abbot family. A couple of calls to locate the extra wives shouldn't alert anyone. The calls went to voicemail.

"Good point," he said.

"Let's check with all the cops we've dealt with this week and with all FBI offices in the states where we have missing families and see if anyone has ever received a series of texts that make no sense or a flash drive with a puzzle."

"Do you think our Unsub has tried to this before?"

I nodded. "It's an elaborate way of making contact. Not everyone would've followed up on it. We didn't. Until the flash drive appeared. I'm picking people will remember a series of single-word text messages."

"Have we got a list?" Sandra said. "I can do some checking because these programs of mine will run until they get all possible results, and so far, I hate to say," she took a breath, "our pieces of completed puzzle have netted a big fat zero. No matches to any photographs found so far."

"Doesn't sound hopeful," Dane said.

He was right. It sounded as if the Unsub used his own photos and not ones available on the big old web or maybe we weren't searching the right places.

"Deep Web," I said. No need for me to explain that.

"I hate messing about in there," Sandra said, pushing her glasses higher on her nose. "But I've got the perfect piece of software for the task."

Sean walked in with his coffee. "Someone say Deep Web?"

"Have you got bionic ears?" I said, moving sideways so he could sit next to Sandra.

"Only when I hear something that sounds like fun," he replied. "Deep Web? Why? What are we doing?"

Sandra filled him in about her problem finding a match for the image segments and how the portion of the Deep Web known as the Dark Web might hold more images and therefore more of a chance.

Not all criminals use the Deep Web or Dark Web, but sometimes it doesn't feel like that.

Chapter Eighteen

Everyday

I walked upstairs and checked on the sleeping babies. Peaceful and angelic best described them while they slept. Such content wee faces.

Argo looked up from his nursery bed near the door. I bent down and ruffled the fur behind his ears then straightened up again. He watched me. I used hand signals to tell him he was a good boy and to stay.

It wasn't my idea to allow him to sleep upstairs in the nursery, but Mitch made a good case and I reneged on my no dog in the bedrooms rule.

Faint noise from the kitchen and the office mingled. The low hum of male voices and the occasional clink of china or cutlery and quiet laughter. If we had to work, at least we were having fun with it.

I left the nursery and ran down the stairs.

Dane walked toward me from the kitchen, holding a ringing cell phone and handed it to me.

"Special Agent in Charge Iverson."

"Special Agent in Charge, this is Officer Grimmer, I'm at the hospital with the male who allegedly stabbed Agent Davenport."

The footage we have indicates it isn't allegedly at all. He definitely stabbed my agent.

"Yes, Officer?"

"Letting you know the man we have tentatively

identified as Ken Green, died from injuries sustained in the altercation with Special Agent Davenport."

"Thank you, Officer. Is there anything else you need to tell me regarding the death?"

"Don't think so, ma'am."

"Did he speak at all?"

"No, ma'am. He never regained consciousness."

"Did you get a statement from Special Agent Davenport?"

"Yes."

"Have you gotten witness statements?"

"Yes, ma'am. Witnesses corroborated Agent Davenport's account that he was attacked from behind by the deceased and Agent Davenport's reaction was consistent with self-defense."

Good to know. Not that I doubted Lee's account for one second.

"Do you have any objection if I speak with the next of kin?"

"Not at all, SAC. If you can find a next of kin would you pass the information on to us at Metro."

"You've had no luck then?"

"He wasn't carrying a wallet or any formal identification. There was a piece of paper in his pocket addressed to Ken Green written on it. That's all we have to identify him."

"I take it you ran his prints?"

"We haven't had a result."

Then we definitely need to take a run at identifying

the deceased.

"Send me the images from the fingerprint scan. We can run those for you."

"Thank you. I'm hoping the coroner will find something. Or maybe someone will report him missing."

If you're lucky. Do you feel lucky? I clamped a lid on the internal rumblings that sounded very like Clint Eastwood.

"Thank you for the phone call."

I hung up. Dane waited until I looked at him before speaking. "He died? The guy who stabbed Lee."

"He did."

"Do we know who he is and why he stabbed Lee?"

"He might be Ken Green. But as to why he targeted Lee, no idea."

"Is this related?" He waved a hand toward my home office. "Could it be?"

"It could be." People do all manner of weird shit all the time. Who knows if this is related to our crypto-puzzle situation? Great, now I'm making up words. "At this point Dane, we need open minds. Discount nothing."

"Got it."

"Along those lines, I want to know why Ken Green attacked Lee. Deep dive into his life. I want answers and a proper identification."

"We'll get them," Dane said with a half-assed salute. "Starting tonight, right?"

"Sooner the better. Just in case there are other lunatics thinking about coming for another one of us."

I didn't doubt we'd get answers and along the way find out all there was to know about Ken Green. We could go so deep, we'd find things about his life that even he didn't know.

Every time I thought about him a series of synaptic pings occurred. Pretty sure I'd never come across him before, so the pings were a tad confusing. If it was important, it'd show itself before long. The fingerprint scan images arrived on my phone. I forwarded them to Dane.

"El!" Sean's voice rose to float above the murmurs and life noises from the dining room and office.

I popped my head into the office. "Right here," I said following my head through the doorway. "Did you want me for something?"

Sean motioned for me to come closer. "While I was scrabbling around inside the guts of that puzzle program trying to get it to run again or show us hidden files, this popped up." He leaned sideways so I could see the screen. A small image hung in the top left corner of the screen. Not quite a thumbnail in size.

"Can you ..."

"Nope, this is as big as it gets."

"All right then. Shove over and let me get in there."

Sean shuffled his chair along the desk, inching closer to Sandra. I dragged another chair over and sat close to Sean. He positioned the laptop between us. I reached over to my left and pulled open a drawer to locate a magnifying glass. With a smile I used the glass on the small image on the screen. It didn't really help. The image was pixelated. Small and pixelated. Not great combinations.

The more I stared at it, the more I saw something I'd seen before. A reddish, maybe pinkish, open-weave check pattern. A shirt. The sort of pattern you see on a flannel shirt down on the farm. I stifled a yawn causing my eyes to water.

"The man in the jigsaw," I said. "This could be him?"

Sean took the glass and looked at the image himself.

"Could be. It's such a crap image." He opened the picture of the man and kid in the jigsaw. "Not much better. And we can't confirm it's the same image."

But with one eye closed and the other one squinted it looked like the same guy.

Chapter Nineteen

Sledgehammer

Morning came with howls of hunger. I grabbed the edge of my pillow and folded it over my head in an attempt to block the noise. Mitch groaned next to me.

"What time did we go to bed?" He mumbled, rolling toward me.

"Four-thirty, or just after," I said, squinting at the bedside clock from under the pillow. "It's six. No wonder they're making a fuss."

The delightful yet noisy twosome was usually eating breakfast by now.

Dragging myself from the warm comfort of Mitch and our bed, I stumbled to the door, hooking my robe from the ottoman at the last moment. We had house guests. The whole team plus Sean and Mike crashed at our place sometime after four.

Argo greeted me with a wag and semi-accusing look. Guess he wanted me to get up and feed the little people sooner.

"It's okay, pal. I'm here. Go on downstairs." I touched the top of his head.

Both girls stopped their noise and looked at me. They were standing in their cribs. All their bedtime toys were on the floor. I picked up Grace's blanket and put it back in her crib. She threw it over the side.

"Really?"

She smiled and nodded. "Mama!"

"Let's get you both changed and go down for breakfast," I said, taking clothes from their dressers and tugging diapers from the full bag in the cupboard under the changing table.

The next ten minutes were a no-holds-barred wrestling match as I changed Grace from her pajamas and dressed her while she tried to escape. Isabella looked on, amused, but quiet. When I set Grace free she took off down the hall.

"Mitch! Grace is running." Knowing he'd intercept her before the stairs. We removed the safety gates at night. A couple of midnight falls suggested we do that.

Isabella's turn took very little time and effort. Her cooperation bordered on resignation but at least it wasn't a wrestling match. I lifted her into my arms for a cuddle and she whispered in my ear, "Un-cool Lee?"

"Mommy will get dressed first then we'll go downstairs." She nodded. I hurried her into our bedroom and sat her in the middle of the now made bed. "Wait for Mommy, Isabella."

"Yes." She sat with her hands in her lap.

I grabbed what I needed and had a super-fast shower. My hair would survive a few days without washing. Dressing at speed had become a specialty of mine.

I shut our bathroom door behind me and smiled at Isabella. "Let's go see if Uncle Lee's awake?"

A beaming smile burst from her tiny face. "Un-cool

Lee! Un-cool Lee!" She bounced on the bed, I lifted her down and set her on her feet. Instead of running, she took my hand and tugged. "Mommy. Find Un-cool Lee." I picked up my phone from the dresser on the way out.

Grace's voice carried through the house and up the stairs, then Mitch's voice, followed by an excited bark. Drawn by the noise we descended the stairs, Isabella's little hand gripped my fingers.

She looked up at me at the bottom of the stairs. Her smile grew as she heard Lee's voice in the kitchen. And with that, Isabella took off running. I followed, with a lot less energy and enthusiasm.

Lee scooped the giggling child into his arms and spun around the room with her. Her laughter hung in the air like fairy bells. I tapped the camera icon on my phone and took a video of the kitchen scene. I never wanted to forget her joy at life.

A light cough from the door told maybe someone did notice. Kurt came into the room behind me, he grinned. "Coffee? I can smell it." He looked around. "There must be some somewhere?"

"On the counter by the stove," I said. "Sleep okay?"

He nodded. "A few more hours wouldn't hurt."

Mitch ran past the kitchen window. Argo's bark sounded like a laugh and almost drowned out Grace's squealing.

"What's happening out there?" Dane said, emerging from the office.

"Hi-jinx," I replied. "Mitch is playing with Argo, and Grace is trying to keep up." I turned my attention to the men and Isabella. "Pancakes?"

Everyone nodded. I may not be the world's best cook but I make excellent pancakes.

There was something soothing about having a pancake breakfast with my team on a Saturday morning. All of us around the table, eating, talking, relaxed.

We used the dining room instead of the kitchen because the dining table was big enough for all the adults and highchairs.

"I have information on the deceased Ken Green," Dane said, between mouthfuls.

"Share," I said, sipping my coffee and passing another piece of banana to Grace.

"It's not his name. I don't know why he had something addressed to Ken Green but the deceased male is Simon Kreg."

Lee placed his fork on the edge of his plate and wiped his mouth on a paper napkin. "Simon Kreg? You're sure?"

Dane nodded. "You know him?"

I glanced at Mike, the surprise on his face told me he knew a Simon Kreg.

"The Simon Kreg I knew was killed in Iraq."

"You served with him?" I watched Lee and Mike.

"Yes. Both of us." Lee inclined his head toward his brother. "He was killed in a firefight."

"You are absolutely certain?"

Lee nodded. "He died. I was with him."

I knew Lee was a medic and said nothing else.

Dane frowned. "Must be another Simon Kreg. There was no mention of him being Army." His frown fell away, replaced by a smile. "Or dead."

"How was the body identified?" Kurt chimed in. "I'd rather not have another case with the dead returned."

Pretty sure none of us wanted that.

Lee grimaced then growled, "We are not going there again." He glanced sideways at Dane. "How was the ID done?"

"Fingerprints," Dane said, passing his phone to Kurt. "The police sent us the prints they took from the body. They had zero luck getting an ID from them when they sent them through."

They probably didn't even try.

Kurt looked at Dane's phone. "Date of birth makes him a couple of years younger than you, Mike. What about his Social Security Number?"

"That'd be about right for Kreg?" Mike said, nudging Lee.

"Yeah, he was a bit younger than us."

"I have the SSN," Dane said. "Two hundred and seventy, Seventy-six, eight, three, one, four."

Lee shoveled more pancake into his mouth. He chewed, swallowed, and said, "Where was that number issued?"

Dane's brow furrowed. Sean had his phone in his

hand and within seconds had an answer for Lee. "Ohio."

"Simon was born in Oregon."

"Oregon numbers until twenty-eleven were five hundred and forty to five hundred and forty-four," Sean said.

Dane floated a sigh of relief. "Different person."

I felt his relief as it hung in the air. No one wanted the dead to return, especially in this instance. No zombie's today, thanks.

Half a smile settled on Lee's lips. "Why did Simon Kreg from Ohio stab me?"

The million-dollar question.

"Why did he have a letter addressed to someone called Ken Green?" I countered. "And while I'm at it, who the hell is Ken Green?"

"Haven't we come across a Green in this missing family investigation?" Dane said, placing his phone on the table and resuming his breakfast. "These pancakes are great."

Chapter Twenty

Copperhead Road

Saturday required a lot more sleep and energy than it got. Energy came in waves of coffee brewed by Mitch while he starred in his role as super husband and dad. I saw him scoop up a crying Grace and soothe her while keeping an eye on Isabella as she ate the last of her mid-morning snack. If anyone was likely to choke, it was our Isabella. Argo divided his time between us all, managing much-needed nap breaks when he could.

I allowed my attention to return to the investigation, satisfied that the little people in our lives were well looked after.

"El, I'm not having any luck finding Ken Green." Dane sighed, rubbed his temples, and looked at me over the screen of his laptop. "Let me change that sentence up a bit. I've found a ballpark figure of one hundred and fifty-two people in the US named Ken Green. It's going to take a while to locate the right one."

"Good chance he's not Ken but Kenneth," Kurt said. "That might help."

Dane searched again then looked up. "Yeah … it didn't. Two thousand two hundred and seventy-seven Kenneth Greens in the United States."

"Who knew?" Kurt said with a smile.

"Could be worse," I said. "We could be looking for

John Smith."

Dane arched an eyebrow at me. "Do you want to know?"

"Go on," I said.

"Forty-seven thousand three hundred and change."

"See? I said it could be worse." Helpful. "What other information do we have regarding Ken Green?"

Dane frowned. "Nothing just a letter addressed to him."

"Who was it from?"

"Someone called Rochelle."

"Nothing else? No postmark, no letterhead, no address?"

He shook his head. "It's a piece of printer paper, folded into thirds. There is no address for recipient or sender."

"And it says what? Because usually, people write things in letters."

"Attention Ken Green. The photographic proofs were emailed to you on December six. And it's signed Rochelle."

"Signed?"

"Well, not with a signature. It says Rochelle. I think this letter was a copy-and-paste from an email."

We pretty much had nothing. Except we knew Ken Green wanted proofs of photographs and they were apparently emailed to him.

"Search photographers with the name Rochelle?" Lee offered. "Might be a smaller pool."

"Worth a shot," Dane said, chewing the inside of his cheek. He stopped chewing. "Why would Simon Kreg have a letter that was meant for Ken Green and why stab you?"

"Photographs." Sean reached across the table for an apple from the fruit bowl. "The jigsaw is a photograph of sorts."

He was right. Didn't help, but he was right.

Dane stood and stretched his arms over his head, dodging the light fittings like a pro. He walked around the table then back to his seat. I watched his mind race, the energy bubbling and wisps escaping into the room from all around him. I saw images as his thoughts came together. It was about photographs. Everything is linked to photographs. But what of? What is so important about these particular photographs? And what are the photos? What are we looking for?

"Dane, we're looking for something that links all the families across five states, something they all did over a weekend," I said, watching his face and knowing he was building a scene in the way I do. As soon as he had, it I could see it. Families getting into cars, laughter, giggling, the occasional discontented grizzle from a child. They were willingly going somewhere. The banter, the light-hearted chatter and happiness exhibited by the parents told us this was voluntary. I waited to see if Dane could follow any of the cars.

We both saw it at the same time. A large building that looked like a warehouse and it was in an industrial area. The first car Dane saw, pulled up outside the warehouse.

"We're looking for photographs of families," I muttered. "That's what Green wanted."

Dane and I looked at each other for a moment. "Do we have a missing Green family? It doesn't sound familiar to me."

Family names spun on a carousel.

"We don't have a Green family, but we have a Green connection."

"Where?" Kurt said, his fingers tapped at a keyboard. "I'm grabbing the info from the smartboard in your office."

"Good thinking. It's one of the Abbot wives, pretty sure she was a Green."

"Got it," Kurt said. "Yes, the last wife was a Green and from Ohio."

"Our dead guy, Simon Kreg, had an Ohio Social Security Number. That can't be a coincidence," I said. It can't be. I don't believe in coincidence. "Okay, so we have two connections to Ohio, one missing and one dead. Let's search for Ken Green in Ohio, then. That should narrow it down."

Sandra spoke from the other end of the table. "I have a warrant for social media accounts belonging to the Abbot wives. I'll start with the latest wife, Andrea Abbot née Green. See if we can find Ken Green on her social media."

I crossed my fingers. Just like that, we had what felt

like a lead in the missing families cold cases.

"Lee, I want you to look into the second wife's social media. See if you can dig up something that links her to wife three and any mention of photographs."

"On it, Chicky."

"Kurt ..."

"Iverson?"

"We're going to visit a body."

Words buzzed from around the table as my team worked, compared notes, and dug into social media accounts. Kurt followed me from the room.

I let Mitch know we were going out for a while and that everyone else was working. Well, everyone except Mike. He was outside playing with the girls and Argo.

Given a choice, that's what I'd be doing too.

Chapter Twenty One

Pictures Of You

The morgue was not my favorite place. Cold, clinical steel surfaces reflected an absence of life. By the time bodies arrive at the morgue all sense of self is lost. I worked better with the recently dead, still inhabited by remnants of consciousness.

Kurt pushed a heavy door open and held it for me. "You okay?"

"Yeah. Just this place."

He nodded.

A voice from a desk set near a wall grabbed my attention "How can I help?"

I showed my badge. "Here to view Simon Kreg."

He consulted the screen in front of him, then looked back at us. "Follow the yellow line down the corridor to viewing room four. I'll have his body brought through."

"Thank you."

Room four was pleasant as far as viewing rooms went. There was a door on the left as we entered, I expected the gurney containing the body would emerge from there. A small stained-glass window in the wall on the right gave off a soft glow, sending green-, blue- and red-tinted light into the room. Chairs sat against the wall by the entrance from the corridor. I crossed the room and twitched a long dark blue curtain that hung on the far wall. Curiosity. Behind it was a window into another small room. Sometimes it's not advisable to let family or anyone else close enough to touch the body. A shudder ran through me as I remembered Qu and how close we came to a global pathogenic disaster. A noise from the interior door jolted me back to present day.

I rejoined Kurt.

The door opened and a man in scrubs pulled the gurney into the room. He maneuvered until the sheet clad gurney was under the small stained-glass window.

"Agent, this is Simon Kreg," the man said. He bent down and removed a plastic bag from under the sheet which he handed to Kurt. "His personal belongings."

"Thank you." Kurt held the bag in his hands, looking at the contents through the thick plastic.

"You're welcome," he said and disappeared through the open door, closing it behind him.

I turned back the sheet and exposed the face of Simon Kreg.

"Now this is interesting," I said, staring at his face. "I've seen him before."

Kurt stepped closer. "Where?"

"Dunno, but I recognize him despite the *pallor mortis*." And it wasn't from the surveillance footage from our cameras. It was somewhere else.

Short hair. I gave it more thought. I'd seen that particular cut more times than I cared to remember. Military. High and tight. A niggle in my gut turned into a roar of words that sounded like Marine Corps. I settled it with common sense. It was also a popular hairstyle among wannabes, actors, and law enforcement in general.

"He look anything like Lee and Mike's age?" I peered at his hair. Not a gray to be seen and no real lines on his face. Although death changes faces.

"He looks about ten years younger." Kurt put the plastic bag on the body and opened it. He passed items to me. "Wallet."

I held Kreg's black leather folding wallet in my hand. The leather felt soft, worn, well used. I opened it. A couple of store cards bearing numbers but no name. No identification. He had to have done that on purpose. Two hundred dollars in small bills.

I set the wallet aside.

"One pair of jeans."

"Nothing in the pockets, as you'd expect." I refolded them and placed them on the body, then held my hand out for the next thing.

A long-sleeved button-down shirt. A denim jacket. I checked the jacket pockets. Nothing. Dried blood caked the cuff on the right sleeve. Lee's blood. I pushed it aside. Lee was okay. Moving on. Socks. Underpants. Good to know he didn't go commando. Boots that looked like military issue.

"What do they call this color?" I pointed at the boots.

"Coyote brown, I believe." He held one and I held the other. "RAT boots."

"Marine, right?" I spun the boot in my hand looking

for the eagle, globe, and anchor that would confirm they were regulation boots.

"Yes," Kurt said as I found my proof.

"Holy fuck balls are we looking at the body of a dead Marine?" A collection of memories jarred and sent my consciousness scurrying for cover. I hooked it by the back of the neck and dragged it back into the middle. Stay. You got this. "If he's a Marine, why no identification?"

Kurt said nothing. He put the boot down carefully.

I pulled my phone out and took a photo of Simon Kreg. Then called Lee.

"Did you get a look at the guy who attacked you?"

"Not really. I defended myself and he fell facedown. I was bleeding and didn't hang around. FBI uniformed were on the scene within a second or two of the incident."

"Police show you a picture at the hospital?"

"No. They just asked if I knew him. I said I didn't really get a look at him."

"He might be a Marine. Sending you an image."

"Shit."

"Yeah."

I heard his phone ding.

"Got it. I've seen him before." Lee fell silent for a few beats. "I can't place him in a Marine context, though. But I've seen that face before."

"I'm gonna make some calls and see if we can find out who this guy really is. If you work out where you've seen him, call me back."

I hung up.

"This Kreg thing has pushed peculiar out of the park," Kurt said, putting all the belongings back in the plastic bag. "Lee and Mike served with a guy called Simon Kreg who was killed in action. Years later another Simon Kreg stabs Lee outside our building in the middle of a city and ends up dead on a slab. And now this Simon Kreg might be a dead Marine ... or not because boots and a haircut do not a Marine make."

"Good point, Henderson. Why did he stab Lee in the back?" Keeping it cowardly not exactly what I'd expect from someone who was military. Also, if he intended to kill Lee, he could've, easily.

"Death wish," Kurt said with a half-assed smile.

"Why did he have a piece of paper with Ken Green's name on it?"

Kurt shook his head. "No idea."

"I think this dead dude and his behavior has knocked weird right out of the fucking state."

Kurt covered the body and stood for a moment before turning to me. "Who was the bumbling Keystone cop in charge of this investigation?"

I uncovered a foot and read the toe-tag to confirm the officer's name. "That would be Officer Grimmer."

"You're kidding me?" Kurt muttered on an undercurrent of disbelief. "Maybe he should accept his fate and become an undertaker."

"Let's see if he carried on trying to contact a next of

kin, because he wasn't having any luck when I asked for the fingerprints and he was sure this guy ..." I touched the body lightly on the shoulder. "... was Ken Green."

"Let's hope he hasn't because if he has—"

"It's the not the right kin and there is someone out there wondering where this guy is." I dropped the sheet over his foot. "Sorry pal. We're pretty sure you're Simon Kreg of Ohio and we will notify your family as soon as we find them."

I scrolled through recent calls and called Grimmer back.

"It's Special Agent in Charge Iverson here, about the body you identified as Ken Green."

"Ma'am, yes, ma'am. What about it, ma'am?"

Wanna chuck another ma'am in there anywhere?

"Did you find a next of kin?"

"No, ma'am." He paused. "Well, yes, ma'am, but no, ma'am. We found a bunch of Ken Greens and didn't get far on narrowing it down."

Uh-huh.

"You know when I called and said we'd take a run at it?"

He exhaled loudly in my ear. "Yes, ma'am."

"We believe his name is Simon Kreg, not Ken Green."

"I don't even ..." Another pause. "I've been on the job four days. I'm sorry, ma'am."

"You were partnered with an experienced officer?"

Pretty sure they don't let the newbies out by themselves.

"Yes, ma'am. Officer Carl Denton."

And then it all made sense. Carl Denton. Lazy bastard number two and former partner of Eddie Conway, my former now-deceased brother-in-law. A little smile tweaked as I remembered how he died but not the part that made me Suspect Number One. I didn't want to remember that bit. Thanks.

"Hey, Grimmer, don't sweat it. We got this. Tell Carl to go have another donut."

"What do I do with the file again?"

"Send it to me at the Hoover Building."

"Okay. I can do that." He paused. I heard him breathing. "Thank you."

I hung up and shoved my phone in my pocket. Kurt sat on one of the chairs waiting for me to finish.

"Send it to Delta," he repeated. "There's a world of trouble in that statement."

"I know. We shouldn't be touching it. But the criminal investigation is over. Self-defense. No contest. This is us helping out a fellow LEO who has a shit partner and will be spinning his heels for the next six months trying to find the next of kin in this case." And they have zero interest in finding out why this lunatic attacked Lee. They'll kick the file around for months then eventually it'll land on our desks anyway.

Kurt rose from the chair. "Yes, that's true. We need to make sure that this investigation into Simon Kreg

175

and whoever Ken Green is, is transparent. You don't need to be accused of white-washing anything this early in your new role."

His concern was expected and yet still touching.

"We got this, Kurt. We're better at it than most of the cops. Our resources are vast. Let's just find his next of kin, and work out if our dead dude is military or a wannabe, and who Ken Green is and hopefully, along the way we'll find out why he stabbed Lee."

Life-ending moves on the street in front of our building were not the norm.

Chapter Twenty Two

My Bloody Valentine

An alert prompted me to open the CCTV app on my phone. Four images loaded. Mikki's driveway, front of her house, side of her house and back porch. A male dressed in dark clothing walked up the driveway toward the house. He wasn't Carlos. He crossed from the driveway camera to the front-of-house camera and peered in a front window.

"What the hell?" I muttered and sent a text to Diego then watched the screen to see if the male looking in the window checked his phone. He did not.

Diego called me.

"Yo, El. Casey and I are with Ms. Falacco. Casey's driver today."

"Where are you?"

"On our way to a bookshop. Ms. Falacco is running a workshop this morning."

"Okay. Kurt and I are going to Mikki's."

I hung up. Kurt flicked the indicator and took the next exit. His hand reached forward and flipped on the grill lights. He used intermittent blasts of our siren to clear traffic that didn't notice the big black Suburban with flashing lights up their backsides.

"Wonder where Carlos is?" I said, watching the male appear on the side camera.

My phone rang in my hand. Mikki's name sat on the

screen.

"Hey, having fun?" I said.

"Is there something wrong?"

"No. Just checking in." I paused as the car swung around a bend and straightened up. "Is Carlos at your place today? Thought I'd drop a little something off for you."

"He was going to the garden center this morning, he'll be home by lunchtime." Curiosity crept into her voice. "You could leave it with Christelle."

"I'll do that then." Before she could ask any questions, I hung up. Kurt flicked off the lights as we turned down Mikki's street. "Park a few doors back. Let's approach on foot."

Kurt nodded.

The car doors closed without drawing attention despite it being a quiet, sparsely populated street. The size of the homes set on large parcels of land indicated wealth. I doubted the occupants were cash poor, which was the case in some areas. Nice houses but no money, which struck me as a hard way to live.

Kurt checked his weapon then adjusted his jacket to cover his appendix carry holster. I pulled my tailored leather sports coat on and my side holster disappeared. My badge attached to the front of my belt, easily visible as I walked but not flashing in people's faces.

Checking the app as we walked, the male was on the back porch. He peered in windows.

"Wonder where Christelle is," I said, showing Kurt

the screen.

"Inside and out of harm's way, I hope."

At the top of the driveway near the house, Kurt motioned that he would go first. I checked my phone again. The male was not in view. I held my hand up to Kurt and shook my head. He needed to wait until I found the male. Getting caught in the tree-lined tunnel to the back gate wouldn't be a good idea. No telling how wacko the dark clothed male was.

The male appeared on my screen and the porch swing moved. He'd been sitting in it. I watched for a moment. He stared at the door. Maybe he was willing Mikki to come out.

"Okay, let's go," I whispered. The dirt on the path would deaden our footsteps and make a silent approach possible. I hoped he'd hear movement and think it was Mikki. He couldn't escape the yard without going toward us but we had no cover from the gate to the porch.

I held my breath. Kurt swung the big gate open. It made no noise. We could step through the gate unseen but once the trees ended we were visible and vulnerable. I exhaled. Kurt closed the gate. Shoulder to shoulder we slunk from cover, checked the male was still on the porch then ran.

He spun around as we thundered up the steps.

"Who are you?" he said. "You shouldn't be here!" His eyes narrowed as he stepped back. I detected some fluster in his bluster.

"Homeowners. Who are you?" I replied. It wasn't a lie. We both owned homes.

"You don't live here," he scoffed.

"And you do?"

"Not yet," he said. He'd regained some composure.

Not yet. I bit my lip to stop a smirk. Not ever. Mikki was correct in her description. The man in front of me was unkempt, sweat-stained, unshaven, and hadn't seen a shower for a day or so. Boyfriend material, no doubt about it. I resisted the urge to reach out and slap him upside the head. I'd need gloves. Physically he reminded me way too much of my ex-brother-in-law.

"Name?" Kurt said, stepping toward him.

The male backed away and trapped himself between the porch swing and the house. He wasn't going anywhere in a hurry.

"None of your business. I'm a friend of the homeowner. And you are not the homeowners."

"A friend," Kurt repeated. "A good friend?"

"Yes."

"Funny that we've never met," I said. "Where did you meet Ms. Falacco?"

Deep furrows appeared on the man's forehead. "Ms. Kennedy lives here. Who are you even talking about?"

I paused for a split second. His frown deepened. "Of course, sorry. I meant Ms. Kennedy."

The creases eased as his expression softened. He thinks of Mikki in terms of her pen-name, not her actual name.

"A long time ago. I said we are friends. Who are you?"

I smiled. "Friends of the family," I said. "We go a long way back."

"Can't be that good friends," he muttered. "You got her name wrong."

"Sometimes people make mistakes," I said.

He stepped out of the corner he'd backed into. Kurt and I moved to allow him room. No way was he getting past us.

"I'm here to check on Mikki," he spouted in a spray of spittle. He inched nearer the door and reached for the frame. His knuckles rapped once. The net curtain twitched. Christelle. I shook my head. She moved away from the window. He rapped again.

"No one is going to answer the door," Kurt said. "And your name?"

He huffed and puffed and shuffled sideways trying to peer in the window.

I waved a hand near his face to get his attention. "Move away from there. What's your name?"

His eyes flicked to me then back to the window and then the door. Desperation oozed from his pores.

"Ellis, my name is Ellis." He tried for the door again. Kurt blocked him and turned him to me.

"Ellis. You need to focus here," I said, circling my hand in front of my face. "Because no one is answering the door. You are not welcome."

He angled back to the door. Kurt grabbed his arm

and twisted it behind his back.

"*Ow. Ow.* Stop it!"

"Pay attention, Ellis." Kurt growled from behind him. "We're done playing nice."

"*Ow.* Let me go!"

"Hey! Settle down." I snapped my fingers in his face, he blinked, and shut up. "I'm Special Agent in Charge Ellie Iverson, and the agent behind you is Special Agent Kurt Henderson."

Ellis tried to twist and jerk his arm from Kurt's grip. "I go to Krav Maga!"

"Outstanding," Kurt said, tightening his grip and nudging the back of Ellis's knees. Ellis dropped, Kurt let his arm go.

"That hurt," he whined. "Mikki won't like you being rough with me. We're friends!"

"Why do you think we're here?" I said, looking down at him. "Coincidence?"

"I don't know. Where's Mikki!" He crawled, trying to get to his feet and hollered, "Mikki!"

Kurt joined me. For a few moments, we watched Ellis try to get Mikki to open the door and save him. Pathetic.

"That's enough," I said.

Kurt leaned close to me and said, "He is not processing anything we say or do. He's only interested in whatever bullshit is happening in his head and what he wants to happen next."

"Is this shit dangerous?" I waved a hand toward the

man pleading to a closed door for Mikki to help him. "Because I'm seeing a truckload of pathetic."

"It's not normal and, yes, this level of disassociation from reality is potentially dangerous."

"Okay, our next move is?"

"A mental health facility for an assessment or he gets trespassed."

"Mental health facility. Trespassing people is fine if the person doesn't intend to go back. Look at him."

"Yeah. He's coming back then we have to rely on us or police getting to him before he can potentially hurt Mikki."

Kurt dragged Ellis away from the door and handcuffed him. He kicked, yelled, complained, and begged for Mikki.

Kurt marched him away from the house and waited for me. I knocked on the door. Christelle moved the curtain, saw me and opened the door.

"You have him?"

"This is the man who harasses Ms. Falacco?" I stepped aside so she could see him.

"Yes. He is loco."

"I think you're right. We'll take him away, he won't be back. Are you all right?"

She nodded. "Carlos will be home soon."

"Tell him we have Ellis in custody. I will call Ms. Falacco now and let her know."

"Are Diego and Casey staying on?"

I nodded. "For a little while. Just to make sure."

"Good. They are good people."

"Look after yourself, Christelle. Keep the door locked."

She smiled and closed the door. I heard a metallic clunk as the lock slotted home.

I ran across the lawn and joined Kurt. Ellis kicked out, hitting my leg with his sneaker-clad foot, almost unbalancing himself.

"What was that for," I snarled.

"Mikki is going to be pissed when she finds out what you've done."

"I don't think so," I said. Kurt pushed him forward.

Ellis turned his head toward me almost tripping over his own feet. Krav Maga indeed.

"We're writing a book together."

"I have an idea," I said. "Shut up." Keep your freaking fantasy to yourself. I slipped past them and opened the gate.

"Iverson, hang back, and let Diego know what's happening. I'll get this gentleman into the car and call ahead to George Washington Emergency Department to let them know we have a psych case coming in and he needs urgent assessment."

"Okay." I waggled my eyebrows at Kurt. "Watch out for him. He's done self-defense."

Kurt grinned.

Ellis squealed and tried to get out of his grip. "I don't need an assessment." He attempted to kick backward and lost his balance. Quite the expert at Krav Maga. No doubt the Israelis will be begging him to join their army any minute.

Kurt stabilized him. "Be careful. You don't want to hurt yourself."

He wrenched his body sideways, that too failed. "You're going to be sorry. Do you even know who Mikki is? She's famous and she'll be angry."

The whining continued through the tree tunnel and down the driveway. Proving that Ellis was better suited to being a kindergarten student than a fighting force. I stopped at the top of the drive and watched Kurt put him in the car while I called Diego.

"Hey, Ellie, tell me something good." Beyond Diego's voice I heard talking and laughter. The noise faded. A door closed.

"We have Ellis. We're taking him to GW for a mental health assessment."

"Good news."

"Yeah. Tell Mikki she should be okay now. But you and Casey stay on. I'll check with Sean. But until this guy is medicated and locked up I want you both to remain on active duty with Mikki."

"Happy to stay for as long as we're needed."

"Figured you would be."

Chapter Twenty Three

Roller Coaster

Most of the day dripped by on the dribble coming from Ellis's mouth. If I ever came across him again it would be too soon. He was locked in a secure unit at George Washington for at least twenty-four hours then he'd be moved to a different psychiatric facility.

At least we'd made progress somewhere – one less ball in the air. Juggling. Clowns. Carnie folk. I jammed the brakes on that series of thoughts. No clowns. We'd found no evidence of circuses present in the towns at the times the families disappeared. A frightening laugh filled the air and a clown slithered down a drain.

Grace barreled toward the front door as I opened it. For someone with little legs, she was quick. Her arms tackled my knees, I bent over and picked her up, upside down. Legs waving in the air. Giggles falling on my boots. I swung her around until she was upright in my arms.

"Again!"

I spun her around until she was upside down and giggling up a storm, then righted her again.

"Mommy is done now, Grace." She pressed her forehead into mine and looked into my eyes. My child became a cyclops. "Off you go and play," I said, placing her on the floor. Kurt chuckled. "Suits you, this whole motherhood thing."

I watched Grace run down the hallway. "There are times when it's actually fun," I said, giving the front door a shove and listening for it to click. "And times when it's petrifying."

The thought of someone putting my precious little people inside a snow globe and watching them suffocate was appalling.

His chuckle became a laugh. Mitch stepped out of the living room, halting our movement.

"How many for dinner tonight?" He glanced at his watch before catching my hand in his. "It's almost four. Shall we find out and maybe order pizza?"

Kurt and I both said, "Not pizza."

"Suggestions would be welcome then," Mitch said. "What is it with you and pizza? We never have pizza I thought it'd be a nice change."

We shook our heads. Images of human eyeballs nestled in mozzarella and tomato sauce sent bile to my throat. We don't eat pizza.

"How about fish and chips?" I said, swallowing excess saliva. There was a place not far from us that did pretty good fish and chips, not New Zealand good, but still good. Anything was better than pizza.

Lee stepped out of the living room. "Big 'no' to pizza but I'm in for fish and chips."

"Fish and chips," Kurt said. "Really?"

"Yeah. Remember, Arthur Treacher's battered fish with thick-cut fries?" I said.

A light went on in Lee's head and back lit his eyes.

"Treacher's creatures, isn't that what Mac called it?"

"Yep. What happened to Treacher's creatures here?"

"Closed," Kurt said. "I'm keen on thick-cut fries with aioli."

"And lemon wedges," I added.

Damn, I wanted battered fish. Now. That's dinner then.

"All right," Mitch said. "I'll get an idea of who is still going to be here for dinner and get a take-out order placed."

"Uber-eats," Kurt said.

"Definitely," Mitch replied.

Dane called out from the office. "Ellie!"

I hurried to him, leaving Mitch, Lee, and Kurt in the hallway talking about something.

"What?" I said to Dane, who was waiting at my desk. Sandra sat along a bit and was still working using her laptop.

"I found a Ken Green of interest. He's Andrea Abbot née Green's brother and he works at the Navy Yard, he's an IT specialist and a sergeant with the Marine Corps."

That just opened things up and gave us a link between Lee's stabbing and the missing Abbot family. But it was still freaking weird. IT was part of the Information Dominance Corp and one of the few ratings that allowed people to work in other fields within the Navy. Green could've chosen SEALs or SeeBees or almost anything but he chose the Marines and our dead guy was wearing Marine boots.

"Awesome." I thought for a second then spoke to Sandra. "Do we have any connection between Lily, Jennifer, and Andrea Abbot, beyond their marriages to Joseph Abbot?"

Sandra shook her head then pushed her glasses into place.

"Social media shows very little regarding Lily Abbot and the kids. No likes or comments from either of the other wives." She paused, I detected a but and waited. "But, Messenger tells another story. Lily and Andrea chatted regularly. There is, however, nothing to suggest they knew they shared a husband. Likewise, nothing to suggest they didn't know."

There was enough to make Andrea Abbot a tentative suspect in the disappearance of the family.

"Keep digging," I said and touched Dane on the shoulder. "You're with me. Let's go."

If we were lucky, we'd be back in time for dinner.

I turned and smacked into Sean. His hands gripped my upper arms and he lifted me sideways.

"Funny," I said, as he let me go.

"Always will be," he said looking down at me with his steel-gray eyes. "Diego called."

A glimmer of sparkle flashed in the gray. "This Ellis guy is locked up?"

"He is. And I've suggested the CPD stay on, you okay with that?"

"Yes. I'm heading to Mikki's for dinner tonight. We'll

talk tomorrow?"

"Absolutely."

"Thanks, El," Sean said with a wink. "Thanks for being there for her."

"No thanks required. Are you going to be here much longer?"

"Here, here?" He waved his hand around the room. "Or Northern Virginia here?"

"Here here."

"I'm lending Sandra a hand for another hour or so then I'll go visit my little sister."

I nodded. "Dane and I are going to find Sergeant Green."

"Any more text messages?"

"Nope. I still don't know what the hell they have to do with anything."

"You'll figure it out, El."

Nice that he had faith. Not sure I had much.

Babble and chatter came from the kitchen. I followed the sound to where Isabella and Grace were playing next to each other. Mitch and Mike sat on the floor with them, Lee was at the kitchen table working on his laptop. Working on the weekend was normal for us but this time felt a little more relaxed and it was nice having everyone close. Even Mike. Argo looked up from his bed. I nodded. He stretched, walked over, and then sat looking up at me. It was a look that said I was his human. So much trust in his brown eyes.

"I'll take Argo with me, about time he did some

work," I said to Mitch. The girls looked up briefly then carried on with their respective games. Isabella's continued play made me smile. Not so clingy today, that had to be a good thing. Perhaps having Uncle Lee around helped.

Mitch grinned. "You could take my car that has a Defense pass attached."

An eyebrow lofted. Juggling cars to get Mitch's out of the garage didn't thrill me. I grinned. "Don't think we need a pass. We all carry Federal ID cards and mine says Special Agent in Charge."

Mitch tilted his head. "Did you say federal or feral?"

My grin splattered laughter across floor. "Federal but really ..."

"So close," Mitch said. "Okay Mrs-Special-Agent-in-Charge, have fun but not too much fun."

"Thank you for holding the fort here." I planted a kiss on his lips.

"You're welcome," Mitch said, handing a block to Grace.

"Any of you seen Kurt?" I said. Mike and Mitch looked up, but it was Argo who gave Kurt away. He looked sideways for a second then refocused on my face.

"Right behind you, Iverson." Humor surrounded his words. "You didn't jump this time."

A laugh escaped. "The dog saw you first and told me."

"Where are you three headed?"

"Navy Yard. Dane found Sergeant Green and he seems to be the Green in the letter Kreg had on him."

"Room for one more?"

"Of course," I said. "I'll meet you outside." I hurried down the hall and up the stairs to our room. I grabbed my messenger bag, checked my wallet was in it, and took a lanyard from the bag and dropped it over my head. May as well wear my ID. There would be a Marine guard on the gate and possibly a detection dog. Security tightened a couple of years back after a lunatic exploded the Navy Museum. I sucked in air and tried to shove the memory back in the box it escaped, from but it fought back.

The room rocked. I stumbled blindly across the floor. Dust filled the air. Feeling my way with my hands, I found the edge of the bed and sat. A voice came from somewhere. Was it me?

"It's over."

My lungs ached.

"This is not happening."

Breathing hurt.

"You survived. You are safe."

... The world tipped. My fingers grasped at the bed quilt. I pushed my feet hard against the floor. A reddish-brown patch on my shirt front spread. Acrid smoke mingled with blood, blanketed sobs, and final breaths. A gap in the haze formed. Just big enough for me to see a little boy. I pushed wood off him. He didn't cry. He just stared. Fine particles of dirt clung to his eyelashes.

I scooped him up. So light. The ability to process stopped. I held him in my arms. His head fell back. His black curly hair gray from concrete dust. His brown eyes stared up at me, not blinking, not reacting. Maybe my mask scared him? All of a sudden, life kicked back in and tried to make sense of his small battered body. Where were his legs? My head turned. Where was his mom? Filthy fingers clawed at rubble. A hand emerged. A voice cried out in pain. Dropping to my knees with the small broken body cradled in one arm, I pulled hunks of concrete out of the way. A face. Tears carved clean streaks toward her matted bloodied hair. A rasping voice said, "My baby."

I pulled as much debris from the woman as I could and placed the boy in the arm I'd freed. She clutched the small lifeless boy and took her last breath ...

My eyelids fluttered. There was no smoke. I breathed. There was no dust. Confusion and disbelief swirled around me. My bedroom came into focus.

"I'm at home?"

My hands shook, my mouth watered, black spots danced in front of me, as I tried to control the rising tide of bile.

Breathe.

Kurt's voice reached me. He didn't sound close.

"Hey, Iverson, you coming?"

I struggled to my feet and took stock.

No blood.

No grime.

No injuries.

My legs didn't want to move. It took concentration to take a step. Then another. And another. I found myself in front of the mirror. I stared at the accusing blue eyes looking back at me. Why now? Why this again?

"Mirror, mirror on the wall. Who's the most fucked of them all?"

The blue eyes didn't blink.

"Get your shit together. You've got a job to do."

Chapter Twenty Four
Don't Stop Thinking About Tomorrow

Kurt waved his keys at me from the front door. He was driving then. Suited me. The jittery feeling left behind from the flashback worried me and I needed to get us an escort into the Navy Yard and in particular Building One-Nine-Seven where NAVSEA resided. And to get a grip. The new memory that surfaced around the Navy Yard was hard to dislodge. Today was the first time I'd remembered the mother. Part of me wondered what else I'd remember while the rest of my brain tried to bury it all.

"You okay?" Kurt asked as I joined him, Argo, and Dane at the door.

"Of course," I replied, with what I hoped was a decent smile. Liar, liar, pants on fire.

Argo leaned against me. I looked at him and he looked up at me and gave me a nudge with his nose. That was his way of calling bullshit but only he and I knew that. And he would keep my secret. Dogs are way better than humans at keeping confidences.

No one said anything else until we were in the car and on our way.

"Which gate?" Kurt said as he drove toward the city.

"6th Street on M," I replied. "We shouldn't have any trouble getting into the Yard."

Kurt smiled and said nothing.

I made a call to NCIS, also housed in the Navy Yard. We had a long-standing relationship. My dad was retired NCIS. A good friend of Delta's was a senior agent with NCIS and now an FBI asset. And once upon a time I had the former Director of NCIS arrested. It was a time-honored occasionally turbulent association with the Navy.

Julie answered the phone.

"Special Agent Julie Evans."

"Hey, it's Ellie Iverson. We're headed your way and need an escort."

"Wow, look at you calling ahead," she said with a laugh. "I'm in the office today and am happy to be your escort."

"Thanks. We need to talk to a Marine Sergeant who works at NAVSEA."

"Give me his name. I'll make sure he's on base."

"Sergeant Ken Green, he's an IT specialist."

"I'll find him and set up a meeting. What time will you be at the gate?" She paused. I almost heard her mental machinations. "I take it you are going to sneak in the 6th Street Gate?"

"Meet you there in twenty minutes?"

"I'll be waiting."

That wasn't so hard but did nothing to alleviate the troubling images that had surfaced before we left and continued to circle like vultures.

Dane tapped my shoulder. I dropped my phone in my lap and swiveled to see what he wanted.

"Okay back there?"

Argo sat a little straighter, ears perked. He was happy at the prospect of work. Dane smiled.

"I ran a hunch and discovered Andrea Abbot flew into Columbia Regional Airport on November fifteen. Columbia is the nearest major airport to Jefferson City, Missouri."

"And November fifteen was the last day anyone saw the Abbot family."

That definitely put her on the suspect list. Andrea Abbot stuck on a blank page in my mind with a big red pushpin. Wasn't so much a suspect list as a big nothing.

"See what else you can find about Andrea Abbot's trip before we meet with her brother. I want to have playable cards in hand." My thoughts gathered momentum. "She didn't answer her phone when I called." I passed Dane my phone. "I added her number to contacts. How about you give it a try from your phone?"

He found her phone number and gave her a call with the speaker on.

Her perky voice filled the car. "This is Andrea, leave your name and number and I'll get back to you."

"This is Dane Smith. Give me a call. It's about your brother."

He hung up.

"Nice touch," I said.

"Figure if she's checking her phone that will get her

attention." He passed my phone back to me. "I'll see what else I can find about her arrival and if she flew out of Columbia at any point."

I faced the front again and watched traffic.

"Wonder who else flew into town that day?" Kurt said, glancing at me.

Yeah, me too.

"Dane … check for any travel by Ken Green or Simon Kreg into Columbia that day?"

"On my list, doing it, along with Jennifer Abbot."

Dane was undeniably an asset to Delta A, and Delta in general. As the boss of Delta teams, this did not go unnoticed.

My phone rang. Claude from Delta B.

"Special Agent in Charge," I said.

"We have an agent down."

My heart dropped. "Is this ongoing? Are you safe? Details, Claude, go."

"One suspect is in custody. One in the wind. Charlotte Hunt is wounded. We are waiting on medevac."

I skimmed over the week's briefings but couldn't remember what Delta B were working on.

"What case are you on?"

"Theft from an interstate shipment."

Ah, yeah. The trucking company which had two truck and trailer rigs fully laden with goods stolen. One hijacked between South Carolina on the way to Virginia, and the other hijacked in Tennessee, also heading for Virginia.

"Can she speak?"

"She's not too good at it, but yeah."

"Can she hear me?"

"Hang on, putting you on speaker now SAC." There was small pause. "Okay, go for Charlie."

"Hey, Charlie, it's Ellie."

I listened for a response. "Ellie. Sorry," she said, her voice cracked. In the background, I heard a familiar *thwock, thwock, thwock*. Any minute we'd be drowned out by the incoming helicopter.

"Nothing to be sorry about. Sounds like your ride is approaching. You'll be in safe hands in a few minutes."

"I ... I know." A hint of a smile found its way to me. "Hey, we got ... one of ... them."

"Good work. I'll be by to check on you in the hospital."

Claude came back on the line, background noise faded. I guessed he took me off speaker. "The helicopter is setting down."

"Before you go, did you recover any of the stolen property?"

"The trailer was empty when we found it."

"What was the load?"

"Cages filled with plastic bottles of HCHO."

"And HCHO is?"

"Formaldehyde," Kurt said without missing a beat.

"All good, Kurt's with me. A shipment of formaldehyde. Now why would someone want that?"

"Not sure but we'll find out."

"I know you will. Be safe. Keep me informed. Tell Charlie the best stories start with a medevac."

In truth, they start with tequila but a medevac often leads to tequila, so there's that.

When I took note of our surroundings again we'd stopped in the gate to the Navy Yard. I had no idea how that happened. A Marine checked our identification.

"State your business."

"We're here to conduct an interview and notify next of kin."

The Marine nodded and handed our identification cards back.

"Stay in the car, please," he said, from the driver's window. "We have a detection dog with us today."

Argo perked up and angled himself to see out the windows. A handler directed a black Labrador. The dog sniffed all over the car exterior with joyful enthusiasm. A few minutes later, we were given the all-clear.

A figure stood near a building on our left. A hand waved. Kurt pulled over and zapped his window down. "Julie. Thanks for this."

"No problem. Room for me?"

"Yeah, dive in," I said, starting to feel more like my usual self. It helped knowing there was a sniffer dog working at the gate.

Dane reached across and opened the door for her. Argo readied himself for fond greetings.

Julie settled beside the dog. "Nice to see you too,

Argo," she said, scratching under his chin. He lapped up the attention.

Chapter Twenty Five
Devils And Dust

Julie guided Kurt to a car park close to the Humphreys Building. It pleased me to find Building One-Nine-Seven had a name. I briefly wondered if all the buildings in the Navy Yard had names. Names were less intimidating than numbers. I attached Argo's short leash to his harness. No need for his long working leash inside a building. We were here to have a conversation not to chase anyone. That thought felt like I'd jinxed our afternoon. But probably not as much as those hidden memories had. Above the street, a glowing silvery seventy-four hung in the air. I looked away and it moved with me. My eyes closed for a split second and it was gone. Seventy-four deaths in the Navy Museum explosion.

There are dogs on the gate. No one explodes today.

Dane nudged me as we walked to the main doors of the building. "Hope that's not a famous last thought."

"Get out of my head," I said with a frown. "It's no place for you." Especially with remnants of old memories resurrecting. I was glad he didn't pick up on the moment I'd had at home. I did a mental shrug to push the remnants further away. Seventy-four people, mostly children.

He laughed, but behind his eyes I saw a glimmer of concern, a hint of knowing. Kurt and Julie looked over their shoulders at us. Kurt's head shook slightly as he swung the door open and held it for us. Julie thanked him.

Nice.

She pressed the button on the elevator. I took a shallow breath, Argo's eyes on me. He knew. Not just him and Dane this time. Everyone knew. Julie turned to me. "The stairs are over there." She pointed to the set of double doors about ten feet away. "Third floor. We'll wait for you."

I wrapped my hand tighter around Argo's leash. Wait for me? I don't think so. Argo and I were through the stairwell doors and halfway up the first set of stairs before the elevator announced its arrival on the ground floor. We ran until I stopped at the door with a big blue three. I pushed the door open and looked around. No one there yet. Argo and I walked to the elevator doors. The elevator pinged.

Kurt greeted me when the doors slid open.

"Fun?"

"Yep," I said. Argo yapped once. Low key but definitely affirmation of the fun we had running up the stairs. I shifted my attention to Julie. "Where are we going?"

"Follow me. He should be in his office down this hallway."

A few moments later, she knocked on a door before swinging it wide. A man in a Marine uniform sat behind a large L-shaped desk working. The shortest part of the desk faced the door with the longest part against the wall, reaching back to the window. On that side were three screens and a keyboard; from where he sat he could reach the keyboard on that side and the laptop on the other by swiveling his chair. His fingers tapped on the keyboard. The screen changed to screensavers before he acknowledged us.

"How can I help?"

"Sergeant Ken Green?" Julie said holding the identification she wore round her neck out for him to see. "NCIS. I called earlier."

Green stood. He was maybe two inches taller than me which put him at five feet eleven inches. His body type leaned a little more toward nerdy IT guy than the door-breaching world-saving *Semper Fi* type I associated with the Marine corp. Ooh Rah.

I moved into the room with Argo. "Special Agent in Charge Ellie Iverson, FBI." Kurt and Dane stepped in behind us and closed the door. "Behind me are SSA Kurt Henderson and SA Dane Smith."

Sergeant Green cracked a smile and looked down at Argo. "And this is?"

"Agent Argo," I said.

"How can I help the FBI and NCIS?"

Julie stepped aside. "I'm here as an escort. The FBI have a few questions."

Green scanned the room. "Don't think we have enough chairs."

"That's fine. We're good standing."

Green came around our side of his desk. He reached over and shook my hand. "How can I help the FBI, Agent Iverson?"

"Do you know Simon Kreg?"

A frown crinkled the middle of his forehead. "He's my ex."

"When did you break up?"

"A few months ago."

"Any idea why he'd have what we think is a copy-and-paste from an email addressed to you?"

"No, ma'am."

"Do you know where your sister is?"

"Andrea," he whispered. "I wish I did."

"When did you last hear from Andrea?"

"November fourteen." He reached over a monitor on his desk and picked up his cell phone. Scrolled, then handed the phone to me. A phone call on the morning of November fourteen. I handed it back.

"How was she?"

"Good. She was away for the weekend and was excited about coming home and a photoshoot. She said she'd have the proofs sent to me on the Monday."

"Nice. Did you get the photos?"

He shook his head. "No. I got an email from the photographer but the photos weren't attached. There was a mix-up."

His answer buzzed in my bones. It was more a partial truth than an outright lie.

"And Andrea?"

"Been unusually quiet. We didn't talk every week but we tried to talk every month." He rested his hip on his desk. His eyes moved rapidly around the room. "What's this about? Is my sister all right?"

"We don't know, yet. But something has happened to Simon Kreg."

He blinked slowly but maintained eye contact with me. "What did he do?"

That's an interesting reaction. "What makes you think he did something?"

A small sigh escaped. He straightened up. "Because Agent, he could be difficult. And he decided Andrea was in trouble. His behavior was erratic, at times unstable."

"He thought Andrea was in trouble?" Kurt clarified.

We thought she was a suspect.

Ken nodded. "Simon and Andrea were close. She used to say if he weren't gay, he'd be the perfect man for her."

Must be weird being attracted to the same people. "How much contact did they have?"

"Several times a week. That's why Andrea and I didn't need to talk a lot. Seemed redundant."

"And he thought she was in trouble, but you didn't?" I said.

"I figured she was busy. We all get busy sometimes." He adjusted his line of sight and looked into my eyes. "Has someone hurt my sister?"

I shook my head. "There is no evidence that your

sister is hurt."

"Okay. Then what is this about?"

"Simon stabbed one of my men in the back."

Ken's eyes widened. Guess he didn't expect that.

"Was he ever military?" Dane asked.

Ken's head shook. "No. He worked in an electronics store. He was a troubled soul."

"What does that mean? Troubled?" I said.

"Everyone has demons, Agent."

Above his head, a silvery seventy-four hung in the air. I dragged my eyes down until I could see his and not the number over his head.

Yes. Everyone has demons.

I attempted a smile. It failed. "Tell us about Simon and his demons."

"If he'd put as much effort into dealing with them as he did hiding from them, we might not be standing here now." Ken sucked in a ragged breath.

"I'm sorry. This is not easy, but we need to understand what happened."

"He'd been hard to communicate with for a few months before we broke up. No real appetite, unable to sleep, irritated, angry for no apparent reason. A couple of times he said he missed me and didn't feel safe when I was deployed."

"Was he ever diagnosed with a mental illness?"

Ken looked at me. "Not as far as I know. But truthfully, I felt he was in denial. Every time I broached the subject, he declared he was stressed. Work was stressful but other than that he said he was fine. Then he'd calm down again for a few weeks."

"How long had he been using meth?" Kurt said, after reading something on his phone. He tipped it so I could see. Toxicology report from the pathologist.

"What?" Ken stepped back with his right foot and sank onto the edge of his desk. "Meth? You're sure?"

Kurt nodded. "Pathologist ran bloods. We're sure."

"I don't know. I never thought of drugs." He looked bewildered. "But that makes sense, I suppose."

"When did you see him last?"

"I shipped out on November eighteen … when I got back last month he'd moved out."

"Okay, so you deployed overseas. When you left the country, Simon was still a functioning human?"

"Yes," he said without hesitation. "I Skype called home twice a week if I could, or at least once every week, and I noticed as time went on that his irritation grew. I could tell he wasn't sleeping. He was wired and jumpy, visibly losing weight. I tried to get him to see a doctor, but he said he was okay."

"He wasn't, was he?"

"Seems not, Agent. I thought it was about me being deployed. He didn't like it when I was away. Then I thought it was about Andrea. He'd said a few times he thought she was in trouble and that she'd dropped off the map, but maybe it was about drugs."

Maybe it was all of the above. "Let's talk about your sister."

His lack of concern bothered me. I'd like to think my brother would at least try to find me. Perhaps turn over a few stones. Not carry on with life as normal when there could be something very wrong.

"Can we get a coffee?" Ken said. "And sit?"

I nodded. I spun around and spoke to Julie. "Where's good for coffee and can we talk there?"

"My office," Julie said. "Ready when you are."

"Okay, let's go."

We waited for Sergeant Green to shut down his work station then escorted him to the NCIS building and Julie's office, where they still made coffee as if Noel Gerrard was there.

Dark, smooth, strong; if you tried to stir in sugar or cream the spoon almost stood up by itself. Perfect.

Green puzzled me. He had an angry dead ex and a sister that his ex thought was in trouble, yet he was calm. I wondered what it would take to rattle him.

Argo drank from a bowl Julie set on the floor near him then sat by my leg. Once we were all seated, all had coffee, our eyes and attention turned to Sergeant Green.

"Tell me about your sister," I said, kicking off round two.

A smile flitted across his lips, fading before it had chance to settle.

"She is two years younger than me, head strong, capable, good job, married."

"Married," Dane said. "Have you heard from her

husband?"

Green shook his head. "No. Don't expect to."

"Why?"

"Don't like him."

"So you know him?" I said.

"We met once. At their wedding." Everything behind his eyes darkened.

That wasn't just dislike. "What exactly do you not like about him?"

"He never seems to be around. He's disappointed Andrea, over and over again." He took a sip of coffee. "She makes excuses for him."

"You were at the wedding?" Kurt said.

"Yes." He turned his head to focus on Kurt. "Andrea asked me to walk her down the aisle."

"Church wedding?"

"Was supposed to be but it became a registry office wedding." He shrugged. "No aisle."

"Why did they change their minds about the wedding venue?"

"He changed the venue. She wanted a church wedding." Green was clearly unimpressed with his brother-in-law. "It was all about him." He clenched his jaw. "She didn't even get the wedding dress she'd talked about. He took away her wedding and replaced it with five minutes at the courthouse." His jaw clenched and unclenched. His right hand did the same. The Marine took over and the IT guy vanished.

Interesting. I got the impression he would like to do

serious harm to his brother-in-law.

"What does her husband do?"

"I think he's with a telecommunications company, but I'm not sure. He dodged questions as if he were CIA."

I brushed a strand of hair from my face. "Not forthcoming then?"

"Not at all. The only good thing I could see was that Andrea loved him and was happy."

Obviously, he had no idea why that was the case. Argo stood, stretched, and approached Green. He rested his head on Green's thigh and waited for his hand to find him. His job was to relax Green. Argo was hard to resist, so he was resting his head on Green's thigh until Green got the message.

"What's his name again?" Green rubbed Argo behind his ear.

"Argo," I said. "Give us a minute? You hang with him, okay?"

Green nodded. Argo never moved.

Julie stayed in the room as Kurt, Dane and I stepped out.

"El?" Dane said with a look that suggested he knew I was thinking something, but not what.

Blocked.

"He's holding back. Let's give Argo a few minutes to work his doggy magic and then we'll go back in."

"What do you think he's holding?" Kurt said. "I'm not saying you're wrong, by the way, just interested in what you've picked up."

"There's more to Kreg's behavior than he's saying. He knows more about Kreg and what he wanted, why he lashed out and connected with Lee in such a violent way."

Dane paced for a minute, then came to a stand-still in front of us.

"If Kreg and Andrea were as close as Green says, then she might have been privy to his secrets."

"Possibly," I said. "She's potentially missing and he's dead."

"Are those things connected?" Kurt peered in the semi-frosted security glass panel in Julie's office door. "He's still petting Argo."

"He hasn't asked what happened to Kreg," I said. "We told him he stabbed one of us but he hasn't asked if Kreg is all right."

Dane shrugged. "Maybe he genuinely doesn't care. Maybe he's not over Kreg moving out while he was deployed. Could be anger there."

All good points. "Back in we go," I said, pulling on the door handle.

Chapter Twenty Six
Blowin' In The Wind

Green looked up when I entered the room. Argo wagged his tail but stayed where he was. He wasn't done with his job yet. Chill and relax the man.

"You okay?" I said, and took my seat. Green nodded. His hand stayed on Argo. "Is there something you want to tell us about Simon Kreg?"

His eyes dropped to the dog. "He had some strange ideas."

Here we go.

"Like what exactly?"

Green petted Argo; his eyes remained on the dog.

"Simon believed *The Handmaid's Tale* was happening." He looked at me then back at the dog. "He believed that women were being pushed out of top positions, that gays were being persecuted, that the borders would close, that the military would turn on the people we're supposed to protect. Our own people would be subjugated." Green made eye contact with me. "Simon told me on more than one occasion that it had already started and he said it all revolved around the birthrate decreasing."

Yeah, well, he may not have it entirely wrong. He was right about the birthrate, I'd just read about our decreasing birthrate and the speculative reasons for the decline for the third consecutive year.

"I see." I'm not blind, but I am a government employee. No comment was the safest route. I was a woman who worked hard and had put up with bullshit concerns about my ability to do my job while pregnant. Another woman proffered the opinion that I should've taken extended leave or perhaps a desk job. I would not miss Owen's particular fucked-up brand of leadership. It was too easy for all the things we'd fought for to be taken from us. I shoved the thoughts and feelings on the subject into a deep pit and dropped a lid on it. Now was not the time to explore anything regarding *The Handmaid's Tale* being a prophecy. A robot hollered, "Danger! Danger!"

I refocused on the present. "He was anti-military?"

"No. He was scared," Green said. A statement, not a judgment.

"Of you, did he believe you would turn on him?"

Green shook his head then stopped. "I hope not." He ruffled Argo's fur. His voice dropped, "You're lucky, pal. You have a job and a home, and no one will tell you you're not good enough to be part of society."

Sounded to me as though he thought Kreg was on to something with this theory or maybe he was smart enough to see the writing on the wall; many of us had. Seeing it is one thing. Knowing how to stop it is something else. Run? Is that our only option?

Danger!

"Do you think he persuaded Andrea to cross the border? Was that what he was doing?"

He nodded. "His opinion was that no one was safe."

"Is Andrea in trouble or has she left the country?"

"I don't know." He rubbed Argo's ears. "I hope she left," he said with quiet resolve.

That was my answer. He'd seen what we'd all seen. He knew Kreg wasn't altogether wacky with his observations.

"And you didn't want to tell us because?"

"I don't know if she listened to him. I don't know if she went." A little glimmer of something sparked in his voice. "I don't know who I can trust."

"Sergeant," Kurt said, attracting his attention.

"Sir."

"You can trust us. In this room, you trust us all." Kurt circled his finger in the air. "This is a safe space. You are among like-minded souls here."

Argo placed a paw on Green's thigh. Green smiled and nodded. He exhaled, his shoulders dropped. For the first time, I sensed a willingness to talk.

"What else do you know about Simon Kreg?"

"He was buying cryptocurrency. Had been for the last three years."

Cryptocurrency. How very interesting. "Bitcoin?"

"He said he wanted a universal currency for when ours imploded. He diversified. He had a digital wallet for some currencies and others he kept on a thumb drive."

Again, not a stupid idea. "We need to talk to you about Simon."

His fingers disappeared in the thickness of Argo's fur. "He's dead, isn't he?"

I nodded. "I'm sorry for your loss."

"I lost him months ago, Agent."

"We've been trying to get hold of your sister. And having Kreg attack one of my men feels connected." I let that sink in for a second. "Do you believe Andrea left the country?"

"No, I guess I don't. I hoped she had."

"Do you have keys to her home?"

"Yes. She lives in an apartment. I have a key."

I was getting a strange picture from Green. If he hadn't heard from his sister in months, why wouldn't he be concerned? Maybe they had a fight, maybe they were estranged. Yet he had keys to her home.

"What happened that caused a rift between you and your sister?" May as well just put it out there.

He looked a little surprised but recovered well.

"She married Abbot."

"And?"

"I told you already. We don't get on."

"Yes, you did. There's more to it. Why would a brother cut contact with his sister?"

"I didn't. Abbot did. I said a few things. Along the lines of her being able to do so much better. Abbot didn't like that."

Okay. "And the photos? What is that all about?"

He sighed. "Simon told me they were having professional photos taken and that I would be getting proofs. She wanted me to see how happy they were." He dropped his gaze to the dog and ruffled his fur. "It was supposed to be a surprise." His head lifted. "It was a fucking surprise all right."

So he did get the photos. "In what way?"

"Andrea and Abbot were not the only ones in the photo. There were two other women and three little kids."

"Abbot's sisters?" I suggested.

"Abbot's wives," he growled. "I was right about the asshole. When I saw the pictures, I tried to get hold of Andrea to tell her to leave, but she wasn't answering her phone. Figured she knew how I would react and blocked me." His eyes met mine. "Or Abbot controlled her phone."

Or she's dead. Or she killed them all and is on the run. There were a couple of options floating in the ether.

"You saw the pictures," I said. Then what was with the note we saw?

Dane tapped his foot into mine. Him too, then.

"Who sent you the pictures? How were they sent? And do you still have them?"

"Andrea. Email. And yes." He pulled his phone from his pocket, unlocked it, opened an app and handed the phone to me.

I stared at the photos in front of me. Smiling happy people. Smiling. Happy. People. In a fucking snow globe with a backdrop that resembled Little House on the Prairie. I swiped left and viewed the rest of the photographs. All three women appeared happy, in their olde time clothes. Camera magic maybe. I would not be happy to discover I was one of three wives. But, they're not me. Whatever paddles their canoe. White water gushed from a narrow opening between rocks. Three canoes careened down the narrow turbulent waterway until the first smashed into a rock. Spray hit my face. I blinked. Wiped water away. The phone in my hand came into focus. Green watched me from his chair.

"It's a lot to take in," he said with a nod.

It certainly is. I handed the phone to Kurt. As soon as he saw the first snow globe picture, his brow creased.

I'll be squashing any ideas my in-laws have of snow globe pictures.

"Do you believe Andrea knew about the other wives when she married Abbot?"

He shook his head. "She didn't like to share anything, Agent. That's why this came as such a shock."

"What about Simon, did he know?"

"Possibly, later on. If so, he didn't tell me." Green's jaw squared. "He was allowed some contact with her. I was not."

"Where were you on the weekend of November fifteen last year?"

"I deployed on the eighteen. I was getting ready for my deployment."

"Can anyone vouch for your whereabouts that

weekend?"

"No." His eyes flickered. "Yes. I was supposed to have on leave that weekend, but I ended up working here. We had a problem with one of our systems and I worked all weekend, coordinating with a colleague in Germany." He breathed a sigh of relief. "I logged in Friday evening, but I didn't log out again until Sunday night. Also, the cameras would've picked me up."

"You were on base all weekend? Didn't go home to eat or sleep?"

He shook his head. "I slept in my office for a few hours on and off. We have a cafeteria which is more like a restaurant in our building."

"Did you go outside at all?"

"I probably walked down by the dock. Helps me think. I stood where DS Barry was moored until they towed her away for scrap." He grimaced. "Funny what you miss. I never thought I'd miss a big hunk of gray steel, but I do."

Yeah, me too. Display Ship Barry was a fond memory that now resided in the inactive ship facility at the Philadelphia Naval Shipyard all because of money and a bridge.

"Do you often stand in that particular part of the dock?"

"Yes."

Julie interjected, "I see a lone male standing down there sometimes, just staring at the water. Is that you?"

"Probably, ma'am. But I'm sure other people use the

dock."

"How about Andrea? Do you miss her?"

His eyes darkened. "Of course I miss her. She's my sister."

Kurt held the phone toward Green and pulled a business card from his pocket. "Can you email us these images?"

"Of course." He took the phone and the business card Kurt handed him.

"Sergeant Green, is there any reason you can think of for Simon Kreg to be in the vicinity of the Hoover Building four times two days prior to attacking one of my men?"

Green made direct eye contact with me and held it. "Absolutely none."

"Did he have any close friendships other than you and your sister?"

"Not that I know of." A light drifted across his eyes. "Yes, there is an old friend he used to mention sometimes, Alana. I haven't met her."

"Do you know her surname?"

"No, sorry."

A few seconds later, an alert came from Kurt's phone. He checked it and thanked Green.

"I think we're about done here," I said. "We'll be in touch. You're not shipping out any time soon?"

He shook his head. "No."

"I'm sorry for your loss. If you think of anything either contact us directly or let Julie know. We're particularly interested in anything that you remember that could give us a motive that explains why one of my men was stabbed by your ex." I paused for a moment. "He didn't pick on the smallest guy." He chose a walking wall. There's gotta be a reason. Death wish maybe. Suicide by cop? "If you hear from your sister, let us know."

He nodded.

Argo enjoyed one last ear rub then joined me at the door.

"Agent Iverson."

I turned to Green. "Yes, Sergeant Green."

"Find my sister, please."

"She's on my radar. We will do our best." I opened the door. Argo and I walked into the outer office and waited by the front door for Kurt and Dane.

Julie called out to get me to stop before I left the building.

"Problem?"

"Not at all," she said with a hefty eye roll. "I'd like to be read in. This case of yours looks like it might involve Sergeant Green."

"Pretty sure I didn't say that."

"Pretty damn sure you asked if he was deploying any time soon. Read me in, Ellie."

What the hell. The more the merrier, right? "You win. I'll send you copies of the investigation paperwork that contain references to Green."

"Thank you," Julie said with a smile. "That wasn't so

hard, was it?"

"Not at all. Hey, let Green go back to work and I'll fire off the email when I get back to the office on Monday."

Could've done it from home. Today. But Monday will do fine.

Chapter Twenty Seven
So Much Trouble In The World

Our phones rang before we even got near the car. I checked the number before answering mine. Hoover Building.

"Special Agent in Charge Iverson."

"Ma'am, we have bomb threats in two locations."

"Where?"

"Navy Yard."

Nope. We're not doing this again. A puff of smoke rose like a signal then dissipated. That's right, brain, we're not going there again. My thoughts caught my memories and jammed them back in the box they escaped from. No time for that shit now.

"Security is tight. There are explosive detection dogs operating at ... at least one gate." One, because I don't know what's going on at the other gates, but I imagine the security is equal to the 6th Street gate.

"Ma'am, I'm going on the information in front of me."

Okay. Someone's screwed up. My index finger crossed my middle finger.

"Both threats? Because I'm standing inside the Navy Yard, right now." My eyes roamed the area. Don't know what I expected to see. A bad guy in a black mask carrying a round bomb with a sparkling fuse sticking out? No such luck. "Where?"

"Sicard Street South East at the chapel and one-three-three-three Isaac Hull Avenue."

I turned and looked back at the chapel from where I stood on Patterson Avenue. I spun around, looking for an open area. Toward the river on my right was a green space. In the same direction on the left, was Willard Park; on the left of that was a large parking area. Willard Park was trees and green space sprinkled with cannons and guns removed from ships. The thought of being in a building when everything collapsed again, did not thrill me. Concrete and metal raining from the sky displeased me greatly. Willard Park and its contents felt like somewhere to avoid. But the parking lot was mostly empty. We could run down Sicard to the river trail, turn left at the parking lot there and get to the bigger parking lot opposite where the DS Barry used to reside. Our route avoided the chapel.

I surveyed the area. No sign of anyone nearby. Saturday. Most people were not at work. For maximum impact, it'd be better to explode a building during the work week. Same as last time.

My arm in the air, I pumped my fist twice and pointed down the road to the river. Double-time the hell out of here. With a clear thought, I sent directions to Dane. He nodded when I made eye contact with him.

"What is the building number on Isaac Hull?" I said into my phone as I unclipped Argo's leash and whispered in his ear. "Go to Dane." I'm not losing my dog to some fucktard who may or may not like to play with explosives. Argo glanced at me once then ran and caught up with Dane.

I joined Kurt. We ran and I talked on the phone.

"One-three-three-three—"

"That's the street address, I want the building number."

A few mouse clicks got lost in my breathing.

"Building One-Nine-Seven."

"This is not good."

"Ma'am?"

"That's NAVSEA. Is this threat credible or some crackpot craving attention?"

My gut back-flipped. It was real. I knew it. But how did anyone get inside the Navy Yard with explosives?

They didn't?

"IB think it's credible. They picked up chatter in the last twenty-four hours. Metro got four calls over the last half-hour all saying there were bombs."

"Chatter? Between whom?"

"They're not saying, ma'am."

This smacks of bullshit. "If the Intelligence Branch knew about it why are we just hearing about this now? Even hearing about it twelve hours ago would've been helpful."

"I only know what I know, SAC."

"And someone is going to act on this Intel anytime today?" I stopped dead and made sure Argo and Dane were over the other side of Willard Park in the parking lot near the Anacostia River. I stopped. Through the trees stood the NCIS building. Right there. Set back a little from the chapel. Dammit.

"What?" Kurt said. He'd noticed and returned to my position.

"Julie and Green."

Kurt called Dane and told him to stay where he was with the dog.

We ran through Willard Park, avoiding trees, installations, and sticking to the paths as much as possible. I swung through the double doors into the NCIS building, stopped and scanned for Julie. I did not want to be in here in another explosion but I also wanted to see Sergeant Green. Bombs, right now, felt a little too coincidental. My phone made tapping noises in my hand. I still had an open line to the office. I lifted my phone to my ear. "Agent. Bomb Squad status?"

"On the way. First team is five minutes out. Second team is seven minutes out."

"Keep me updated." I paused then issued another instruction. "Inform the teams I am on the ground." And I do not want to go bang. "No one dies today." I hung up.

Julie looked up from a desk with a phone in her hand. She nodded at me.

"Tell me your bomb squad is on the way?" Julie said.

I gave Julie a nod. She spoke into the phone in her hand then hung up.

Stillness blanketed the room. I centered myself. We

got this. No one's going to die today. My positivity took me by surprise. Good to know I hadn't lost my inner Pollyanna. Kurt tapped my shoulder.

"Right, Julie, this is yours. What do you need from us?"

"I need you all out of harm's way. While I make sure the Humphreys building and surrounding area are evacuated, and the chapel and surrounding buildings."

This building included. It's right next door.

Sounds good to me.

"Okay, Dane and Argo are by the river in the parking lot." I pointed. "Where the Barry used to be. We'll join them."

"Pretty sure we have people evacuating buildings but I'm checking," she picked her phone up and made a call while grabbing a backpack from under her desk.

Green stepped out of the hallway that led to the bathrooms.

"You're back," he said. His tone gave nothing away.

Kurt waved him over. "We'd like a word. Walk with us. Outside."

I did a quick tour of the ground floor looking for anyone else. And hollered a few times. No one. Upstairs was the same. I ran down the stairs. Kurt and Green were walking across the road. Julie was still talking on the phone. She slung the backpack over one shoulder, handed me a red sign for the door, and opened the front door for me.

I slapped the sign to the inside of the unopened side

of the door. Building Clear. Do not enter.

Julie shoved her phone in her pocket.

"Where is everyone?" I said, with a nod of my head toward the NCIS building as we crossed the road, veered left, and headed over to the path that Kurt and Green took that would take us to the parking lot on the other side of the trees.

"Only Kath and I were in, catching up on paperwork, enjoying the peace. She left before you arrived."

Sirens wailed through the air. That took longer than I thought.

"Everyone's evacuated?"

"Evacuation was in progress by the time you got back to me. Should be all out by now."

I smiled.

"What are the odds of a bomb scare at the Navy Yard while we're here," I mumbled, more to myself than to her.

"At least this time we had warning," Julie said, her voice dropped to a whisper, "And there're no kids, El."

My phone rang. A loud 'Good morning, Vietnam!' blasted from my pocket. Julie laughed. I grinned and answered the call from Tony, the best bomb disposal tech I'd ever worked with.

"Tony, tell me something good."

"We're on the ground."

Julie looked toward the museum before we left the street and pointed to a man clad in green waving at us from the intersection.

"Well, I guess that's good."

"Wave back, El. I look like a dick standing here waving and being ignored."

I waved at Tony. "Two teams?"

"Yep, and Andrews is coming in as support. We have some Navy boys with us."

Good. SWAT and Navy. That should cover things nicely. "And the dogs?"

"Got military dogs with our teams. Where's yours? I don't see him."

"With Dane down by the river," I said.

"Good place for you to be too, Iverson. We got this."

"Be safe."

I heard him laugh as he hung up.

The conversation with the office rolled back. Chatter. That felt wrong. Chatter in our intelligence community was a sudden increase of intercepted communications. Email and phone conversations, internet message services, any of the ways people communicate and also includes suspicious movement of suspects, the transfer of funds and information from live sources. If IB detected a surge in chatter, who were the suspects they were monitoring and why didn't we know about this yesterday?

"Kurt!" A louder holler than I intended crossed the empty parking lot as I walked toward him. He was with Green, Dane and Argo stood a few yards away by the wrought iron fence and its red brick pillars that separated the parking lot from the river trail and the now-empty dock.

"Iverson, you yelled?" he said when I reached his position.

"Chatter?" Chatter made no sense. "What the fuck?"

Green squinted at me but said nothing.

Kurt nodded and made a call while walking over to Dane and Argo. Green stood still.

"Why would someone want to blow your building today?" I said.

"I don't know. You mentioned two bombs?"

"The chapel."

Green took a step back. His brows knitted. "Humphreys building and the chapel?"

"What does it mean?"

"Every day I'm at work, I walk from the Humphreys Building to here." He swept his arm across the pathway beyond the fence. "Via the chapel."

"That sounds like it might be connected to you, this bomb threat."

"But it makes no sense. And here?" He met my gaze. "If someone wanted to kill me Agent, there are easier and more accurate ways."

That was true.

A bullet would do the job just fine without a whole lot of collateral damage. Unless the point was collateral damage. Kill Green and other people. Retaliation for something.

Kurt was still talking, animated with his gestures.

"Could this be related to your last deployment?"

"I'm a computer specialist. I build systems and troubleshoot. Probably not."

Julie called my name. I glanced at her, then back at Green as fragments and red mist exploded from the side of his head.

Chapter Twenty Eight
We Didn't Start The Fire

My knees jarred as I dropped to the ground near Green's body. Small stones dug into my knees, fingers on autopilot felt for a pulse in his neck. Zilch. Shit. Kurt crouched on the other side. I shook my head as he too searched for a pulse.

"Dammit," Kurt muttered.

"Where did the shot come from?"

An explosion hit the air as a rumble shook the ground. Argo whined. Dane threw an arm over Julie and pushed her down. I turned. Smoke, dust, debris fell from the air. It can't happen again. Time slowed. A single blink took an eon. My eyelids lifted to reveal Kurt in front of me. His mouth moved in silence. A hand wrapped around my arm, like an anchor. The world around me moved in slow motion. I pushed Kurt's hand off my arm, and scrambled to my feet.

With a *bang*, sound and speed returned. I clicked my fingers. Argo jumped to his feet. His eyes on me. I sprinted toward the clouds of smoke with the dog next to me.

Kurt's voice followed me, "Stop!"

"Stay there!" I yelled over my shoulder.

The closer I got, the harder it was to see. A voice in my head questioned my wisdom as I ran toward chaos. I growled internally. "It's what I do. Back off."

My phone rang in my pocket. It mingled with the noise, easy to ignore. Ten yards from the explosion zone a bulky person intercepted me. Stopped in our tracks, Argo reacted with a protective growl but waited, unsure.

"Argo," the male said, his voice muffled slightly by his gear. A gloved hand landed on the dog's head. "Friend not foe."

"Tony."

Argo shoved him with his shoulder. He recognized the voice.

"Stay where you are, Iverson. Let us get in there."

"Anyone hurt, trapped?" I didn't want to ask if there were dead in the chapel.

"The chaplain was with us. As far as we know, no one was in the building except two of my men. They're talking. We'll get them out."

"The other bomb?"

"Haven't found it yet."

So it could still go bang.

"Where's the chaplain. I want a word."

Tony lifted a bomb suit clad arm and pointed toward his truck. "Back there. Good place for you to be as well, Iverson."

"I'll go have a word, see if he saw anyone new over the last few days."

"Good."

"Did you get his name?" I didn't want to call him Chaplain.

"Lieutenant Commander Dan Gordon."

"Thanks."

Argo and I left him to his task. As soon as I knew I could be seen by Dane, Kurt, and Julie, I waved. We got this. I knew Kurt and Julie would've called in Green's death and asked for a forensics team and a Marine recovery team. Although getting to the fallen Marine would be high priority, it would be difficult for any of the teams to complete their assignments in the current situation. All Dane, Kurt, and Julie could do was sit tight and try to stop any scene contamination. Hurry up and wait. Meanwhile, Argo and I had a Lieutenant Commander to talk with.

"It'll be fun." Argo looked up at me. "It's okay, boy." His eyes told me it wasn't okay. He needed more reassurance. I adjusted my tone to suit. "It won't be *that* much fun. It'll be okay."

I bashed on the side door of the mobile command center, also known as Tony's truck. It's a bit fancier than just a truck.

The door opened.

"Come on up, Iverson." A hand reached out for mine and helped me up the four steps. I've learned a few things over the years and one of them is never knock back an offered hand. Doesn't hurt to be polite. Once inside the truck. Carl let me go and looked at Argo who'd followed me in. "Welcome aboard, Agent Argo."

"You got Lieutenant Commander Gordon here, Carl?" I stood in the artificially lit area. It always surprised me how much room there was. Computers, communication equipment, and monitors covered a long bench and half of one wall. The smell of coffee overlaid several layers of scent, including laundry detergent, carpet cleaner, and the more subtle stick-type male deodorant. Bet Argo enjoyed the many smells associated with a confined space like the mobile command center. Carl petted the dog. "Carl, Commander Gordon?"

"Sure. The chaplain is down the end. He's a bit shaken." He scratched Argo under the chin. "Go on back and have a word."

"Argo, let's go," I said, paused and made eye contact with Carl. "You okay?"

Carl was usually in the midst of the chaos, not in the truck.

The wiry man grinned. "Yeah. Short straw. I'm on comms today." He ruffled Argo's fur. "See you soon, pal."

I knocked on the interior door that led to a separate quiet area.

A voice called out, "Come."

I poked my head around the door. "Lieutenant Commander Gordon?" Our eyes met as I pushed the door open. He looked familiar.

"Yes, I'm Chaplain Dan or Lieutenant Commander Gordon, or just Chaplain if you prefer."

Argo waited until I entered the room properly before he made his presence felt.

"You're a fine-looking animal," the Lieutenant said, as Argo presented his paw.

"Lieutenant Commander Gordon this is Argo and I'm—"

He looked up and smiled. "Gabrielle Conway."

Whoa! What?

"Sorry, have we met?"

"A long time ago."

I studied his face, I took in his silver-gray hair, wrinkles, crinkles, the sparkle in his green eyes, and the general weathered look he wore with humor, then tried to replace it with a younger version. Funny, I'm good with faces and names, but his eluded me.

"I'll take your word for it."

"Would it help if I told you that you were in college last time I saw you."

I spun back to my college days. Nothing jumped out. But he was Navy. And I knew that would be the connection. His throaty laugh caught me by surprise and triggered a memory.

"You know my father." Lieutenant Commander Gordon nodded. Then I placed him. "The Navy booth at the career expo in my last year." College felt at least two lifetimes ago.

"I was surprised you chose the FBI. Figured you for Navy like your old man."

I didn't. They chose me.

"Good talk," I said with a smile. Subject change time. "Today. Can we talk about today?"

"Sure." He squinted at me. "You're married now, I see."

I reached forward and shook his hand. "Ellie Iverson."

"I see you had the good sense to take your husband's name."

I chose to ignore his remark.

"Tell me about today." I sat down and shuffled the chair closer. "Anyone come into the chapel?"

He nodded. "No one I didn't know."

Yeah, but it doesn't have to be a stranger. In fact, I'd be surprised if it were. We're on a Naval base.

"Why is the FBI in the Yard? NCIS take care of Navy investigations."

"Usually, yes, I was here on an unrelated matter." Not a lie. I was definitely not here because of a bomb, initially.

I passed him my notebook and pen. "Names of everyone who came in over the last twenty-four hours, please."

When he passed it back, I saw four names and one of them was Sergeant Green.

"Thank you." I read the names again. "Sergeant Green, what can you tell me about him?"

"He's a frequent visitor. Quiet. Comes in and sits with his thoughts."

"Roughly how long does he spend with his thoughts?"

"Ten to twenty minutes. Almost daily when he's

here."

Guess he had a lot to think about. "Anyone ever talk to him?"

"Never seen him with anyone in the chapel." Lieutenant Commander Gordon stopped petting Argo. "He goes from the chapel down to the water. I asked him once why. He said he likes to be near water."

"Anyone else do that?"

His head moved like it was about to shake, then stopped. "Not usually. But yesterday, I was walking to my car and I saw Lance Corporal Jenkins standing by the fence and talking to someone on the other side."

I glanced at the list in my hand. There he was.

"What time?"

"It was late, almost dusk."

"Jenkins was talking to whom?"

"A woman. I thought she passed him something. She was smiling. They were comfortable with each other. I thought perhaps she'd packed him snack, and they'd arranged to meet there."

Possible. Could just meet at the gate like most people. Unless he didn't want her seen by the guard or she didn't want to be seen by the guard.

"Did you see him again?"

"This morning. That's how he got on the list."

I relaxed my tense shoulders and breathed.

"Do you know if there is any video surveillance down there that would've picked up the woman?"

His brows knitted as he frowned. "It's possible."

"Was the woman at all familiar?"

He shook his head.

"Jenkins ever visit the chapel at the same time as Green - before?"

"Maybe. I can't recall."

"Where can I find Jenkins?"

"He works in Navy History and Heritage Command. I don't know exactly what he does."

"He worked today?"

"I don't think so, he was in civvies."

Okay, so he wasn't in uniform and probably not working. Why be in the Yard? An urgent desire to repent? A sudden need to pray?

"What did he have with him?"

"A backpack and before you ask, he left with it."

Yeah, but did he leave with the contents?

"You didn't notice anything left in the chapel?"

He thought for a moment. Frown lines appeared. "No."

"You're absolutely sure?"

The light in his green eyes faded. "Agent. I. Am. Perfectly. Sure."

And yet I didn't believe him. His reply did not give me the slightest confidence. None whatsoever. Why didn't I believe the Lieutenant? What was it about him that gave me pause? He's a freaking Chaplain. Maybe that was it. Maybe the whole man of God thing was all too much. A spark flared. Perhaps he was telling the truth.

What I needed was Chance. I glanced around the room. No Chance. Fuck it. Wishing he was here wouldn't make it so.

"Is there anything you'd like to tell me before I go look for Lance Corporal Jenkins?"

He shook his head. "If I remember any details I'll call."

I passed him one of my business cards. "I'd appreciate that." Argo joined me at the door. We exited the room. I pulled the door closed behind me with a click.

A thought burgeoned and mumbled words tumbled over my tongue. "The trouble starts when someone believes their intelligence is superior to everyone else's."

"All right there, Iverson?"

I looked up to see Carl's bemused expression. "Keep an eye on him." I jerked my thumb over my shoulder. "I need to locate someone."

"Wandering around the Yard is ill-advised right now. I'll get you an escort." His eyes roamed over me. "You should be at least wearing a vest. Where is yours?"

"In our car, inside the cordon."

Carl opened a cupboard. He passed me a vest which wasn't a bad fit. Carl turned his attention to Argo. "At least you're kitted out, pal." He gave the dog a hearty pat on the side.

Argo wore his stab-proof vest that doubled as a

harness to keep him safe in the car.

Carl had a radio in his hand. He spoke quietly into the handset as he sat back in his chair. Argo and I waited by the door. I knew better than to insist on leaving before he had a chance to find us that escort.

"Okay, Iverson. You're good to go. Paul Dixon put up his hand and will meet you outside."

A smile maneuvered around my lips. Paul was Jerry's brother. The Dixon boys were good people. "Andrews's team is on site."

"Yes. Dixon is here now. I'll see you when you get back."

"Thanks, Carl."

I swung the door open.

"Agent Iverson," Dixon said, with a grin. "Where are we headed?"

"To the parking lot down by the river for starters. Got an NCIS agent over there with Kurt. I need her help to find a Lance Corporal who may know something about that." I pointed to the dust, smoke, and rubble that used to be the chapel. I wrapped Argo's leash around my hand and gripped it hard. Stay together. Stay safe.

Dixon spoke, his voice quiet and not intended for me. He talked to his comms and letting them know where we were on the move.

Chapter Twenty Nine

Lucky Man

Kurt looked up as we approached. He gave an understated wave. A shiny silver survival-blanket covered Green's body, affording the dead man some dignity. The waterfront area closed, Marines secured the gates. They'd closed the Navy Yard section of the river trail until further notice.

I pointed to the fence. "A woman handed a man called Lance Corporal Jenkins a package. It may have been his supper or a snack. Whatever it was, it was passed through the bars of that fence. Jenkins was also in the chapel prior to the explosion."

"Hey, Paul, short straw?" Kurt said with a laugh, then followed my arm to the fence line.

"Volunteered," Dixon replied.

"Adrenaline junkie," Julie responded with a grin before turning to see where I pointed.

"Why would anyone deliver a package through a fence?" Kurt said.

"Not difficult to drop off a forgotten lunch at the gate," Julie said, looking from the fence back toward the smoky street. "Unless it's something you don't want vetted."

"That's what I was thinking," I said. "Cameras?"

Julie nodded. "Parking lot surveillance cameras should pick up the fence line, and some sections of the trail have cameras." She held her arms out. "All along here. This is Navy land, we let the public use that section of the trail, but it's ours. We monitor it."

Not that closely, obviously. "How do we view that?"

"I'll take care of it. It's a Navy thing."

Fair enough.

I looked out over the river. Fuck this for Christmas. I wanted answers. Yesterday.

Questions fired so fast, I felt dizzy. Who shot Sergeant Green? Why did the ex-boyfriend of a now-deceased Marine Sergeant stab Lee from behind? Why did Lance Corporal Jenkins receive a package through the fence? Did he place a bomb in the chapel? Why would anyone do that? Is there another bomb? I spun around. Where in God's name was Green's sister, Andrea? Did she know about the other wives of her dear husband? What happened to the Abbot family? What happened to the other families? And what the actual fuck was with the jigsaw puzzle? Who sent the puzzle? What is the damn connection with Delta? Or am I imagining that?

The last questions gave me pause. Why do I think the Chaplain is involved in something shady? What is really going on here?

"Iverson?" Kurt's voice rattled in my head.

I glanced at him. "Yeah?"

"You okay?"

"Sure."

Paul Dixon gave a half-assed laugh. "None of us are that stupid."

I laughed as I said, "Are ya sure about that?"

A sparkle caught my eye. Sun on the water. I squinted. A boat on the water. I capped my sunglasses with my hand and looked again. Shit! "Down!"

Everyone dropped, including the dog. A muzzle flash. A round thumped into the edge of the dock just above the water. Whoever was shooting needed to adjust their line of sight and trajectory if we were the targets.

Dixon yelled at the Marine standing at the locked gate. "Gun on the water!" The Marine dropped to his stomach, his rifle training out to the river.

"That boat out in the middle of the river," I hollered while belly crawling closer to Dixon, Kurt, and Dane. Argo followed me, crawling.

"Yes, ma'am," came the distant reply from behind the rifle.

Julie was near the parking lot on my left and made a call. Her tone made it clear she was calling for reinforcements.

"We need to get out of here," Dane said.

No kidding, Einstein. "Just stay down."

"Is this the same shooter that shot Green?"

"No idea. There wasn't a boat on the water when Green was shot. Or if there was, I couldn't see it."

"Used a cloaking device," Dane mumbled.

Yeah, that makes about as much sense as any of this. I wriggled closer to Julie. "There should've been a team here by the time I got back. There's a Marine down and no guard or recovery."

"In case it escaped your attention, we're fighting fires all over the Yard," she said, without animosity at all. "I had two teams coming for recovery, but now they're coming in hot."

Somewhere in the skies, a dull *thwack* vibrated the air. Another muzzle flash on the water was met with gunfire from the Marine by the gate.

Green's body jerked under the silver foil blanket as a round struck him.

Downriver, two helicopters came in low and fast. The rotors smacking air out of the way and sending noise vibrations across the area. The air rippled and stacked before sound exploded. Firing from the boat continued. Green jerked again. Paul and the Marine fired back, distracting the shooters' attention away from the incoming gunships.

Lying on the cold concrete, I watched two helicopters hover a hundred yards from the boat in either direction. The surface water spread like rings rocking the boat. We heard the megaphone from one of the helicopters.

"Drop your weapons or we open fire."

Muzzle flashes from the boat told me they didn't feel like disarming. Within a split second a series of shots blew the boat to pieces. One helicopter lifted and moved toward us, the other stayed where it was. Two Marines dropped from ropes into the sea, looking for survivors or bodies.

I sat up, stopped watching the water antics, drawn by the helicopter setting down in the parking lot. Dust flew in all directions. Wow, concrete is dirty. Made me grateful for the protection of my sunglasses.

Four Marines disembarked and moved toward our position.

My foot shot out and connected with Kurt's.

"You wanted something?" he said, making eye contact.

"What if Green and the chaplain were targets? Not just Green." This is overkill for one guy.

"What do we have that suggests that could be the case?"

"Nothing really." Dead Marine close to the chapel. Maybe they thought we'd bring the chaplain down to administer last rites once they somehow realized the chaplain didn't die in the explosion.

And that might have been the case if there hadn't been an explosion and I hadn't had a hinky feeling about Lieutenant Commander Gordon. I couldn't even explain it to anyone. Nothing new there.

"What?" Kurt said, his blue eyes holding mine. "What is happening in the dark recesses of that head of yours, Iverson?"

"A gut feeling that this is connected to the chaplain as much as anything else."

Julie met the Marines five yards away from our position and spoke with them. Out on the water I saw a body winched into the helicopter.

Julie joined us. We gathered ourselves together and moved away from Green's body. The Marines would take over now.

"Two bodies in the water," Julie said. "They opened fire on to the Yard This is our jurisdiction. Problem?"

"Joint investigation?" I said. We needed all the help we could get. We'd gone from having a chat to a Marine about his dead ex and missing sister to bombs in the Navy Yard and utter chaos.

She smiled. "I can live with that."

"Then you should know, Lieutenant Commander Gordon is a person of interest."

"Ah, crap," Julie said with a groan. "What the hell is it with clergy?"

"Maybe it's historical ... clergy being involved with all manner of dirty dealings pre-dates the Inquisition. The real question is, why are we always so surprised by their behavior?"

"Cynical, Ellie."

"Realistic, Julie."

She nodded. "I'll find Lance Corporal Jenkins. You okay?"

"Yeah. I'll be in touch."

Chapter Thirty

In the Navy

I called my father.

"Hey, Dad, how you doing?"

"Good. Have Bob over."

Mac's dad. My ex-father-in-law. He and my father worked for my foundation. The Butterfly Foundation supports kids of mentally ill parents. It was a project born from the childhood parallels Mac and I shared.

"Say 'hi' from me."

"Consider it done. We wanted to update you on the Dragonfly Club."

"Okay. Shoot." Perhaps a poor choice of words considering the last hour but whatever.

"The initial invitations were sent three days ago, uptake is at eighty percent so far."

"Impressive. And the opening of the premises?"

"Formal invitations go out next week to the opening gala."

"Is Grange involved?"

"Yes. They will play on the night."

Of course they will. Rowan Grange and his band were supporters of the Butterfly Foundation. I was pleased we could at least remain civil and conduct a working relationship like grownups for the sake of the Foundation. Personally, I kept my distance, he was my past and I didn't want him in my present.

"Do you need me to do anything?"

"Just be there, with Mitch on the night. You're speaking."

"Crap on a cracker. Better write some notes then."

I'm kinda used to public speaking now. Microphones hold no fear anymore. There are worse things out there than talking to a room full of strangers and friends. We were about to open the Dragonfly Club, a drop-in center for teens where they could hang out, join groups, play sport, and access free medical care and counseling services. Dream realized. It felt good to know we'd achieved so much toward providing for at-risk youths.

"I called with a question, Dad."

"Let me have it then ..."

"How well do you know Lieutenant Commander Dan Gordon?"

"Well enough to not like what I see. Why?"

"His Navy Yard chapel blew up."

"Can't believe he's still around," Dad muttered. "Shame about the chapel. Watch your six, kid."

"He's a Chaplain, Dad."

"He's always had an agenda. Tread carefully."

Interesting. "Thanks. Dinner next weekend?"

"Whose turn is it? Yours, mine, or Mitch's folks?"

"Yours."

Dad chuckled, Bob called out 'goodbye' right before Dad hung up.

A chaplain with an agenda? Dad's remark made me

glad it was a Navy problem and not mine.

Back in time for fish and chips seemed like a crazy notion as we drove through the city and headed home. I should've known better. The best we could wish for as darkness deepened and street lights cast their eerie glow was that they'd save us some dinner. I wanted I'd be able to say goodnight to Isabella and Gracey more than I hoped for leftover fish and chips.

My stomach grumbled.

"Past dinner time, Iverson?" Kurt said with a chuckle. "We don't need a clock with you around."

It's true. "I could eat the north end of a south-bound polecat."

Laughter bounced off the windscreen and pooled in the corners of the dashboard.

"I haven't heard that in a long time," Kurt said, as his laughter subsided.

"You people are very strange," Dane said. He leaned forward from the back seat. "Do you genuinely think the Chaplain is involved in whatever got Sergeant Green killed?"

"I don't know what to think. I'd like to just find these missing families, and leave the weird-assed military shit to NCIS." That what I'd like to do but the weird-assed military shit landed on my desk because of Green's ex-boyfriend. Why the fuck did he stab Lee?

My phone rang. The Rolling Stones, 'Angie,' filled the car. "Hey, Sandra, what's up?"

"O Genie of the Mighty Deltas. I have something. I

found a file."

"When you say found?"

"I extracted a file from the mess created by the jigsaw puzzle implosion."

Hot damn, she was one talented techy. I never ceased to be impressed and amazed by her abilities. "Okay, and?"

"I might have something in front of me that we can use."

"For?"

"Remember steganography?"

"Uh-huh."

"I might have found a password. I saved that thumbnail before the implosion. I was working on trying to see if I could get it any clearer and I realized it's bigger than it should be, file-size wise."

"We're on our way. Wait for me?"

"Absolutely. We're saving you three dinner. Trust you're hungry."

"Starving."

Sandra laughed and ended the call.

Before I dropped my phone back in my lap it rang again. This time, Kiss's 'Psycho Circus.'

"You're kidding me," Dane groaned. "Whose ring tone is that?"

"Sean O'Hare's," I replied, laughing and answering the call. "Hey, Sean."

"Where are you?"

"On my way home."

"I'm heading back to yours in about an hour. We need to talk."

"Everything good?"

"Not exactly. We'll talk when I get there."

"Mikki?"

"Safe."

Well, that was something. "See you later." I touched the red icon and ended the call as a frown embedded in my brow. Weird.

Kurt glanced at me before changing lanes. "Problem?"

"Not sure."

"Just say yes," Dane said from behind me.

A small chuckle fell from my lips. "Yes. Potentially."

Kurt laughed.

Silence enveloped the car interior until we were almost home. Loud vibrations from Dane's phone filled the car like a swarm of blowflies on warm dog shit.

"We do have a problem," Dane said, passing his phone to me over my shoulder. The email app was open. "Three more families."

I read the first email. A family disappeared in Springfield, Illinois on or about May fifteen, twenty-fourteen. The next email gave me another missing family, this time from Indianapolis, Indiana. April ten, twenty-fifteen. And the last email said a family disappeared without a trace from Cincinnati, Ohio on February ten twenty-seventeen.

I passed the phone back to Dane. "Ask for those

files, please. Let it be known that we think their missing families are linked to our case."

"Doing it now, Boss."

I sat back in my seat and pulled up images on my phone of the map on my whiteboard. Holy shitballs, Batman. It's an actual trail across America. But not coast to coast. What did that mean?

Do we have missing families we don't know about yet, or is whatever this is still happening? The timeline wasn't linear. The dates and years jumped about but there was still a trail across America.

Kurt pulled into my driveway, zapped down his window and entered a code into the box by the gate. My car and Mitch's car have chips and open the gate on approach. Kurt, Dane, and Sean have individual gate codes. The codes change frequently and the security system registers all activity. Having two houses blow up made me a little cautious.

I watched the gate close behind us in the wing mirror. Habit. If I watched, then I knew without a doubt that no one seized the opportunity to sneak in with the car. All the tension ran from my body. We were home.

The nice thing about being the boss was being able to say we were working through the weekend and using my home as a base.

A cold case probably wasn't the best use of my overtime budget. I flung the door open as the car stopped outside the front door. A little voice reminded me that Lee's stabbing was not a cold case. The bombing and death of Sergeant Green were not cold cases. And our mystery text sender and jigsaw creator was also a current happening.

Argo ran past me and over to the shrubbery in the dark beyond the security lighting. Nature called. The front door opened while I waited for Argo to return. Warm yellow flooded the doorstep and porch, casting a shadow across the surfaces. Light spilled onto the path and diffused when it reached the brighter white from the outdoor lights.

"Glad you're back," Mitch said from the doorway. "You look like hell."

"Charming," I said, walking toward him, brushing dirt and dust off my clothes. A dark area on the knee of my jeans refused to budge. Dammit.

Mitch wrapped his arms around me. "I take it things didn't go as planned." He dipped his head and whispered in my ear, "Is that blood on your jeans and is it yours?"

"Plans are more of a rough guide." I looked up at him. "I think so, and no."

"Okay."

"Babies?"

"Asleep."

"Did they miss me?"

He laughed. His breath ruffling my hair. "They have Uncle Lee here. We are both surplus to requirement."

True. I got the feeling it wasn't a bad thing,

especially with the current mess heating up.

Argo emerged and shook. He bounded toward us like the goofball he can be.

Mitch laugh, then coughed, and extracted long strands of my hair from his throat.
"You'd think I'd know by now."

I pulled my hair back and tied it with the hair tie from my wrist. "You'd think."

Chapter Thirty One

Every Breath You Take

Mitch plated up fish and chips for us. He'd kept our meals warm in the oven. Judging by the shriveled condition of the fries, it was good thing we weren't much later.

I carried my plate into the office.

"Hey," Sandra said without turning around. "Got enough aioli there?"

I glanced from the generous creamy deliciousness that smothered my fries and fish and then at the back of Sandra's head. "I thought eyes in the back of the head were a parental thing."

She laughed. I slid into the seat next to her and placed my plate on the desk. Her eyes flicked to my dinner. Another laugh rippled. "I get you like aioli, but wow."

"I've never been bitten by a vampire." I pulled a coated chip from the middle and shoved it in my mouth.

"While you eat, I'll show you this development."

Mike spoke from the doorway. "El, when you get a minute, I need a word."

I turned toward him to gauge how urgent the word was. His eyes held unease. "Your word is … yes."

"I'll be in the living room."

There was no time to wonder what Mike wanted to

discuss. Sandra's fingers on the keyboard demanded my attention. At times, there wasn't enough of me to go around. Cloning myself would be a great idea.

Sandra's fingers tapped again then she said, "And here we have the image file and what I believe is a password."

"Great. Now what?"

"This—" She opened a browser window and a website, then dragged the image file onto the screen. "This will tell us if there is another image hidden in the file. If not, then I need to work out what program was used to hide whatever is in it."

"Kinda hope it isn't another image," I said, licking aioli off my fingers. A paper towel would've been handy.

Sandra scrolled down. "It's not an image. So, now, let's find out what it is."

I ate and watched. She opened apps and tried the file and the potential password. Four apps later she stopped and looked at me.

"Why am I assuming this was created by an app or program that resided on someone's computer?" Sandra sighed. "It could easily be created online by one of the many steganography websites for free. You don't even to sign in to a lot of them."

"Worth a try."

Sandra had a dozen tabs open by the time I got halfway through my drenched piece of fish, and the file uploaded to each of them. The third tab yielded a result.

"I got it. Look."

There on the screen was a text file ready to download.

"Do it. Let's see what it contains."

Neither of us spoke as Sandra opened the file. We stared at the words on the screen for at least a minute. Technical information.

"What am I even reading?" Sandra said, scrolling through the three-page document until she reached the bottom.

I chewed another chunk of fish and searched my memory banks until I found a match for the information I'd just read. It sounded familiar because it was. A long time ago, I'd read about a technique that preserved human bodies indefinitely. Plastination.

And I know damn well it has a correlation to now. "It's a document that outlines the standard technique for plastination."

"What is plastination?"

"A way of preserving bodies and organs for educational purposes."

"And why would this file be inside the image of the man and child, hidden in a jigsaw puzzle that we had no chance of completing?"

"Because someone hoped one of us was smart enough to find the file and the key."

Sandra typed on the keyboard while I called Caine. I managed to eat another couple of fries before he answered. Eight rings.

"It's the weekend," he growled.

"Yeah. We're working through."

"You're not in the office."

"Technically, I am in *my* office."

"You've got Delta A at your place?"

"Yeah. Working, like I said. I thought we had a cold case. It's warming up."

"What do you need?"

"Freedom. I need more people than Delta has available. I need to coordinate with FBI in every state and town that has missing families that fit our brief and, despite being approached, they're not giving this the attention it deserves."

"Have you heard back at all?"

"From one agent, saying they weren't officially consulted beyond the local police wanting to know if one of the families was under Federal protection."

"And the answer?" Caine's voice rumbled.

"The agent didn't know and made no further enquiries."

"Give me a list of all towns and states involved, I'll get our agents on it, and have them report back to you."

"Thank you."

"What did you have to do with the bomb in the Yard?"

"Nothing. We were there interviewing a sergeant regarding Lee's stabbing and the sergeant's sister who may be a person of interest in Operation Disney."

"Who's handling the bombing?"

"NCIS. They're working with us on the death of Sergeant Green."

"Green is?"

"You'll have a full report by morning. But Green was the sergeant we were interviewing. And someone shot him."

"I'm looking forward to *that* report," Caine growled with about as much enthusiasm as a tired grizzly bear.

I hung up.

Sandra was waiting for me with questions. They danced behind her glasses. "Is the jigsaw maker also the crypto-text sender?"

"I think so."

"Has this happened before in any investigations into the missing families?"

"Haven't heard." Good point. I'll chase that. "I think Dane was looking into it."

The smell of freshly brewed coffee drifted on a slight breeze, closer and closer. I turned in time to see Dane walk into the room with a coffee mug in each hand.

"Thought you two might need this."

Now that's anticipating and forward planning. "About the crypto-text guy, did you find out if any other police involved with any of the families in Operation Disney got weird texts?"

Dane passed me a mug and set the other one down next to Sandra.

"As far as I know, there are two missing families' cases where police said the lead officer on the cases received a series of texts. They match those we were sent. No one followed up. It didn't seem to be related and it stopped."

"No one else?"

He shook his head. "Neither cop made a connection and until now, no one had a clue these cases could be related."

"Anyone received flash drives?"

"No. Just us."

"Thanks, Dane."

"What did you find?"

"A document that outlines the steps for plastination." I glanced at the screen where the document sat open. "In particular, the S10 technique."

"Thanks for the answer but I don't want to ask any more questions," Dane said.

Sandra piped up, "Apparently the S10 technique is used for whole specimens and thick body and organ slices to obtain a natural look. They also use Epoxy resins for thin transparent body and organ slices, and polyester-copolymer is used for brain slices to gain distinction between white and gray matter."

Dane backed toward the door. "I was right. I don't want to know."

"But I do. Why was a document about the S10 technique inside a photo of a man and child?" And then it was right there. "Fuck. What if they were plastinated?"

"Is that even a word?" Sandra said.

"It is now," I replied. "Could that be what happened? People turned into teaching aids in universities?" Or mannequins in a private exhibit? Whoa. Where did that come from? "Would anyone know if they were donated bodies or not?" The private exhibit idea circled. Would anyone know if they were wax figures or real people in a display of some sort?

Sandra's eyes darted across the screen as she read, the words reflected in her glasses.

Dane moved closer and sat down. Guess he decided he did want to know after all. I tried to imagine if this could be what happened to the families. The screen in front of me blurred into a dull haze. As my vision cleared a huge truck shuddered and screeched to a halt on a highway, armed men came from everywhere. A truck? Gunfire erupted. Over my shoulder I saw agents take on the armed men. Charlotte Hunt from Delta B fell beside one of the black SUVs. Claude grabbed her under the arms and dragged her into cover.

"El?" Dane tapped my hand. "What was in the truck?"

"Formaldehyde," I said without thinking. "A shipment of formaldehyde."

"Who would need a lot of that?" Dane said.

Sandra took a sip of her coffee before replying. "I have no idea what happens in your head when you go quiet, Ellie, but formaldehyde is one of the chemicals used to preserve bodies."

"If you killed an entire family," I said slowly. We looked at each other. "Crap on a cracker." If you killed a dozen families, that's probably more formaldehyde than you can buy without raising suspicion.

Dane jumped to his feet so fast his chair careened across the room. "I'm on it. I'll check with Delta B and find out what else has been stolen. There were more trucks hijacked, right?"

"Yes." I still needed to visit Charlotte in the hospital. "Hey, Dane, find out how Charlotte is and when I can visit her."

He nodded and left the room.

All of a sudden, it felt like progress. I didn't like where this path headed, but at least it was movement. I chomped the last few lukewarm fries scooping all the aioli from my plate in the process, then finished my coffee.

I emailed Caine the details for the missing families included in Operation Disney and formally requested help from FBI field offices in the relevant cities, towns, and states. Troops mobilized. Then I thought about trucks and stolen loads. We wouldn't necessarily know if a shipment of anything wasn't intended to cross state lines, and stolen. I fired off another email to Caine, asking that the field offices talk with local police and state police about missing or stolen chemicals. I sat back and thought for a moment. I doubted we'd hear anything until Monday. So maybe we could have a

Sunday like normal people. A small laugh bubbled within me.

"What?" Sandra said.

"I just thought we might get tomorrow off."

Sandra chuckled. "Nice idea, but I think the execution might need work."

Lifting my cuff, I noted the time. "Yeah. I need to go talk to Mike before Sean arrives." I stood and stretched. "Take a break, Sandra. You must be tired. Have a glass of wine. Pretty sure there is wine in the wine rack. Or coffee, whatever you like."

"I think I will. I'll be along to make my selection soon. "

I left her to whatever she was doing and deposited my dishes in the kitchen sink before I joined Mike in the living room with Lee.

"Hey, you doing okay?" I said to Lee.

"Much better. I think Isabella has secret healing powers."

A smile broke forth. "Wouldn't surprise me. What happened to Kurt and Mitch?"

"I think they're in the dining room with Dane."

I sat next to Mike on the sofa. "What was it you wanted to talk about?"

"Sandra," he replied, his voice hushed. "She's met someone online, and there's something strange about the guy."

"Strange because you like her and it's not you?"

"No." He stretched his legs out. "I do like her. We get

on well, but that's not what this is about."

"Okay. So what is it about?"

"They've been talking, you know, chatting online for about three months. She's never met him. He's an excuse maker. Always a reason why he can't meet for coffee or whatever. She's never seen a picture of him. Again, excuses. He avoids questions he doesn't want to answer by disappearing for a few days or changing the subject."

"He's probably married."

By the frown I got from Mike, he didn't think that was the answer.

"He knows a lot about Sandra and she knows nothing about him."

"How do they communicate?"

"Through a dating app on her phone."

Ah, that's why she checks her phone so often. "When did she sign up to a dating whatsit?"

"Three months ago."

Yeah, okay. "Sandra is a smart woman. If she's okay with the situation, I'm inclined to leave it alone."

Mike sighed. "It's like he's got a hold on her."

"It's been my experience that no one is who they say they are online. Might not be a him." Probably doesn't help much. "What do you want me to do?"

"Talk to her?"

"If I do that, this conversation is going to come out. Do you want that?"

"She's vulnerable, El."

"I'm aware." Having your fiancé murdered in the midst of wedding preparations is the kind of thing that leaves a woman vulnerable, but part of working through something like that is allowing yourself some joy. "Maybe she just needs a bit of fun, and that's all this is."

"I'm worried. She's going to get hurt."

Sure, I could see how that would bother him. No one wants anyone they care about to be hurt, but we can't dictate their lives accordingly. That's not fair. In my mind's eye, I saw Sam and Sandra holding hands and laughing. It wasn't fair the way Sam was ripped away from her. Sam's warm deep voice filled the crevices in my mind. "No one said life was fair, Chicky Babe. It is what it is."

"And you are okay with this conversation coming out?"

He shook his head then changed his mind. "Can we talk to her together?"

"Yes. Let's go. We're doing this now. I've got Sean coming in soon to talk to me." It felt like I'd been running all over hell's half-acre and getting nowhere.

Mike hauled himself to his feet, and reached his hand out to me to help me up. Hard not to smile. He was a thoughtful, kind, person who just happened to be an award-winning actor.

"You two on a secret mission?" Lee asked.

"Yeah," I said. "See you in a bit."

Mike strolled into the office with his hands in his

pockets. Casual. I followed. Sandra was texting. A glass of red wine sat on the desk by her.

"Good choice," I said, and motioned to the glass.

"It's hitting the spot," Sandra said, switching the phone for the glass. "What are you both up to?"

Mike and I grabbed chairs and sat down. I scrambled for a way to start the conversation. If ever there was a good time for Chance to appear and take me away from all this, it was now. Not a sign of a sketched outline anywhere. Damnit.

"We were talking about dating," I said. "Mike said his hot property status has worn off." Could've handled that better. Let's bring up death, even if it's imagined.

Sandra smiled. "I doubt that's true."

Mike nodded. "It is. It's been a few years since my wife died." Mike nudged me. "And I think everyone's forgotten I was a grieving widower."

"You never were a grieving widower Mike, I'm right here." But then, he fictitiously married Laura Graham, my alter ego, and not me. Poor Laura died of shellfish poisoning at her wedding reception. We do have some fun sometimes.

Sandra laughed. "You were great though, Mike. Most believable." She raised her glass to toast his acting ability.

"Are you dating anyone, Sandra?" Just putting it out there. "You deserve some fun."

"Not really." Her eyes held Mike's. I recognized the look on her face. She was trying to determine if he'd said something to me. Sandra broke her gaze and focused on me. "Signed up to a couple of dating sites."

"Any luck? I imagine men would be flocking to you." Trying to keep it casual was killing me. I just wanted to blurt out what Mike told me.

"Been out for coffee a few times. They have big shoes to fill, and no one's measured up so far."

Sam was six feet six inches tall and built like a muscular wall. They legitimately had big shoes to fill.

"Not surprised," I said. "I can't imagine using an app to find a date. Guess we've investigated too many cases where people have misrepresented themselves online to make that a thing I'd be comfortable doing."

Mike nodded. "Online isn't for me either. I did try once. Couldn't tell if they wanted to date me because they recognized me, or because they were genuinely interested in me as a person."

"Couldn't be both?" Sandra asked.

"I suppose it could. Just never seemed to be."

Sandra shook her head and then sipped her wine. "Mike told you about Sebastian."

"Yep."

She attempted to glare at Mike but failed because he grinned. "Okay, let me have it. Give me the speech you gave your niece about giving out information online and how people aren't who they seem to be."

"Do I need to?"

An eyebrow arched in my direction. "What do you think?" Her phone buzzed.

"Is that the mystery man?"

Sandra nodded. "Sebastian."

"Invite him over."

Sandra's mouth wobbled into a smile, but it didn't last. "Okay."

She picked up her phone and replied to the message.

"What do you think will happen now?" Mike asked when she placed her phone back on the desk. "Will he come?"

"He'll disappear for a few days because I pushed."

"How does that make you feel?" I said.

"Little anxious."

"How do you feel when he messages you?"

"Happy."

"How about when there's nothing for hours?"

"Anxious."

"When you hear nothing for days?"

As I watched her, a realization dawned. "Honestly, progressively more anxious." She sighed. "We've been talking for months. I don't understand why he won't meet up or why I get so upset when I don't hear from him. I won't ask questions now that might cause him to vanish. And I know that's not right for me."

"Do you see a problem with this?" Because I do. He's controlling and he's got all the power. "Does Sebastian have a surname or anything traceable?"

She shook her head. "I haven't tried too hard to find him," she confessed.

That's about to change. "Can you download the

message history? Do you trust one of us to read the messages and try to locate this guy?"

She blinked slowly. "Of course. Can I ask for Lee?"

"Yes. I want you to take your phone and your laptop and go see him. He's in the living room. Talk to him, Sandra. This," I waved my hand in a circle over her, "is not healthy. We all want you to have fun, but, with someone who appreciates how amazing you are, not someone who hides behind a screen collecting information and giving out zip."

"You must think I'm pretty foolish," she said, her eyes filling with unshed tears.

"No. I do not. We do not."

Mike reached over and touched her knee. "Sandra, it's okay. You're going to be okay."

She nodded. Wiped an escaped tear from her cheek and stood up with her glass and phone. Mike picked up her laptop. I sat for a minute after they'd gone. No one is safe, no matter who they are or how smart they are. Predators will find that small crack and exploit the shit out of it. I closed my eyes and willed Sam to help Lee. Find the prick and make him pay for toying with Sandra.

I went into the kitchen and poured a drink. My phone buzzed with a text from Sean saying he was here as Argo jumped up off his bed, and ran down the hallway toward the front door. I followed him. Tail wagging, fur flying. The front door opened.

"Argo, good to see you," Sean said, giving his side a

good pat. He looked up as he pushed the door shut and greeted me with a smile.

"Drink?" I held up my glass.

"Please. Quiet here," Sean said as he joined me in the kitchen. Argo went back to bed. I handed Sean a glass of wine.

"For a house full of people I suppose it is quiet." A low murmur of voices in the dining room and more voices in the living room, but apart from that, it was pretty quiet. A comfortable kind of quiet from people who truly liked and respected each other. "Any objections if we hang in the kitchen?" As a change of scenery from the office.

"Not at all."

I sat in the window seat and motioned to Sean to join me there. Argo could've got in on it too if he wanted.

"How was dinner?"

"Good. But I think we have another problem in Mikki's world. I think a stalker piggybacked into her world on the back of the original stalker." Sean settled into the cushions.

"You're fucking kidding me?"

"Nope. She's uneasy about the friend she told you about, the one who helped her see what was going on with Ellis."

"Maybe that's something she could have mentioned when we were there talking about the other friend."

Is there something in the water that's causing people

to behave like bigger dicks than usual all of a sudden?

"She's sorry she didn't. To be honest, I don't think she was ready to admit what was happening."

"Understandable." Imagine it made her feel silly for not picking up on it sooner.

"Advice, El?"

"Keep the close protection detail with her, at least until her husband gets home from his latest trip. And we'll take a run at the woman." I sipped the wine and enjoyed the rush of warmth.

"Do you think this woman is dangerous?"

"Not enough information in front of me to determine her potential behavior."

"It's all starting to sound a little too *Single White Female*."

I smiled. "Usually me that makes the movie or TV reference. You've been around me too long."

"Probably."

"You sure it's not more like *Misery*?"

Sean paused with his glass halfway to his mouth. "Oh, God. I hope not. Definitely keeping the CPD in place."

"Question—"

"Go ahead."

"Does she identify with Mikki's main character?"

"Mikki said she likes her a lot and mentions her often. Texts her saying that her character would love this or should do that, or wouldn't this be a great storyline."

Bet that goes down well. Mikki's been writing her series for over fifteen years and as far as I knew never discussed plots or storylines or what her characters may or may not do with anyone. She certainly did not allow input from outsiders. A few times over the years, I'd been asked for advice regarding something her characters did, but it was research-based and I wasn't influencing anything, simply offering believable detail, or a fact check.

"What else does she do?"

"Buys her gifts all the time. Comments on everything her Facebook page. Hasn't quite figured out that most of those posts are not from Mikki herself but her PR team."

That amused me, maybe more than it should. "Is Mikki communicating with her via those posts?"

"No, but she thinks so. Most often the replies are text messages rather than public replies on Facebook and Mikki often has no clue what the texts are about because she didn't write the post."

Okay, that is funny. "Name of this woman?"

"Shelly Morton."

Confirmation it's the same woman who sidled up and tried to become her savior regarding the Ellis situation. Life is a twisty chocolate-coated pretzel dipped in nuts. The name felt familiar. Not just because Mikki told me her new friend was called Shelly, but from before, from my past. "And she is?"

"A photographer."

"Mikki is finishing her series soon? Thought I read something about that?"

"She's about to start work on the final book."

"If she kills her main character, we may have a full-on Stephen King *Misery* scenario."

"That's fucking comforting, thanks for that, El."

Shelly Morton was a name I'd seen or heard before. Long boney fingers scrabbled about in the dark looking for a light switch. A pool of light illuminated a series of photographs hanging on a wall. The Newseum. Pictures of comedians on tour. When did I see it? Why was it important? Google is my friend.

"Don't move. I need my iPad." I hurried upstairs and grabbed my iPad from the dresser and checked on the babies. Both sleeping. I left the room and my cherubs in dreamland to rejoin Sean.

Settling back into the window seat, I entered the photographer's name into Google. The top result was her exhibit. It was eight years old. Interesting. No big exhibitions or anything noteworthy since then. Not even a blog. So what was Shelly Morton doing for the last eight years? I set aside what she was potentially doing..

"I've seen Shelly Morton's work. An exhibit in the Newseum and according to Google, it was eight years ago." Time sure flies. "Her exhibit was called 'Mediating Dissent: Locality and Complacency.'" She was a talented photographer and foreign correspondent. I opened the page on Google about the exhibit. "She was the photographer on tour with a group of comedians, Niles Palacio, Griz Kleinmann, Hadlee Lewis, and Karissa Silvetti. The tour was organized by Armed Forces Entertainment. They went to Germany, Japan, Guam, Hawaii, Turkey, Afghanistan, and Spain."

"And this is the same woman who is all over my sister like white on rice?"

"Does Lee know you're using his sayings?"

Sean smirked. "I don't think he invented it."

"So we have an accomplished photographer who has befriended your sister."

"Does that make you less likely to look objectively at these behaviors and assess the risk?"

"No. I'm just saying I know who she is." I'm not saying she couldn't be a raving lunatic. Going into war zones is not something regular people do. It takes a special kind of person to work in those conditions.

The reason the exhibit stuck with me was one photograph. I searched the site to see if the photo was there. It was. Niles Palacio in a body bag. The bag was open, revealing the cold mask of death. I scanned the blurb under the image. "While they were on the tour, Niles Palacio died suddenly. His body was sent back from Afghanistan. Part of his standup routine was a skit about death and what he wanted to happen once he died."

"Morbid," Sean said. "Did he know he was going to die young?"

"Maybe. Some people have an inkling."

Sean shot me a look. "Enlighten me."

"He wanted to be stuffed and sat on the couch in his living room to freak out potential boyfriends as his daughter grew up."

Sean chuckled. "That would do it."

"Yeah, I don't think human skin is suited to taxidermy, so the kid was probably safe from that horror."

"How'd he die? Is there anything other than 'suddenly'?"

I opened a tab and typed his name. "No, but his *Everipedia* page says the comedian died of a brain aneurysm." It also said he had a history of severe migraines. I chose to keep that to myself.

"His brain exploded," Sean mumbled. "His corpse was intact."

"Yes, but I doubt he was stuffed and seated on the sofa in the family room."

Shoving the thoughts of brain explosions aside, I dragged it all back to Shelly. The comic's death was tragic, but Shelly was the person of interest here. We were looking for a photographer with a connection to the disappearance of the Abbot's.

"The photography thing reminded me of something, gimme a sec." I jumped to my feet and searched out Dane. "Hey, how far did you get looking for photographers called Rochelle?"

"I have a list, hang on." He picked up his iPad and

found the list. "Nineteen photographers working in their own businesses called Rochelle nationwide. No idea how many could be working within other businesses."

"Can I see?"

He passed me the iPad, and I scanned the list. Shelly could be a nickname derived from Rochelle. None of the photographers on the list were Morton's, or in the vicinity of Washington D.C. I handed it back. "Have you contacted any of the women?"

"All of them. Waiting to hear back. I asked them all if they had a client called Abbot."

"Thanks."

I disappeared back to Sean in the kitchen.

"What was that?" he asked.

"Wanted to make sure we hadn't come across a Morton in our enquires. We've been looking for a photographer called Rochelle. No surname. She may have taken the last-known photos of one of the missing families."

"At least you have something to go on in that case."

A small sigh escaped. "The case isn't as cold as we thought and is growing warmer by the hour."

"You ready to talk about this friend of Mikki's some more?"

"Lay it all on me. Happy to do the risk assessment. Kinda my job."

"After talking with Mik at length, I came up with a few things. First up, no peer friendships."

"And that means?"

"Shelley never talks of friends or anyone she's known for any length of time. Certainly no one from school or work."

"Okay." I opened Pages on my iPad and typed notes from Sean's account.

"Creating reasons for contact. This is constant ... all day and into the night."

"That'd be fucking annoying."

Sean smirked. "And this one, an inability to tell the truth even over something small. Mik is constantly catching her out."

"Any reason for the lies?"

"She can't think of any. And immediately elevated Mik to best-friend status. Full on."

"Needy."

"Big-time needy. There is always drama. Even when there is no drama, she will manufacture drama."

"I like her less and less all the time. Keep going." And it didn't marry with the image she once had as a photographic journalist.

"Jealousy."

Now I was super interested. Jealousy is destructive. "In what way?"

"She's jealous of everything Mikki does. Her traveling, her love of wine, her beautiful tea sets, her husband."

I was using both hands on the virtual keyboard to keep up. When I got to her husband, I stopped and looked at Sean. "Exactly what does that mean, jealous of her husband?"

"You've seen them together. They're fucking adorable. They dote on each other and genuinely like each other."

True. Theirs was a wonderfully supportive marriage full of love and laughter. But nothing is perfect and I was sure like all people, they had their moments and their arguments.

"They are cute as fuck."

Sean grinned. "You and Mitch remind me of Mik and Ed." His grinned faded and he told me the next thing he'd written down. "Shelly sucks up over everything. The minute she says anything about work, this chick is all over it raving about how fantastic she is. Mik reckons she could write a load of crap and this woman would still say it's better than cream cheese frosting on carrot cake."

"Over-the-top fanatic then." But with all the other stuff, I wasn't so convinced that she was a fan. "Next?"

"Always praising her friendship. With phrases like 'you're such a good friend.' Mikki says its crap. She's not that good a friend. She's mostly preoccupied with work or Ed and has very little time to be a good friend. Her longtime friends all understand and don't need constant attention."

Like most people.

Just when I thought he was finished, Sean continued. My hands were getting tired., "She has the same experiences as Mikki. Always. The biggest thing was when Shelly found out Cait was killed, all of a sudden her sister had been killed, but it was a few years before Cait."

"That's easy enough to find out." I added a question mark to my note. I'd check later.

"Remember when Mikki was researching the bomber and went missing?"

Not something I'd forget. We found her with blood sugar so low she almost died. That was in all the newspapers.

"Shelly made up a similar story, but she was kidnapped while taking photos and rescued just before she died."

"She could've been, she went to some dodgy-assed places." Benefit of the doubt an' all.

"She wasn't. I checked that one before I came over. That would've been a story carried by all the news outlets. And I still know people in the CIA. There's nothing to it." He waited a second for me to catch up again. "She downplays or outright denies family relationships. Not close to her siblings and jealous of Mikki's family relationships. Estranged from her mother and father. But Mik caught her out on that one as well and came across recent photos of them together, just hanging playing happy families."

"What the fuck is the point of lying about that?"

"Poor little me syndrome? We always had a good relationship with our mom and dad. If they were still with us, we still would."

I knew something that many people did not. Sean and Cait's biological mother was killed in the line of duty when they were six years old. Their dad remarried a few years later. Mikki came along a couple of years after that. So when Sean said mom, he meant step-mom. Had a feeling Shelly did not know that.

"Are we done yet?"

"Nope. They have nothing genuine in common. Everything is manufactured to appear as though they have stuff in common. They don't even like the same music or hang out in the same circles. Except now, all of a sudden Shelly loves the same bands as Mik."

"Now are we done?"

Sean smiled. "Impatient. And no. She gives long-winded explanations of inconsequential events based on lies or embellished truths. They seem to be to throw off suspicion and pull the focus away from the original statement. And the final nail ... creation of a common enemy."

I finished writing and then read it back, twice. "Houston we have a problem."

Sean drained his glass and set it next to my empty one on the side table. "I thought we might."

"You could refill those," I said, pointing to our empties, "while I think."

I closed my eyes and let all the information slosh around. When I opened them, a page turned. As it moved the kitchen disappeared, replaced by a pencil drawing of an office. Another page turned. Chance stepped from behind a large wooden desk. That was different. His desk was usually a glass-topped modern piece of furniture.

"Chance, you've got redecorated?"

"Old school. Think it suits me, yeah?" It did. He could blend into old school or modern. Didn't matter. Chance was a chameleon. "You summoned me, O Genie of the kitchen?"

He's been listening to Sandra. "Guess I did. I have a couple of things that are or should be unrelated, but it doesn't feel like that."

"I'm listening."

I gave him the Reader's Digest version of current events, including the new information regarding Mikki and her friend.

"I have a question regarding the Mikki situations. What reason or motive would Shelly have for playing up Ellis's behavior to the point that he's institutionalized?"

"Explain that, I thought he was an oddball all by himself."

"Yeah, maybe, but it feels like Shelly was hyping the situation up."

We looked at each other for a beat.

"Because he knows something and she wants him discredited."

Chance nodded. "That would be my go-to response. But what would he know that was worth all this effort?" He pulled a chair closer to sit right in front of me. So close our knees touched. "She's clearly not a great liar, so is either hoping Mikki is too stupid to see through the lies, or perhaps believes all the flattery distracts her, or—"

"Mikki has challenged her and caught her out several times, from what Sean has told me." I stopped. "What's your 'or'?"

"Or it doesn't matter, because she believes Mikki will still be her friend, maybe not a friend, but will still do whatever it is she wants done."

"Or she's fucking delusional and doesn't realize her lies are not getting the desired response."

"There's that."

"But why is she doing this?"

"That's what you need to find out, El. The motive. People do things for two reasons—"

A smile tweaked the corners of my mouth, I'd heard him say that before. "One is altruistic and one is self-serving."

"Yeah, you just need to figure out what the motive is here. What is she getting out of it?"

"She could be insane, and this is her losing the plot. Fixating on Mikki or Mikki's main character."

"What'd you just say?"

"Fixating on Mikki or her main character."

"Talk to Sean. Do it now. I think it's the main character thing. That should unlock what the hell is going on."

Christ, this is becoming a Stephen King *Misery* scenario.

Chance dragged the chair back to his desk, with a wink he turned and left. Colors ran and mingled into a dirty watery brown before fading into the wooden floor of my kitchen. I blinked. Sean passed me a glass.

"You all right?"

"Yep." I took a sip. "Did Mikki mention anything about Shelly identifying with her main character?"

Sean's head moved in tiny increments. A very small nod. "Yeah. That was one of the first things she said to Mikki was how much she identified with Elisabeth Korsman."

"In what way did she identify with her?"

His mind spun in his eyes and it made me dizzy. "Um—" He hauled in the conversation. "She said they had the same childhood and early years." The hamster wheel behind his eyes spun some more. "There was something about the men in their lives. Neither made good choices."

"Fill me on where we are at with Elisabeth and the story, I'm about three books behind." I held up my hand. "But no finale spoilers, thanks."

Sean laughed. "Couldn't if I wanted to ... Mikki doesn't talk about what's coming up."

"Okay, what was the last book you read, I'm sure you keep up with your sister's output."

"The one that came out a few months back. Last I recall, Elisabeth married her childhood sweetheart and all was set for a happy ever after, until someone she used to know came back into the picture and told her the love of her life wasn't so loving."

"Uh-huh, and all this happens inside a thriller?" Because I never noticed a romantic thread when I read her books. Perhaps that was just me.

"Yep."

"So the actual latest story, not the romantic thread, is something about a crime?" I concentrated on the latest work because this person Shelly, upped the anti recently which suggested she was modeling something from a recent book.

"A series of art thefts from collectors."

That didn't feel like it was going anywhere. Maybe it was about the men. I thought about Ed and Mikki. Devoted. A shudder ran through me when I thought about Ellis and his creepiness. Yeah, nah. He was never going to be in the running. Why was he behaving like he was? Because Shelly was stirring the pot. Feeding him information that wasn't true about what she supposedly knew about Mikki. Just like she did to Mikki with information about Ellis. Thing was, he was weird and over-the-top creepy. It wouldn't take much to push his buttons and make him think he was right and Mikki did want him.

So why was Shelly playing Ellis and Mikki off against each other? What possible reason could she have for fucking with their lives? Did she ultimately want Ellis locked up? What would that achieve?

Hero syndrome. A phenomenon I'd seen before, but last time it was a firefighter lighting fires so he could save people and property. People who seek heroism or recognition, usually by creating a desperate situation that they can resolve. Crap on a cracker!

If I was right and she wanted to be the goddamn hero and save the day, then that would, in her warped state of being, put Mikki in her debt.

"Sean, did Mikki say much about Ellis?"

"No, not personally but said that Shelly mentioned several times how lucky it was that she could help her put the pieces together before something awful happened."

"Stand back a bit and assemble all the things you know about this situation." He nodded. "Could this be Hero Syndrome?"

A light went on behind his eyes. The gray lightened. "Starting to look like it."

And just because I could, I tossed a cat among the pigeons. "Alternatively, she could be angling to be a character in a book," I said, lifting my glass and taking a generous swig. Felt more like the hero thing. "But I feel like she wanted to swoop in and be the hero and it failed because—" I pointed at Sean then myself. "We ruin everyone's fun."

Sean laughed. "We're certainly good at it."

"Which begs the question, has Mikki ever mentioned who you are? Does she know Cait was the Director of the FBI or did she come in too late to know that and not make the connection?"

Sean called Mikki. I listened to his side of the conversation and drank my wine. By the time he hung up, I knew Shelly did not know about Mikki's family, beyond that she had a brother and her sister died. Different surnames were a definite bonus in that regard. Even if Mikki had mentioned her maiden name, it wasn't O'Hare. O'Hare was Sean and Cait's mother's name, not their father's. No doubt there is a story there, but I was not privy to it. Mikki was a Kennedy. Shelly knew Mikki's husband was a movie director. Mikki keeps things close, giving away just enough to appear friendly. I also knew Mikki hadn't mentioned to the so-called friend, Shelly, that I was her friend and that she had a close protection detail. I stretched my hand out for Sean's phone.

"Hey, Mikki, it's me."

"El, thank you for helping us."

"No thanks needed. Question time ... you told me the other day that Ellis and Shelly work together?" And that seemed like a stretch.

"That's right. They've both told me they work together."

"Where?"

"In a hospital emergency room."

That didn't seem right. "Hold on. Explain that."

"Ellis is a hospital porter and works in the emergency department. Shelly has been working as a medical photographer in the same hospital."

Interesting.

"Thanks for clarifying that." Next question. "Has Shelly been pressuring you for anything, or to do anything?" An audible swallow. This can't be good.

Mikki cleared her throat. "For the last month or so she's been talking about a series of photographs. She keeps saying she wants to immortalize me in images. Do an exhibit centered on the life of an author."

"Uh-huh."

"Can't think of anything more boring." Mikki tried to deflect her nervousness with a light laugh. "Here's the author sitting at her desk typing. And here's the author backspacing. And here we have the author drinking coffee and doodling in a notebook. Except they'd be static images. It'd just be me sitting at a laptop." She paused. "Why would that appeal to anyone?"

She painted a dull picture. "How keen is she?"

"Very. To the point where it's annoying. She wants to shoot these pictures in her studio while I'm writing the last book."

I shook my head at Sean. "Nope. Not happening. Anyway, why would someone do that, it's not a study of you if you're not in your natural environment."

"That's what I said, and she ranted about being able to control the lighting."

"Okay. Do us a favor, do not go anywhere with her."

"How worried should I be?"

"Not at all, you have a team. They will keep you safe until we can figure this out."

"Thanks, Ellie."

I passed the phone back to Sean and waited while he said goodbye.

My teeth chomped into my lower lip as I considered the situation. "Be worried Sean, be very worried."

He nodded.

I stood and stretched. Argo opened an eye and watched me then closed his eye and went back to sleep.

"What now?" I asked Sean, taking the empty glasses to the kitchen counter.

"I'm going back to Mikki's. Her spare room is pretty comfy."

Chapter Thirty Two
Wishing (I Had A Photograph Of You)

Photographs. Kurt. The photos from Sergeant Green.

A check of my email revealed the forwarded images from Kurt. Snow globes. The whole thought of being inside a snow globe filled me with dread. I tugged at my collar, pulling it away from my neck. Ain't happening.

As I looked at the images of the snow globes, parts of the photo looked not super familiar, but tweaked something in my memory. I hustled through the house poking my head around doors looking for Sandra. I found her still deep in conversation with Lee.

I left them to it and went back to the office.

The browser on the PC had a bunch of tabs open. I flicked through them to see what had been happening research-wise while I was gone. My phone buzzed. A text from our buddy the crypto-texter.

And we were back to single words again: `Cryptozoa.`

Kurt appeared before I'd put my phone down. "Cryptozoa," he said.

"Small animals that like high humidity and darkness," I said. "Slugs, woodlice, centipedes, earwigs, and other such delights of nature." And all of a sudden it made sense.

Holy crap balls.

Kurt pulled up a chair. "What? I know that look on your face. What?"

"What if the crypto words are telling us something we don't know, because we haven't dug deep enough in the right places? What if they're jobs or interests of some of the missing people?"

"Then that would prove that this crypto-nut is connected, no doubt about it."

"Dane was looking into the families' backgrounds, how far did he get?"

Kurt shrugged. "No idea. We've been fragmented for days with unrelated events."

Time to call this.

"From now, consider everything that has happened since the email from Carl asking for an opinion to be related to our missing families, however tenuous the connection."

"All teams or just us?"

Formaldehyde popped into my head. "All teams ... I need to talk to Claude and see Charlotte, she's still in hospital?"

Kurt nodded. "She'll be there a couple more days. Let's worry about that in the morning along with Claude." Kurt shifted in the chair. "What about the Mikki Falacco situation?"

"Which one?"

"Say what?" His brow furrowed. "We had the Ellis guy removed from the equation. What don't I know about?"

"Remember the other friend Mikki told us about, the one who helped her piece what Ellis was up to together?"

"Yes." His shoulders slumped a bit. "You're kidding me?"

I shook my head. "Turns out she's a photographer by the name of Shelly Morton."

"Why do I know that name?"

I let him think for a moment. But then my impatience got the better of me. "Got it yet."

"No."

"We saw her exhibit at the Newseum a few years ago. It was titled: 'Mediating Dissent, locality, and complacency.'" And I still have no fucking idea what that actually means.

Kurt nodded slowly. "She was the photographer on tour with a group of comics and one of the cars was hit by an IED."

"Correct." I watched him still retrieving information from the recesses and crannies.

"Soldiers in the first vehicle were injured. No fatalities but a day or so later one of the comedians died suddenly." He paused. "I can't recall why."

"His brain exploded."

"Brain aneurysm, Iverson."

"Yeah, whatever. She could've chosen a better name for that exhibit. Do artists have to be so obscure?" Do they learn fancy-schmancy ways of obfuscation while at college?

Kurt smiled. "And this renowned photographer is now a lunatic?"

"Seems that way."

"Is there something in the water? Because we're coming across a lot of weird behaviors lately."

A small electrical charge fired in my bones. Last time there was something in the water it killed a lot of people. I watched the thought skitter across an icy surface and plummet over the edge. A small head shake brought me back to the present.

"You okay?" Kurt asked. He studied me for a moment.

Doctor Henderson was in the house. "Yep. Fine." I held his gaze with a stare that dared him to argue. "Are there more strange behaviors than usual?"

"I think so."

"Then maybe it is the water." Not helpful to our many branches of investigation within this case.

Kurt broke eye contact and shifted the subject. "Why do you think Shelly Morton is involved in our missing family cases?"

I took a deep breath. "I wouldn't go that far, yet, something is so far off with her, I don't quite know what to make of it, and it's not going away."

"Speak the words, Iverson. I can't see in your head in the way Dane and Mitch can."

"She's putting pressure on Mikki to be photographed in her studio. She wants to do a series of images, day-to-day life of a writer, type thing."

"And?"

"We're looking for a photographer because Andrea Abbot sent her brother photos, snow globe photos."

"Okay, seems a bit of a stretch, even for you." Kurt scanned the room. "Is Chance here?"

I shook my head. "No. It's a gut thing."

"And your gut is telling you that Shelly Morton has snow globes and wants to put Mikki in one?"

That sounded pretty stupid when Kurt said it. "Not exactly. It's telling me that she wants to photograph Mikki, but not at Mikki's house, and that we are looking for a photographer." It's really telling me nothing useful.

"And we need to do what with this lack of information?"

"Follow the trail," I said, there was more hope in my tone than I intended.

"Let's concentrate on the snow globe aspect, if you think that's a link to the Operation Disney families."

I sighed. That made more sense. Mikki was safe for now. No one was getting past her CPD and Sean. "Okay."

"There can't be that many photographers using snow globes. You have a leaflet from one kicking around here."

Time to stop ignoring what was in front of me. Like it or not. "Yeah, I do."

I jumped to my feet and hurried to the living room, the last place I saw the leaflet. Sure enough it was on the coffee table; I hurried away before Lee or Sandra commented. I sat down in the office and laid the piece of paper on the desk. Kurt had the photos from Andrea Green open on his phone. I found the screen with the jigsaw puzzle pieces still on it.

Time ticked by as we compared the three images in silence.

"That slight curve on the jigsaw piece could be to edge of a globe," I said, pointing to the piece on the screen.

"I suppose it could be. There's no color match, even without running one of Sandra's programs, I can tell there is not a color match between any of these images."

"Yeah."

"Do you know what we need?"

I shook my head. "What?"

"Sleep. We all need sleep. Let's pick this up again in the office tomorrow."

Maybe he was right. Would it hurt to get a night's sleep and start again tomorrow? No, it would not. "The Navy Yard?"

"Not our problem. NCIS are handling it, let's let them do their job and fill us in tomorrow. Green is dead. His ex-boyfriend is dead. Pretty sure that means neither of them will be stabbing anyone from Delta anytime soon."

He had a point.

Before I could go find Dane he appeared next to me.

"Boss?"

"Everything you have on all the families. I want it on my desk and anything you think is relevant investigation-wise added to the smartboard tomorrow morning." We need to know their stories to understand their lives and figure out where they fell over.

"I'm on it."

"Nine a.m."

"Sure thing, Boss."

"Go home, get some rest."

Dane left the room.

"Lee?" Kurt said.

"We have plenty of room, he and Mike are welcome to stay."

"That's a good idea."

Really? I watched him for signs of discord. For anything that suggested he was concerned about Lee. For once, he was hard to read.

"Why is it a good idea?"

"I think he'll heal better here."

Of course, the amazing healing properties of toddlers. I laughed. "He's lucky the girls sleep through the night now." I pushed my chair back and stood up. "You wanna give Sandra a ride home?"

"Is she okay?"

"She is."

"You're not going to tell me?"

"Sandra will tell you herself. Not my place." I knew she would. We don't have secrets for long. What affects one of us affects us all, eventually.

"You are no fun when it comes to gossip, anyone ever tell you that?"

All the time. "Sean left?"

"I think so."

"Okay, get out, take Sandra with you. I'll see you in the morning. We're going to get answers."

Before anyone tries putting my babies in a snow globe. We are going to get answers.

The chair slid backward as I stood. A cloud of thick dust and smoke billowed toward me. I turned toward it. Heart pounding. I blinked. The cloud vanished.

My eyes darted sideways, another cloud billowed. Surely Kurt could see it? The dust parted in the middle I saw broken concrete and twisted steel. Muffled cries lay under screams that burst holes through the dust ceiling. No. This is not happening. Not again.

"Iverson." Kurt's voice fell under a final breath wrapped in a tortured scream. "Hey. Iverson. Look at me."

His words suffocated in the dust. Gasping and writhing on the broken ground. Another voice, stronger, more insistent, came from within. "Breathe. Just breathe."

"Navy Yard." I sank onto my chair. Tremors in my hands vibrated into my wrists. "I'm there again."

He crouched in front of me. "*We*, Iverson. We *were* there again." Kurt's hands rested on my knees. His eyes held mine. "Breathe. You're safe. We're safe."

"No kids this time." My voice shook more than my hands. I swallowed hard, but the lump in my throat stayed.

"I can still hear the cries."

"Me too." I looked into Kurt's eyes, past the blue, and into the deep dark beyond. "Why do we put ourselves through this hell?"

"Because someone has to be there when the world turns upside down." A half a smile. "Penance. Dunno what we did in a previous life, Iverson, but, it must've been bad."

"Wish I'd been a better person."

A ball of tightly wound rubber-bands bounced around my rib cage. One flicked off; I sucked in air as it hit a rib. Kurt's fingers gripped my knee.

"Breathe. We survived."

I nodded. "Does Rachel know, about the—" I breathed. "The Museum bomb. Did you tell her what we did?"

He used my knees to push himself up, then motioned to me to scoot over. He sat, we angled toward each other, knees touching. "I thought about it a lot, but no matter how I tried I couldn't find the words."

"Yeah, I get that."

"When do I tell her? Breakfast? Date night? In bed? While we're talking about Olivia and her day?"

"What would you even say?"

"I have no idea."

For whatever reason, it was comforting to know Kurt

didn't know how to talk about the Yard either. "She must notice."

"She does. I tell her I've had a hard day. I don't want her carrying what I see. This is mine to carry."

That I understood. "It's ours to carry. You and me. At least we're not alone with our memories." It just feels like it some nights. Another rubber-band fired from the ball. I jerked.

"What's happening?" Kurt's hand reached for mine. Warmth seeped from his hand to mine. "If we can't talk to each other, Ellie, we won't make it."

"Before we left today for the Yard, I was back there, in the middle of it. The little boy, the first one. This time I saw his mom. I haven't remembered that part before."

He closed his eyes, then opened them slowly. "It's not surprising. We were about to go back there."

"I've been over there since the bomb."

"I know, but, Ellie ... today is the anniversary."

My head shook. "It can't be. Don't they do something to mark it?"

"They did it on Friday. A wreath-laying ceremony at the Museum."

A brilliant white spotlight hit a thought. "That was why the package was passed through the fence. The gate was too risky, security would've been tighter."

"You're right."

"Why did no one mention it?"

"What? The security?"

"The anniversary. Why didn't anyone tell me?"

As soon as the words left my mouth I realized they did. Julie said it in her office after the explosion. Why didn't I hear it then? I rolled back to the comment she made as we left the building: 'Ironic that it should be today.'

Kurt's fingers tightened around my hand. "We'll get through this. Together."

The white-hot penny dropped right through the sofa in front of us. "That's why the whole team is happily working from my place." I looked into Kurt's eyes for confirmation and saw it. "Did you arrange it?"

"Lee, it was Lee."

Of course it was. He got Mike out here and knew I'd invite him for dinner. Guess if I hadn't turned it into a team dinner Lee would've invited everyone over anyway.

"And that's why you didn't go home to Rachel and your daughter?"

He smiled; it stopped short of his eyes. "I can't share this with her and I needed to be with you as much as you need to have us all here."

"Why is it so bad now? It's three years, I shouldn't be circling back like this."

His eyes widened, disbelief crossed his face. "You know better than that." He dropped his voice an octave. "The little boy was eighteen months old."

Grace and Isabella's age. "That makes sense."

"Yes, it does. We'll ride this out. We're okay."

Water washed over me. Pink frothy bubbles swirled around my feet. Pink drips ran down the glass walls. Soap overpowered the blood for a moment before the metallic stench returned. A hand tightened on mine. The shower vanished. His eyes scrutinized me. "There isn't enough water to wash it away."

Kurt's eyes locked on mine. Blue on blue. I felt his breathing. Rhythmic. Slow. Deep. Following Kurt's lead, I breathed. Kurt's cologne hit the back of my throat. *Cool Water*. He'd worn that cologne for years.

He held my hands up. "What do you see?"

"Our hands." No blood. No dirt.

"There is enough water."

"For now."

"Forever."

"This is hard."

"Yes. It's better when we stick together. We will get through this. We have to keep talking, Ellie. We. Talk."

"It takes a lot of energy to prevent Mitch from seeing what I see and knowing everything I know."

He nodded. "I know. He knows you block him."

I nodded. He'd asked me not to on several occasions, but the girls need one parent who isn't a psychological disaster.

"Why is Mike here?"

"Remember when he disappeared off the plane, and you found him, and he was in the middle of a PTSD episode. He wanted to be here for you, for us. He figured this one would be tough."

301

As much as I wanted to stamp my feet and tell everyone I was fine, I wasn't and more than that, I appreciated having people in my life who understood and were there.

"You're not going home tonight, are you?"

He shook his head. "I'm taking Sandra home and coming back."

"Go home, Kurt. Go home to Rachel." I squeezed his hand. "Wouldn't you rather be with your family?"

"I am. Anyway, I can't go home to Rachel."

"Whoa, what?"

He grinned. "Rachel and Olivia are at her mother's for the week. She knew I needed to be with you." He caught himself and frowned. "With Delta."

"I'm still not her favorite person." Even though Kurt and I never were an item, and I'm married with children. "If you slip up like that around her, then I understand why she sticks pins in my voodoo doll."

His eyes smoldered for a second, then returned to normal.

"I'll be back."

"Thank you."

Chapter Thirty Three
Manic Monday

Breakfast was a grounding experience. I didn't get a lot of sleep, judging by Kurt's appearance nor did he. Lee, Mike, and Mitch cooked breakfast. I got the girls ready for the day and Kurt had a FaceTime call with Rachel and Olivia. Life returned to normal for the most part. If I turned my head too quickly, smoke and dust swirled but far enough away that the smell didn't reach me.

I packaged up what we knew about the recent Navy Yard bomb and put in a mental drawer marked 'not our problem.' We knew that the Navy Yard bomb was passed through the fence because the security was tighter than usual at the gate, and now, we had to let Julie deal with the Navy part of the equation while we got back to Operation Disney.

Find the families. Think. Explore. Live another day.

I drove into the office with Kurt and Argo.

Lee was off for another day; he and Mike opted to hang out with the toddlers and Mitch decided to work from home. The drive into the city was non-eventful.

At my desk, I drew a big red mental circle around the booking my in-laws had for Friday evening with a photographer. They wanted Mitch and me there too. Lack of sleep made me more determined to put an end to any notion they had of surprising us with a family portrait taken in a giant transparent plastic coffin. I sat staring at the smartboard.

What happened to all those families?

Could a photographer handle killing an entire family? I guess the oxygen line could deliver a poisonous gas and take care of the death part. But then what? A single person disposing of between three and seven people at a time? That's a lot of dead weight to shift. And what about their cars? What happens to them? They had not been seen again either as far as we knew.

Disposal of bodies like that is not happening by someone working alone.

I rolled my thoughts back. We had nothing to suggest they had all met with or considered meeting with a photographer. One family that we knew of did have dealings with a snow globe photographer. A singularity. It's not buildable.

The Abbot case wouldn't quit, nor would the snow globe scenario. That family definitely climbed inside a large plastic snow globe. But, Andrea sent the photos to her brother, so, wouldn't that mean they didn't die then? Or at least she didn't? Or maybe she's working with the Unsub. Or the Unsub sent the photos from Andrea's phone after the fact?

A serial killer targeting families? That wasn't usual behavior.

Whatever happened to the missing families was organized to an astonishing degree. They vanished, and so did their vehicles. What would it take to make an entire family disappear? I stopped myself thinking about their deaths. There was nothing that said anyone was dead. I picked up the phone on my desk and called Sandra.

"Hey, you got the phone numbers for Carl and the rest of the police or sheriffs who've sent us missing family info?"

"I do, O Leader of the Pack. What would you like?"

"Video conference call with as many as you can get, in an hour."

"I'll set up the Delta conference room for the call, I take it you want Delta A present?"

"Yep, I also want the SSAs of B and C."

"Charlotte is doing better and the hospital expects to discharge her by the end of the week."

"Good news. Schedule me out of the office to visit her this afternoon. I'll take off at four and see her on my way home."

The fingers of my right hand crossed without my bidding. That's right, fingers crossed, I'll be out of here by four.

"Done."

"Thanks Sandra."

I replaced the receiver and studied the smartboard for a few minutes, then Julie from NCIS appeared in my doorway.

"Coffee? I don't see any?" A smile settled on my lips.

"Thought we'd step out and get some from that coffee shop you like so much," she replied. "Walk with me, El?"

I grabbed my jacket and snapped the leash on Argo, Julie waited in the outer office.

"All right, what's up that makes you want to walk?" I said, holding the door open for her.

"Stairs or elevator?"

As if she actually needed to ask that question. Julie giggled as we headed for the stairwell door.

"We've been annoying Frank big time lately by running down the stairs. Apparently, it's noisy." Argo looked up at me; he agreed.

"Shall we?"

We ran, the three of us neck and neck down three floors, I took the lead feet from the ground floor door and laughing, charged through with Argo, followed closely by Julie.

Frank walked around the desk toward me. "Having fun, SAC?"

"Yes thanks, Frank," I said as Julie and I walked to the door. "Catch you when I get back. Coffee?"

"That'd be fine. Americano will do nicely." Frank turned back to his desk.

"See you soon."

The warm sun hit me when I stepped from the building. I pulled my sunglasses from my jacket pocket and put them on before leading the way toward the coffee shop. Again I was aware of the prevalence of security cameras.

"All right, spill the beans. Why are we going for a

walk?" Sun warmed my shoulders. Argo sniffed a tree. Couldn't say I was unhappy to be out of the office but I knew Julie and there was a reason.

"Sergeant Green was the intended target of the explosion at the chapel."

"You're positive?"

"We found the person who passed the package through the fence. It was a prearranged drop. You were right about the increased security. They planned it for that weekend to coincide with the anniversary."

"Why target Green?"

"You know Green was gay, right?"

"Yes."

"The bomber didn't like that."

"Green's not the only gay man in the Navy." It took maximum effort to not hum along with the Village People.

"No, he's not, but he is the only gay man who questioned the bomber's sexual orientation."

Ah, sensitive. "He was okay with murdering bystanders to get one man ... that's excessive. What about the chaplain?"

"He was warned."

"Warned or he helped?"

Julie stepped in front of me, stopping me in my tracks. "My thoughts exactly. I did some digging. Hate crimes have followed the chaplain throughout his career."

"Unfortunate."

"Looks like he handpicks likely scapegoats, picking at them until they reach breaking point, then suggests a target."

I motioned to her to keep walking. Coffee called. "And this is only obvious now?"

"He carries on like a regular chaplain for a few years before he starts up, then is off on a new posting around the same time as the scapegoat attacks someone. His timing couldn't be better."

"Can you bring charges? Court martial?"

She held the door to the coffee shop open. The smell of fresh roasted coffee beans floated in the air. Warm, rich, deep, and life-sustaining.

The barista waved at me. "Your usual, Ellie?"

"Please, and an extra Americano, and ..." I looked at Julie and waited.

"Cappuccino with cinnamon," she said.

"On your tab, Ellie?"

"Thank you."

The barista nodded.

We moved away from the counter to a quietish corner and sat down. Moments later, a bowl of water appeared in front of Argo. He drank with gusto.

"Can you prove the chaplain was behind any of the attacks?" I watched Argo drink.

"His word against the bombers. But I think we'll get the evidence," Julie said.

"Excellent." I tucked hair behind my ears. "Weird thing, Green's former partner. Was convinced *The*

Handmaid's Tale was a thing. That we were heading down that path and the military would turn on the people they're supposed to protect."

"And you want to know how that ties in with the chaplain?"

"Does it?"

"He's been quietly preaching his anti-gay, anti-women in the military, anti-everyone who isn't a white male holding positions of power rhetoric for many years to a select few. His inner circle," Julie said.

No wonder he wasn't what I'd call a friend of my dad's and why dad balked at my having to deal with him.

"How would that impact on Green's ex?"

"I don't know yet. But I will find out," Julie said.

"Keep me in the loop."

"Of course."

The barista waved me over. Coffee time. He placed all three cups in a cardboard holder.

In less than ten minutes Frank sipped his Americano, Julie headed back to the Navy Yard and Argo snoozed on his bed.

Chapter Thirty Four

Everybody Hurts

With Julie investigating the chaplain connection, I could edge away from that situation and free up synapses for the photographer slash-snow globe-slash missing family case. It felt right to lump those things together, evidence or not. Allowing myself to think only about the snow globes turned up interesting avenues of thought.

Where did the snow globes come from? Someone was making them. Someone was supplying them. So who and where? Why did I think it was about the snow globes? Because I'm paranoid and I don't want my kids in a death chamber. Wow. Even for me, that was dark.

I grabbed my bag and took off out the door, Argo on my heels. My mother-in-law, June, said she booked with the photographer at Fair Oaks Mall. I needed to satisfy my inner paranoid crazy chick and make sure the photographer was not involved in making families disappear.

Shit.

Making families disappear. I spun around and went back into the office, followed by Argo.

We knew they were not in WITSEC, but what if they were in some kind of protective program within their states?

I dropped my bag on the floor and sat down. We

didn't know they weren't in custodial care. My eyes roamed the smartboard.

As I stared at the board, dates glittered and jumped. With a blink, I focused again. The dates sparkled, jiggled, and danced. The pen on my desk rolled toward my fingers. I wrote down the dates in the order in which they jumped and worked out the time lapse between disappearances.

Eleven months, nine months, five months, eight months, eight months, six months, three months, sixteen months, six months. The pen circled five months and three months. They stood out above the rest as anomalies. If I took them out of the list I was left with eleven months, nine months, thirteen months, eight months, fourteen months, eleven months, and six months. Eight families. I scribbled what I knew about the families I considered to be anomalies.

Miles and Caroline Davis with their eight-week-old son, Jeremy, from Colorado Springs. Scott and Kirsty Gatewood and their twelve-year-old twin daughters, Josephine and Julie. Scott had cancer; he was iffy in my book as soon as I knew that.

That took Colorado and Nevada off the board. For now.

I really needed to talk with the LEOs involved in all the cases. A horrible, sick feeling blossomed in my stomach. If Colorado Springs and Carson City are off the table because they don't fit, then maybe the Gatewood family drank the Kool-aid and maybe

WITSEC is involved in Miles and Caroline disappearing. The families would not know if that was the case. They'd just fade into the ether with new names, and new lives. No way of finding them. The only people who would know were the Marshals responsible and from experience, it was easier to get blood from a stone than an answer from a Marshal regarding people in their protection. Good, unless you have an anomaly in a case.

I called our resident expert of creating new lives. Debbie Barnes or Michael Addison. Someone answered on the fourth ring.

"Sub Basement Dungeon, how may I help?"

"It's Ellie. Who did I reach?" I learned a while ago to not assume the identity of the person on the end of this particular phone.

"Debbie."

"I need to pick your brain about a ... let's call this a hypothetical situation," I said.

"Sure. What's the problem?"

"Working a wide-reaching case. I have two families that don't fit tidily into the timeline. One I think drank the Kool-aid but the other could be a WITSEC situation, they're throwing the timeline out and clouding everything. I'd like to remove them." I'd like to find them all, but removing anomalies is a good start.

"I take it you looked for crimes that happened before the disappearance and found nothing?"

"Yeah."

"That might mean it happened a while ago, and they were already under protection."

Of course. Doh!

"They had a baby. The wife's brother was deployed. The husband's parents lived in California. They had been in touch prior to disappearing, and even talked about a surprise."

"That might be the answer. They broke the agreement and have either been moved again, or whoever they were hiding from found them." Fingers tapped on a keyboard. "Or maybe they thought they were going to be able to go home."

"How often does that happen?"

"Never."

"That's what I thought. They could be dead anyway, just not related to the rest of this investigation?"

"Could be. Send me everything you have on the family, I'll see what I can find out."

"You can do that?"

"Not officially, but I know what I'm looking for, so I have more likelihood of seeing something that could point to potential government involvement."

"Thank you."

"You owe me a glass of wine and some baby time."

"The girls would love to see you. Make it Sunday and come for dinner, Mitch does a roast on Sundays." Threw that in there to let her know it was safe. Puts people off if they think I'm cooking. Just as well I have a thick skin.

"Done. I'll get back to you when I've found something regarding this family."

With a smile, I hung up and sent the little info I had to Debbie.

If the other family was a murder-suicide situation as I suspected, then the bodies could be in the vicinity of their intended campsite.

I wrote notes regarding the Gatewood family to remind me to speak to the officer from Carson City, Nevada, during the conference call. Specifically, I wanted information regarding the camping trip and to know if anyone checked the area for them. Pretty basic stuff but I knew never to assume people did the obvious.

Sandra appeared in my doorway. "Almost time, O Fearless Leader."

"Great. Delta all ready?"

"Yes, indeed. Just waiting for you."

I smiled and gathered my notes and iPad. Sandra led the way to the conference room. The video screen waited for the calls to come in. I love technology. I love that we can talk to twelve places at once and we can all see each other. Or at least we can see all of them. Not all police departments had the tech we possessed. I had a moment of gratitude for the budget we worked within.

The table, positioned across the room, a space kept for me in the middle. I slid my stuff onto the large table and sat, Kurt on my right and Dane on my left, where Lee usually sat. Claude and the SSA of Delta C sat next to Kurt. Sandra had it set up so the camera on the wall showed all of us to whoever was watching. A united front: this is who we are and we are here to help. An electrical charge ran up my spine. I hoped we could help.

Chapter Thirty Five

I'm Gonna Miss You When You're Gone

One by one, the twelve squares on the screen filled with uniformed officers. I introduced myself and my agents to the serious faces scattered across the country.

"Thank you all for taking the time to meet with us, regarding Operation Disney." Faces smiled, murmurs of inclusion filled the air. "Two things straight away, who is here from Carson City, Nevada?"

A hand waved in the right corner of the screen. "That'd be me, Agent. I'm Officer Logan Johnson."

"Nice to meet you, Logan, although the circumstances could be better. Has anyone checked the campsite for the Gatewood family?"

The officer nodded. "No sign of them in the area they said they were going to be in."

"They didn't arrive?"

"No, they did. They checked in with the ranger station, but haven't been seen since."

"And their vehicle?"

"Also not been seen."

"It's our opinion that a more thorough search should be carried out for the vehicle and family."

"Yes, ma'am."

Foaming white water rushed through a narrow gorge crashing over rocks and into deep pools. Spray filled the air; underneath the whitecaps and mist, I glimpsed a shiny white surface. I glanced at my notes. The missing vehicle was a white SUV. Damn. Seemed prudent to offer a search zone. "In particular, search waterways. Fast-moving rivers with deep pools."

Dane dove in. "Logan, it's likely there was a murder-suicide situation at play. Deep water is a good place to hide a vehicle full of bodies."

My phone buzzed, providing welcome relief from any more questioning looks. A text from Debbie Barnes advised me the Davis family were in WITSEC. The winky smiley face at the end indicated she confirmed with someone in the Marshal's office. I replied with a thank you and the poo emoji next to the grin emoji: my version of a shit-eating grin.

"Colorado Springs, where are you?"

A hand waved. "Ma'am. I'm Emma Shute, Jim Kowalski couldn't be here today."

I had a vague recollection of a memo saying Jim was giving evidence in court. "We can now confirm that the Davis family are under the protection of the Federal Government."

The officer frowned. "WITSEC?"

"Yes."

"Thank you."

"No problem." Kurt slid a piece of paper to me. I glanced at it. It had one word on it. 'Text.' A little reminder for me. "How many of you received text messages around the time the families disappeared, from an unknown caller and that contained only one word?"

Knitted brows looked out at me. Maybe a little help then. "The text messages we are interested in are single words and all begin with 'crypto.'"

A finger waved from one of our virtual guests. "Illinois PD here. Officer Sarah Albright. Maybe a day or two before the Brown family were reported missing I received a text from an unknown caller and it said 'cryptozoa.'"

"Did you get any others?"

"No, ma'am."

"And you are certain of the timing?"

"It was a few years ago, but yes, I am."

Another hand moved. "Yes, you're California?" I said.

"Yes, ma'am, Officer Ralph Montego. I recall a text message that made no sense to me maybe a day or two before the disappearance of the Martinez family in Redding." He swallowed while flipping through a notebook. "Found it. Just one word. 'Cryptozoology.'"

I liked how prepared he was. Bringing his old case notebook with him was smart.

"Now, think carefully. Was it before the family went missing or before they were reported missing?" Kurt said, making notes.

He flipped pages again. "Before the missing person's report was filed with us, but they were likely already missing for a matter of some days. What is the relevance of the text messages?"

I smiled at the police officers and sheriffs looking out at me from the screen while I composed a reply I hoped would not alienate them, or make them feel they hadn't done their jobs to a high enough standard. "We think someone was trying to alert law enforcement and maybe wanted LEOs to take an interest and follow up on the odd texts."

"The texts are linked to the disappearances?" Ralph asked, his frown lines deepening.

"Potentially, but let's see where they lead, shall we?" I glanced at the notes in front of me. "Alejandro Martinez of Redding California had a particular interest in things like Sasquatch. That field is known as cryptozoology."

Montego frowned as he thumbed through more pages in his notebook. "That's not in my notes."

"Check again," I said. "Carefully."

We waited. Other officers searched their notebooks and devices. Nice that they suddenly wanted to look deeper into their respective cold cases.

"There is a reference to a hobby that took him out of state. He spent holiday weekends in Oregon and was a member of a group called The Wilderness Team." I held up a photo of Alejandro wearing a T-shirt with the words 'Gone Squachin' in large letters on the front. "The Wilderness Team were a group of people who spent their vacation time searching for Sasquatch. Alejandro was active within the group for many years."

"And the person who sent the text knew this about

him?" Montego said. "And perhaps knows what happened to the Martinez family?"

"That's a possibility."

A hand waved from the other side of the screen. "Carl Broderick, Utah. Two officers investigating the disappearance of the Andersons reported text messages. They received two simultaneous text messages from unknown callers. The first said 'cryptomnesia' and the second 'cryptosporidium.'"

"Time frame?"

Carl checked his notes before answering. "The first text arrived two days before the department opened a missing persons' file on the Anderson family and the second arrived four days after we started investigating."

"Was there any context surrounding the first text?"

"No."

"And was there any follow-up?"

"Apart from knowing they were from the same phone, there was nothing in the way of location or any other information available."

"Did anyone try replying?"

He shook his head. "Initially, neither officer mentioned the first text, both thinking it was a wrong number."

So did we. Understandable. "What do you think now?"

"That there is a link."

"Sherrie Anderson is a psychiatrist. Her speciality is

cryptomnesia."

Carl nodded. "I'd like to think that if we had received the texts the other way around, we would've followed up, with vigor."

I'd like to think that as well. It took us long enough, and there were four of us getting the same texts over a period of days.

Logan spoke, "So what does this mean?"

"It means that someone knows what happened to at least some of our missing families and that person is reaching out, albeit not very forcefully, until now."

"What does that mean?" Emma said. "Until now?"

"Once we started looking into the cases, the Unsub lifted his or her game. All four of us received texts and then a flash drive arrived at my home." I paused, took a sip of water from the bottle near my hand, then continued. "Whoever this person is, they can't make direct contact."

"Or don't want to," Emma said.

"Or that."

Dane spoke, "It feels like this person is an insider. They know, they potentially help or are involved in whatever happened the families."

"How do we find them?"

"We're working on it," he replied.

I pulled up details from the hijackings. "Do any of you have any hijackings of trucks containing chemicals in your states?"

"What sort of chemicals?" Emma asked. I could see

her phone in her hand.

"Acetone, formaldehyde, dichloromethane, and silicone S10, or large quantities of a polymer resin."

"What on earth is going on, Agent Iverson?" Carl said, as he typed quickly onto a tablet in front of him. "And how much of each product?"

"Entire shipments."

"Usually, hijackings are food, booze, or electronics," a gruff male said. I didn't recognize the voice and searched for a face to match on the large screen. I picked him within a second. A mustached, grumpy, gray-haired officer at the bottom left corner of the screen.

"And you are?"

"Ty Elliot, Indiana."

"Anything reported stolen in Indiana from trucks?"

"Plenty, but as I said, usually food, booze, or electronics. Just last week a shipment of those fancy flat-screen TVs vanished."

Murmurs of agreement rumbled from the wall.

"We're particularly interested in hijacked chemical shipments."

Ralph waved. "We had a weird one back in twenty-sixteen, had us in stitches. A couple of lunatics hijacked an interstate shipment of blow-up dolls and snow globes."

Chuckles and sniggers came from various officers. No harm to have a laugh. Dane turned his head to look at me.

"Seriously?" Kurt's voice dropped as he nudged me.

"Pretty fucked up," I whispered. And creepy. Very creepy.

"We've had some odd ones," Emma said. "But blow-up dolls and snow globes, makes your mind boggle."

"Did you catch them?" Lee gave Ralph his full attention.

"Nope. Although we did find the truck in an old barn about two months later."

"Fingerprints?" Hope sprang from my voice before I could hide it.

"The truck was clean. Do you think this is related? Blow-up dolls?"

Not the dolls. I chose to ignore his question for a moment. "How many of you have seen a pop-up type shop in a shopping mall advertising family photographs, or know of a corporate event or school ball or whatever that used a professional photographer and a gimmicky, cheesy set of backdrops?" I worked hard not to say snow globes.

Everyone said they'd seen a booth such as I mentioned somewhere.

"Okay, thinking about when the families disappeared, do you recall any photographers in the area doing special deals, or maybe a fundraiser or whatnot?"

Silence rained down as everyone cast their minds back.

Someone we hadn't heard from raised a hand. "Sir?"

"Jimmy Larsen, Wichita PD. The snow globe truck story jogged my memory. One of the local elementary schools had a photographer as a fundraiser ... some of the proceeds went to the school, must've been about when the Johnsons vanished. My sister had a family photo taken inside a snow globe. She and the kids were dressed up like early settlers. I might have it on my phone." He scoured his phone for several moments; when he looked up, his grin beamed from the screen. He held his phone up and turned it so we could see the picture.

"Would you email that to me, please?" I said, returning a warm smile.

That was two snow globe photos in two different states around the time of families disappearing.

Dane spoke, "Do you know exactly when that photo was taken?"

"December seven twenty-eighteen."

Dane underlined the date the Wichita family was last seen. December fourteen. Exactly a week later.

"Do you know who the photographer was?"

He shook his head. "I'll check with my sister, she might remember, or the school will have a record."

"We'd appreciate that."

"Anyone else?" Dane said.

"Noah Allen, Cincinnati. There was a Valentine's dance at a community hall in our neighborhood with a snow globe photo-booth."

Dane slid his iPad closer so I could read the date the

Cincinnati family was last seen. On February ten, twenty-seventeen. That's close to Valentine's Day. Too close.

Fuckadoodledo, I was right about the snow globes all along.

"Can you find out who the photographer was?"

"Absolutely. The neighborhood organized the dance, with community police also involved and on the organizing committee, I know who will have that information."

"A couple of the photos would be helpful too."

"I'll send some."

"Do you know if the Hamiltons attended the community dance?"

He shook his head. "I'll find out."

Three instances of snow globe activity in the vicinity of missing families, and in the days leading up to the disappearances. Synapses fired. Electricity surged sending shocks through my skeleton. I had zero doubts about the snow globe connection. Zero, and that no one would find the families alive.

But I could not fathom a reason anyone would want to murder entire families. And these particular families, nor did I imagine they were the only families who climbed into a snow globe; in fact, I knew they weren't. Jimmy Larsen's sister braved the dome of death with her cherubs and survived. What was the trigger for those who never returned to their lives?

"I want all of you to please dig around and see if

your missing families had their photographs taken prior to vanishing." I chose a time frame. "Let's go with within two weeks of their vanishing acts."

Emma's hand rose. "Even me and Nevada?"

"Sorry, didn't catch your name, Nevada. Yes. Even you and Logan Johnson in Nevada." If they could place a snow globe using photographer in the area where those families lived, then maybe we'd make greater headway.

Kurt eyes asked for a sit-rep. I smiled. "I'm good. Let's get this done. Then it's a field trip out to Fair Oaks Mall."

The flyer said that's where to make bookings for a photo in a death dome. I clenched my fists until the shudder that ran through me dissipated.

"Officers, I really appreciate you being here today and your help with this huge case. We do need a few more things from you all. We've compiled a list of all the vehicles that are missing. Complete descriptions and the tag numbers. I want to find the vehicles." I smiled up at the officers looking at me. "I need ..." Rephrase. "We need. We, all of us, we need to close the cases and I don't believe there will be happy endings for anyone. Closure for the families and friends is the best we can hope for now. So, let's find out what happened to the cars. Search Craig's List, newspaper classifieds, online classifieds, Facebook Market Place, anywhere cars are sold privately, put out bulletins, contact car yards, and also check out storage facilities nearby, and areas where cars can be abandoned. Make sure you all do this for all the cars."

"Not just the cars from our state?" Noah asked.

"Nope, all the cars. It's a big job." I headed the questions. "If I wanted to make a family disappear and they had a vehicle with them, I'd do one of two things. I'd store it close to where I took them, or I'd sell it in another state."

"If they were taking the cars interstate, it'd need to be before anyone reported the family gone," Sarah Albright said.

"Or, they load it onto a car transporter or into a covered truck," said Gary Singe. He'd been quiet so far. Gary introduced himself to the group. "I'm Gary Singe from Missouri. Looks like our family is the only one with a bigamy link."

Everyone chuckled.

"The Missouri family were also the first to show a snow globe connection," Dane said. "And a link to that family and their interesting life choices stabbed our colleague Lee Davenport."

A sharp intake of breath came from the screen in front of us.

Dane shot me a wide-eyed look before he said, "He's going to be fine. Lee is recuperating for a few days."

"Yep. The Abbots in Missouri have opened a can of worms and even led us to explosions at the Navy Yard."

"You've been busy," Gary replied. "Hope Agent Davenport is on the mend."

"He is, we can't say the same for the other guy," I said.

"You said an explosion at the Navy Yard? Was it something to do with the third anniversary of the bombing?"

Kurt reached for a pen. "The timing was deliberate but it's a Navy problem, not ours," he said.

I interrupted the chatter. "Your assignments are to find those cars and gather information regarding photographers working in the areas when the families disappeared. Logan, please look closely at the waterways where the Gatewoods went camping."

"If they're there, we'll find them," he said, his voice flattened.

No one wanted to look for potentially waterlogged bodies. Ever. There's nothing appealing in a waterlogged corpse situation.

Chapter Thirty Six
Photograph

Kurt leaned on the hood of the car waiting for me to alight from the vehicle. I held up a finger and finished my call to Mitch before climbing out.

"Everything good?" Kurt asked, pressing a button on the fob. The car chirped and lights flashed.

"Yep. Mitch confirmed this is the mall where his mother picked up that flyer. Upstairs from CVS."

"Escalators," Kurt said, "No running up them."

"Whatever. Point is it's not on the ground floor or wasn't on the ground floor." So up we will go however that happens.

We avoided groups of young people meandering in the mall and dodged clusters of older folk stalled in the main thoroughfares. A small child holding a helium balloon on a string bounced past me, her other hand clasped firmly by a young woman. I slowed my gait letting them get further ahead. Not the world's biggest balloon fan my eyes roamed the mall for tell-tale clown signs. A young woman with multi-colored hair gave me pause. False alarm.

Kurt looked over his shoulder and smiled. "You coming?"

Two strides and we were shoulder to shoulder. From the escalator I surveyed the floor below us. People shopping. I broke that down into chunks: Small family groups. Groups of friends. Women with shopping-bag-laden strollers. Children running around. It added up to nothing of note, and importantly, nothing that looked like a circus escapee.

Satisfied I stepped off the escalator after Kurt. "All right let's see what we find," I said while I walked toward the smell of coffee. When in doubt follow the coffee.

"Coffee, Iverson, that's what we'll find." Kurt, low key, pointed to a kiosk about four shop fronts away. "Check it."

"That was easy," I muttered, veering away from the aroma of roasted coffee beans and toward the kiosk that proudly displayed a banner featuring snow globes. A raw gnawing began in my stomach. The closer we got, the greater the feeling of impending doom until it rang every bell I had.

"You doing okay there?" Kurt said, stepping in front me. "Iverson?"

"What? I'm fine." I shrugged off his question. So I lied. Unfortunate, but not unexpected.

"Your pale clammy look indicates a considerable lack of truth in your statement."

"Shhh, I'm good."

"Iverson." He shook his head; resignation hung in the air. I waited for it to drop and splash on my boots. It didn't. Huh?

We were right by the kiosk and the snow globe banner. I forced down a shudder.

The brunette woman behind the small counter smiled and spoke, "Hi, we're offering a discount this weekend on a portrait session."

Kurt picked up a brochure and showed it to me. Just like the one in Grace's backpack.

"Great," Kurt said to the lady and smiled. He hooked his arm through mine. "My wife and I wanted to get some anniversary photographs. What would be a suitable backdrop for that, do you think?"

"Let me see what I can find, sir. I'm Christine, and you are?"

Not Rochelle then.

"I'm Kurt," he replied without introducing me.

She ran her finger down a list in front of her then looked at us before making a suggestion. "I can imagine you two in something like the American Civil War era globe."

"I don't feel very Civil War era," I said.

"Or something from the sixties. We have a spectacular moon landing set?"

Yeah, nah. I tugged Kurt's arm. "Are you sure about snow globes, Sweetie, it's all a bit cheesy."

He shot me a dazzling grin. "That's the fun of it, Doll Face."

The lady perked up. "How about Chicago during the twenties, a speakeasy from the prohibition era?"

"See?" Kurt said. "That's more like it."

"I'm sure you could pass as a Made Man," Christine said to Kurt.

I stifled a chuckle. Not so much. He's kinda the opposite of a gangster and a member of the Mafia.

"Look, if we did this." I pursed my lips, then relaxed my mouth. "If we did. What sort of time frame are we looking at?"

"Photo shoots themselves can take two or more hours, depending on the costumes and makeup required. We generally get the proofs out to clients within twenty-four hours. You make your selection, and we send the image files without the watermark for you to have printed."

"You don't print them?"

She shook her head. "Keeps the costs down this way."

Imagine it would. "And where does the photo session take place?"

"We have a fully equipped studio in Reston."

"With the costumes and everything?"

"Yes."

Kurt slung an arm around my shoulders and gave me a squeeze, while focusing on Christine. "Do you have appointments available this weekend?"

"This is our last weekend here ... we have one or two spots left." She looked at the iPad in her hand and tapped something.

"Anything on a Friday?"

Christine gave an apologetic smile. "Sorry, Friday evening is reserved for families with children. We have a Saturday morning and a late Saturday afternoon for adults and couples."

Kurt squeezed my arm again. "How about Saturday morning, honey?"

"Sure, let's book that in."

Kurt smiled broadly at Christine. "Are you the photographer?"

"No. I make the bookings. You'll meet the photographer on site." She handed him a card with the address and time of our appointment on it. "You're all booked in. We'll see you on Saturday."

"Great," I said, with as much enthusiasm as I could muster. None: zero enthusiasm.

"Come on, it'll be fun, you'll see," Kurt said, grabbing my hand. "Come on, I think you need coffee."

Nope. I need tequila. Lots of it.

Once out of earshot we stopped walking. I leaned against the railing and watched mall patrons go about their busy shopping day. It took a few silent seconds before I uttered the words, "Friday is reserved for families with children."

"That's what she said."

"We think our missing families vanished without a trace on Friday afternoons or evenings."

"We do."

"How were the Friday vanishing acts confirmed?" My gaze followed a young mom and two small children as she tried to divert one from a tantrum.

Pages in Kurt's notebook rustled. "By last recorded sightings and last bank account activity in the majority of the cases, with a phone call and text messages being the last contact in two cases. All of these things were on Fridays."

"Mitch's mom is planning to stick my babies in a snow globe on Friday." I turned around to look at Kurt. "We have until Friday to work out if this snow globe photoshoot is the death bubble I suspect it is."

Kurt checked the appointment card Christine handed him. He turned it over in his hand twice. "There is no address on this card. There is a message to text a phone number with the appointment time and your name the evening before the appointment." He passed it to me.

"Why so secretive? Do they have a lot of people gatecrashing photography sessions?"

"I imagine Joan has such a card, and that means on Thursday sometime, she will know where the studio is," Kurt said, taking the card from my hand and pocketing it. "Unless we can find out for ourselves before then, we might have to rely on her telling us."

"Mitch said she wanted us all there, so, no doubt she'll share."

"You'll be identified at the session if that Christine woman is there."

"There will be no fucking session. As soon as we get an address, we move on it."

I can't even imagine a scenario where a photography session would take place with my children in a snow globe. A frozen hell sprang to mind, with Christine

334

dangling by her hair over an icy precipice. Happy to let go and make her death a reality if anything looks the least bit dodgy regarding the whole family photograph thing.

"Do I need to remind you that we have no evidence to back this?"

The pesky need for evidence causes so much work. "Let's put some pressure on a few of the tentative links and see what cracks."

Or shatters ... and what if anything turns into a diamond from the stress? I'd be delighted for my theory to be nothing more than the overactive overprotective slightly paranoid ramblings of a serial-crime-investigating mother.

"Let's go, before you go back and hang Christine over the railing."

"Excellent idea. A dangling we will go!" Kurt clamped a hand on my arm and shook his head. I stifled a sigh. Sometimes he took the fun out of being me. Kurt maneuvered me toward the stairs. Guess he decided the escalator put me too close to Christine.

He knows me quite well.

* * *

A healthy swig of tequila right from the bottle and then I placed the bottle back in the liquor cabinet and closed the door. Mitch waited, his eyes on me, the myriad questions swirling in his mind all too obvious. To stop him probing for answers, I clanged the door shut

I turned with a small smile on my face. "It was a day."

"I can tell. Wanna talk about it?" A small frown wrinkled between his eyes. "What's going on?" He pivoted his arm from the elbow, and flashed his hand across the gap between us. "It's like there's a wall here."

Imagine? "We need to stop your parents going through with this snow globe photo idea they have."

"Why?"

"Because I have a bad feeling." I opened the cabinet door, took the bottle, unscrewed the cap and chugged another big gulp of tequila.

"Mom wants to do something nice for us, create a tradition."

"I know." I nodded. "And I appreciate the sentiment."

"This is more than you not liking confined spaces, isn't it?"

"Yeah."

"Whatever this is, it's the reason for the wall I can feel. Tell me, El."

"Three of the missing families have links to a photographer and snow globes."

"And you don't think that's a coincidence?"

"There's no such thing." I saw the machinations of his thoughts in his eyes.

"Is that why you wanted to know where Mom found

the flyer?"

"Yes." I wanted another slug from the bottle.

"How about I fix us a drink and you can catch me up. Unless you just want to stand there swigging from the bottle?" He wrapped his arms around me, expertly removed the bottle from my hand, and planted a kiss on the side of my head. "Go check on the girls."

I hefted my bag from the floor, slung the strap over my shoulder, kissed Mitch, and walked quietly up the stairs. Quiet sounds of breathing in stereo floated from the girls' open door. I flipped the light switch inside our bedroom door then dropped my bag on our bed and pressed in a passcode on the bedside drawer. My gun, holster, belt, other bits and pieces, fitted neatly into the drawer. The lock caught automatically when I shut it. My fingers scrabbled through the bag on the bed until they connected with a phone case. I stuffed the phone in my back pocket and snuck into the girls' room. The nightlight on the wall allowed just enough soft glow to see our little blonde angels asleep in their cribs. Watching long enough to decide they weren't about to wake up, I rejoined Mitch downstairs. He'd migrated with drinks to the living room. Flames licked at fresh kindling in the fireplace.

"This is nice," I said, dropping on to the sofa next to him. "They're sleeping. When did you put them down?"

He glanced at his watch. "Half an hour ago."

Down for the night then. As much as I loved the pre-bed routine and cuddles, I appreciated the time with

Mitch.

"Talk," he said, and handed me a glass. "Tell me what you think is happening to families and why."

I sipped the drink and chose my words with care before telling Mitch what I suspected. I couldn't add the why, I had no clue why someone would want to kill entire families, but I was sure they were dead. By the time we'd finished our drinks, Mitch was in camp Ellie.

"As soon as your mother gets the address, I need it," I said, placing my drink on a coaster on the coffee table. "I tried the phone number but it goes straight to voicemail."

He nodded.

"They want us to meet them there, so Mom will call."

"She'll know the night before. However you get that information is up to you, but we can't wait until your parents and our daughters are en route the next day."

He nodded again. "What time frame are you looking at?"

"I want to hit the place that night. As soon as Joan gives us an address, we move."

A horrible thought rammed home. Other people had photos taken and lived. Did they have two studios? One you go to and live, the other a death chamber? They'd probably have two, otherwise, anyone could accidentally discover their operation.

I picked up my phone and tweeted: Anyone done those Snow Globe photos at the mall? #AskingForAFriend #FamilyPhotos

#Snowglobe

I don't know why I didn't think of going to social media earlier. I scrolled through my Twitter feed to see what the #ButterflyKids were doing. Some were using the hashtag Dragonflyclub. I showed Mitch.

"That's great. Your initiative is working." A smile lay on his face. His eyes twinkled. "You should be proud of the Butterfly Foundation and everything you've put in place to help the kids. It's fantastic."

Warmth glowed inside my chest. For a split second, I wondered if that was pride. A tweet alert interrupted my pondering.

@Changling: Mom had us do the snow globe thing last week. #NotFun #Donotrecommend

Yes!

@EllieIverson: Where did you do it? Is there a special studio? Why didn't you like it?

@Changling: We went to a photographic studio in Fairfax Corner, not far from the Pot Belly. Claustrophobic. The photographer was okay though.

@EllieIverson: Thanks. I'll pass it on. Who was the photographer? #Curious

@Changling: Shelly someone. Not sure. Mom was all gushy over her, she was famous once or something.

I swallowed a mouthful of tequila, placed the glass back on the table, willed my hands not to shake, clanged some mental doors shut to keep Mitch out of my head, and took a screenshot of the conversation thread. Without saying anything, I sent it to Kurt.

"What's the matter?" Mitch asked.

"We have a lead." I downed the last of my drink and stood up. My phone buzzed: Kurt. He'd be at our place in twenty minutes.

A brief internal argument took place. Do I tell Sean or not? Shelly. Not an unfamiliar name. Was it Shelly Morton? I made a call as I walked down the hallway with Argo on my heels. Mikki answered on the eighth ring. "Sorry to disturb you, but do you know where Shelly Morton has her studio?"

"Not exactly. I think she said, Market Commons Drive, Fairfax."

Twitter exploded in my ear. I looked at the phone in my hand, touched the speaker icon, and tapped the tweet alerts. "Does she travel, this friend of yours?"

"She said she does."

Tweets came from Indiana, Ohio, Utah, Indiana, Illinois, Virginia, West Virginia, California, a bunch from Nevada, and seven replies from Missouri. All places we had missing families except Virginia and Nevada. We'd accounted for the Nevada family, the unfortunate murder-suicide. On the thread where @Changling and I talked about the name of the photographer, people commented that she was either Rochelle or Shelly.

"Ellie?" Mikki's voice rang from the speaker. "Why

did you ask that?"

"I can't say. Its work related." More replies popped up. I saw one from Colorado. We didn't have a missing family there, that family was in WITSEC.

"What are you on? Is that Twitter?"

"Yeah."

I heard her tap something. Guess she was curious. I kept reading the tweets about the snow globe. Shit. Just shit. Why didn't we think to dump this in social media earlier?

"Ellie!" Mikki's voice crackled through my name.

"Are you following this conversation?"

"They're places she's mentioned. All of them."

"In what context?"

"She told me she was a staff photographer for a magazine."

"She ever mention the name?"

"No. I thought it was strange but with hindsight, I thought she was lying or possibly embellishing the truth. It appears to be her modus operandi."

Sure does. "Understandable considering what Sean has told me."

"What's the carry on with the snow globes?"

"I'm not sure, but it's a line of inquiry I need to follow. Can you narrow down her studio?" More tweets landed. More people talking about how cool it was to be photographed in the snow globes.

"Somewhere close to Whole Foods. She's mentioned how handy it is to her studio."

"Thanks, Mikki, I'll talk to you soon."

"Be careful, El."

"Always."

I ended the call and watched Twitter go nuts. A fluffy yellow duckling popped out of my phone. It quacked once then pulled a string of wriggling words from the Twitter feed, gobbling them up before they squirmed away. The duckling shook its little tail and disappeared in a poof of yellow fluff.

I made another call. "Sandra ... I need you to dig deep into Shelly Morton, the photographer. I want to know if and when she was in any of the states and cities or towns on my whiteboard. I need that info A-sap."

"Yes, O Leader of the Befuddled."

"Did your fancy software find anything we could use from those jigsaw pieces?"

"Nothing that you don't already know about."

"Thanks."

Chapter Thirty Seven
Chained To The Rhythm

Kurt leaned over and opened the passenger door for me. "Thanks," I said and waved at Mitch as I climbed into the car.

"Where's her studio?" Kurt said.

"Market Commons Drive."

"I'm going to need more than that," he said, exiting the gates.

"Close to the supermarket. It's mostly big chain stores along there, shouldn't be hard to find a photography studio."

The silence overwhelmed me as we drove and blanketed the questions and confusion in a soft fluffy nothingness.

"Whole Foods?"

I jumped, startled from the clouds that surrounded me and back into the car interior. Kurt chuckled. "Yeah, near there."

"I'll cruise to the end of the road and back, let me know what you see."

Between the supermarket and a sporting goods store I saw the studio or a studio.

"Might be the place with the fucking ginormous snow globe in the window," I said. "How have I never noticed that before?"

"No idea, Iverson." Kurt parked the car. He swiveled in his seat to look at me. "This is the part where I ask if we know what we are doing?"

We had a lot of Twitter activity saying how cool the snow globe photos were and how nice the photographer was and that her name was Shelly or Rochelle. What we didn't have was actual evidence that Shelly Morton was involved in anything more than photography and was a bit odd toward Mikki.

"We're winging it."

Kurt's head shook. "If we wing it and screw this up …"

"I know. So, we're not going to screw it up. We're just going to talk to Shelly about that fucking giant snow globe in her studio window."

My phone pinged. A text from Sandra with the info about Shelly Morton and travel. She flew to Cincinnati in February twenty-seventeen, Sandra found credit card records suggesting she flew to Wichita, December twenty-eighteen and Indianapolis April twenty-fifteen.

And ask her when she was last in Ohio, Kansas, and Indiana. Because the months and years corresponded to families vanishing off the face of the earth and I don't believe in coincidence.

"Look," I said, showing Kurt the text.

"We've still got Illinois, California, Utah, Missouri, and West Virginia with no link to Morton."

"So far." I texted Sandra back and asked that she keep looking.

"Let's go see if Morton is in her studio," Kurt said, swinging the car door open.

We stood side by side and watched the studio for a minute. A glow from a light emanated from beyond the snow globe. I took a photo with my phone and sent it to Sandra with a note to compare it to the photos taken from the jigsaw. The way the light illuminated the top of the globe … I'd seen it before.

"We going to knock?"

"Yep."

We strode across the road and I rapped my knuckles on the glass door and peered inside. Something crossed the path of the light creating a momentary blip. The blip became a shadow and moved again. Seconds passed. A figure emerged from the semi-dark becoming whole and human as it progressed toward us.

Kurt had his credentials in his hand. He held them to the glass. The woman smiled and unlocked the door, pulling it inward. "Hello. Can I help?"

"Shelly Morton?" Kurt said.

"Yes."

"I'm Special Agent Henderson and this is Special Agent in Charge Iverson. We'd like to talk to you about your business."

"You're interested in photography, or am I in trouble?" She gave a small laugh and stepped aside. "Please come in."

"Right first time. We are interested in photography," I said, with a smile; it didn't pay to spook people outright. "What's with the giant snow globe?"

"Bit of a gimmick, but people love it." She didn't sound as though she loved it.

"And you?" I said, as we followed her through the front of the premises into an office out the back. I noted we walked past two closed doors.

"Have a seat," Morton said, waving at a group of four armchairs in the corner covered in a faded yellow and green floral fabric, and clustered around a small battered occasional table. The chairs felt comfortable enough. Morton sat opposite us. "In answer to your question. The snow globe thing is fun. Not sure I'm the world's biggest enthusiast."

"What sort of photography do you prefer?" Kurt asked, flipping his notebook open and preparing to take notes.

"Something with more backbone to it. Studies in humanity and the human experience."

And dead comics. "How did an award-winning photographer like yourself end up taking frivolous pictures of people in snow globes?"

She eyed me with a modicum of suspicion. "It pays the bills." The index finger on her right hand traced a flower on the arm of her chair. "Art doesn't pay well, Agent."

"Where do you get giant snow globes?" Kurt asked.

"There is a supplier in Richmond. I have them shipped from there."

"Are they expensive?"

"Two thousand dollars each."

Wow. Must need to take a few photos to recoup that expenditure. "Do you have many?"

She shook her head. "I have two. The one in the window and one set up in a studio."

If she has two, then she probably doesn't have one dedicated as a gas chamber. Enough. You don't know that's happening. "How many people are using snow globes, do you know?"

"There is a company that rents them out for events and I sometimes fill in for their photographer. There's a knack to taking great photos through a plastic bubble. Not everyone can pull off consistently usable images."

"That's interesting," Kurt said. Making notes. "The other company is?"

"Arianda Enterprises."

"Based?"

"They have an office and permanent studio space in the city."

"You have an address for that?"

She stood and walked over to desk. A few seconds of rifling through paperwork followed. She handed Kurt a piece of paper. He jotted down the address and handed the paper to me.

It was a document asking Shelly to travel to West Virginia and take photos for the company. I handed it back. "Do they use you a lot?"

"Maybe a dozen times in the last four years."

"Do you know who their regular photographer is?"

"Rochelle Coombes."

Kurt's pen moved across his notebook. "Do you have contact details for Rochelle Coombes?"

She shook her head. "What is this about?"

"Are you using your snow globes and taking bookings for family photos?" I asked, maintaining the smile on my face. Or are you taking bookings for Arianda?

She nodded. "Yes. I have a student set up at the mall who takes bookings. People like to get a head start on holiday season photographs."

"And this is you, by yourself, not affiliated with Arianda Enterprises?"

"That's correct. I have Northern Virginia. It was a condition of my employment."

A little sigh of relief hissed out of an internal crawl spac; before it could become anything, a cold dead hand grabbed it around the neck and hauled it back into the dark.

"Why don't you tell the clients what your studio address is at the time of booking?"

She smiled. "I have this studio and I use another when necessary. It depends what I have on where I set up the snow globe."

Seems reasonable. Or does it? "Where is your other studio?"

"Monument Drive."

"What reasons would you change studios?"

"Sometimes I lease space to other photographers. It helps pay the electric bill."

Fair enough, although having two studios would be dearer than one. "Wouldn't it be better to have one studio?"

"I sublease space when I need it at a cheap rate. This is my main studio."

"Arianda Enterprise sends you out of state?"

She nodded. "They fly me all over the country."

"And you just take photos of people in snow globes?"

"Yes."

"And the people are alive?" Well, that just popped right out.

She faltered. Her mouth opened and closed. "Yes, Agent, the people are alive."

Good one, Ellie. "Good to know."

"What is this really about?"

"A line of inquiry to do with a case," I replied. "Can't give any details." I sensed her closing down and her cooperation dissolving. "Can we see your studio?"

"I don't think so," she replied, folding her arms across her chest. "I think we are done here."

Shit. I rose. "Thank you for seeing us." I went ahead and asked another question. No harm, we were already leaving. "Do you work anywhere else?"

A smile crossed her lips then vanished. Her arms relaxed. "In my other line of work the clients are not always breathing," she said. "I am a staff photographer at a hospital."

"That must be interesting and terrifying in equal parts," I replied, sitting back down. You'd need a strong stomach for that job, and that's just going by what we see on a fairly regular basis.

"It is. Sorry for the attitude, Agent. I understand you can't give me details when you're working a case."

"I'm sorry I didn't phrase my question better."

And we were back.

She made eye contact with me. "I've seen you in the news. Not recently, but over the last few years."

I had nothing to say to that. Most often when I'm in the news it's delivering a media update on something horrific or a story by a less-than-reputable journalist ripping into my life.

"You dated Rowan Grange."

Oh. She means that far back. Great. Not so much news as gossip column then. "I did."

Kurt jumped in. "How long have you worked as a hospital photographer?"

"Four years. Entering my fifth year now."

"Your last exhibition ..." he started.

"... we saw it at the Newseum," I continued. "Are you planning anything now?"

She smiled. "Actually, yes, I'm working on the last two image sets for a new exhibition."

"Have you titled it yet?"

"'Arbitrary still life: the disjunction of fear.'"

"Fascinating." A question I'd long wondered reared. "How do artists come up with their exhibition names?"

She smiled. "To tell you the truth, I used a random art name generator."

Of course. How else would they do it? "Now I know, thank you." With my curiosity sated in one regard, I continued being interested and chatty. "How long before it will be viewable?"

"Four weeks. As long as a writer I know agrees to let me shoot her working for the last section."

"If that doesn't happen?" How would she proceed if everything hinged on Mikki doing what she wanted her to do?

"I doubt she'll refuse. We're close."

No back-up plan then.

"Who is the writer?" Kurt asked, leaning in, and using his friendliest tone. "Can we ask that?"

She smiled. "Michaela Kennedy." She focused on Kurt. "Have you read her books?"

"Agent Iverson is a fan," Kurt said.

Her gaze switched to me. "That's great. She's amazing, right?"

I nodded. "I'm a bit behind, though. Haven't read the last book yet." I fought the impulse to cross my fingers. I was at least three books behind.

"A true fan," Shelly said with a smile.

"Guess I am. Have you been friends long?" I spiraled into a fact-finding mission, and she came along for the ride.

"Not in real life, I suppose. I've been a fan for a number of years." Her eyes flashed and face brightened. This was a topic she liked. "When I discovered her work, she was five books into the series. I binged and caught up."

I waited for a few beats before speaking. "You get to know someone quite well reading their work, don't you? Sometimes I think Kennedy and I would have a lot in common." I brushed it off. "But of course, I know its fiction and not really her."

Bingo. A light went on behind her eyes. "I'd say you do get to know a writer through their work. They put a lot of themselves into their creation like any artist." She was loving the topic. "I've read all her books multiple times now. I like to re-read the whole series before the next one comes out. I always see different things. It's clever how she does that."

Maybe if you read them properly to start with.

"You must really enjoy her stories," Kurt said, capturing Morton's attention.

"I do." She dropped her voice. "We have a connection. You know?"

Kurt nodded. "Uh-huh."

"Sometimes I offer suggestions regarding characters and plot threads."

What now? "And Kennedy uses them?" I tried hard to keep any skepticism out of my voice. The look on Kurt's face told me I failed.

"Yep." Shelly nodded. "She's very open to suggestions. We have a very close relationship."

She must know a different Michaela Kennedy

because the one I know keeps all talk of plot and characters to herself until the book is almost ready for release.

"Has she ever written about you?" Kurt jumped in, giving me a moment to discipline my thoughts which were in danger of spilling all manner of unhelpful phrases from my mouth.

Shelly glanced around as if afraid she'd be overheard. Her voice dropped again, this time to a loud whisper. "Her main character is *me*."

"Wow." Didn't have to feign astonishment. It was real. Fuck, she was delusional. "I imagine it must be cool seeing your name mentioned in the acknowledgments of the books. They do that right? Authors thank people they've garnered inspiration from?"

Skin furrowed on her brow. "She's discreet and a private person. She doesn't need to thank me."

Kurt held out his phone to me. On the screen was the latest of Mikki's books. I'm not the only fan on the team then. He'd opened to the acknowledgment page at the back. She'd mentioned a few people but only used first names or nicknames. I recognized all four names. Sean told me once that Cait used to refer to me as 'Cait point one'. And Mikki thanked 'Cait point one' for the helping with a few technical scenes. No mention of Shelly.

"What are you looking at?" Shelly asked.

"The last book Michaela Kennedy wrote. Just

wanted to see who she thanked."

She didn't seem bothered. "She just thanked some publishing people," she said with a dismissive wave. "Her editor and manager, that kind of thing. It's what writers do."

"Wonder who Cait point one is," Kurt said with amazing deadpan delivery.

I passed the phone back to him. "Wonder who Cait is," I replied. "Must be a Cait if there's a Cait point one."

"Probably people who would be offended if they weren't thanked. Some people are like that."

"Not you though, right?" Kurt asked.

"I know how important my input is ... I don't need other people knowing."

Of course. And she's such a close friend she doesn't know who Cait is which confirms she has no idea who Mikki is, beyond Mikki the author.

"How did you meet her?" Let's poke the bear and see what happens. I watched close enough to see a smile suppressed before it could establish itself on her lips.

"At a book signing. We got talking and found we had a lot in common."

"Must be great to know an author like that." Sincerity coated my words like hot caramel sauce.

"It is. but there is more to it." She leaned forward slightly. "I was lucky enough to notice something out of the ordinary and bring it to her attention."

"That was good of you. Was it in a story?"

"No. Not at all. Someone was acting oddly, and I thought she should know. Seemed like a stalker situation developing."

"Whew, lucky you spotted it then. We know just how ugly stalkers can get," I said, flashing a glance at Kurt.

"Yes, we do. We just dealt with one."

She leaned closer. "It's a good feeling when you can help someone and avert disaster, isn't it?"

Yeah, because that's what you did. You unhinged woman.

"Sure is," Kurt replied.

"I'm sure she was very grateful," I added.

Shelly nodded and attempted humble. "She's thanked me numerous times. I'm just glad I saw what was happening and could help before it became anything awful."

Well, look at that, we have a hero in our midst. "Thank goodness you were smart enough to stop it," I said, with a relieved smile. "And has the situation resolved?"

She smiled, but it failed to reach her eyes. "I hope so. He was bothering me before he turned to Mikki." She shook her head. "So sad when people latch onto someone and make more of it than it is."

Oh, boy! Kurt and I shared a quick look of disbelief before I spun the conversation back to work topics. "Great that you were there to prevent trouble." I flipped back to a warm smile. "Do you have any more work for Arianda in the next few weeks?"

"No. Their usual photographer is back and I'm concentrating on getting my exhibition up and running."

"Thank you for your time, Ms. Morton." I stood. "Good luck with the exhibition."

Her manner changed. The smile slid from her lips. An air of panic surrounded her. My sense pinged off the change in her like a Geiger counter sniffing out radiation.

"Would you like to see my studio?" She stood quickly, steadied herself with a hand on the back of the chair and blurted, "I have a snow globe set up."

A little voice in my head voiced a thought, 'What the hell is this change all about?'

"We'd like that, thanks," Kurt replied.

"Follow me."

She moved ahead of us. Down the short hallway, she opened a door. Another short hallway led to another door. She opened that door and we followed her into the room. A spacious room containing a huge snow globe, with lights and reflectors set up in various places in front and behind it. On the far wall was a screened area.

"What's behind the screen?" Kurt asked.

"Costumes and a changing area for clients. Some like to use our costumes and some bring their own."

"How do you change the backdrop?" I said, staring at the globe taking up a good deal of the large room. The saloon frontage and hitching posts felt like a step back into the wild west. I walked over and inspected it. Nope, my kids are not getting in one of these. Not now. Not ever. "This is huge." I looked at Morton over my shoulder. "The backdrop isn't an image, it's built."

"Yes, I have a few custom builds. They're made of cardboard and foam board. You can't tell can you?"

"No, well, I can't. Looks like aged wood and realistic." The backdrop looked pricey. My eyes roamed the expansive bubble. "Where's the door?"

"Hidden in the side is a seam. Within the seam is the zip. It's sealed so the globe doesn't deflate."

I now knew more than I ever wanted to about bubbles of death. "How do you breathe in there?" I walked around the back, stepping over light cords taped to the floor. Before she could say anything I said, "Found it." A flexible pipe that joined into a connector at the back near the floor of the globe. The pipe ran to the back of the studio and disappeared behind another screen. I followed it. Air tanks. Beside the air supply was a compressor.

Morton spoke from behind me. "When the door is open, I have the compressor running, it keeps it inflated until we seal it behind the clients."

"We?"

"I have an assistant. A local student. It's a two-person job, managing the globe, clients, and setting up for a shoot."

I imagined that killing entire families would require more than two people. Removing dead bodies from a globe would not be easy.

They're heavy.

They're awkward.

And then what?

Are there studios with dead bodies in them all across the country? Imagine the smell.

"Thank you for your patience," I said, shaking Morton's hand. "We'll leave you in peace." Her grip wouldn't let up, forcing me to extract my hand from hers.

"It's no trouble. I'm around if you have more questions." She smiled. "You can just drop in, that's fine."

Kurt and I left the building.

The car beeped on our approach. I opened the passenger door and slid into the seat. We stared at each other for a beat.

"What the fuck was that about?" I muttered, looking over at the studio. Shelly stood waving in the doorway. I gave a half wave and looked away.

"I think she wants to be your new bestie," Kurt said with a chuckle. He turned the key. The engine rumbled to life.

Kurt drove in silence.

Lights flashed deep within my head as scenery flew past. Why was I so sure the missing families died in snow globes? It made little sense once illuminated by daylight, but inside my head it was real.

I called Sean. "Hey, Morton is sure Mikki will say yes

to her request to be photographed for her new exhibition."

"And?"

"Keep the CPD with her."

"Why?"

"Remember our conversation about Morton being a hero?"

"Yes."

"She also thinks Mikki's main character is modeled on her."

"Jesus."

Yeah. We all knew that character was loosely based on her sister, Cait O'Hare, at least that's how it was when she conceptualized the first book.

"I have no proof she means Mikki harm, but she was telling lies and that is hinky as fuck."

"Good enough. You'll figure it out."

"Thanks for the vote of confidence."

My finger pressed the end call button. Will I though? What if this whole snow globe thing is me having a meltdown and nothing more than a wild turkey chase? My stomach grumbled. I'd really love a turkey sandwich. I leaned down and picked up a snow globe photography flyer from the footwell.

Everything blurred. I blinked to clear my vision. A pencil scribbled shading in the corner of a page. A black pen drew outlines, moving from the edge to the middle of my vision. A desk and chair emerged from the trail of the pen. My shoulders relaxed, breathing slowed, calmness followed every stroke of the pen. A page turned to reveal a familiar and comforting scene.

Chance grinned and walked around the desk toward me. "El, thanks for coming."

I looked around the room then down at my legs and boots. They were real. Chance was real. Everything around us was drawn, reality in a comic-book setting. "I had a choice?"

"Yes."

"You did this?"

"I did."

"Why?"

"You're struggling. I heard you. You needed some clarity."

"I need evidence."

"What did you think of Morton?" Chance stepped closer, his hands reached out and grasped my shoulders. "What are you thinking?" His pale blue eyes searched mine. "What's happening inside that head of yours, El?"

"There's something about Morton, but I don't think she's involved in the missing family situation."

"Why?"

"I don't know."

"Was she in the cities where families vanished at the time it happened?"

"Yes, well, for some anyway. Not sure about all."

"Could there be another photographer?"

"There is another photographer."

"And?"

"I can't prove any of it. I shouldn't be trying to prove my theory. I need to follow the evidence."

"And the evidence points too?"

"Zilch."

A buzzer sounded. "Try again."

"A few of the families had their photos taken in a snow globe. The text messages we received are linked to some of their occupations or interests. The puzzle was impossible to solve but sent by the text message person, who knows what happened to the families but likes playing games or doesn't want to communicate directly for whatever reason."

It's possible that a piece of that puzzle is an arc at the top of a snow globe, but that's not confirmed.

"Your gut says?"

"The Unsub likes playing games and it really believes this is all tied to snow globe photography."

Chance nodded. "I concur with the game playing." His eyes searched mine. "Dig deeper into the community surrounding those families, El. You're good with people. Face-to-face a few of them, see where you get."

"The last person who had a link to a missing family member that I got face-to-face with was killed."

"Ah, the Marine. The sister of a missing family member."

"Yeah."

"Is his death tied to his missing sister or something

else?"

"Navy says a hate crime."

"The guy who stabbed Lee?"

"Tied to the dead Marine and the missing family member. We may never know why he stabbed Lee. But he had a letter addressed to his ex on him, and it mentioned photos." Everything twisted back on itself.

"Do you think he knew or suspected something?"

"He was upset ... we don't know what about."

His dead body was too dead when I saw it, and no chance of a chatty corpse. So we'll probably never know what went on in his head.

"Sit down," Chance said, pressing my shoulders until I sat in the chair behind me.He perched on the edge of his desk. It always amazed me how the drawings supported us.

"He had a letter that mentioned photographs," Chance said. "And the Marine's sister is missing. Did you see the photos?"

I nodded. "Yeah, snow globe photos. They were sent from the sister's email account to the Marine after the family disappeared."

"One of two things happened, Ellie. Either the sister sent the photographs and did not disappear that weekend at all. Or?"

"Someone else had control of her phone or laptop and sent them to make it look like nothing out of the ordinary happened that weekend."

"Can you get the original email?"

I nodded as I smiled. "Thanks, Chance."

"One last thing. What is it about Morton?"

"She's a liar, but I don't know why she's telling lies."

He waved. All around me the colors and ink ran. They joined to form the words: Trace the origin.

Chapter Thirty Eight

Roll On Down The Highway

Paying attention to my surroundings again, the hum from the buildings in the city pulsated. People created energy. "Kurt?"

"Almost there. Nice nap?"

"I wasn't sleeping. I was thinking." I was listening to Chance.

"And?"

"Our dead Marine sent you the original email with the photos ... Sandra might be able to find the origin."

He smiled. "Now that's a positive forward thought." He pulled into the garage under the building and parked. Together we ran up the stairs to our floor. I won.

Sandra watched us from her desk as we strode along the hallway. "How can I help, O Mighty Leader of the Rebellion?"

Kurt handed her his phone with the email app open.

"Can you trace the origin of that email?" I said.

"Possibly, how far back do you need to go?" She scrolled and tapped on the phone screen. "It's a forward."

"All the way back, we'd like to know where it came from."

"IP?"

"Yes."

"If we're lucky, we can trace back to an owner but it's not always the case."

"I'm feeling lucky," I said with a smile.

"Send me the email, Kurt, and I'll try some Sandra magic."

"Thank you," he said, taking the phone from her and forwarding the email.

"About how long do you think that will take, Sandra?" I leaned a hip on her desk. "Long enough for us to get coffee?"

"Ah, nope," she replied. "I have it."

"You're kidding?"

"Not about this. The IP origin of this email is a broadband connection in Louden County, Virginia."

"Thank you. Who is it registered to?"

"A company called Arianda Enterprises."

Proof, that Arianda was involved in something. I looked at Kurt. "Road trip, get Dane and Lee."

My phone rang. Kurt left as I answered the call. And I walked to my office talking on the phone. "Special Agent in Charge Iverson."

"It's Julie at NCIS."

"How's it going?"

"Not great. The chaplain is a piece of work. We're finding a trail of destruction with his hands all over it. Every posting. Every time he moved on, something horrible happened to someone or multiple someones."

"He was perpetuating hate crimes?"

"Yes. He particularly hates homosexuals and women

in the Navy."

"Glad he's yours and not ours," I said. "Did you find anything out about Green and his ex-boyfriend?"

"He was a victim of the chaplain's hateful rhetoric. I've been through his quarters and nothing points to any reason for his ex to stab Lee."

"Okay, thanks for trying. I don't expect to get an answer."

"Sorry I didn't have good news."

"You kinda did. At least the chaplain can't hurt anyone else."

"Yeah. Wonder if we could gag him in the Brig, just to make sure."

I laughed. "Don't see why not."

"Take care, Ellie."

"You too."

The call ended. I made a conscious decision to set anything to do with Green the Marine and his ex aside.

The whiteboard loomed over the room. My phone rang. I tapped the speaker icon as I answered.

"Agent Iverson, it is Gary here. Gary from Missouri. One of my officers just reported a traffic stop, and it feels off."

"Okay, I'm listening." Kurt waved from the doorway. I beckoned him in. "You're on speaker, Gary."

"Half an hour ago, one of my officers stopped a refrigerated truck. Routine license, insurance and manifest check."

"Uh-huh."

"The truck was carrying cadavers. Paperwork said they were donated to a laboratory in Virginia."

"People do donate their bodies to science, Gary."

"The manifest said five adults and five children."

"All right, I'm interested. What are the odds of families donating their children to science?"

"Not good," Gary said.

Kurt nodded in agreement. As a parent, the thought was abhorrent.

"Where did they come from?"

"Two adults and two children originated in Idaho." I heard a page turn. "One adult and one child came from Wyoming, and two adults and two children from Nebraska."

I searched the whiteboard. None of those states had reported missing families. Yet.
"And the paperwork?"

"All in order as far as the officer could tell, roadside."

"Send me everything, including his body cam footage."

"Done. I'll link you to the server where the body cam footage is stored."

"Great, thanks."

"Could this be how the families vanished, someone kills them and ships them out of state?"

"We don't know they're dead." Not for sure. "I don't know, Gary. We'll check it out and get back to you. Did the manifest have names attached?"

"Yes. According to the paperwork, none of the cadavers are related."

So it could be a shipment of bodies for science and not at all related to our investigation; the trucker could be picking up cadavers on his way across the country.

"What do you think, Gary?" Inclusive, I am.

"I think you could intercept the truck for a closer look at the contents."

"That's a very good idea. I'll let you know what we find."

The call ended. Kurt shot me a questioning look.

"I'm thinking."

I generated my own form of white noise to help my thought processes. That white noise sounded a lot like my mom nagging. What worked, worked. I tuned the repetitive drone out and let a map fill my mind. If this was connected to our missing families, then picking up bodies from consecutive states was a ballsy move. The crypto-Unsub could've been more helpful.

California, Nevada, Utah, Colorado, Kansas, Missouri, Illinois, Indiana, Ohio.

Idaho, Wyoming, Nebraska, Iowa … the line continued, Illinois, Indiana, Ohio, Pennsylvania, New Jersey.

A large, clear balloon inflated. Bigger and bigger until bang! Glitter fell like sparkly snow. I shook my head to clear my vision.

"Iverson?"

I looked at Kurt. He was sitting in front of me.

"Yeah?"

"I'm not liking these long silences and the mid-distance stare that goes with them. What's happening in that head of yours?"

"There's another pattern. What if the Unsub is collecting people from every state?"
What about Hawaii? Nothing's come in from there about missing families. Or Alaska.

Where is this even coming from? Another image filled my mind: a snowy scene inside a globe. Glittery white snow piled around a log cabin. In front of the cabin, wrapped in winter clothes stood a family of four, their clothes modern ski wear. Skis leaned near the front door of the cabin and two children held ski poles. A mom and dad, smiling, the man had his arm around the woman. I took step back. A plaque on the outside of the stand read: Robinson family Christmas vacation 2015, with a logo to the right of the plaque. It said OSC with stylized mountains above it.

"Iverson? You okay?"

I refocused on Kurt. A frown deepened on his forehead. I wrote everything I'd seen on my desk blotter, including a rough sketch of the logo. "I'm okay."

"That's not going to wash. Something's up."

He studied me, his eyes seeking answers. He'd flipped the switch and was in doctor mode.

"I'm fine, Henderson. I saw something."

"What?"

"A family in a snow globe. The Robinson family. It was the Christmas of twenty-fifteen and they had skis."

"Then we better work out what's happening."

I reckon. I searched the missing persons database for a missing family during winter months of twenty-fifteen; while that was running I snapped a picture of the logo I'd drawn and ran an image search.

Seconds seemed like months.

The computer pinged. "The logo I saw, Omaha Ski Club."

Kurt's eyes met mine. "Nebraska."

The computer pinged again. "The Robinson family. Mom, dad, a seven-year-old daughter and a nine-year-old son. The report was filed on January fifteen, twenty-sixteen." I dug into the missing persons reports regarding the family. "Last seen on December twenty-six, twenty-fifteen. It was a Saturday." A Saturday. All our other families were last seen on a Friday. But Friday that year was Christmas Day.

"I don't get how I saw that family now. They're hardly likely to be the cadavers on the truck. Not four years later." Yeah, that's what I don't understand ... not that I can see it at all. What if they are the bodies of the Robinson family?

"Your mind is a wondrous place, Iverson."

"Could they be the Robinsons?"

"On the truck?" Kurt didn't miss a beat. "Perhaps."

Woah. What? "Really?"

"Potentially," Kurt said.

"Cryogenics?" Or an industrial freezer and lots of cling wrap.

"That's a possibility but I was thinking plastination."

Of course you were. "Jeez."

"Yeah."

"Let's see what Gary sent us." I printed the files Gary sent then opened the link to the body cam footage. "Wanna watch?"

Kurt joined me on my side of the desk. I read the time stamp from the email and scrolled to that point in the timeline. The minute we got a clear image of the driver, I paused the video and snapped a screenshot. We continued watching. The driver handed the police officer his license, logbook, and then his manifest. He did not appear rattled or concerned. Once the officer sent him on his way, I stopped the video. Kurt was writing in his notebook. I ran the screenshot of the driver. It came back with an ID and his driver's license. Charlie Batton. He drove for a California company: Carson Brothers. A quick Google told me the company specialized in long haul refrigeration, cold storage, and cadaver transportation.

"If they were plastinated they would not need refrigeration," I said.

"That's correct. But what better way to move bodies, plastinated or not?"

No risk of anyone wanting to look at the cargo. "If they were moved as a display or in a display case." Snow globe. "Then a curious cop might ask to look inside the truck."

Kurt raised his eyebrows. "Exactly. But no one wants to look at bodies."

"I want another search done. We might have a lot more missing families than we know about already."

Kurt straightened up and headed for the door. Over his shoulder, he said, "The truck?"

"We're stopping it before its final destination. I'll get access to the LoJack." I circled the registration number of the truck and the driver's name on the papers in front of me, and punched in the long phone number for the company that owned the truck and waited while it dialed through.

A perky receptionist answered. "Carson Brothers, how may I direct your call?"

"This is FBI Agent Iverson in Washington D.C, can I speak to the owner, please?"

"Yes, ma'am."

Music followed a click. While I listened, I messaged Sandra to get a warrant for the LoJack data in case the owner didn't want to play nice. The second song started as a man answered. "This is Kevin Carson-Wilson. How can I help you, Agent?"

"I'd like access to the LoJack on this truck." I read out the registration number.

Fingers typed. Stopped. Tapped again at computer keys. "Charlie Batton is driving that rig. He's one of our most experienced drivers. Why is it you want access to the LoJack?"

"It's part of an ongoing investigation. I am not at liberty to say."

"Does this involve Charlie?"

"No, we don't think that at all. We're interested in the load he's hauling."

Tapping again. "He's on the way to Louden County, Virginia. A scientific facility."

"Great. How many more stops is he going to make?"

"One, he has a pick-up in Iowa."

My cell phone buzzed on my desk. A message from Sandra. Being an SAC had perks. Warrants were fast. "I'm forwarding you a warrant enabling me to access that LoJack."

"Thank you."

I sent it to the email address I'd found on the website. "You can send the link in the return email," I said. No choices offered. "Who is the client?"

"Arianda Enterprise."

"How often do you deliver cadavers for Arianda Enterprise?"

"Once or twice a year."

"Have you worked with them long?"

I listened to typing. "Six years. And before you ask, yes we deliver to the same facility to Louden County," he said. "I have your warrant, Agent Iverson. I'll return the link to the LoJack and the required log-on information."

"How many cadavers would you deliver in one shipment to Arianda?"

Mouse clicks filled the silence. "Average shipment is seventeen."

Seventeen bodies twice a year. Thirty-four bodies times six. Two hundred and four bodies. We knew of thirty-nine missing people. Forty-three counting the Robinsons. And that was after I'd removed two families from the equation due to murder-suicide and WITSEC. We potentially had one hundred and sixty-one bodies we knew nothing about.

"Could you send me the information you have on file for every shipment for Arianda, please?"

"Email okay?"

"Yes."

"Do your trucks pick up the Arianda cadavers from the same locations every time?"

"Yes. There are five pick-up points across the country for Arianda."

"Do you pick up bodies for any other facility from those points?"

"No. Usually we pick up from hospitals, county morgues, or funeral homes."

"Anything else different about the Arianda jobs?"

"No. What's this about, Agent? Because I'm gleaning something unsavory regarding Arianda and if that's the case I need to protect my company."

"As soon as I know for sure, I'll let you know." Another thought popped up. "How many other medical research companies do you ship for?"

I didn't want to be responsible for the company

going under if I could help it. They don't deserve to be caught up in this killing spree. Unless of course, they did. I left a small shiny question mark hanging over their name. For now.

"We have contracts with one hundred and forty-three research facilities, we also work with two hundred independent funeral directors, seven large funeral home franchises, and have two government contracts." He paused. A door opened then closed before he spoke again. "We also facilitate in the repatriation of Americans who've passed away overseas."

A warning bell sounded. "Is that part of your government contract?"

"No. Usually its private citizens, very occasionally we are asked to assist the Armed Forces in repatriation of fallen personnel."

"Have you retrieved American citizens from Hawaii and or Alaska on behalf of Arianda?"

He tapped quickly and then responded, "Not Hawaii, but there was a pick-up in Alaska five years ago."

I made a note.

"And you ship other things too, right? Across the country?"

"Yes, anything that requires cool storage or freezing."

In different trucks, I hoped. "Business is good?"

"Yes."

"The government contracts?"

"The Centers for Disease Control and Prevention and the Defense Department."

The CDC I could understand, but the Defense Department? I did not want to know why they wanted bodies.

"Thank you. You've been very helpful." I guess when you're in the body-moving business, helping law enforcement is a smart idea, even smarter if you hold the sort of contracts they held.

"Everything I have on Arianda will be in your inbox within the next ten minutes, Agent."

"I appreciate that." I hung up, leaned back in my chair, and stared at the smartboard.

One hundred and sixty-one people we don't know about yet even without including potential Alaskan bodies.

My eyes closed for a moment. Six years. How could this be happening for six years and we're only piecing it together now? Unbelievable.

I reeled my inadequacy back in, we've only just become involved. We needed to go wider. Reach out to states we hadn't heard from and ask them to dig deep for missing families as far back as six years ago, and our only criteria was that they were last seen on a Friday. I circled Alaska on my desk blotter. Five years ago. Big place. Low population. Then again, might not be from Alaska. Could've been people on vacation.

A proviso: special interest in anything regarding

snow globes or photographers.

My eyes pinged open. We had no evidence of wrong doing going back six years. Nothing that said the families were murdered. My gut would not hold up in court. I was amazed we got a warrant for the Arianda information.

A rap at my door jam jerked me from my thoughts.

Lee. "Boss ... I might have something."

I beckoned him in. "Whatcha got, Lee?"

"Someone with a large collection."

"I'm going to need more than that."

"This person collects snow globes."

"A lot of people do." The vital fluid in my body chilled. It felt like my core temperature dropped.

"She's the daughter of the comedian who died in Kandahar."

"Okay." I gave him a look that asked for more.

Lee placed a folder on my desk. I opened it. Photos of small furry animals in snow globes assaulted my eyes. "Taxidermy," I muttered, and flipped more pages. Each page contained five photos of mice in various poses inside snow globes. I never did like taxidermy. Always seemed to make the animals appear terrified or terrifying. "Why would anyone collect animals in snow globes?"

Lee shrugged. "Not my thing." He sat in the chair opposite the desk. "Didn't her father want to be stuffed and seated on the sofa in their living room, forever?"

I nodded. "It was one of his jokes. One of his most

famous." I turned over a few more pages. "When did this obsession with keeping dead things begin?"

"Not long after her father died. He used to buy her snow globes for her collection when he traveled."

"Great. I imagine they were tourist-type snow globes, not little bubbles of death." Bet he didn't expect this to be the outcome.

"Each globe is custom made."

"Figured. It's not exactly the kind of thing you see in gift stores." I turned another page. "And they're all small animals." I paused with the next page ready to turn. "I'm not about to find a dog or anything?"

"Mice, hamsters, and rats, all doing fun activities."

"How did you find this?" I waved a hand at the now-closed folder.

"Google." Lee's eyes met mine. "I Googled snow globe collections and found her Facebook page." Before I could comment, he grinned and said, "It's public, so no warrant required."

"Does she say where she gets these atrocities?"

"Her mom. She makes them for her."

Fun family. "What do you know about mom?" I rested my wrists on the desk and laced my fingers together.

"That she creates freaky things in snow globes for her weird kid and she studied Plastination in Germany in the nineties at a place called The Institute For Plastination, in Heidelberg, Germany."

"Gunther von Hagens," I said slowly. "They also call

him Doctor Death."

"Why do I know that name?"

"Hagens or Doctor Death?"

"Von Hagens."

"Because he invented plastination and his exhibitions tour the world. He curates the *Body World* exhibitions. And he famously asked his wife to plastinate him after his death so he could become part of their newest exhibition."

"Jeez," Lee said, "What is it with these people wanting to be preserved?"

I shrugged, and pulled up the newspaper story I'd read on the terminally ill doctor. "He has Parkinson's disease. He's also had a controversial career. He even performed a public autopsy."

"Sounds like a fun guy."

"Hence the name Doctor Death."

"And now we're looking for a homegrown version?"

"I think we are." There are some fucked-up people in the world.

I called Kurt and Dane. "Get someone to find that truck and a suitable place to stop it. I want a thorough search and hold the driver for questioning. He might know a bit more about his cargo than head office."

"Claude wants that job," Kurt said. "I've briefed the Delta SSAs in on evolving situation."

"Great give it to him. I'm going to see Charlotte now, then I'll be back. We'll go knock on the door of a lab in Louden."

"SWAT on standby?" Dane asked.

"Can't hurt," I replied. "I'll be back in an hour. Lee, keep Argo with you."

As much as Charlotte would love to see him, better to keep dog hair and whatnot away from someone recovering from gunshot wounds.

Chapter Thirty Nine
Crash Into Me

Traffic moved at a steady pace enabling my trip to the hospital in almost record time. The only way to get there faster would've been with lights. Even the car park angels smiled on me.

I knocked on the door frame of Charlotte's room and poked my head in. An IV pump pushed fluid into her left arm. "You up for a visitor?"

She smiled. "Thanks for dropping by, SAC."

I walked in, pulled up a chair on her right side, and sat down. "How're you doing?"

"Getting there." She passed me a small clear container. It rattled as I took it from her.

"Three bullet fragments, impressive." I handed it back.

"Thinking of getting them hung on a charm bracelet."

"Good idea." I surveyed her pale face for a moment. "You remember much about the shooting?"

She nodded. "Everything."

"Has our psychologist been in?"

"Yes. She's helpful."

I nodded. That's the right answer. "Looks like the truck jacking is linked to a case Delta A is working. We're close to wrapping it up. I'm hoping you'll be out of this place in time to enjoy a Delta night at

Murphy's."

"A couple more days, and I'll be going home."

"Good. Take it easy. Healing takes time, make sure you allow time."

"Yes, SAC."

"Keep in touch. Anything you need, let Sandra know, and we'll make it happen."

"Thanks, SAC."

"No problem."

I put the chair back and left the hospital, satisfied my agent was healing. The trip back to the office looked set to be another record. Go Washington. The lights changed at the last intersection before the Hoover Building. As I entered the intersection, movement to my right caught my eye. Fuck! The vehicle slammed into my passenger door. The impact drove me into my door. Airbags smacked into me as the front fender of my car crashed into a light pole.

Fast diagnostic time: I could move my feet and hands. My vision blurred as the airbag deflated. Blood splattered across the whiteness. The windscreen had myriad cracks and splatters. Crazy paving. Noises outside the car matched the racket in my head. I reached for the radio. Pain surged in my right arm. I forced my hand to close around the radio and lift it to my mouth, gasping at the effort to depress the talk button.

"Break, Break. Special Agent in Charge Iverson requiring immediate medical assistance."

I let the button go and closed my eyes for a second, dropping the radio handset in my lap. My head bounced on the headrest. One Mississippi. Two Mississippi.

"Go for Agent Iverson, over."

Using my left hand to depress the button and circumvent the shooting pain and lack of compliance in my right hand, "I'm in a car wreck about two hundred yards from the Hoover Building."

"We have your position, Agent. Paramedics are on the way. Over."

Yay, for GPS locators. "Roger that."

The radio slipped from my fingers and disappeared from view. Blood ran from my mouth, dribbling down my chin and onto my shirt. I tried to release my seat belt, but it wouldn't budge, or my hand didn't work anymore. I attempted to release the belt with my left hand. I couldn't move easily. Non-compliance all round. In the glove compartment was a seat belt tool. I reached out. Regret followed sharp deep pain. Again with the non-compliance. There was no glove compartment anyway, just a jumble of metal, plastic, glass, and deflated airbag.

My phone. Where was that? I turned my head; my neck protested. The passenger seat was a mess of twisted metal and leather with bits of door, deflated airbag, and I think part of another car. Several bouts of confusion followed. Why did my arm hurt? What could've hit my arm? I was driving, my hands were on the wheel. No, my left hand was on the wheel, my right was resting on the console between the seats. When I looked for the console I understood why my arm hurt and why I couldn't move much. It was under shit, somewhere. Everything was shoved against me and the driver's seat. Thank fuck I was in an SUV. There'd be nothing left of a smaller car.

My eyelids battled to stay open, my right eye unable to cooperate at all. There was nothing to look at but a broken, confusing scene. Sirens wailed beyond the wreck. I heard people talking; no, yelling. I wanted to flash my badge and tell them to take a step back and breathe. Everything slipped sideways. I felt it. Everything moved at least ten feet. Not a good time to start thinking about time slips and parallel universes or binge-watching *Fringe*. But how handy would it be to go back in time an hour and change the outcome?

I rested my eyes. Apart from blurry vision, a sore arm, crick in my neck, and maybe a cut lip, I was okay.

"Iverson! Hey! Open your eyes!"

Kurt's voice filled my head. He felt close. Opening my eyes was problematic. They were tired.

"Iverson. Can you hear me?"

That was a different tone. Fear linked his words. My left eye opened. Progress. "I'm okay."

Kurt smiled. The door opene and he leaned into the car. "Sure you are. Can you open both eyes?"

My right eye wasn't playing. I touched it with my left hand. Felt odd. Gappy. What the fuck? I looked at my fingers. Blood.

"I'm not sure there is an eye there," I said, without realizing what the words were that came from my mouth. "Where the fuck would it go?" Oh, shit! "Is it sitting on my cheek? Is that what I can feel? Is that why my vision is blurry because my fucking eye fell out?"

Cool hands cupped my face. "Iverson, it's okay. It's not on your cheek."

"I lost it?" Who the fuck loses an eyeball? Are they actually balls that can roll away? I don't think so.

"Hey, your eye is where it belongs. You have a gash down your eyebrow. Your eye is swollen shut. It's the gash you felt." His eyes probed my one functioning eye. "You're okay."

"I have an eye?"

"Yes."

"I can't see out of it."

"It's full of blood from the gash and swollen. You're going to have an impressive black eye."

The seat belt released. Instead of trying to move, I waited for instructions. No way for me to tell what was trapped and what wasn't. And the eye thing freaked me out a bit.

Kurt helped me out of the wreck. Then he climbed into the car and found my phone and my bag. He guided me to a waiting ambulance. From there, I looked at the wreckage. Holyshitballs it was a mess. I was lucky to be alive. I was lucky I didn't have the girls or Argo in the car. A jittery feeling grew until my innards were shivering. Someone wrapped a blanket around my shoulders. The arm that did it stayed. Kurt.

"What hit me?" Part of a vehicle hung out of my car.

"You were T-boned by a driverless car."

"I thought they were safe?"

"Not this one," he replied.

Guess that's why I didn't hear injured people sounds from that heap of twisted metal. I just thought the driver was dead.

Someone placed a big white piece of gauze on my eyebrow. So my eye did kinda work.

"Let's have a look at that arm," Kurt said, moving the blanket out of his way. My muscles tightened. Ready. He didn't touch my arm, instead he turned his head and spoke to a paramedic. "We need to splint this arm."

"I can handle that for you, Doctor Henderson."

"Thanks." He looked at me. "Let's get some pain relief onboard."

"You don't have to get carried away," I said.

The paramedic spoke, "Ketamine?"

"No. Give me morphine."

Kurt laughed. "You heard her. Morphine. Then splint and transport."

Dane ran up to the back of the ambulance. "El! You okay?"

"Been better."

"Eye patch is a good look."

"Aargh, me hearty. That it be." A sharp prick in my

left arm surprised me. "Dammit I don't need a line, just hit me with the morphine and let's get on with it."

Dane grinned at me. "I feel sorry for them already." He thumbed toward the wreckage on the road. "Lee and I will process the crash scene. We still going to Louden?"

"Hell, yes." Cool liquid flowed into my veins. "I'll get this mess taken care of and then we'll go on over."

"Don't think there's much of a rush. They're not going to be any less dead."

True.

Chapter Forty

Because The Night

I stepped out of the ambulance using all the reserves I had to prevent my legs from buckling and dropping my ass on the ground. Mitch stood in the ambulance bay, hands in his pockets, a frown etched into his brow. He walked toward me, slow deliberate steps. His energy swung from concern to relief and back.

"Hey," I said.

He stopped in front of me. "Hey, back." His mind roamed mine, searching for a crack and a way in. "Can I hug you?"

"Yeah, watch the arm." Securely splinted and in a sling, tucked safely under the blanket that hung from my shoulders.

Mitch angled his body to hug me and wrapped one arm around me, not both. I breathed in his scent.

Kurt spoke to the paramedics. I wasn't listening, I knew the drill. They'd walk me in, hand over to Kurt in the Emergency Department, and be on their way. Kurt would stay with me and take over care. It's how Delta A worked. I also knew an orthopedic specialist would be on standby for my busted arm. And Leon Kapowski would be on hand to do a neuro exam. Because my skull likes to fuck me over at every given opportunity. All up, I could kiss the rest of the day goodbye and I really wanted to get over to Louden and check out the premises belonging to Arianda.

"On the bed, Iverson," Kurt said.

I looked around with the one good eye. I'm not in Kansas anymore. No, idiot, you're not in the ambulance bay anymore.

"What's the smile about?" Kurt said, while washing his hands.

"Nothing. Morphine maybe."

Mitch lowered the bed so I could sit on it. At least he was thinking. "Tired?" he asked, moving pillows. "Put your legs up. May as well get a nap in, we'll be here a while."

Not even up to arguing. Not a single murmur of annoyance. A gentle blanket of warmth crept slowly through my veins. Ketamine. My last thought hung on a bridge above a stream for what seemed like hours, words sparkling in the air. Fuck you Kurt.

Water babbled under the bridge. I checked for trolls. No sign of any. Paper floated just under the surface of the river. Images formed on the paper. I leaned over the rail to get a better look. A crack then a crunch, and the rail gave way. Tumbling through the air, head over heels. Sudden cold hit me. Gasping for air, I struggled to the surface, spitting out water. Sodden photos floated nearby. I grabbed at them but they evaporated. Evaporation. Nice idea. Rolling over, I leaned into the water until I floated on my back. My eyes closed as the water carried me downstream, bobbing amidst photographs of the missing and the lost. It would be so easy to slip under and drift away.

A car slammed into the water, sending a wave crashing over me. I surfaced, struggling for air. Before real thought kicked in, I dove down to the car, searching for the driver. No driver. No passengers. No steering wheel. Autonomous. Really?

My good eye opened. No water. No car. Hospital. "Henderson?"

"Right here," Kurt replied from nearby.

"Was it driverless or autonomous?"

There was silence for a beat. "Autonomous. Our forensic cyber techs are working on finding the cause of the crash."

"Am I okay?"

"Yes." He moved closer. His hand touched my wrist. A smile filled his words. "I learned a long time ago that it takes more than a broken arm and head laceration to keep you down. You're going to be fine."

My heavy eyelid closed.

Chapter Forty One

I hope you find it

Arianda Enterprise wasn't housed in a single building. It was a complex. At eight in the morning, the front gates stood wide open, with no one to prevent entry. Lee drove through the gates. Dead ahead, we saw a large building with a striped canvas awning over the entrance. On either side, two nondescript buildings. In front of the building sporting the awning, were parking spaces. Yellow letters painted on the asphalt read *Visitor Parking*.

"That's us," Lee said, parking his car. He looked over his shoulder at Argo. "Ready boy?"

The dog whined softly.

My phone rang. "Wait, Argo." With some effort I wriggled it free of my pocket and answered, "Henderson?"

"Iverson, the autonomous vehicle was hacked. Techs found a fun little piece of additional software hidden inside the computer system."

"Hacked. And they said these cars would be safer than human-driven vehicles."

"Techs think the car was controlled by someone. That someone would need to see the car and you."

"And me." Fuckadoodledo. "Did they hack into the city surveillance cameras or use drones?"

Pages turned. I imagined Kurt's grim expression as he leafed through the tech's report.

"Their money is on drones."

"And the car is owned by?"

"Christatech."

"That's a Virginian company. I recognize the name." Why? Electrical impulses zapped. A technology expo a couple of years back. That's where I'd seen the name. I went with Mitch because his company had a booth there. Bits and pieces assembled to provide a clearer picture. Christatech was a small new company, more involved with software development than manufacturing hardware, whereas Iverson Technologies did both and held military contracts. "Christatech was developing software a couple of years ago. Guess they've moved right along."

"You want to know who owns the company."

"Yes. I do."

"Christina Palacio."

"Ain't that just peachy."

"Thought you'd like it. Alert and safe."

"Alert and safe." I touched the end call icon. Lee and I stared at each other. "Did you hear it all?"

"Yep. Did she hack her own car and drive it into you, or did she hire someone to do her dirty work?"

"Let's go find out, shall we?"

Lee grinned. "Looking forward to it."

"No leash, Lee." I wanted Argo free to move, and I was one-handed. I reached across myself to open my door. My fingers fumbled the door handle twice, then the door swung open and Lee stood there grinning at me. Argo wagged his tail.

"Thanks." I turned around, swinging my legs out of

the car to stand. One of the reason's I like SUVs is the height of the seats.

"You're welcome."

"Let's go see if anyone's at work this morning. Argo, heel," I said. The dog turned around and placed his shoulder gently against my right leg. I tried to move my hand to check my weapon. Nothing happened. My heart skipped a beat. It's on the other side. I lifted my Glock from the holster, hooked my back sights into the top of my gun belt, racked the slide, and slid the Glock back into my holster. "You'll be pleased to know I've been working on my left-hand draw."

"That statement right there fills me with confidence," Lee replied with a smile. "I'm liking the one-handed rack." His eyes roamed the area. "This is a lab, isn't it? White coats and experiments?"

I wanted to nod, but my neck had other ideas. Like no.

"It's a lab, or at least that's what all the company documentation says." I stared at the collection of buildings. No vibes. No tortured souls rattling chains. So far so good.

Lee opened the door. I expected a buzzer or bell. Neither happened. The carpeted reception area swallowed our footsteps as we approached an unmanned desk. I poked around for a bell or intercom, something that would summon the genie from the interior of the building and provide a starting point. Zero communication devices. Not even a camera on the walls. Argo stuck close.

"Either they don't care who comes in, or no one comes," Lee said. "A place that gets no visitors?"

"Someone drops cadavers at this address," I reminded him.

"Maybe truck drivers use a different entrance."

I couldn't imagine a truckload of corpses unloaded and hauled through a reception area. "So what is the purpose of this," I said sweeping my left arm around the room. "And what's behind doors number one and two?"

"They're big doors," Lee commented.

A stack of printer paper on the desk caught my eye. The top sheet was white but skewed, with a picture on the next sheet. I flicked the top piece of paper and it slid off the stack revealing a snow globe and the words, *Arbitrary still life: the disjunction of fear* from award-winning photographic journalist, Shelly Morton.

The world tilted and then straightened. Nausea bubbled up. I blew air out my mouth and breathed in through my nose. Twice. Fingers fumbled for my phone. Another deep breath in through my nose.

"Ellie?" Lee touched my shoulder. "What's wrong?"

"One sec."

I pressed two numbers and waited. Kurt answered before the fourth ring.

"You okay?"

"Nope."

"Talk to me."

I snapped a photo of the poster on the desk and sent it to him. "We're at Arianda now, this is on the reception desk. A big stack of those posters."

"Morton is hired by them … perhaps they're helping distribute posters."

"Or …"

"She didn't mention she wanted Mikki in a snow globe, did she?"

"Not to my recollection."

"And if anyone would recollect that, you would."

"Find Morton."

"I'll take Dane. You and Lee be careful."

"We're fine."

"No, Iverson. You're fresh from a car wreck and he was stabbed last week. You shouldn't even be teamed together." He stalled. "One day you'll stun me by listening to my advice."

"We're fine. We've got Argo." I hung up and shoved my phone in my back pocket.

"What's going on?" Lee asked. He leaned on the wall by the mysterious double doors.

"The poster. It's advertising the new exhibition by Shelly Morton. She's worked for Arianda over the last few years taking photographs, and she wanted to put Mikki Falacco in the exhibition."

"In a fucking snow globe?" His voice dropped to a harsh whisper.

"She didn't mention that part to us."

"Is she someone of interest in Operation Disney?"

"Damn straight she is."

"Wanna see what's behind doors one and two?"

"Yeah, let's do it. We've hung around in here long enough and no one's found us. Perhaps they're behind the doors."

Lee pressed the lever handle down and pushed open one door. He held it for me. Once Argo and I stepped through, he moved up beside us and let the door close. We stood side by side, letting our eyes, or in my case eye, become accustomed to the low light. Floor lights ran under heavy drapes. The whole thing reminded me of a theater. Along the back wall near us were long plush seats and wall-mounted lights spaced about six feet apart on the wall. A warm light emanated from the bulbs and cast soft pools on the carpeted floor.

"What is this?" Lee muttered.

"I don't know." Doom laced with sinister feelings flowed over me. "I don't think it's anything good."

"Neither do I."

"What's through the curtains?"

Lee strode over, he checked the lighting on the floor and chose a likely place to part the curtains. I followed him through. There we stood dumbfounded. The whole time I thought Operation Disney was something to do with snow globes, I never let myself dwell on what that meant. And here it was. Right in front of me.

"Inconceivable," he murmured.

"Yep, except someone not only conceived this idea but acted upon it."

I counted four rows and thought there could be more. Four rows. Giant snow globes. Holy fuck balls, batman. The things were huge.

Holy bat shit this is insanity. I walked over to the nearest display that faced into the wide aisle on the left. The base. Round and smooth and about three feet high, looked wooden. I tapped on the globe part. Not glass. Perspex possibly. Not inflatable then. That just put the cost up.

Carefully, I circled the display and the wooden base, doing my best not to read the plaque or acknowledge the contents. Flatter on the back, the globes were more domed at the front, so not a sphere. I tried to gauge the size using Lee as a reference and adding the base. I figured the dome was about eight feet high at the highest point, on an almost three feet high base. The width was just under eight feet at its widest and five at its deepest. I couldn't see in from the back of the monstrosity because of the backdrop.

"What the actual fuck am I looking at?" Lee whispered while squinting at the contents of the giant snow globe display case.

I swallowed before speaking, and forced bile back to my gut. We gazed at an environment best suited to centipedes and slugs. Wet dirt, decomposing leaf matter, rocks, and a woman crouched, looking at something. I peered closer. She was looking at a centipede. The more I looked, the more bugs I saw. None of them moved. Sitting on a rock behind the woman were two small girls. Beside them holding a slug in his hand was a man. One of our missing families was a biologist named Christine Brown. Her specialist field was Cryptozoa. I read the plaque and confirmed my suspicions.

"The Brown family. She was the biologist. Look at the date."

"Twenty-fourteen."

At least they had skin and clothing. And hair. Unlike the *Body World* exhibits. The inhabitants of the display were eerily lifelike. Reminding me of figures I'd seen created by Weta Workshop in an amazing Gallipoli display on our last trip to New Zealand.

"How do you think they do the hair?" I said. "I don't imagine hair does well during the plastination process. If indeed that's what happened and we're not in a new version of Madam Tussaud's Wax Museum."

"I'm inclined to go with you on the plastination stuff, Ellie."

Yeah, me too. "The hair is amazing. Wonder if it's theirs, and how would they do that?"

"Shave it off and turn it into wigs?"

Yeah, maybe. "Or scalp them and preserve the scalp with hair intact."

"Wouldn't there be shrinkage as the scalp dried. Be hard to put it back on and have it look right." He walked around the side of the globe. "They almost look as if they're made of wax. Maybe they get wigs made like you would for a wax figure."

I liked that idea better than the scalping scenario. "Incredibly real, aren't they?"

He nodded. "There is real skill involved here with the makeup realism. Even more than you see in a funeral home, and those technicians are highly skilled."

I snapped a photo with my phone; Shelly Morton was right, it's not easy photographing the contents of a reflective globe. Then I called Sandra.

"How can I serve, O Finder of the Lost?"

"The photo I sent you. Take it to Caine. We need a warrant. It'd be a bit too easy for someone to say these are wax figures that just happen to look like and have the same names as one of our missing families. I want warrants now. We need to turn this place upside down and inside out."

"I'm on it, Boss. Also sending back-up to your location."

"Thanks. Where's that truck?"

"Staties and FBI should stop it in about half an hour."

"Keep me posted." I hung up and looked around for Lee. He was further down the row. I caught up, trying not to look at the scenes in the globes I passed. The hink factor was off all known scales.

"I've found the Johnson family from Kansas. Wonder what the winter-themed dance is about."

Barren trees wound with LED ropes. A family in formal wear, standing on a glitter-covered mirrored floor. Father and daughter in the middle, with mom and the young son off to one side, watching the father and daughter. The little girl stood on her father's feet, as if they were dancing. Deep in my gut, a tug turned into a memory. I danced with my father like that, only he wore dress whites and a sword. Memories of a Navy ball twirled around me in time with the music from a string quartet.

"What's with the button next to the plaque?" I raised an eyebrow.

Lee shrugged and pushed it. Glitter swirled around the globe, the middle of the floor turned. It reminded me of my mother's music box. Twenty or so seconds later the swirling glitter fell and the dancers returned to their places, facing forward, frozen in time.

"Don't push any more buttons," I said. "This macabre place is giving me the willies."

And that's saying something; I've been to an art gallery where all the exhibits were painted with human blood. Human snow globes were in it to win it. I inspected the dome with care and saw a thin line and see-through clip closures on the bottom near the base of both sides. "Lee, look up for me and check for clips or fasteners of some sort. I think the dome things come apart."

He circled the structure. "They do, there are clear closures near the top of the dome."

We walked in silence down the rest of the row then up another. Halfway along, I stopped. Stylized Bitcoin hung inside the globe above the family who were all on laptops. I didn't need to read the plaque to know I was looking at Constance and Daniel Ash and their two children, fourteen-year-old Eli and twelve-year-old Madison. Constance was a developer for a cryptocurrency company. A movement caught my eye. A laptop screen flickered. They were working?

"Lee."

"I saw it." He moved closer, cupped his hands on the dome and pressed his face to his hands. "They're all working." He stepped back. "They're mining bitcoin."

"There are cooling pads under those laptops, power cords are plugged in." I walked behind the structure and found a power outlet on the floor with a cord from the globe plugged into it. "This has to be drawing a lot of power. Four computers mining non-stop."

"How do they get in to fix anything that breaks?" Lee walked around the globe tapping on the Perspex. "Surely they don't have to open this dome, dismantle the entire thing?"

"The base." I leaned down, knowing that if I crouched, I wouldn't be getting up without help. One armed, one eyed, and achy as fuck. "Look, is that an access panel?" I pointed at an area near the cord.

"Screwed shut," Lee said, crouching next to me. "Don't think I'd fit inside that." He stood and looked into the globe. "There's another access cover in the floor behind the man, Daniel?"

"Yeah, Daniel."

The bases of the globes were at least two and half

feet high but they weren't sitting on the floor so appeared higher.

"These are all high, like, too high for people to fully view the displays." He smiled. "Not everyone is six feet six."

Then maybe this is a storage facility. A very attractively laid out storage facility.

"How big a gap is underneath the globe?"

He knelt on one knee and used his phone to determine the gap. "Six inches."

"They must be sitting on something."

"If they wanted to move these things they'd need a gap for lifting."

"Good point. Even if they can somehow pull those bases apart and dismantle everything, they'd still need to get in there to pick the base up."

We continued walking up and down rows of globes lit by underfloor lighting and strategically placed spotlights. It felt like a museum. The carpeting on the floor stole our footsteps, rendering our movement silent. Rows of death domes and families posed forever. Each unique and fucked up.

"How many do you think there are?"

"I counted ten in a row, I think there are four rows, but I'm becoming disorientated."

"Jesus."

"Yeah." I paused at an exhibit; this one had more people than the others. "I found the Abbot family."

They really were a museum piece. The death of

Andrea Green and her brother wiped their line out. Extinction.

A door closed. I spun around.

"We're not alone," Lee said, drawing his weapon.

My eye darted left then right. Another noise. Scraping. Heavy sounding. It came from our left. The light in the room changed. Filtered daylight spread across the side of the enormous room. I pointed with my left hand. Lee nodded. I drew my weapon. We moved toward the new light and the origin of the noise. An engine started, the vibration thrumming through the floor. Using the exhibits as cover, we edged closer to the light and the noise.

Lee whispered, "Forklift."

"Are they bringing in one of these exhibits or taking one out?" I wondered aloud.

From our position, I saw a large brown object moving. It appeared to float high in the air in the middle of the enormous doorway. That account for the scraping noise. Big doors pulled open. The half-round brown object hovered in place. A woman wearing a hard hat slipped past and gave directions. I scanned the object. Looked like half a base. So that's how they moved them, in pieces. I was right. They came apart completely.

"Take this to row five, bay nine. We're assembling the new exhibit later today."

"Row five, bay nine," the operator repeated over the sound of the engine.

There was another short exchange of words.

I touched Lee's arm. "Let's go."

He smiled. Instead of our usual palm slide and finger grip, he tapped the edge of his hand on my left wrist. "Alert and Safe."

I moved right. Lee went left.

Covering twenty feet, I emerged from between two displays and in front of the woman and the forklift.

"FBI. Hands where I can see them." Look at me being all authoritative with one arm in a sling. The woman's eyes slid to my arm and back to my face then my weapon.

Her jaw dropped and expression spun through surprise, confusion, fear and back to surprise. Slowly her hands rose, elbows out, palms up. Lee secured the forklift operator.

"What's this about?" The woman asked, her voice shaky.

"Multiple murders," I said, keeping my voice low. "Who else is here?"

She shook her head. "No one."

I found that hard to believe. "Are you the owner of this enterprise?"

"Yes."

"What's your name?"

"Christina Palacio."

We have a winner. "Any relation to Niles Palacio?" As much as I wanted to holster my Glock, I didn't.

"He was my husband."

And Shelly Morton toured with him and based an entire exhibit around that tour and his death. Her posters sit in a stack at the front desk of this weird-assed storage facility. And now we have a freak show in snow globes. I was done with playing connect the dots.

The human race is fucked.

"What is your involvement with Christatech?"

She blinked slowly. Her lips curled into a small smile. "That's one of my companies."

"Aren't you entrepreneurial," I muttered.

"What happened to your arm and face?" Palacio's cold smile remained.

"One of your autonomous vehicles happened," I said. "Wasn't terribly clever to make an attempt on my life using one of your cars."

The smile disappeared.

Lee encouraged the forklift operator to join Mrs. Palacio.

"Your name?" I said, using a pointed stare to encourage speech.

"Paul." His eyes dropped to his feet.

"Paul what?"

"Crestley."

Somewhere beyond the forklift and its cargo, a door shut with a bang. I looked at Christina Palacio. "Seems someone else is here."

She shook her head. "Just us."

Liar.

"What's back there?" Lee asked.

"Workrooms," Paul answered. "Storage."

"One of those workrooms a laboratory?"

Crestley nodded. "I don't go in there."

Palacio's head swiveled to Paul. She openly glared at him. If she wanted my attention, she had it. "Who else is here?"

"No one."

"And yet a door closed ... and I don't feel you're being truthful."

"There's no one."

Still lying like a rug. "So when SWAT move in, in about two minutes, they won't find anyone?"

She shook her head, her eyes on the ground.

"Best be very sure ... they don't like surprises."

She swallowed hard and focused her gaze on me. "My daughter."

"Better if you tell the truth the first time," I said with a cold stare. "Who else?"

"I'm not sure."

"Try again. Surprises get people killed."

"A couple of technicians and a makeup artist."

There had to be more people. Lee spoke into his phone – running booted feet followed his directions. I spoke to Siri and asked her to place a call to Kurt.

"Pick up Shelly Morton. We confirmed the owner of Arianda is Christina Palacio. Shelly Morton is a person of interest."

"I'm there now."

Siri ended the call and I turned to Palacio; her

expression remained impassive. "So is your husband in one of these globes?"

She stiffened. Was that a yes? "Where will I find him?"

Inquisitiveness got the better of me. I wanted to know if he was sitting on a sofa in a replica of their living room, but really I did not. I love my husband but no way in hell would I consider keeping his body around for eternity; it turns out everyone isn't me.

"Not here," she squawked.

Details of his most famous joke came back to me. Perhaps he was sitting on the sofa in her living room? Just chilling, scaring guests.

"Siri call Sandra."

"Calling Sandra now, Agent."

"Hey, I need you to add to the warrant. Include Mrs. Christina Palacio's residence and all business properties."

"And you're looking for?"

I made eye contact with Lee before walking out of earshot. "Anything related to the murders and plastination for at least forty families from across the country. We need to seize computers and electronic devices, including phones. Locate any properties out of state and secure warrants for them too."

"Do you have a suspect in custody?"

"Not yet. Detained for questioning. Have the DA meet us when we come back in. This is huge, Sandra."

"Writing the warrant amendments now. Have used

previous warrants as reference."

"Thank you. Also, media blackout until we can notify all next of kin."

"Got it."

The call ended and I rejoined Lee. Voices came from beyond the large doorway. I holstered my weapon and released the handcuffs from the pouch on my belt. This was likely to be tricky. I poked the cuffs just inside my sling, grabbed Christina by the left wrist, and pulled it behind her.

"Don't move," I said. Letting her wrist go and grabbing the cuffs. I snapped one on then asked for her other arm. She resisted. "You're wasting time," I growled. "Arm!"

Reluctantly she put her hand behind her back and I snapped the cuff on.

"Am I under arrest?" she asked, as I turned her around to face me.

Nope, I just like torturing myself putting cuffs on innocent people, one-handed. "You have the right to remain silent. Anything you say can be used against you in court. You have the right to talk to a lawyer for advice before we ask you any questions. You have the right to have a lawyer with you during questioning. If you cannot afford a lawyer, one will be appointed for you before any questioning if you wish. If you decide to answer questions now without a lawyer present, you have the right to stop answering at any time."

"What am I being charged with?"

I hauled in the exact part of the Virginia Code that I required. "Code of Virginia Eighteen point two dash three-two-three point zero-two, prohibition against concealment of a dead body, eight counts. Other charges pending." I leaned close to her ear. "I advise you to get a good lawyer because even without murder charges you're looking at, at least forty years in prison." I straightened up and smiled. "Something else to consider. First-degree attempted murder. I'm a federal agent, we're in Virginia, that's a minimum of ten years. I don't have to push much for the District Attorney to put the death penalty on the table." My smile remained steady. "You can expect more charges as we continue."

Dane's voice rang out. "FBI, coming in."

He appeared beside the forklift in the doorway. "You want me to lower this thing?"

"It is part of the base of an exhibit," Palacio said with a bristle.

"You can operate a forklift?" Lee said; a hint of surprise registered in his voice.

"Yep. Used to move stock around my father's warehouse when I was a teenager. Could you all move back about six feet please?"

We moved.

Dane climbed into the cab, started the engine and carefully lowered the base to the ground, and jumped out with a smile on his face. His eyes roamed over my shoulder. The smile faded as he came face-to-face with the reality of the grim warehouse contents. His eyes met mine.

"We have Sophie Palacio in custody and two lab techs." He glanced at his notebook. "There are four people unaccounted for. I've sent units to their addresses."

"Did you find the office?"

"Sure did."

This was a big operation and expensive. I wondered for a moment about funding. Taking photos in blow-up snow globes didn't seem like a multi-million-dollar business. But maybe it was? I had a feeling there was more to it.

"Is this a private exhibit?" I asked Christina Palacio. She blinked. Her lips remained clamped together. "Do you make these to order?"

She remained stony, mouth a tight thin line.

"Lee, I'm going for a walk," I said.

"Take Dane, I'm fine here." He ordered the woman and forklift operator to sit on the ground.

"Okay."

Dane fell into step beside me. I'd noticed numbers on some of the exhibits and wanted to see if any were missing.

"Are these in any sort of order?" Dane asked.

"I guess so, otherwise it'd make tracking inventory harder than it has to be."

I felt his eyes on me. He mentally repeated the word 'inventory.'

"Let's start from this end," I said, pointing to the

door Lee and I entered. We'd walked through a foyer, so that made that end feel like the beginning or the front.

"I'll start over there," Dane said and pointed to the farthest row with a head tilt.

"If you see a light switch ..."

"Yeah, I'll flick it. This soft lighting is creepy as fuck."

He wasn't wrong. The first stand I came to had a four at the bottom of the plaque.

I called out to Dane, "Hey, have you got a one?"

"Nope. It starts with ten over here."

I moved toward Dane. An exhibit grabbed my eyes. A farm yard scene. Two little girls scattering chicken feed. Chickens peeking the ground. Chickens and kids. No adults. It was the first one I'd seen without adults. I spun around. Directly across from the chickens and kids I saw an exhibit containing two adults sitting on a porch with mugs of coffee watching something in the mid-distance. A creepy set. Shaking off the double whammy, I concentrated on the numbers starting with the chicken dome. The numbers went four, five, six, ten. The next row coming back started with eleven then jumped to fourteen. Dane pointed out one with a small pond. The detail was incredible. Dragonflies hovered above the pond. I expected to see them whiz past but they didn't. A boy in a checked shirt sat on a rock and beside him, kneeling, a man in the same patterned shirt. There was no denying the incredible skill that went into producing each of the strange, creepy, snapshots of life. We walked up and down several rows then rejoined Lee in silence.

I stepped into Christina Palacio's space and looked down at her.

"Where are numbers one, two, three, seven, eight, nine, twelve, and thirteen?" A lot more than that were missing but I had to start somewhere.

She dropped her gaze to the floor.

The forklift operator spoke. "Twelve and thirteen shipped out last week. I loaded them onto the truck."

"How are they shipped?"

"Wooden crates with packing pellets."

"How many crates per exhibit, approximately?"

"Each figure is moved in its own crate, then the interior display, the dome halves, and the base pieces." His lips moved as he counted. "Twelve crates maybe, it varies for each display."

Christina flashed her eyes at him. He ignored her.

"Where did they go?"

"I don't know. I just load the crates onto the trucks when I'm told to."

Already he was distancing himself from the situation. Bit late. "What do you know?"

He brought his eyes up to mine. "I know they're popular. It's the fourth time I've loaded those particular exhibits."

There must be a few people whose job it is to take down and reinstall the displays.

Christina looked at me, her lips moved, then stopped. Guess she changed her mind about speaking. Can't say I blamed her. She was neck-deep in shit.

"Who takes the displays apart?"

He shook his head. "I just move the boxes."

I turned to Dane. "The daughter ... take me to her."

Christina flinched.

Chapter Forty Two
The Chronicles Of Life And Death

The daughter, Sophie, sat on a desk chair in the middle of an office. Her hands cuffed behind her back. A Delta Agent stood just inside the door. I took in the overall image of Sophie. Cropped bright purple and teal hair. Piercings in her eyebrow and lip, multiple ear piercings with a mixture of studs and hoops on display. She wore a black fitted long-sleeved top, short red plaid skirt, fishnet tights, and knee-high Doc Martens.

I acknowledged the agent first. "Agent Hanson, any problems?"

"No, ma'am. Quiet as a mouse."

The photographs of Sophie's mouse collection flooded my mind. I didn't want to see anything in a snow globe ever again. "Has she been Mirandized?"

"Yes, ma'am."

I crossed the floor to the young woman with Argo. "Sophie Palacio?"

"Yes," she looked up at me. Brown eyes glistening with unshed tears.

"I am Special Agent in Charge Ellie Iverson. Do you understand your rights?"

She nodded.

"How old are you?"

"Twenty."

Good, no need for a chaperone or parent. "Are willing to speak to me?"

She nodded again. So far so good.

"Can you use words, please?"

"Yes. I am willing to talk to you without a lawyer present."

"Thank you."

Dane rolled a chair across the room. Less intimidating than having someone stand over her. Argo sat next to me and waited. "When the globes are shipped out, where do they go?"

She swallowed. "Different places."

"Do you know how the exhibits are made?"

"Yes. It's similar to the Body Works exhibition. Plastination."

"Where do the people come from that are plastinated?"

"They're donated bodies," she said without hesitation.

"They are?"

She nodded. "We get them sent from all over the country."

"The exhibits have family names on them, and they look like family groups, how is that possible if the bodies are donated."

She frowned at the question. "They're not really families. Mom, Doctor Palacio, she makes the families for the exhibits."

"So, it's a coincidence that the families we know are missing are represented in those exhibits?"

"Pardon?" Her brow knitted. "I don't understand the question."

I left it. She could think on that later, she'd have plenty of time. "When did this all start?"

"After my dad passed."

"Where is he?"

"He's in the cemetery," she said. "That's where most dead people end up."

But he didn't. I was sure of that. "You're positive your father was buried?"

She nodded. "Why would you even ask that?" A spark flew across her eyes, leaving a bright trail. "Oh, is this because he used to tell his audience he wanted to be stuffed and seated on our sofa?" She shook her head. "He was joking. How creepy would that be?"

Dane and I exchanged glances. Because that's the creepiest thing we've heard of all day? Try again. "Can we talk about your animal collection?"

"Sure, what about it?"

"Why?" That's all I wanted to know.

"Mom made them for me. Dad used to buy me snow globes when he traveled and then one day, mom made one with a mouse sitting in a chair, and it was so cute."

"How'd she make the mouse? I've seen your website and they're super lifelike."

Awes filled her voice, "She's really amazing at sculpting wax, isn't she?"

"They're wax? All of them?"

She shook her head. "Some are real animals that she

found at a taxidermist's."

"She certainly goes to a lot of trouble with her creations." I smiled, trying for friendly. "She must love you very much."

She gave a half a smile.

"Dane, can you take the cuffs off Sophie, please."

He did as I asked. She dropped her hands in her lap and rubbed each wrist in turn.

"Do you like dogs?"

"Yes."

"Would you like to have Argo here sit with you?"

She smiled. "Is he allowed to do that, he's not going to bite me?"

"He's not going to bite you as long as you don't try to hurt me."

"That's fair."

Argo's tail brushed the carpet as it wagged. "Go on, boy." He stood and gave a small shake. A second later, his head was on Sophie's thigh, waiting for attention. I let them get acquainted before I began more questions. She stroked his head and ears.

"I have some plastination questions. How long do the bodies take until they're ready for exhibiting?"

"About a year for each body. We have six laboratories, so we can handle quite a big load."

Six. Crap on a fucking cracker. "Are they all in Virginia?"

She shook her head while fondling Argo's ear. "Only two are in Virginia. We have this one and one in Richmond."

"And the others?"

"I know there is one in Colorado, one in Missouri, and I think Utah, and Nebraska."

Dane walked away. I heard him making a call before he left the room.

"I have a question about the snow globe photography. Arianda Enterprise hires out snow globes and a photographer for functions and balls and so forth, and they also have studios and book clients for photos, yes?"

She nodded. "That's correct."

"Is there one particular person who is on every team that takes the photos?"

I wanted our puzzle lover. I wanted whomever that was, bad.

And Morton's work.

"We have two photographers. Shelly Morton and Rochelle Coombes. They both have their own businesses and contract to us."

"Is there anyone else who would be at every photographic session involving the snow globes?"

Her eyes moved as she thought, then came back to me. Her head nodded up and down. "The production manager. She oversees the bookings, the globe interior's used in each shoot, and coordinates the travel and crews and everything."

"What's her name?"

"Alana Forrester."

Alana. Alana. Green. No. Simon Kreg, he had a friend called Alana. "Where can I find Alana?"

"She was here today. She's here somewhere. Mom had a meeting with her about an hour ago."

I shifted to Dane. "Did you round up Alana Forrester in the sweep?"

He checked his notebook. "No."

I looked at Agent Hanson. "Find her, Agent Hanson, turn this place inside out if you have to."

He nodded and left.

Turning my attention to Sophie and Argo again – he was doing a wonderful job of calming her – I said, "Do you know what the meeting was about?"

"Not really, but I know Alana was unhappy and she asked for the meeting."

"What makes you say that she was unhappy?"

A small smile flicked across her face. "Alana always has a complaint. She's wired like that, you know?"

"And you don't know what the meeting was about?"

"No."

"Did you see her afterward?"

"No."

"Is that unusual?"

"Not really. She could've gone out the other door. Mom's office has two doors. Sometimes Alana goes straight out into the courtyard and not back through the building."

Okay. A prickle in my gut sprouted into a thorn. "Where is Alana's office?"

"Back down the hall you came in." She paused, "Third door on the left."

"Thank you, I'll be right back."

I motioned to Dane and he followed me to the door. In a whisper, I said, "Simon Kreg had a friend called Alana. Keep an eye on things here, I'll be a few minutes."

"Okay. Hang on. Glove."

Good thinking. The whole place was a crime scene. Dane took a glove from his pocket and pulled it onto my left hand for me. I walked down the hall until I came to the third door on the left. I turned the handle and pushed. The door opened without resistance.

A tidy desk faced the door. I noted the laptop was open. Brushing a finger across the trackpad brought the screen to life and revealed an open spreadsheet. I scrolled up the page to find the headings. A stock sheet. Locations of where all the globes were currently. I clicked on one missing from the main storage area. The globes were shipped to private collections. Some were permanent placements some were temporary; none of them ever installed in public places. There are a lot of disturbed people in the world with money.

I left the spreadsheet and opened her email, looking for a connection to Simon Kreg. Nothing. I opened her drawer. Two phones.

Who has two phones?

Someone with a work phone and a personal phone.

One wasn't locked and I checked the messages. All

work related. A lot of back and forth from Christina. But that was to be expected. Nothing about murdering families.

The second phone beckoned, locked with a pattern lock. I drew my finger tip in a 'Z' shape on the screen and smiled as the phone unlocked. I whispered, "You need to be smarter at security, Alana."

Her messages revealed many chatty correspondences with her friends and family. One in particular stood out. Shelly Morton. Imagine? I looked for her emergency contact information and up popped Shelly Morton again. They were married. Shelly had neglected to share that bit of information. I returned to the text messages and scrolled through the names of people Alana conversed with, and eventually found a Simon. When I opened the conversation, I scrolled through screeds of texts about movies and whatever until I found one that contained a phone number. Nothing else. I knew that number: the number that the crypto-texter used in my own phone.

She had the number. She gave the number to Simon. Where's the phone?

I scrabbled around in her drawer and found nothing. My attention turned to the cupboards in her office. In one, I found a backpack and a purse.

Would she leave without her purse? Doubtful. No matter how annoyed she was after her meeting. In the purse, I found her wallet, keys, personal items, no phone. The backpack. I put it on the floor and awkwardly tipped the contents, one-handed, onto the rug. Gym clothes and sneakers. A small zippered bag, which contained deodorant and moisturizer. A key lay on the rug. I picked it up. It looked like a locker key.

Did they have a gym here or did she go to one in town?

My hand delved into the many pockets in the backpack. No phone. Locker key in hand, I went back to Dane.

Sophie was still petting Argo, while Dane looked on.

"Sophie," I said.

She looked up. "Yes."

"Is there a gym on site?"

"There is, yes. If you go down the western hallway to the end, you'll find it."

"Thank you."

Dane nodded as I glanced at him and mentally threw words into my head. "Careful, El."

In the women's changing rooms, faced with twelve lockers I sighed and tried the key in each lock in turn until I felt a click and the door popped open. Inside was a folded pink towel and inside the towel I found a phone. There were no texts on the phone to me or my team, but plenty to and from a person named Simon.

Taking the phone, I hurried back to Alana's office and checked the laptop. She had three internet browsers. Chrome, FireFox, and Tor. Then I found TunnelBear, a secure VPN service. Alana was our mystery text message person?

Kinda made sense. Maybe she developed a conscience or didn't buy the line spun by her boss about how the bodies were donated because she'd seen the people first-hand, having their photos taken. Or maybe she was in on it from the beginning. Either way, I wanted to speak with Alana.

On my way back to Dane, I called the forensic team and told them Alana's computer and office needed close examination. I had the phone I'd liberated from the gym locker.

Dane met me at the door and found the thought about Alana and Shelly. His eyes locked onto mine. A short sentence hit my mind from his: That's interesting.

Dane cleared his throat and said quietly, "Want me to take the glove off for you?"

"Yes, please."

He pulled it down over my fingers, encasing the phone, and put it in his pocket.

With a light smile inserted in my voice and I spoke to Sophie. "Sophie, you all right?"

"Yes."

"Do you know Alana's wife?"

Bewilderment flew across her eyes and disappeared as a frown took over. "I don't think so."

Maybe it wasn't common knowledge. "Where can I find Rochelle Coombes?"

"I don't know. You'd have to check the bookings on Mom's computer."

"Thank you, I will." I watched her for a few seconds. She didn't appear worried or nervous. My next statement would change that. I watched carefully as I said, "I have arrested your mother for concealment of dead bodies. There are more charges pending."

The words hung between us on a thick rope. As Sophie processed the sentence, a noose formed and jerked the words high into the air.

Confusion and disbelief raged a battle across her face. Argo shuffled closer. "I don't understand. Who did Mom conceal? The bodies were donated, she didn't hide them!"

Dane heard her question and held his hands up to me from the doorway. He signed. Forty-four. Confirmed.

"Forty-four people that we know of."

A look of utter disbelief froze on her face. "What other charges?"

"We have a raft of charges coming to light, including trafficking in dead humans and homicide, and attempted murder of a federal agent."

Her mouth opened and closed. No words emerged.

My phone rang. I stood, removed it from my back pocket, and joined Dane near the door before answering the call.

"It's Claude. The bodies in the truck are plastinated and packed posed in wooden crates. We've done a photo identification and they match two missing families. We have located the Robinson family from Nebraska and the Geraldson family from Idaho."

"Hold the driver."

"We are. He said a lot of the pick-ups for Arianda are packed in wooden crates and require a forklift."

"Not all?"

"Sometimes they're packed in ice."

Crapadoodledo. "Make sure you get the addresses of the pick-up points from his logbook."

"Thank you."

I hung up.

Sophie's voice crumbled. "Why would my mom kill people?"

I spun around, crossed the room and sat on the chair in front of her again. "I don't know. That's a question you need to ask her."

Her breathing changed. Shallow, fast. "Why would she do that?"

"Hey, look at me. Slow your breathing down." Her eyes met mine. "Breathe in through your nose, and out through your mouth. Slow. With me." I took an inward breath then exhaled slowly. She followed suit. "Think about Argo and breathe." Her breathing calmed, I spoke again. "You're twenty, right?"

"Yes."

"Are you in college?"

She nodded. "English major."

"Breathe."

She nodded. Argo moved his head, rubbing his face on her thigh. "I just ... I can't ... why, why would she?"

"It's a lot to process. It's a lot for us to process and we're used to coming across bad situations."

"Can I see her?"

"No."

"When then?"

"In a few days." I tried to offer a reassuring smile, but the sheer extent of her mother's crimes threatened to overwhelm me. "We're going to take you in for questioning."

"Will you be questioning me?"

"No. It will be someone else."

A tear slipped over her lashes and rolled down her cheek. "Will Argo be there?"

"Yes."

Agent Hanson appeared in the doorway and motioned to me. I joined him. "Okay?"

"There's something you need to see."

I turned to Dane. "Back in a bit."

He nodded. Sophie's attention remained on Argo.

I followed Hanson from the room. He paused, allowing me to fall into step beside him. "We're going to the CEO's office suite," he said as we walked.

Hanson turned down a corridor, the opposite way from the gym and walked another few yards before pointing out a door.

"This is us," he said, his mouth set in a grim line.

He swung the door open. Two of our forensic techs were inside. They acknowledged us with quick smiles and continued bagging items as evidence.

"This way," Hanson said opening another door. It led to a bathroom, the walls tiled in a zigzag pattern with two-inch black and white tiles. A large mirror hung over the vanity. To the left was a half-wall partition and the toilet. On the far right a glass encased shower. Hanson walked to the wall between the vanity and the shower. Fascinated I watched him reach over the edge of the vanity, press a tile, and shove the wall with his latex gloves. A panel opened to a room beyond.

"Come on," Hanson said, stepping through the gap.

My heart pounded with trepidation. Enclosed spaces are not my favorite. Curiosity won. I stepped into the softly lit interior of a small room. I turned slowly on the spot and took it all in. A tiny living room complete with a comfortable sofa, floor lamps, a plush rug, two end tables, and the body of a man sitting on the sofa. A living room with nothing living in it.

I snapped a photo of the man for our records even though the techs would do the official evidential photography. He looked like Niles Palacio. "I think you've found the missing husband."

"Thought this person was important," Hanson said. "Someone went to a lot of trouble to set this up and keep him hidden."

"The wife is an unusual woman." On the end table nearest the plastinated body, was a coffee cup, complete with dregs. "Pretty sure he didn't drink this coffee." Time to leave.

"You think she spends much time in here with … with him?" Hanson crossed the threshold into the bathroom.

"I don't know. But I do know it's pretty damn impossible to move on if you don't let the dead go."

Silence swallowed our thoughts on the way back to Dane.

Chapter Forty Three
She's So Cold

I spun a pen on my desk until it spiraled off the edge and landed on the floor. From the drawer, I took another pen.

Same process.

Ten minutes later, there were no pens left in the drawer. They littered the floor in front of my desk.

I took the sling off my arm. It felt okay with the cast, even though it wasn't the final version. I had a couple of days before the bright yellow waterproof cast would go on. This one was plain white plaster. My fingers were coming back to life, meaning my arm wasn't entirely useless.

A yawn threatened to make my head a flip-top. Six a.m. starts are not my favorite especially when they start with a meeting. Caine and the new Director, Craig Jones, required briefing. It took two hours to give a comprehensive report on Operation Disney, Arianda Enterprise, and Christatech.

The second meeting followed ten minutes later with the Delta teams. After that, I spent an hour talking to police officers in a conference call. I briefed them on the case and received updates regarding their parts of the investigation. The cars were gone. Most officers suspected they were sold to chop shops and disappeared into the parts market. Never to be seen again.

We'd know more when we waded through all the company records.

We couldn't find Alana Forrester at the complex and her wife hadn't heard from her; I feared for her life. The forensic team found her. She was dead and shoved inside a freezer. I doubted Christine Palacio did that by herself. Probably destined for a snow globe display once the fuss died down.

Alana's text messages with Simon Kreg made interesting reading. His agitation grew visibly during the conversation threads. He suspected a covered up and that something had happened to the Abbot family. He and Alana appeared to have met in person several times since the Abbots' disappearance. The conversation jumped a fair bit, so provide a complete record of what he thought was happening or if Alana had confessed to him her part in any of it. Three days before Lee was stabbed, Simon sent a text to Alana saying he was going to the FBI. A few more text messages followed. It didn't look like she tried to stop him. There was no way of knowing if he knew she was sending us text messages.

Going to the FBI. Not going to stab a member of Delta A.

As much I hated it, I had to admit we might never know what flipped Simon Kreg's switch.

Morton was arrested. Coombes arrested. The snow globes Morton photographed for use in her latest art exhibit contained families. A lucky break for Mikki; she could've been one of them. It took almost a year to prep a body for display, so I couldn't imagine how Mikki would be in an exhibition due to open in a matter of weeks. It bothered me.

Palacio refused to speak.

Across the country, we made eighteen arrests in connection with the murder and subsequent plastination of missing families, and there were a lot more arrests pending. The media were in a frenzy. It would take months to return the dead to their families and for memorials and burials to get underway.

And still I didn't know the one thing I wanted to know. Why? Why turn people, families, and lives, into exhibits? If it were a case of wanting to exhibit slices of life, then a photograph would suffice or a series of photographs, or wax figures. Anything but murdering families in inflatable gas chambers and then plastinating them. It was the most horrific, expensive, and time-consuming option. It made the least sense. Since when did serial killers' minds make sense? I knew I had to let the need to know why and what drove Christina Palacio, go, at least until she started talking.

I circled back to the expense of the whole operation. The cost of the chemicals wasn't off-set by the truck hijackings because people were involved and people like to get paid. I took a pencil from my drawer and scribbled a dollar sign on my blotter with my left hand. Less than stellar. I leaned back in my chair and closed my eyes for a moment.

My eyes pinged open at the sound of a pencil lead moving against the blotter surface. A pencil stood, supported by an invisible hand. With precision it sketched lines. Each line created a warm familiarity. My breathing slowed, and eyes closed. When I opened them, Chance stepped through a newly drawn door in the smartboard wall.

"Nice coloration around that eye," Chance said, scrutinizing my face. "How many stitches?"

"Thanks," I replied. "At least the swelling's gone down. Five stitches, I think. Collecting scars again."

"What do you need, El?" His pale blue eyes twinkled as he lowered himself into a deep blue leather armchair.

It wasn't there a second ago. Sometimes I love my imagination. Blue leather. Always a favorite. Maybe we should look at updating our living room suite.

"El, you didn't summon me for my taste in furniture," Chance said softly. "Did you?"

"Maybe I missed you. Maybe that's why you're here."

He grinned. "I'd like to think you do miss me." Chance tapped his fingers on the arm of the chair. "Try again."

"What am I missing, Chance?"

"We talking about this whacked-out snow globe case?"

"Yep. I don't get how they're funding this bullshit."

Chance nodded. "Okay, you think it's about money?"

"Yeah. The loan-out fee of the exhibits is high, but

not high enough to keep the enterprise running."

"True, but it's not the only money coming in, is it?"

"No. Six labs across the country, all had legitimate work in research and in preserving body parts for use in universities and the like."

"That's probably the most legitimate part of their income. What else?"

"The photography part of the business."

"There you go … that's already three separate revenue streams in play."

"Yes, but think about it, Chance. There are six labs. Six fully equipped labs that came into being over the last eight years. That's a massive drain on resources."

"I wouldn't want Palacio's loan repayments."

Yeah, and it's not her only business. Christatech was a separate company in experimental technology; on paper it was in the black but not by much. "Come here and have a look at the files with me."

Chance dragged a chair around the side of my desk. It wasn't the blue leather armchair he had a moment ago. It was an executive style leather office chair. Nice. I shuffled my chair over a bit.

Chance shot me a grin. "Show me yours and I'll show you mine."

We both sniggered, nothing like schoolboy humor.

I opened my laptop and pulled the files up. I scrolled and scrolled, hoping whatever it was that twisted my gut into a tight ball would pop up. Report after report on the bodies discovered so far. Family photos, individual photos, all attached to the files along with the after-pictures. The stillness of the plastinated bodies at odds with the lifelike expressions on their faces.

A jumble of words fell from the air and mounded on my keyboard. One by one they oozed from the pile, stretching languidly across my blotter. Lung. Heart. Kidney. Eyes. Liver.

Fuckadoodledo. "Chance, did you see that?"

"Yeah. Little bit hurt that you did that without me." He bumped my arm with his and grinned like a loon.

"Yeah, you look hurt as fuck." I stared at the screen for a moment. "Okay, I got this."

Chance leaned over and planted a warm kiss on my cheek. "Yes, you do."

When I looked up, he was by the drawn doorway. My voice followed him as he waved and stepped into the wall. "Thank you."

The drawing dissolved into a puddle of silky colors that swirled down a drain in the carpet.

I made a call to Kurt. "We need to verify the origin of the organs Arianda plastinated for research purposes. Did they use legitimate donated bodies? Did the organs come from the missing families? Are all the organs present and accounted for? Notify all teams working on Operation Disney."

"Where are you going with this?"

"Revenue stream. Blackmarket organ trade."

"That might explain how they continued to grow despite the overheads."

"Would anyone know if the organs were sold off prior to plastination, once the bodies are posed and whatnot?"

"Not unless they were cut."

I swallowed. "Cut?"

"We need a circular saw and the more teeth on the blade, the better."

Spots danced in front of my eyes. Circular saw. Jigsaw. I blinked hard trying to dislodge the spots and clear my vision. Gray closed in. I leaned my forehead on my desk.

"Iverson?"

Meat and blood splattered across my internal screen. Bile swelled as the memory took hold. My world fell away. Flies buzzed in the air, banging into each other and me. I swatted them away. A second's reprieve before they buzzed around me again as I dragged one of the metal workshop doors open. The stench of rotting meat hit me full force. I gagged and pulled my T-shirt neck up over my mouth and nose. It didn't help. I'd walked about ten feet into the room before my eyes grew accustomed to the dim light and the horror hit me full force. I turned, stumbling in my haste, and thrust my hand out to steady myself on a bench. My hand connected with a sticky mess. Staggering to the doorway I vomited, clutching the edge of the door for support. The handiwork of Hank 'Saw' Creole would never leave me.

Hank liked puzzles. He liked to make puzzles out of

people. When we arrested him, he told me he'd like to make a puzzle out of me. Everything blurred and swayed as the horror took over.Every image associated with Hank and his fascination with jigsaw puzzles and scroll saws flooded back. He liked to use a reciprocating saw first, then move to a scroll saw for the more intricate patterns. Two of his victims were sliced up using a band saw in welder's workshop. I'd never seen a mess like it and hoped I never would again.

A voice broke through the gray and red disaster. The residual smell of death overpowered by a subtle cologne as a hand touched my arm. "Iverson."

Argo whined and pushed against me.

"Iverson."

I opened my eyes, pleased that both worked. Raising my head was harder. The room tipped and slowly rotated as I sat up straight. The movement stopped before I spoke.

"Henderson," I said, hoping my voice held weight.

"What's going on?"

"We were talking on the phone," I said, with as much innocence as I could muster. "And now you're in my office."

"I'm in your office because you stopped talking and ten-seconds later Argo appeared at my desk demanding I follow him."

Clever dog. I glanced down. His head was in my lap. I brushed his ears with the fingers of my cast arm. "Good boy," I whispered. He nudged my leg.

"What happened?" Kurt asked, perching on the edge of my desk. He reached out and rubbed Argo behind the ears.

"I had a moment." Not wanting to say much, I looked up at him and said, "Hank Creole."

Kurt frowned.

Dane darted into my office. "What the actual fuck did I just see?" He dropped into a chair, his face pale. "Who the hell is Hank Creole?"

Oh, man. The last thing I wanted to do was spread the love from *that* case. "I'm sorry, Dane. I'm really sorry."

He didn't reply. Argo gave me a long reproachful look. "I'm sorry." Seemed right to apologize to the dog. Argo stood and wove around Kurt's legs to reach Dane.

Kurt leaned close to my ear and whispered, "I'll get the Medical Examiner to check for organs."

A sigh escaped. "Thank you."

"Are you okay?"

"Yeah."

"Been a rough week, Iverson. Hang in there."

Rough week. Yeah. Let's go with that. And now for something completely different.

"Can we connect Christina Palacio to the death of Sergeant Green?"

"Where did that come from?" Waved his hand around. "Is he here?"

"Green is dead," I said, with the straightest delivery I could manage knowing full well he did not mean Sergeant Green's ghost.

"Not him," Kurt grumbled. "Chance, is he here?"

I shook my head. "This is all mine."

"What makes you think she could be responsible for Green's murder?"

"Simon Kreg knew her assistant Alana." Let's not allow any wriggle room on that. "Alana was our phantom crypto-text messenger. It wasn't a secret that she was unhappy at work. A liability even. Palacio tied up that loose end. She didn't need to tidy away Simon, he did that himself. Why not clean up Green and move on?" For all we knew, Alana's wife might be on her clean-up list.

"She had a go at slowing you down as well," Dane said. "Makes sense to get all those loose ends squared away."

Kurt dragged his phone from his pocket and called Julie over at NCIS with our observations. "Hang on Julie, I'll put you on speaker." He placed his phone on my desk and pressed the speaker icon. "Say that again for Ellie and Dane."

"The bullet that killed Green did not come from either of the weapons recovered from the river."

"So there was another shooter?" I said, leaning forward.

"It looks that way." Her voice faded then came back. "We're searching the park across the river."

I conjured an image of where we were standing in relation to the river. "How far across is it? About five hundred yards?"

"Five hundred and twenty-eight is my estimate," Julie said. "Not far enough for it to require a huge amount of skill."

She was correct. An experienced hunter with a three-oh-eight could take out a mountain goat at six hundred yards without much fuss. Key word being experienced.

"Let us know if you find anything."

"Will do, El."

Chapter Forty Four
Stuck In the Middle

Late afternoon sun warmed my back. Argo's tail thumped against my desk leg, bringing my attention back from the misery inflicted by Operation Disney and Arianda Enterprises. We had an answer. Organs were sold on the blackmarket. Cyber dug up a trail that wound through marketplaces in the Darknet and created a very profitable revenue river. The ME sliced a few of the bodies and confirmed that tradable organs were missing. The records of plastinated organs for research purposes didn't match the number of organs available from the missing families. Parts of the missing lived on in unknown recipients. Cold comfort.

I looked up to see Sandra and Mike in my doorway. Something was going on. An image flashed: the pair of them sitting under a tree. They were an item. The couple smiled at me.

"Did a pen box explode?" Sandra asked, gesturing the floor.

"Yeah, let's go with that."

"Can we take you for coffee?" Sandra said, she crouched and retrieved the pens, placing the bundle on my desk blotter to prevent them rolling away. Her eyes sparkled with mischief. "Or did you want them on the floor?"

"There's fine, thank you." I can always spin them off

my desk later.

"About the coffee?" Her eyes landed on the unopened bottle of turmeric latte concentrate on my desk. My office-warming gift from Mike. "Or did you want to try that?"

"Coffee, and Argo needs a walk," I replied, eyeing the bottle. "I'm working up to that." Change doesn't happen overnight. I pushed my chair back and reached across to open the drawer containing Argo's leash.

Mike's hand took the leash from mine. "Let me," he said, and bent down to clip the leash to Argo's harness. "Come on, boy. Coffee time."

Argo stood, but waited for me. "I'm coming," I said. "It's okay."

For the first time in a very long time, I walked down the stairs sedately and out into the atrium.

Frank looked up. "Wondered what it would take to slow you down, SAC. Hope you heal fast, it just ain't right not hearing your boots running down those stairs."

I smiled. "I'll be back to my old self soon enough, Frank."

He grinned and mock-smacked his head into his desk.

Outside the building, Sandra fell into step next to me, as Argo and Mike dropped behind, there were trees to sniff and replies to leave.

"What's up?"

"We're dating," she replied.

"I know."

"You do?"

"Uh-huh."

"It's okay, right?"

Sam would want her to be happy. I wanted her to be happy. Not up to me where or how she finds her happiness.

"Of course. I'm glad you and Mike found each other."

"I really like him, Ellie."

I'd seen the look in his eyes when she was around. He really liked her too. Good outcome. "He's a good guy." I smiled at her. "Just be careful, the spotlight takes a toll."

My phone blared Poison's 'Every Rose has its thorn.' Julie. I stopped walking and took the call. "Good news?"

"Good news El, we have a casing. Three-three-eight Lapua."

Not a point three-oh-eight then. A three-three-eight Lapua could easily make the shot from across the river. "So someone using a rifle, potentially a military-style sniper rifle, shot Green from across the Anacostia but did not police their brass? Amateur hour."

"Which makes me think it wasn't the idiots we pulled from the river, trying again from a boat. Whoever shot Green had to have been nested and waiting, took the shot and vanished."

"Yeah, that makes sense. Especially now we know

our suspect is very tidy person."

Julie chuckled. "I wonder if the shooter had any idea that he or she nearly got away with it because of the chaplain and his goons on the river."

"Unless you can pull prints off that casing, they might get away with it."

"El, it's me. I wouldn't ring with half the news." A lightness in her voice brought a smile to my face. "The person we wanted wasn't in the system at first. Seems he was only recently arrested and fingerprinted."

"Someone we picked up as part of Operation Disney?"

"Remember arresting Paul Crestley?"

"The forklift operator."

"The very same. We'd like a word with him."

"You're welcome to him."

"Take care El."

"You too, Julie."

The end.

Under Glass

Inside the bubble
Time froze
Trapped forever

Slivers of life
Never age
Immortality achieved

Lost in the moment
Museum pieces
Picture perfect

Exhibitions of art
Follow death
Beyond understanding

Under glass
Forever now
Forever mine

Continue reading for a preview of
Vaporbyte:

Chapter One

Let's Dance

The barista looked up and smiled as I walked toward him. "Hey, Ellie. Usual?"

I looked right at him, deadpan, and said, "Make it a black decaf, Jake."

He didn't miss a beat. "On your tab?"

"Please."

Jake had made my coffee every day for six years.

The male on my right added, "I'll have a breve. Put it on her tab." His head tipped toward me.

Jake glanced at me for affirmation. I nodded. I kept my hands in sight. Not once did I venture toward the gun on my hip. Better to play it out than risk innocent bystanders. For now.

"Name for the cup?"

"John."

"With an h or without?" Jake held a black marker pen over the cup.

"With."

"Okay."

He busied himself then hurried out the back. He returned with milk. I waited. Jake's phone buzzed. The idiot with the gun in his pocket waited.

Jake carried on with the coffee orders in front of him. No surreptitious glances in my direction. Jake's phone buzzed a few more times. He checked the messages.

John, the idiot with the gun, leaned on the counter, keeping his right hand in his pocket and watched Jake as he checked his phone. "What's with the phone?"

Jake showed him the screen without even looking up. "People text their orders, dude. It's the capital ... if you haven't noticed everyone's in a hurry."

I scanned the phone screen super quick. Three messages in a row.

Tony S: `Black.`

Kevin C: `Black.`

Dean W: `Double shot low-fat soy latte with cinnamon.`

I really appreciated the names Jake had chosen to use on his phone for Lee, Kurt, and Dane. Guess I wasn't the only one who saw Grange's lead guitarist, Kevin Costner, and Dean Winchester when looking at Delta A. For a split second, I wondered what he called me. I made a mental note to ask him one day.

"I'm about done here," I whispered to John with an 'h', hoping my voice did not betray the smile I felt growing. Typical Dane. Double shot low-fat soy latte with cinnamon, my ass!

John's eyes darted to me. "That's a shame."

"You've made a mistake. I can still help you correct it."

He snorted with derision. "There's no mistake here, Agent Iverson."

"I'll make sure that's carved on your tombstone."

"Pretty sure of yourself, given the situation." John wiggled the gun in his pocket. Jake clanged a milk jug, distracting the idiot's attention. "What's taking so long?"

"Coffee is a science. You want it good, or you want it fast?" Jake replied with a grin. I'd never seen him rattled by anything and he'd seen me first thing in the morning and well under-caffeinated.

And we waited.

Other patrons came in, picked up phone orders, and left. Something pinged off to the side of my right eye. A flicker. My team.

"Where to next?" I turned to the man with me. He may have told Jake his name was John for his coffee, but I very much doubted that was true.

"Not your concern, Agent." He watched Jake intently.

"Glad you have a plan."

The flash in my peripheral vision increased.

"Hey, Jake?" Jake looked at me. "You got any of those cupcakes out the back?"

"I let you get coffee, cupcakes is pushing it," the gunman growled.

"You don't wanna be around me if I haven't eaten." I shrugged.

"I'll get you a couple, Ellie," Jake said with a smile and disappeared. There would be no cupcakes.

Back-up was about to walk through the door.

The bell above the front door dinged. Lee crossed

the floor with four easy strides, and stood as if he were waiting in line. He leaned around the gunman.

"Hey, Ellie. Didn't expect to see you here," he said with a grin a mile wide. "We still good for racquet ball later?"

"Looking forward to it," I replied.

Lee's eyebrow danced at the man between us. The door dinged again. I saw Kurt moving into line behind Lee.

Beads of sweat appeared on John's forehead. He craned his neck to see out the back. "Hey, coffee guy, leave the cupcakes. We gotta go."

The door dinged once more. Dane strode in.

He came up behind me, leaned into my ear and whispered just loud enough for John to hear, "Baby, I hope you ordered something special."

Biting back a chuckle, I let my voice rasp a bit as I whispered back May West style, "Double shot. Low fat. Soy latte."

John made a grab for me, but Dane flipped a hand-cuff on his wrist and gave his arm a good twist. Lee reached over and took the gun from his pocket.

"Fucking amateur hour," he muttered, handing the weapon to Kurt.

"You okay?" Dane asked me, while pushing the cuffed man into Lee's waiting grip.

"Absolutely," I said then leaned over the counter and called to Jake. "Hey, it's safe."

He emerged with a paper bag and handed it to me. I

peered inside. Cupcakes. "Put these on my tab. And thanks for being cool."

"My treat. Not every day someone tries to kidnap a federal agent in my coffee shop."

I reached over and shook Jake's hand. "Thank you."

"You're welcome."

Kurt and Lee escorted the prisoner. I heard Kurt reading the Miranda as he placed a hand on John's head while encouraging him into the back of his car. Dane caught up with me on the pavement. He had a tray of coffees and a grin plastered on his face.

"Coffee first then interrogation?"

"I think so."

Kurt and Lee drove off. Dane and I climbed into his SUV and followed.

(to be continued ...)

Acknowledgments

Big thanks to Pete Turner for helping me understand blockchain and cryptocurrency, and for the conversations both on air and off.

Also thank you to the usual suspects for keeping me moderately sane: My kids, My Knight: Geoff, Dad, friends both old and newish - couldn't do this without any of you.

Extra special thanks to the new beta readers who jumped in and gave excellent feedback early on. You were awesome!

This is the first Byte Series book without Rebel ePublishers, but not entirely, because we still have the glorious Jayne Southern and her red pen.

About the Author

Cat Connor is a coffee addict and tequila aficionado who loves greyhounds. She's been described as irresistible, infectious, and addictive – and quite liked it. She believes music is essential to her writing process. She knows where to hide the body and what you did last week.

Connor lives in the Wellington Region of New Zealand with her youngest two children [The Hostile Assistant and ActorKid], Bucky Barnes and Timmy the guinea pigs, and Missy the grey cat.

Cat's greyhound Romeo passed away at home on May 5th 2019, he was a constant companion during the writing of the last 9 Byte Series novels. His presence is greatly missed.

On Sept 6th, 2019, Missy the grey cat joined her best friend Romeo over the rainbow bridge. Together again on their next adventure.

You can connect with Cat in the following places:

her website: www.catconnor.com
Twitter: @catconnor
Facebook: @cat.connor
Instagram: @catconnorauthor

Arctic Romeo 15/09/2006-05/05/2019
Thank you for your help raising the youngest two humans. I can take it from here big guy. You rest.